OUTSTANDING PRAISE FOR
EMILY'S SECRET

"Lovely . . . It's the book I've always wanted to write."
—Marion Zimmer Bradley

"This is a wonderful story handled with great skill. Jill Jones has a fantastic future ahead of her. Charming, intriguing . . . and I loved the characters."
—Barbara Erskine

"A splendid read, with an intricate plot, made all the more viable by research and some intriguing suppositions. I do hope this is the first of many from this author."
—Anne McCaffrey

"Takes the reader on an absorbing trip into the past to solve a famous literary puzzle. A great debut for a talented new writer!"
—Jasmine Cresswell

"Remarkably invigorating! A modern romance Emily herself would have been proud to have authored. Felicitations to a great writer for a magnificent novel!"
—*Affaire de Coeur* (5 Stars)

D0816404

EMILY'S SECRET

Jill Jones

St. Martin's Paperbacks

This is a work of fiction. Only the characters of the Brontë family and Henry H. Bonnell are historical. All other characters and situations in this story are entirely fictional, and any resemblance to any persons or actual happenings is purely coincidental.

EMILY'S SECRET

Copyright © 1995 by Jill Jones.

Printed in the United States of America

St. Martin's Paperbacks edition/September 1995
St. Martin's Paperbacks special free edition/February 1997

10 9 8 7 6 5 4

For Peggy and Val

ACKNOWLEDGMENTS

Excerpts from Emily Brontë's poems are taken from *The Complete Poems of Emily Jane Brontë,* edited by C. W. Hatfield, New York: Columbia University Press, 1941.

Excerpts from *Wuthering Heights* are from the edition of that novel published by Signet Classics, New American Library, a division of Penguin Books USA, Inc., New York, 1959.

I am deeply grateful to the Brontë Society and the Brontë Parsonage Museum Library for making the materials necessary for the research of this book available to me. I also wish to express my gratitude to Kathryn White, Assistant Curator/Librarian, Brontë Parsonage Museum, for her professional and conscientious assistance.

My thanks go to my husband, Jerry Jones, for his research and editing help, his creative ideas and unconditional support; to my stepson, Brad Jones, for his research at the University of Texas, and to Carol Gaskin, Maggie Davis, Glenys Steger, and Virginia Esson for their assistance in assuring the authenticity of the content and suggestions concerning style.

And finally, I wish to express my sincere gratitude to my editor, Jennifer Enderlin, whose thoughtful creativity brought so much to this book.

He comes with western winds, with evening's wandering
  airs,
With that clear dusk of heaven that brings the thickest
  stars;
Winds take a pensive tone, and stars a tender fire,
And visions rise and change which kill me with desire—

Emily Jane Brontë

❧ *Prologue* ❧

DECEMBER 1848

*B*lizzard-whitened winds blasted across the desolate high moor country, enshrouding gorse and heather in a sheet of shimmering ice. Gales surged down the open hillsides and into the churchyard, moaning across the ice-encrusted gravestones that shouldered against one another in the December darkness. Then the winter wraiths combined their attack, encircling the old stone Parsonage at the edge of the village, shaking it and shrieking,

Let me in!

Like relentless, malevolent ghosts, they battered the brittle windowpanes, wailing their demand for the warmth and life inside.

Within, three unmarried sisters huddled by the fire in the dining room, trying to ignore the death call that grew louder with each tick of the clock. Charlotte drew her chair closer to the fire and tucked her heavy skirts around her ankles. She adjusted the queer little spectacles on the bridge of her nose, then resumed reading aloud from the book she had purchased at the stationer's shop the day before. It was the work of an American writer, Emerson, which she found intriguing. Perhaps it would please her sister Emily, who sat next to her large yellow dog on the rug, pale and still, holding onto her rosewood writing box with a kind of quiet desperation. If only Emily would have let them call a doctor, Charlotte agonized, glancing at her stricken sister in the flickering firelight. Then she looked up, and her eyes met those of her other sister, Anne, the youngest of the three at twenty-seven. There she saw a reflection of her own grief. They both knew that now it was too late. There was little they could do for their brilliant but determined sister except stay with her until the end.

Suddenly, Emily's shoulders hunched, and she was wracked by a deep and terrible cough that echoed into every chamber of the house. Across the hall in his study, her father tried in vain to concentrate on reading his Bible, peering at the printed page through a large magnifying glass. His heart was heavy as the snow-laden clouds outside, knowing he would soon bury another of his children in the cold vault beneath the stone church floors.

The spasm subsided, and with trembling fingers Emily opened the writing box that had been her closest friend and confidante through the years. She knew and was grateful that she hadn't much time left. Only one thing remained to be finished in her waning lifetime.

Inside the box lay a slim, red-covered volume that, until this moment, only Emily knew existed. For the past three years she had written in it furtively almost every night. She had kept it hidden beneath the mattress of her small bed, risking exposure of a dark and dangerous secret should one of her sisters discover it. But it was a risk she had been willing to take, because writing was the only way she had been able to sort out her terrifying thoughts. Writing had led the way through the treacherous anger, fear, and despair that had at times engulfed her like the mists on the moors, leaving her lost and helpless. Writing was the rock of sanity to which she clung desperately after a chance encounter on the moors had sent her hurtling into a frightening chaos of emotions that she neither understood nor had the experience to control. With no one to confide in, she turned, as always, to the patient page.

A sob escaped her throat, and the effort sent her into another coughing fit. Surely it couldn't take much longer, she thought. She hadn't known her dying would be so attenuated.

> *I know there is a blessed shore*
> *Opening its ports for me, and mine;*
> *And, gazing Time's wide waters o'er,*
> *I weary for that land divine . . .*

Emily had planned to burn the diary earlier, when the others were not looking, but she'd waited too long. Her sisters had become anxious nursemaids as her illness worsened, hovering around her, not leaving her a moment alone in weeks. The clock on the stairwell chimed the quarter hour. Emily paused. She had no choice but to carry out this final task before their eyes. Slowly, with great effort but steadfastly, Emily ripped away the first few pages, crumpled them, and threw them into the fire. The flame leapt momentarily, consumed the tidbit, then returned to its normal glow.

Startled, Charlotte closed the book she was reading and leaned forward. "Emily, what is that?"

Her sister's only reply was to turn her back squarely to Charlotte, tear more sheets from the book, wad them, and feed them to the flames.

"Emily, stop!" Charlotte cried out in alarm. She knew her sister prized her privacy, but she could not sit by and allow Emily to destroy her work, for there would be no more of her strong and energetic poetry, no more strange and moving novels like *Wuthering Heights*. If Emily Brontë had created more work than what Charlotte had already found, Charlotte felt it her duty to rescue it from the sure death Emily obviously intended for it. The poet might go to her grave, but her poetry must live on. Charlotte sprang from her chair and knelt by Emily's side, eager to see what the volume contained.

Emily slammed the book shut and crossed her arms over it. Charlotte was such an impossible meddler. I should have burned this long ago, she thought, disgusted. She looked up at Anne.

"Help me," she whispered, her words ending in a rattling cough.

Anne looked from Emily to Charlotte, uncertain what to do. She knew Emily was loath to give the outer world so much as a glimpse of her private thoughts, even in her poetry. But did she not recognize her worth as a writer? Of them all, Emily was the true genius. But Anne had long since given up trying to understand her difficult and enigmatic sister. Right now, all she wished to do was ease Emily's pain. Whatever she had written, it was clear her sister did not want it to survive her. "Yes," Anne said quietly at last, and looked at Charlotte. "Let her be."

"No!" Charlotte insisted. "You know how she is. She'll destroy all the beauty she has created. I won't let her do it!"

"It is hers to destroy if she wishes," Anne said patiently.

"It is *not* hers," Charlotte cried, vexed at being crossed by her normally compliant younger sister. "Those poems belong to everyone who loves her work."

Emily tore more pages from the diary and crumpled them hastily. She handed them to Anne, who dutifully threw them into the fire. "Not poems," Emily managed.

"A novel?" Charlotte could not bear the thought. "Is it a new novel you were working on?" She reached out and attempted to wrest what was left of the volume from Emily's grasp but stopped short when her sister's deep gray-blue eyes froze on hers, daring her to intrude further. Charlotte sighed and backed away, and Emily resumed the chore at hand. When the last of the diary was gone, her secret would be safe. Hopefully, the savage wind and rain on the moors would have destroyed the letter she'd foolishly left under the message rock.

Since she didn't believe in heaven or hell, she had no fear that she would burn for what she was doing. Dying now would put a natural end to the horror almost before it began. She was safe. Her family was protected. Her secret was secure. Emily felt light-headed with relief as the last paper blazed and the cover turned to ash.

The flames crackled contentedly, like the purr of a cat with a belly full of cream. Emily tried to breathe deeply the fullness of her release, but consumption stole her breath and allowed only another coughing fit. The clock on the stair struck ten. Emily nodded to Anne in gratitude for her help. Then, without speaking, her two sisters helped her off the floor. She refused further aid and made her way slowly, painfully, up the stairs. She eased down onto the narrow bed in the tiny, unheated room that had been her private quarters since she'd returned home for good six years ago. In the dark, she listened to the wind wailing outside her window.

Let me in!

Throughout the night, the tempest continued its assault on the darkened Parsonage, and the following day, shortly after two o'clock, a windowpane finally burst under the force. The icy wind found Emily on the sofa in front of the fireplace, and without hesitation, completed its mission of death.

❧ *Chapter 1* ❧

*T*hunder shook the sodden skies over London as Alexander Hightower topped the stairs of the Underground, exhausted to his bones. Across the traffic-choked avenue the chimes from Big Ben somehow managed to overpower the street noise below, where red buses roared and taxicabs honked, competing with private cars and commercial trucks in the muddy, endless race of commerce.

One o'clock.

Alex drew the black mackintosh closer around him and moved under the protection of a nearby archway. Above him pigeons clucked and cooed in the shelter of windowsills and alcoves, the rain sending their residue like so much whitewash to the pavement below.

He spotted a display of umbrellas in the window of a nearby souvenir shop and decided immediately on his first purchase on British soil.

"I'll take that one." Alex indicated the largest black one in the lot. He paid the vendor with soggy pound notes, opened the umbrella with a snap, then ventured into the heavy traffic, making his way across the circle and past the park.

One o'clock.

He had exactly two hours. Two brief hours until he had

to face Maggie Flynn. And into those two hours he had to cram what under more leisurely circumstances could easily take him several days.

Damn!

He walked briskly, dodging puddles, wishing he hadn't agreed to this afternoon's meeting. He was in no shape to spar with Maggie Flynn. His clothes were rumpled, travel-worn from the long night spent cramped in the coach class seat on the flight from New York. He was in need of a shower, a shave, and a nap. But as it was, he'd barely had time to check into his hotel and sling his bags into the room before starting off again.

Maggie Flynn, it would seem, had bested him again.

Alex reached the ancient shrine of Westminster Abbey, where a service was in progress inside the magnificent Gothic structure. Organ music swelled to the tops of the intricate arches and reverberated off the smooth stone walls, loud enough to shake the crumbling bones that lay beneath the floors and in the tombs and vaults. Lightning flashed fiercely through the majestic stained-glass windows, and moments later thunder echoed throughout the cavernous cathedral.

Alex felt the hair on his arms stand on end, and he shivered. He was not a religious man, but if there was a God, he thought it likely He might call this place Home.

But it wasn't God he had come here to see. He waited until the music died, the aisles emptied, and a tall man in a red coat indicated that the Royal Chapels would be reopened. Then Alex made his way through the gate among the throngs of other sightseers, paid his three pounds, and entered a time warp.

Tread softly past the long, long sleep of kings . . .

They were all there, virtually every monarch who had held power over Britain since there was a Britain. Edward the Confessor, who established the Abbey, followed by a parade of Henries, Richards, and Jameses along with their wives and consorts and various and sundry relatives. He paid his respects to Queen Elizabeth I, whose carefully carved marble effigy slept peacefully atop her tomb. In the room opposite, given almost equal space, the bones of that throne-usurper, Mary Queen of Scots, reposed restlessly for eternity. Lightning flashed, eerily illuminating the sepulcher.

Alex moved on, filing past the ancient coronation chair and the legendary Stone of Scone. Most of Britain's monarchs had been crowned on this chair, and he was duly awed by the sheer weight of the history that surrounded him.

But it was another kind of hero he'd come to honor today. Royalty of a different sort from whom he sought a silent blessing for his improbable quest.

He stepped into the South Trancept, better known as the Poet's Corner, and allowed the moment to envelop him. Here his true heroes were either buried or memorialized. The giants of English literature. Those whose works he had studied and taught and loved most of his life. Dryden. Dickens. Johnson. Kipling. Hardy. They were all buried right here, beneath his feet. The walls, columns, and floors were filled with memorials, tributes to the likes of Milton, Shakespeare, Wordsworth, Byron, Shelley, Tennyson, Coleridge, and many more.

And then, there to the right, Alex spied an inconspicuous, inornate square framing three names, engraved in plain letters:

Charlotte Brontë
1816–1855
Emily Jane Brontë
1818–1848
Anne Brontë
1820–1849
With courage to endure

Another streak of lightning pierced the afternoon gloom.

Alex stood for a long moment, gazing at the memorial, wondering what these three strange and provincial women would think about having been enshrined here. Charlotte, who sought fame and fortune, would be ecstatic, he felt certain. Anne, in her own quiet way, would be pleased. And Emily, at the very least, would approve of the plainness of the memorial.

Alex allowed himself a small smile. As a scholar of early Victorian literature, he had studied the lives and works of these three writers so long and so intensely he felt as if he knew them intimately. He knew what clothes they wore and what food they ate. He knew much of their suffering, as well as their victories. At times he felt almost a part of the family.

His eye was drawn to the middle name on the memorial—Emily Jane Brontë. Of them all, she was his favorite. Perhaps because she was the most elusive. Little work remained from which to try to piece together the personal and literary puzzle she presented. Less than two hundred of her poems existed, many only fragments, along with one strange and darkly fascinating novel, *Wuthering Heights.* She had lived only thirty years and died after a short illness. It was her death Alex found most inexplicable about Emily Brontë. A young woman. A strong will. A premature death. She died, he theorized, if not by her own hand, then certainly by her own design.

> *O for the day when I shall rest,*
> *And never suffer more!*

His theory, that Emily's death was, in essence, a suicide, was not popular among Brontë devotees.

Although many concurred that in those final months she seemed to have lost the will to live, most attributed it to her grief over her brother Branwell's death, while others offered more complex psychological explanations, including *anorexia nervosa*.

Alex alone among his contemporaries in the world of academe had dared mention suicide. Emily Brontë was, after all, something of a sainted literary figure. A scholar's monarch. One was not welcome to loosely question tradition.

But Alex sensed there was something that had driven this intensely private woman to take her own life, not with a gunshot or a dram of poison, but rather in a way that would not raise the suspicion of others, based on her past behavior.

Through willful neglect.

What else but a deep and unyielding desire for death would cause her to refuse, totally and absolutely, all medical help when she became so gravely ill? Something devastating must have happened to her in those last few months, something so frightful and traumatic that death had seemed the only escape.

Something she had successfully hidden from snooping biographers like himself.

Alex had been vocal about his opinion, both to his students and among his colleagues, and the latter had called his hand. The academic world, like science, scorns conjecture. His peers, Maggie Flynn foremost among them, demanded proof.

Put up or shut up.

The showdown was to be a formal debate that loomed like a menacing storm at the end of the summer.

Having a gut-level feeling was one thing. Finding solid evidence to back it up was quite another. Alex had studied every available Brontë resource in the United States, but still had nothing stronger than a hunch to present, based on his interpretation of some of Emily's work. The only element of her life he had so far been unable to examine was her environment—the wild and haunting moors of northern England which she had loved deeply and which had influenced virtually everything she wrote.

So tomorrow he would travel to Haworth, the small West Yorkshire village that had been her home. He planned to review the material available at the Brontë Parsonage Museum Library there. But more than that, he wanted to walk the rugged countryside she trod, breathe the air she breathed. It wasn't in a library, he felt, that he would find an answer. If he found one at all, it would come from insight gained by personally experiencing the forces that had touched her and molded her life.

It wasn't much to build his seditious suicide theory on, but it was the only strategy remaining. He must uncover Emily's secret, for unless he found arguable proof, in late August, in front of many of the world's preeminent scholars of English literature, he would be torn to shreds over the issue by another expert in the field, Dr. Maggie Flynn.

Maggie.

His colleague.

His former lover.

Alex stared at the letters carved in the cold marble memorial. "Why?" he murmured. "Why did you choose to die?" He ran his fingers across the engraved name.

"Emily," he entreated softly. "Answer me."

Rain, driven by a sharp easterly wind, pelted against Selena's cheeks as she dashed from the old farmhouse. The gale whipped a long strand of dark hair from beneath the knitted cap she wore, lashing it with a sting into one eye. Unsure of her footing on the slippery, sandy mud, she made a careful run for the old Land Rover parked in the drive.

Overhead, gray clouds scudded across the tops of the

moors like large sheep in need of shearing. On the verdant squares of pasture below, real sheep huddled for shelter behind drystone walls that formed uneven geometric quilts over the landscape for miles in every direction. The world was cold and wet from four straight days of rain.

Selena got into the dilapidated vehicle and turned the ignition, concerned whether the square-backed wagon would make it all the way to London and return. The ancient engine bucked and snorted. She ground the starter again. Nothing. She beat her palm against the steering wheel and pumped the accelerator furiously. "Come on!"

At last the car rumbled to life, and after letting it warm up, Selena slipped it into gear and backed carefully up the steep drive into the lane. She allowed herself one last glance toward the house, where a bedraggled black and white border collie sat on the stoop, staring at her with sad, accusing eyes.

"Damn it, Domino. Why don't you have the good sense to stay out of the rain? And don't look at me like that. I'll be back tomorrow. By noon. I promise."

She was apprehensive about the long drive to London and hoped the rain would let up once she was out of storm-riddled Yorkshire. Glancing at her watch, she regretted having committed to visiting Matka en route. Selena had to be at the gallery in London by five.

But she'd promised, and she knew her grandmother would be watching the clock.

The nursing home where Matka lived was new and modern. The receptionist greeted her with friendly efficiency. Matka had reported the food was good and the place clean.

But it hurt to see the woman who, through sheer tenacity of spirit had somehow managed to hold the fragile pieces of Selena's childhood together, confined to a wheelchair, her body rendered mostly immobile by rheumatoid arthritis. Matka's manner was always gruffly cheerful whenever Selena visited, but her granddaughter suspected the brightness was a front, a show put on for her benefit, like the old Gypsy used to do for her customers in the fortune-telling booth.

Selena found her grandmother in her favorite spot beside the fireplace in the Community Room, a small package of a woman sitting in a wheelchair, hidden behind the wall of the daily newspaper she was reading. "Hey, Gran!" She poked her face over the papers and kissed the wrinkled forehead.

"Stars in heaven, child! You like t' a taken my breath. Where't y' come from, appearin' like tha' out o' nowhere?"

"You knew I was coming," she reminded the wizened woman. "I'm on my way to London."

Matka squinted, her clouded dark eyes focusing on the young woman. "London, eh? What'd y'be doin' in London?"

Selena picked up the paper and folded it noisily, impatient at the game her grandmother seemed to play with increasing frequency, the one called I Don't Remember. "You know that, too, Gran. Those paintings of mine I told you about. They've been on exhibit in a gallery there. The show's over, and I'm on my way to pick them up. It's been on a month. Got a lot of good reviews, too. I even sold a few."

Matka snorted and chewed her toothless gums. "Paintin's! An artist, y' want t' be? Wha' kind o' life would tha' be for a girl like you?" Like a locomotive, she was building steam, getting set to roll into her favorite subject. "You ought t' find a nice man and settle down, have children. You'll soon be turnin' thirty, you know . . ."

Her voice trailed off, and Selena said nothing. She found it difficult to defend her choice of lifestyle to her

Romany (and sometimes surprisingly traditional) grand-mother. She pulled an ottoman close to the old woman's chair and took the gnarled, aged hands in her own.

"We've gone over this before, Gran," she said, sum-moning patience. "Think about it. Do you *really* believe that getting married and having a family would be the best thing for me?"

The old woman looked at her with eyes that saw more than what was in front of her. Neither said a word for a long while, each remembering Selena's violent child-hood, the stormy parents who had deserted her at differ-ent times, in different ways. They both knew it was only after Matka had come to live with them that Selena had known any security or happiness.

Selena didn't like to think about those days. In fact, there was much she had carefully buried deeply inside her so she would no longer remember the horror. But she remembered when the old woman's brightly-colored Gypsy van was parked for good in the shed behind her parents' small home. She recalled how sad Matka had been to leave her wandering life on the road, but how glad she herself had been to find one loving soul in her life. The young girl and the old woman had clung to each other as the terror and turmoil of her parents' lives raged around them.

"It's the curse," Matka would swear, wringing her hands.

"No, Gran," Selena would reply under her breath. "It's the whiskey."

Witnessing her parents' unhappiness, Selena doubted she would ever marry, but her grandmother never gave up hope that she would change her mind. Because, in spite of the old woman's superstitious belief that an an-cient curse hung over the family, Matka prayed that one day, by some miracle, the hex would be dispelled and one of her line would at last be free to love without pain.

That one had to be Selena. Because her raven-haired, olive-skinned granddaughter was the only one left, the last descendant of this branch of the ancient line of fabled Abram Wd, King of the Welsh Gypsies.

Selena did not believe in any such curse. Her parents' problems had been caused by nothing more mysterious than financial stress and alcoholism. Matka's story about the curse, Selena felt, was just a Gypsy superstition.

And Selena refused to let her Gypsy ancestry control her life.

Sure, she loved the romantic stories Matka had woven for her as a child as they sat together by the fire on cold nights, tales of the old woman's vagabond life. But Selena knew it was their Gypsy heritage that drove her father's anger, her mother's despair. Her father had left his own caravan behind when he was only a boy, seeking his fortune in wartime England. He had been too young to fight, so he'd gone to work in a munitions factory.

But life for a young Gypsy wasn't easy in the *Gorgio* world. When anything went wrong, he was blamed. When anything was stolen, the Gypsy did it. In his first job, and in every other job, it happened again and again, until he simply gave up. That's when the drinking began, and the fights. And his misery didn't end until he pulled the trigger one dark, rainy night, sending his body to the bottom of a cliff outside of town. In spite of no longer being brutalized by her husband, her mother never recovered from his suicide, and Selena found her one morning, dead of alcohol poisoning.

Matka patted Selena's hands and shook her head sadly. "The curse has a strong hold on our family. No one's escaped it in a hundred and fifty years. Perhaps it has touched y' already, makin' y' lonely, afraid of love." She sighed heavily.

Selena wanted to shake her grandmother and cry out,

"There is no curse!" For intellectually, she didn't believe in such nonsense. That stuff belonged in fairy tales.

She would have pressed the point, if it hadn't been for the paintings.

Selena hadn't shown Matka any of her recent work, even though it was the old woman's money that had paid for her education at the École des Beaux Arts in Paris, because Matka would have spotted the letter in an instant.

The letter.

That impossible letter that Matka still kept, brittle with age, in the drawer of her bedside table at the nursing home. Selena wished she had it now. She would burn it and be done with it. The damned thing had caused nothing but torment and tears to countless of her superstitious ancestors.

And now, it seemed, it was insidiously invading her own creativity, somehow manifesting on every canvas she painted. No, she didn't dare show her art to Matka, for the old Gypsy would insist that the curse was attacking the only thing she loved—her work.

Ironically, it was the continuity of the images in her work, especially the scraps of the letter, that had led Selena to some measure of recognition in London. Actually, the reviews *had* been good. One writer had even compared her favorably to Léonor Fini. The bizarre nature of her surrealistic compositions had captured the equally bizarre taste of trendy London, and she had sold several pieces. Tom Perkins had already asked her to show again in the fall.

But she couldn't keep painting like this—the same picture, in essence, over and over again. It was as if she were possessed when she went to her studio. She'd pick up her brushes, determined to stay away from the mauves and grays, the campfires, the dancing bears, the wild ponies, the monkey's head, and above all, that ubiquitous scrap of letter that made its way onto the canvas regardless. Sometimes it was pounded beneath the horse's hoof. Sometimes it was burning in the fire. Sometimes the monkey reached out with it teasingly, as if handing it to the viewer. Selena wished Matka had never shown her the letter or told her about the curse.

She wished she wasn't a Gypsy.

She wished she could paint a bowl of fruit.

June 2, 1845

> *How beautiful the Earth is still*
> *To thee—how full of Happiness;*
> *How little fraught with real ill*
> *Or shadowy phantoms of distress;*
>
> *How Spring can bring thee glory yet*
> *And Summer win thee to forget*
> *December's sullen time!*
> *Why dost thou hold the treasure fast*
> *Of youth's delight, when youth is past*
> *And thou art near thy prime?*

June 4, 1845

I should not write this lest Charlotte come snooping, for he made me promise not to tell anyone of his whereabouts. And yet it is all so strange I am loath not to record it. I will mark it now, and maybe tomorrow awaken to find it only a mad dream anyhow, like all the rest.

When I was upon the moors today, late in the afternoon, I climbed the ravine along the back hill. I do not know what made me go there today, because it is not common for me to walk that way. I was busy playing at Gondal in my mind and watching the water splashing down the beck, and I did not see what lay in front of me. Neither did I hear anything unusual, until my foot struck a low mound that stretched across the path. Then I heard an awful moan, and I saw that an injured man lay half hidden in the grass. Keeper heard it, too, and came running, ready to attack, but I held him off. I was not frightened, but I picked up a rock and approached him cautiously. He was the most ragged creature I have ever seen, and I guess from his dress he is one of those they call gipsie. He wore a silk kerchief knotted about his neck, and a large earring in one ear. His shirt was dirty and torn and stained with blood from his cuts. He opened his eyes while I stood there staring, wondering what to do about him. He looked up at me, his face filled with pain, and asked if I was an angel! (He thought he was dead.) I told him no, I'm Emily Jane Brontë. I brought him some water from the beck. He told me he had fallen from his horse, but I saw no horse nearby. Perhaps it ran away.

He is badly hurt. I know his leg is broken, and he may have other injuries. He was in great pain, so much that it beaded in sweat on his brow though the day was chill. He would not have me summon help, though I fear for his life. I understand, for the gipsies are not welcome in the village and I, too, do not trust doctors on any account.

I helped him to take shelter beneath a large outcropping of rock and tried to make him comfortable, but when I left, he was pale and not awake. Tonight, I will save some broth and bread, and Keeper and I will steal away after everyone is asleep. I pray he is still alive. This must be a most secret adventure.

✌ *Chapter 2* ✌

Dr. Alexander Hightower at last bade a reluctant farewell to his beloved and long-dead friends in the abbey. Visiting the shrine had been a career-long desire, and he hadn't been disappointed.

Outside, the storm had subsided, leaving only a residue of high clouds and dripping leaves. Alex looked at a small tourist guide book he'd brought along, and decided his next destination was within walking distance. He was used to exercise; it would feel good to stretch his legs and clear his head for his afternoon encounter with Maggie Flynn.

Walking along Whitehall, with its impressive row of government buildings and associated sense of power, Alex tried to concentrate on the historical structures he passed. He noted a female bobby in uniform striding purposefully some distance in front of him. Still farther along he could see Nelson lording his imposing figure over tourist and homeless alike in Trafalgar Square.

But nothing seemed to dislodge Maggie Flynn's persistent presence from his mind.

What was he going to say to her? What could he say? Sorry, but I never loved you? It was the truth, but he couldn't say it any more now than he'd been able to before. Maybe they would just go for coffee. No, tea. This was England, after all. Tea and scones and small talk. And then she would go away, and he wouldn't have to face her again until August.

Somehow Alex knew it wouldn't be that easy.

With Maggie, nothing was easy.

Alex remembered vividly the first time he'd seen Maggie Flynn. She was holding court in the midst of several awestruck male students on the campus where he taught. Her burnished hair was shining in the sun, a glorious reflection of the colors of the crisp autumn leaves swirling around the carefully landscaped grounds. She was a visiting professor from Oxford, and she took the small Virginian liberal arts college by storm, as was her style.

Their affair had started innocently enough. She was assigned to his department and shared his field of expertise, and in her he had found a witty and intelligent companion whose radiance dispelled for a while the gloom of his existence. She was different from the colorless, faceless women he'd dated in a string of one-night stands that did nothing to ease the pain and guilt of his miserably failed marriage.

Alex had been attracted to Maggie, not only because she was beautiful, but also because she was safely out of reach emotionally. She was cold beneath her outward demeanor. Unattainable. Which suited him just fine. He'd spent six years with someone exactly her opposite, someone warm and caring and sensitive whom he'd loved and trusted, only to have his heart ripped out when she left him for another man. He'd sworn then never to invest himself emotionally in another relationship. It simply wasn't worth the pain.

Alex and Maggie had read poetry aloud and talked about things literary that only scholars would deem interesting and important. They debated issues, sometimes hotly, over which they disagreed. They gossiped about their mutual acquaintances and compared the education systems of their respective countries. Maggie intrigued Alex, and for him, friendship was enough. He had no intention of getting involved in anything more serious with her.

But that was exactly what Maggie had wanted, and she was a woman who would not be denied. And as they spent time together, Alex found the defenses he had so carefully constructed against involvement with the opposite sex proved inadequate against her indomitable will.

From the start, Alex had been acutely aware of the sexuality that simmered, barely hidden, beneath the surface of her composed demeanor, and he would not have been male if thoughts of making love to Maggie had not erupted from time to time, ever more frequently as the days passed. By the time she gave up waiting for him to make the first move and assumed the role of seductress, Alex's emotional wall of steel had melted in her white-hot heat. Without examining his own motives, needs, or desires, he allowed himself to be consumed by her burning passion, which obliterated all reason, all pain. He drank in her beauty, swallowed her fire.

Maggie had won.

Maggie always won, Alex thought bitterly as he walked, dodging puddles. That's what Maggie Flynn was all about. Conquest. Victory. Maggie couldn't stand to lose, and the more he gave, the more she took. The coldness that had in the beginning been appealingly safe had turned odious as her calculating and domineering nature surfaced more and more often. Their formerly friendly sparring turned into nastier fights. She took offense if he questioned her authority or knowledge of a subject. She was especially sensitive about her career path. She had clawed and scratched her way to the top at Oxford, and those efforts had left their scars.

Although their sex had been steamy, it wasn't long before his fascination with red hair and milky skin was replaced by a frequent desire to see her on the plane back to England.

Lying in the dark one midnight, listening to the even breathing of his finally sexually sated partner, Alex was suddenly filled with deep self-contempt. Their sex was hot, spontaneous, and uninhibited, but he had no business making love to Maggie night after night. He didn't love her. He didn't even like her. His was an animal, hormonal response, not rooted in any deep emotion, certainly not love. She had become just another woman in his bed, like all the rest.

The only difference was that she had been there more than one night.

Alex got up quietly, put on his pants, and never went back.

He had never told Maggie the real reason for his abrupt exit from her life. She had mistaken his desire for love, and he hadn't bothered to tell her otherwise. He'd made up some excuse about it being too soon after his divorce, and then withdrew into a self-imposed exile, broken only by Herculean workouts every day at the gym that built his body to steel-hard perfection and helped to block Maggie Flynn and all the others from his mind.

It would have worked if Maggie had let it. Instead, she intensified her efforts to convince him that she was exactly what he needed, and after a few painful encounters, Alex realized to his horror that she had fallen in love with him. Either that or she was unwilling to be the loser. Whatever the reason, she'd kept up her efforts until merciful time at last put an end to their mutual misery and Maggie's tenure at the college drew to a close. She didn't call to say good-bye, but she left a note in his departmental mailbox: "My door will always be open . . ."

Lost among these gloomy thoughts, Alex arrived at the front door of the National Portrait Gallery without knowing how he got there. He was early, on purpose. His destination was Room 20 on the third floor. There, some of the names from the Poets Corner were reunited. Portraits of Tennyson, the Brownings, Thackeray, Dickens, and many more famous writers joined artists and musicians in a celebration of the arts against dark green walls. Among them, Anne, Emily, and Charlotte Brontë stared, somber and serious, from the famous "pillar" portrait painted by their only brother, Branwell.

Restoration of this piece had not eliminated the cracks from where it had been folded and stashed away after their deaths, but it had removed what was once thought to be a pillar between Emily and Charlotte, revealing the ghost of Branwell, who for his own characteristically inexplicable reasons, had decided to white himself out. The sisters regarded the viewer with expressionless eyes and pursed lips and appeared to earn their reputation for plainness.

Next to this austere portrait hung another, however, that gave an altogether different impression of young Emily Jane.

Alex gazed at this, the so-called "fragment" painting, for a long, pensive moment. Although some scholars claimed the painting was of Anne, he believed the profile depicted Emily. She would have been only fifteen at the time, but she looked somewhat older, perhaps because of the daring off-the-shoulder gown she was wearing. Alex had often felt that her attire in this portrait was inconsistent with academic studies that emphasized her plainness and inattention to her looks. The Emily before him was far from plain, almost pretty, in a delicate, Victorian sort of way.

"Anyone you know?" The voice behind him was feminine and husky and decidedly British. Alex froze.

Then slowly he turned to face those intense green eyes, that sophisticated curtain of satiny red hair, the too-generous mouth.

"You're early," he said brusquely, hoping to hide any sign that he found her attractive, which he realized to his chagrin that he did. Actually, she was stunning, as always. Her copper hair fell straight and perfect, curling under slightly at the shoulders. She wore an emerald silk suit, cut wide at the shoulders, and a slim, short skirt. Below, long legs stretched, shapely in dark green hose and matching heels. Alex let out a long, slow breath.

Maggie reached out and took both of his hands in her own. "Don't I get a welcome kiss?"

Alex obliged, catching the scent of a familiar perfume as his lips brushed her cheeks. "You look great, Maggie," he said, discovering suddenly and to his surprise that he still had some measure of affection for her. He wished they could be friends, like before, when they first met. They sat down on a bench in the center of the gallery.

"I've missed you, Alex."

His reply was silence.

"So . . ." She searched for a way past the awkwardness. "How long will you be in London?"

"Just today. Tomorrow I leave for Haworth."

"Not going to the British Museum first? There are lots of Brontë originals there."

Alex felt the muscles in his jaw tense. "You know I've always wanted to go to Haworth," he said, determined to stay detached. "It seems the best approach to my research, there in the Parsonage. If I don't find what I need, then I'll come back to London."

Maggie cocked her head and said with a sardonic smile, "You're not going to find what you need anywhere, Alex, because it doesn't exist."

The dragon lady had surfaced. Maggie the conqueror.

He did not relish their confrontation later in the summer.

"Maybe not. But I have to give it a shot."

"Of course, dear." Maggie's patronizing reply stung. She considered her battle already won. Alex had no doubt she believed she would eat his lunch in the debate, and maybe she would. But he didn't like the way she salted her sandwich so early in the game. Irritated, he was about to change the subject when she did it for him.

"I'm glad you came early," she said, looking at her watch. "I want you to go somewhere with me. I have been dying to see an art exhibit everyone in London is hot over, and today's the last day. If we hurry, we'll just have time to make it before the gallery closes."

Alex groaned inwardly. He was already at the only gallery he was interested in seeing. "Look, Maggie, I can't. I mean, I just got in a few hours ago. I think I'll go back to my hotel. . . ."

"Nonsense. It won't take long." She stood up and pulled him to his feet. The reality of Maggie Flynn iced any earlier misguided feelings of nostalgic affection for her and replaced them with contempt. What Maggie wanted, Maggie usually got. Including him, once upon a time. But no more.

"Thanks all the same, Maggie, but . . ." Alex dropped his hands from hers.

"You'll love it, I promise. This woman's work is so far out. It's all the rage. You simply must go with me. I won't take no."

She was already walking out the door, passing the portrait of the three dour-looking sisters without so much as a glance. Perhaps one got used to such treasures when one didn't have to travel across an ocean to see them.

Alex shot one last glance at Emily's portrait, then turned and followed Maggie. Today, because he was so tired, it was simply easier to comply with her than try to

beg off. But, he warned himself, giving in was a dangerous precedent to set.

Thirty minutes later they reached the doorsteps of the
Perkins Galleries, a small, exclusive salon in the heart of
Chelsea. They were the only customers in the shop. A
well-dressed man in his late thirties was busily taking
paintings off the walls and displays, dismantling the exhibit in front of their noses.

"Sorry for the disorder," he apologized, introducing
himself as Tom Perkins, the owner. "I'll leave as many
hanging as I can, but the artist will be here shortly, and I
promised to have started the crating."

Maggie assured him they were just browsing, and then
they were left on their own.

"Well, what do you think?" she asked, as if assured he
would be totally grateful she had made him come.

"I think I need to go back to the hotel," he said, furious with himself at letting Maggie draw him in one more
time.

She looked at him, her face softening. "Poor dear.
Maybe you should. I'm sure you are tired. You look quite
dreadful. Well, we won't stay long." With that she began
a tour of the exhibit, leaving Alex staring vacantly at one
of the paintings.

Either it was truly unusual, he thought dimly, or his
fatigue and anger were creating monstrous distortions.
The size of a large window, the canvas was covered with
what looked like fog, or mist, or a muddy sandstorm.
Bright images jumped out at random, their garish colors
juxtaposed incongruously against the softness of the
mauves and grays of the background. The figures exuded
a fierce freedom, with black horses racing against the
wind, fire burning out of control, an organ grinder's monkey laughing raucously as he seemed to reach beyond the
canvas to hand Alex a note.

The painting itself he found disturbing, but the scrap of paper in the monkey's hand caught his eye. He looked at it more closely.

On the note the artist had painted a message of some sort, spelled out in a tiny, cramped style of handwriting. Squinting, he thought he could make out a few words: *my health . . . it would . . . the misery . . . myself. It is . . .* They appeared to be parts of a sentence or two, disembodied words floating ghostlike on a painted scrap of paper, itself like a piece of a jigsaw puzzle.

"Would you look at this?" he exclaimed in a low voice.

Maggie heard him and returned to his side, smiling up at him, happy that he was finally enjoying the exhibit. As she knew he would. She tucked her hand in the crook of his arm. "What, love?"

Although Alex hadn't meant to call her over, he pointed to the painted image of the written words. "What do you see there?"

"Hmm. That's interesting. Looks like a note or something. I wonder what the naughty monkey has been into?" She laughed lightly. "Isn't this great stuff? Really makes you think, and yet it is so whimsical."

"Maggie, look again. What does the note say?"

She peered at the scrap of paper in the monkey's hand, then gave him a withering look. "You know I can't see close up without my glasses."

"Then put them on."

Maggie gave him an exasperated glance, then fished her glasses out of her purse. With the large lenses on her face, she lost some of her sex appeal, and Alex knew why she didn't want to wear them. To humor him, though, she examined the image again.

"I don't know," she said at last. "The letters are so tiny."

"That shouldn't bother a Brontë scholar," he commented, recalling his own eye strain from hours of work-

ing his way through the Lilliputian handwriting of the
Brontë children's juvenalia. Emily, in fact, had never out-
grown that immature penmanship. "Looks a little like
Emily's scrawling, doesn't it?" he added, jolted at the
similarity.

"Emily?"

"Brontë."

She removed the glasses, looked at him and raised her
eyebrows. "I think it *is* time we got you back to your
hotel."

"Just joking, Maggie," he growled. "But I do think
those are actual words painted there." He pointed to the
top line. "It says 'my health,' then 'it would.' See?"

Maggie considered the painting again, studied it for a
long moment, then replied with a shrug, "I suppose."

Alex frowned. "Never mind."

He moved on to the next painting, and the next and
the next. In each there was a scrap of the letter, a tantalizing tidbit of the whole. A lover of word games, he
wished he had more time, a strong magnifying glass, and
no Maggie to contend with. What would the message
reveal, he wondered, if it were pieced together?

The bell at the front of the shop tinkled, and Alex
turned to see the figure of a dark-haired woman approaching. For a drop-dead moment his pulse came to a
standstill. Alex was often caught like this, suspended if
for only a moment in a timeless space, surrounded by
fear and a dark, nameless pain. It happened when a
woman even vaguely reminded him of his former wife.
His reaction was irrational, neurotic, he knew. It engulfed him in anger and guilt.

And it had gone on far too long.

Alex watched the woman coming toward him, realizing
that except for having long, dark hair, she looked nothing
at all like his girl-next-door ex-wife. She was clad in a
black turtleneck sweater, tight-fitting black leggings, and

high-topped black boots. Over the silhouetting black, she wore a cape of brilliant magenta that fell to the tops of her boots and flowed behind her as she walked. She was of medium height, slender, and, Alex observed with a sudden and acute awareness, very, very beautiful.

She didn't look British. Her face reflected perhaps a graceful Spanish or Italian heritage, rather than the pale and sometimes pudgy Anglo-Saxon features. Her olive complexion was flawless, her obsidian eyes breathtaking. Caressing her high cheekbones and delicately defined jaw was a mass of hair so dark the highlights seemed almost blue.

Alex felt the heat of her body as she passed him where he stood transfixed in the aisle. He turned and studied her from behind, watching her move gracefully to the back of the gallery where, to his disappointment, Tom Perkins greeted her with an effusive embrace and a kiss placed directly on her lips.

"I was getting worried, my dear," he heard the gallery owner tell the woman. "It's almost six o'clock. I've already got a good start packing up your things, although, I must say, if I hadn't already booked the next show, I would hold yours over for another month. You really should leave a few pieces here for me to sell."

Alex realized with a start the woman must be the artist, come to collect her work. He stared. Yes, she had to be the artist, for she was as fiercely exotic and mysteriously provocative as her work.

But what, he suddenly wanted to know, was her relationship to the gallery owner?

"You ready to go?" Maggie's voice slapped him back into reality. It had an edge to it that let Alex know she'd caught him staring at the other woman.

I've been ready to go since we got here, he thought angrily, but he replied with only a nod, noting it had started to rain again.

Maggie steered him toward the front door, but before he left the gallery, Alex picked up a pamphlet about the artist's show. The woman's photo was on the back, her midnight hair tossed by the wind. She had signed it with a single name—Selena.

June 11, 1845

For one week now I have kept secret my patient on the moors. His name is Mikel, and he says he is the descendant of a gipsie king. He is darker-skinned than anyone I have ever seen, and his countenance is rough. I am frightened of him, and yet he is too injured to do me harm. He speaks little, and when he does, it is like a growl. I almost feel as if he is a wild animal. I have braced his leg as best I could with a timber I found, but I know he needs better. He will not have it, though. When I suggested I bring a doctor after all, I thought he would rise off the ground and wrench my neck.

I am uncertain what to do. I cannot continue to hide him. It is too difficult. Yet if I tell even Charlotte or Anne, I fear they would insist I alert the constable. Mikel has done no harm, so far as I know, and yet if the constable is called, I am certain he will end up in prison. I cannot bring myself to impose such injustice.

His appetite is getting better. I am going to have to make more gruel if I am to continue to feed him. It is fortunate that I cook most of our meals, for no one will notice if I make an extra portion.

❧ *Chapter 3* ❧

S elena disengaged herself from Tom's unwelcome embrace. She wished he wouldn't do that. He was an excellent art dealer, the best in London, and careerwise she needed him desperately. But she knew Tom would be more than willing to mix business with pleasure. It was an arrangement in which she was not the least interested, but she had to be very careful in the way she held his seductive intents at bay. He was, unfortunately, in a position to make her career, or break it.

"I'll bring them back for another show if you'd like," she said with a forced smile. "You mentioned the autumn maybe?" She moved away from him, going back onto the main floor of the gallery, putting space between them; professional space.

"Autumn, for sure," he said with a sigh. "Well, love, I'd better get back to the crating if you want to get out of here before midnight. You want to bring me those that are still hanging?"

"Sure." Selena was in no hurry to take anything into the back room with Tom.

As soon as he disappeared through the doorway, she turned and stretched, weary from the long trip. She allowed herself the luxury of doing nothing for a moment, just looking around at her work on display in one of London's top galleries. It was a lifelong dream come true.

Funny how things work out, she mused. The paintings hanging here were the least favorite of anything she'd ever done. In fact, she hated them. They frightened and intimidated her. But they had put her on the map as an up-and-coming talent. Who, she wondered incredulously, would want this sort of thing in their home?

At the moment there were two customers in the gallery, a man and a woman who stood together in front of one of her canvases, talking in low tones. Selena observed them, thinking that neither looked like they were having fun. She hoped it wasn't her work that caused the pained look on his face or the barely suppressed anger and frustration on hers.

The woman was striking, draped in red hair and green silk, and frosted with white, white skin. She appeared elegant, well-bred, refined. But her beauty was interrupted by tiny lines straining from the corners of her green eyes and rigid lips pressed tightly together.

Selena shifted her attention to the woman's companion. His face, likewise, showed strain, but it failed to detract from his strong, handsome features. His hair was dark and thick, combed to one side and back, away from his wide forehead, falling to an even trim at the nape of his neck.

His eyes were also dark, gray perhaps, although it was hard to discern their exact color from across the room. Heavy dark brows slashed across his tanned face, drawn together at the moment in a tense frown. His nose was slender but nicely formed. His lips were generous. A shadow of a beard outlined a strong jaw.

He was, to Selena's artist's eye, decidedly handsome.

A black mackintosh covered most of the rest of him, but it outlined broad, muscular shoulders. He was several inches taller than the woman, perhaps almost six feet in height.

She observed him massage his temples and wondered if he was ill. She might be ill, too, she thought wickedly, if she had to endure the presence of that woman. An odd pair, she concluded, taking down a painting at last. But perhaps it was the oddity of Tom's customers that had made her show such a success.

The following morning the rain was gone, and so was Alex's jet lag. Fourteen hours of sound sleep after he finally managed to extricate himself from Maggie did the trick, and he awoke feeling refreshed and energized. He took a vigorous jog through the quiet park across the street from the hotel, did some push-ups, and indulged in a full English breakfast. Looking out of the third floor window down into the park, he considered staying in London for another day. He felt short-changed at having had to make such an abbreviated visit to a city so enriched with history, but the clock was ticking. He needed to get to Haworth and begin his work in earnest. Besides, London and Maggie were somehow synonymous to him now, and he was ready to leave them both behind for a while.

An hour later he boarded a train for Leeds.

England was pretty in early summer, decked out in blooming hedges and wildflowers which crept to the very edges of the track as the train made its way out of London's suburbs. The population thinned and the engine gathered speed, propelling the train at well over one hundred miles an hour through villages and farmland. He stared out at the passing fields where brilliant yellow rapeseed, cultivated to make cooking oil, covered acres of farmland like buttery snow. Cottages with thatched roofs dotted the landscape, along with occasional herds of dairy cows and sheep. It seemed satisfyingly pastoral, proper for Britain.

The train itself was a study in clean efficiency. The upholstery appeared new and fresh, covering the comfortable seats, and Alex noted appreciatively how much more leg room he had than on the airplane. He had selected one of the seats at the rear of the carriage which faced a table, hoping to get a little work done on the journey. Across the aisle at another table a young couple munched noisily on plough-boy sandwiches purchased at the station. An elderly woman sat at their table, facing him, doing a crossword puzzle.

Alex reached into his briefcase and retrieved a dog-eared copy of a slim paperback, finding it hard to believe that in all his years as a Brontë scholar he had never made this trip. The tiny village of Haworth, nestled on the edge of the West Yorkshire moors, was the source of it all—the poetry and novels they'd written and the myths and legends that surrounded the remarkable Brontë family, all of which had encompassed a large part of his career in academe.

Alex was aware that to some, particularly his father, his career choice was less than macho. A star athlete in high school, he could have gone to college on a baseball scholarship that had been offered to him by a nearby sports-oriented school. Or, had he followed his father's desires, he could have entered medical school.

But from an early age, Alex had been drawn to the written word. An avid reader, his boyhood adventures had been played out with the likes of Robinson Crusoe, Tom Sawyer, and Huck Finn. He had gone on the *Trail of the Lost Tribe* with Tom Stetson, and traveled the world in the Landmark series. He had scared himself thoroughly with *The Tell-Tale Heart* and *Dr. Jekyll and Mr. Hyde*, and found heroes to worship in biographies written for young boys. For Alex, nothing was more exciting than a good book, and he'd never given a damn what others thought about his literary pursuits.

It wasn't until high school, however, that he'd met the most fascinating hero he'd encountered on the printed page—Heathcliff. Passionate. Strong. Cruel. Frightening. Mad. But above all, unforgettable. From that first introduction, Alex's imagination had been held hostage by this darkly brooding, inexplicable character, and as Alex matured and began to consider career options, Heathcliff's vote had counted more heavily than either a baseball scholarship or his father's dreams for his son.

Alex contemplated the book in his hands, a tattered copy of *Wuthering Heights,* thinking about the supposedly celibate, reclusive authoress who had created the story and its dark hero, and in so doing, seemingly had laid claim on Alexander Hightower's soul.

Emily Brontë and her family had moved into the Parsonage at Haworth when her father, Patrick, an eccentric Evangelical preacher, became curate there in 1820. She was just under two years old at the time, and she lived in that same house, except for a few unhappy interludes away at various schools, until she died there twenty-eight years later. Hers had been a short and strangely isolated life, but one that had spawned remarkable poetry and this single volatile novel.

He turned the premise of his quest over again in his mind. Had Emily ended her life on purpose? If so, why? *Wuthering Heights* had only been out a year, published at the same time as her younger sister's novel, *Agnes Grey,* and just two months after Charlotte's hit, *Jane Eyre.* The three sisters, writing under masculine pseudonyms to overcome the sexual bias against women writers in their day, had a promising future as novelists to look forward to. Was the notoriety more than the reclusive Emily could bear?

Alex thought not.

Although Charlotte and Anne eventually came out of the closet and revealed their true feminine identities, Emily remained cloistered in the Parsonage, protecting her privacy solidly behind her pen name, Ellis Bell.

It was true that once Charlotte had had to coax Emily into allowing her poems to be published, but after that, Emily had written *Wuthering Heights* and included it willingly in submissions of all their work made to London publishing houses. It wasn't as if she didn't want to see her work in print.

And although some reviewers were shocked by the content and characters of *Wuthering Heights*, Emily should have been gratified by the fact that the novel was popular with many readers. Apparently, Alex continued his line of thinking, Emily had planned to write another novel, perhaps had even started on it, according to a letter written to "Ellis Bell" from "his" publisher, T. C. Newby, early in 1848.

With so much to live for, why would she want to die? This was the stubborn issue Maggie would use against him in the debate. And it was a valid one. If Emily Brontë did commit suicide, her reasons must have been enormous to outweigh a promising career as a writer.

For, next to nature and the moors, Emily loved writing best.

Maybe she *was* overcome with grief for Branwell. The two had been close all their lives, although toward the end of his, Branwell had become violently self-destructive and a heavy burden on his family, especially his doting sister Emily.

Had the physical exertion of hauling her drunken, consumptive brother up the stairs every night broken her health just as watching his moral degradation had broken her heart? Had he depleted her resources so seriously that she just gave up?

Again, Alex thought not.

Because Emily Brontë had a will of iron. And there was no doubt she'd used that will to control the events and circumstances of her life. Alex recalled that when she was unhappy at being sent away to school, Emily had simply stopped eating and literally made herself sick so she would be allowed to come home. Another time, with stoic resolution, she had cauterized a wound on her own body with a hot iron after being bitten while breaking up a dog fight.

No, Alex believed Emily Brontë had been perfectly capable of controlling anything about her life she chose . . . including her death.

In fact, she'd illustrated this possibility in her novel. He thumbed through the text of *Wuthering Heights* to the scene just prior to the heroine's death. Catherine Linton, in an effort to control the two men who loved her, had willed herself almost into her deathbed. However psychotic this might sound to a modern-day reader, Alex thought, to Emily it might have been a very realistic way out of an unresolvable situation. He read:

> . . . *the thing that irks me most is this shattered prison, after all. I'm tired, tired of being enclosed here. I'm wearying to escape into that glorious world, and to be always there: not seeing it dimly through tears, but really with it, and in it. Nelly, you think you are better and more fortunate than I, in full health and strength; you are sorry for me—very soon that will be altered. I shall be sorry for you. I shall be incomparably beyond and above you all.*

Was this Catherine Linton speaking, Alex wondered, or Emily Brontë? Had she written this purely as fiction, or had she ideas of willing her own final exit?

Either way, Alex was convinced that in the winter of

1848, Emily Brontë made a decision to die and used her implacable will to control her life to the very end.

All he needed now was proof.

Out of the corner of his eye Alex saw the old woman across the aisle lay her crossword aside, and then he realized uncomfortably that she had turned her attention fully and unabashedly upon him.

Involuntarily, he looked up at her, and when he did, he found himself peering into a pair of faded blue eyes, enormous behind thick-lensed glasses. They belonged to a feminine face that had surely weathered more than eighty years and yet managed to maintain a certain beauty. The nearly translucent skin was rouged at the cheekbones, and a bright lipstick seeped through deep crevasses that lined the ancient lips. She was dressed in a chocolate-colored suit trimmed in pink, and a pink blouse with a large bow tie at the neck.

Alex nodded at her and smiled slightly, then tried to return to his book. He could feel her staring at him, however, reminding him of a certain feared English teacher in junior high school.

"I couldn't help but notice what you were reading." Her surprisingly strong voice made its way across the aisle and into his consciousness.

Alex looked at her blankly.

"Wuthering Heights," she elaborated with a pleased smile. "A classic. A real classic. It's so refreshing to see a young person reading something besides those trashy novels they publish these days."

He started to point out that lots of good books were published as well these days, but before he could say anything, she continued. "Are you going to Haworth?"

Her question caught him off guard. "Uh, yes ma'am."

"I thought so, you being a Brontë reader and all. Will you be there for the meeting?"

He was having trouble following her. "Meeting?"

"The AGM. Brontë Society. I go every year. I've been a member since just after the war."

Alex shook his head. He didn't ask what AGM stood for, because he didn't care to encourage her to continue. The Brontë Society, he knew, fulfilled a valuable function in preserving the Brontë heritage, but he wanted no part of the politics that were usually associated with such groups. "No, I'm going strictly for research."

"Too bad. We could use some new blood," she said bluntly, then shifted her line of questioning. "What are you investigating?"

Alex was in no mood to humor what he perceived to be a dilettante. "Oh, the usual. Americans don't get much chance to look at their original work."

"Emily's my favorite," the old woman pressed on. "That *Wuthering Heights*. Don't you know it was scandalous in its day? The grandmother of all shockers. Makes you wonder what that girl was like, doesn't it?"

Alex nodded, amused. But he noted gratefully that the train had at last reached the station in Leeds, precluding further conversation.

He waited before leaving his seat, allowing the old woman to go ahead of him. He retrieved his heavy traveling bag from the luggage storage area, but when he got off the train, he found the woman waiting for him.

"That'll be your track over there." She motioned in the direction of the next platform. "The train to Haworth leaves in twenty minutes."

Together they started walking toward the station. "I'm Eleanor Bates, by the way," she said, stopping and extending her hand.

Politely, Alex shook it. "Dr. Alexander Hightower."

"Hightower!" The old eyes widened. "I should have known it. You're the gentleman who'll be facing off against Maggie Flynn later this summer at the university. The one who thinks Emily killed herself."

Alex felt the blood rise to his face. How had the likes of Eleanor Bates heard about that? "Yes. Uh, yes, that's true."

Eleanor was visibly excited. "I can't wait for that one. I go to them all, you know. There are lots of Brontë symposia here in Leeds. I heard Maggie Flynn once. What a ball of fire!"

His guts contracted. "Well, it was a pleasure meeting you, Mrs. Bates," he said, trying to graciously extricate himself from her enraptured presence.

"It's Ms. Bates. Not married, you see. Husband died in 'fifty-five, and I never found another one I liked as well. But I'm too old to be called Miss. I was glad when that Ms. thing came along."

Alex nodded, attempting to keep a straight face. "Well, then, Ms. Bates, perhaps we will meet again." He turned and walked briskly toward his waiting train, wondering just exactly what he'd gotten himself into in agreeing to this debate.

June 16, 1845

Mikel's strength is amazing. His leg is not mended, yet he manages to move with some agility using his arms and his good leg. He is restless and angry with himself over his predicament, for he will not be able to bring home the money this year he needs for his family. He trades in horses he captures wild on the moors and breaks before taking them to market in his home country. He says he comes each summer to the moors, but has never been this far. His speech is strange to my ear. He says he comes from over the Welsh mountains.

He is unlike the ruddy English in the village. His skin is like bronze from the hours he spends in the open sun. His eyes are large and dark, and his dark hair falls to his shoulders. He wears a kerchief tied around his neck, and his chest is exposed beneath his open (and very dirty!) shirt. His face is strong, with a long nose and craggy cheekbones. He is quite handsome, in a rough way. He speaks little, and although I know he is grateful for my help, he sends me away.

It is my own feelings that I find most strange when I think of Mikel. I am frightened of him and yet attracted to him. I know nothing about him. He could be a murderer or at the very least a thief. I think not, however. His eyes are soft when he speaks of his home and his family, although he has told me little. Such are not the eyes of a felon. Or is that only my wish? I know I am starting to live each day in anxious anticipation of the time when I can go for a long walk on the moors. Charlotte is cross with me because I want to go alone, but I don't care. I will nurse Mikel until he is well enough to return to his home. He will be my secret . . . from them all.

A flash of black and white met Selena's eyes as her dog cleared the corner of the old stone farmhouse and barked eagerly at the approaching vehicle. Selena grinned and rolled down the window. "Get back, Domino. Scoot!" With care not to run over the tail-wagging animal, she maneuvered the rear of the Land Rover close to the door of the barn behind the farmhouse.

"Hey, boy," she laughed. "Did you miss me?" She knelt and hugged and petted the dog, happily receiving its wet licks on her cheeks. "It's okay, it's okay. Calm down now."

Selena often wondered what she would have done for companionship if Domino hadn't shown up. Hers was a solitary and sometimes lonely life. She didn't make friends easily, never had. She knew the postman and the butcher at the market and a few others in town. But no one she could call a real friend.

And her work demanded a great deal of her time and energy, preventing her from having much of a social life

even if she'd been so inclined. So when the stray border
collie had wandered down the moors and taken up residence on her back step, she was pleased to welcome such
a roommate.

She'd inquired around the area, trying to locate his
owner, but no one stepped forward to claim the ragged
canine, who wasted no time in making himself quite at
home. Domino must have put the word out to his homeless friends, because shortly thereafter Peaches arrived,
followed by Hizzonor, two bedraggled, scrawny cats who
now likely lazed fatly in the noon sunshine upstairs, wondering when their dinner bowls would be refilled.

Selena stood up and brushed her hands together, then
opened the back door of the vehicle and pulled a
wooden-clad parcel from among the many that were
tightly packed inside. Might as well carry one of these
upstairs as I go, she thought, eager to check on her cats.

The old wooden steps creaked beneath her feet as she
ascended to what once was the loft of the barn. At the
top of the stairs she lowered the heavy crate with an
audible groan and opened the inner door that led from
the stairwell into the two-room studio. Even though it
was somewhat stark and still in need of many more re-
pairs, the studio was home, and she was glad to be back.

Selena had moved here shortly after returning from
her studies abroad. She could have chosen to stay in
London, closer to the community of British artists, but
she wanted to be near her aging grandmother, who at the
time still lived in the tiny village of Stanbury, in the house
where Selena had grown up.

But the old woman had hired a live-in aide in Selena's
absence, leaving no room for her when she returned. It
was just as well, for Selena was ready to be on her own.
She needed solitude, as well as space for a studio if she
was going to try to make a living in earnest as an artist.

With Matka's help, she had purchased the small farm

from the heirs of the farmer who had died a decade earlier. The abandoned property was like so many others in the vicinity—aging, weather-beaten, run-down. And it was for sale cheap. With a lot of hard work and some borrowed money, she had managed to convert the loft of the barn into a relatively comfortable studio, but the house was still barely habitable. She kept her clothes in the house, and her groceries, but spent little time there.

Most of her waking hours, she labored in the small, paint-spattered back room of the studio, and most of her sleeping ones she spent on the battered but comfortable sofa in the larger front room. She had installed a free-standing fireplace for warmth, a kitchenette with a small sink and a hot plate to make tea, and a tiny bath.

It was sufficient.

Someday, she hoped she would be able to restore the whole place, but that would have to wait until the remodeling loan for the studio was paid off. And that would only come with her continued success as an artist. And that would only come, she thought with growing trepidation, if she could successfully defuse Tom Perkins's amorous interests in her while maintaining his professional regard.

And, she knew, she had to grow as an artist, expand her work into other media, other subject matter.

She had to start painting something besides the Gypsy riders and campfires and pieces of some crazy letter that permeated this series.

The series from hell.

Selena lifted the unwieldy crate and carried it into the front room, leaning it against the wall. Then she reached down and picked up the large orange tabby cat that brushed against her legs.

"Hello, Peaches. Where's Hizzonor? Did you fellows miss me?" She checked out their food dishes and decided both felines were probably on the verge of a ner-

vous breakdown. She could actually see the bottom of
both bowls, although there was enough dry food remaining to sustain even their greedy appetites for another day
or so. Hizzonor showed his gray and white presence then,
materializing from nowhere to stand next to his bowl and
issue a loud protest at having been left overnight.

"You poor, mistreated things," she said dryly, reaching
for the box of cat food from the cupboard. "Here. This'll
tide you over until supper." She topped off their dishes,
then turned her attention to the fireplace.

Outside, the afternoon was warm and springlike, but a
chill always seemed to cling to the damp stone walls of
the building. Selena built a small fire, and Domino curled
up on his blanket nearby. The cats munched noisily in the
corner. She put a kettle of water on for tea. All should
have been right once again in her world.

But all was far from being right.

As long as her paintings were on exhibit in London,
Selena had been able to avoid thinking about the future.
For a time she'd allowed herself to bask in the glow of
her success—the positive reviews and the four canvases
she'd sold from the show.

But standing now in the silence of her studio, the
strong summer light pouring starkly in through the high
northern windows, she was filled with apprehension.

Would she ever be able to paint something else?
Something besides the insistent repetitive figures that
seemed to jump of their own volition from her paintbrush? She shuddered at the thought of starting work on
a new canvas, knowing from experience what it was like
to have some terrifying and powerful force take command of her, sending her into a trancelike state and
painting what *it* willed, not what she desired. She had
fought it in many ways over the past year. Once, she'd
deliberately consumed five cups of strong coffee before
starting work, hoping the overdose of caffeine would

hold the trance at bay. But all it did was make her work that day perceptibly shaky.

Other times she had used a projector to cast images from photos and negatives onto the white canvas, then drawn their outlines in pencil, giving her a preconceived and conscious subject from which to work. But when she'd picked up her brush and palette, the force had simply painted over the lines of her drawing with easy strokes of mauve and gray and prepared the canvas to receive its haunting images in spite of her.

Selena closed her eyes and crossed her arms over her chest, grasping her shoulders and dropping her head. What force was this, what obsession drove her to paint these images? And more importantly, she thought desperately, how could she break free of it?

She had insisted on bringing all of her paintings back from the gallery, thinking that if she hung them all together, surrounded herself with them and studied them closely, perhaps she would be able to discern and understand what was driving her to paint them.

And then maybe she could stop.

With a heavy sigh, she returned to the truck and began unloading the rest of the crates.

Later that afternoon, Selena stood in the center of the studio, surrounded by eleven of the paintings in the series, which, in spite of her personal anxiety concerning them, had generated the first serious recognition she'd received as an artist—not to mention almost two thousand pounds that she desperately needed.

The sunlight suddenly gave way to threatening clouds, as it so often did in this wild, rugged country, and she heard the roar of the wind spilling down the slopes and whipping past the corner of the barn. Large drops of rain began to spatter intermittently against the windows.

Around her the canvases hung on the walls like unanswered questions. The images beckoned, leered at her, dared her to challenge them and the authority they held over her. Stepping closer to one of the larger paintings, Selena stared at the rider on the black horse.

Who are you? she demanded silently. Where did you come from? She'd never been around horses in her entire life. Or campfires or monkeys or organ grinders. She knew those things only from Matka's tales.

She supposed her fertile imagination could have fleshed out these impressions from those childhood stories. But why did they have such a hold on her now, at this point in her life? They were, after all, only figments of her imagination. The only images that might have come from reality were the red roses.

Those, and the fragments of the letter.

She paused, considering . . . It had to be the letter. Something about the letter. That cursed letter.

The curse . . .

Nonsense!

A sick feeling rose in her throat, and she turned away from the painting. Perhaps the source of the images didn't matter after all.

What mattered was getting them to go away.

She had to change directions. Stretch her creativity. Advance as an artist. She had to, if she was to survive.

With no small effort, Selena forced herself to explore the first canvas she had painted when the madness started almost a year ago. It was tame compared to the others. In it, the bit of the letter was larger, easier to read. The monkey's face was comical. The Gypsy rider looked like he belonged on the cover of a paperback romance novel.

She smiled slightly, then compelled herself to move on to the next painting, and then the next, surveying them one by one, slowly moving in a circle. Chronologically, they developed from the almost humorous to the uncomfortably threatening.

They were her fortune.

Her fame.

But they were not her friends.

After one complete circumnavigation of the paintings, anxiety swept over her with such intensity that Selena felt suddenly as if she couldn't catch her breath. Her chest constricted and her heart began to pound. A sheen of perspiration dampened her skin, chilling her to the marrow. "Let me go!" she gasped, staring at the figures in her earliest painting. "For God's sake, let me go!"

Slowly, her heart racing, she began a second turn around the studio. Facing the paintings, she lifted her arms and held her palms face out in front of her.

She addressed each painting as if it were an evil entity laying claim to her soul.

"Let me go!"

She repeated her demand over and over, louder and louder, until the words became a chant and her conscious mind seemed to disappear, melting into a fog of mauve and gray. Faster and faster she moved around the room until she was whirling dervishlike, out of control. The words echoed off the walls and thundered inside her own ears until she heard herself screaming them at the top of her lungs, "Let me go! Let me go! Let me go!"

Then, with a sharp cry, she collapsed into a heap on the floor, dizzy and breathless. Tears streamed down her cheeks and she was wracked by uncontrollable sobs.

Around her, fire burned, horses reared, monkeys laughed.

And Selena knew they had not let her go.

❧ *Chapter 4* ❧

Alex settled into a shabbier, less comfortable seat on a smaller train to cover the final leg of his journey, unexpectedly disturbed by his encounter with the old woman. It was inconceivable that he would run into a total stranger who not only knew about the debate, but was familiar with his name as well. In the United States such an event might draw a few dozen interested parties, mostly from among the academically obsessed, like himself. Certainly not from the general public.

The train chugged along the valley, and Alex stared out of the smudged window, watching farmland replace the smoky factories of Leeds. Overhead, the sky was an indeterminate gray, matching his mood since his conversation with "Ms." Bates.

Maybe Eleanor Bates wasn't from the general public, he considered. Maybe she was also one of the academically obsessed. She had mentioned she was a longtime member of the Brontë Society. She had certainly pegged Emily's *Wuthering Heights* precisely. And she knew Maggie Flynn. Maybe she was a retired professor or some such.

Alex frowned, wishing the old woman hadn't introduced the specter of Maggie Flynn into his thoughts once again. He'd promised himself to forget about her until the debate, and resolutely he forced himself now to keep that promise. With an effort, Alex shoved Maggie, Eleanor Bates, and the debate solidly to the nether reaches of his mind and focused instead on the scenery unfolding in front of him.

Stands of trees were sporadically interrupted by villages and farms on the lower slopes of the hills. Higher up, the crests were hidden from view by a heavy mist that subtly shifted shapes and changed colors. Sunlight strained through the vapors, casting rays of mauve and gray over the faint contours of the trees and houses in the distance.

Misty mauve and gray.

Like the background in the paintings he'd seen last night. The paintings by the woman with the ebony hair and infinite eyes who had breezed into the gallery and drawn his attention like a magnet.

Alex rummaged in his briefcase and found the brochure he'd picked up, hoping the artist might have an address listed, but it carried only the location of the Perkins Galleries. He turned it over and stared at the photo on the back. Even in black and white, Selena's dark beauty beguiled him, filling him with surprising and disturbing fantasies.

He read the copy beneath the photo. "Although working in a remote moorland studio, Selena is recognized as a rising star on the international art scene, and there is a growing demand in London and abroad for her work. Her style is considered by many to be comparable to the great surrealists of the earlier twentieth century . . ."

Alex stared at the photo, spellbound. Then he glanced out of the window again.

Remote moorland studio.

Was it possible Selena was from Yorkshire?

* * *

The train pulled into Keighley Station, and Alex caught a taxi to the Black Bull Inn in Haworth, where he planned to stay until he could locate a small flat for the summer. The old soot-stained tavern perched atop a steep hill on Main Street, next to the church.

According to history and legend, which often intermingle in Brontë lore, the Black Bull was the scene of the nightly degradation of Branwell Brontë, the only son of the Reverend Patrick Brontë. Branwell, Alex recalled as the taxi wheezed up the steep incline, was supposed to have been his father's shining star. Brilliant and talented in both art and writing, Branwell could have, should have, been successful enough at something to provide security for his three surviving sisters, as was the custom of his day.

Instead he lived most of his life in a fantasy world. He never entered the London Academy of Art, as his father had so carefully arranged. He had trouble holding a job, preferring the company of drinking companions to that of coworkers.

The taxi reached its destination, and the driver set the emergency brake. Alex paid the fare and unloaded his bag. Despite the fact that it was early summer, a brisk, chill wind whipped his hair into his eyes, and Alex pulled the collar of the mackintosh closer to his neck. He watched as the cab disappeared down another steep incline, then turned and surveyed the Black Bull.

Poor Branii, he thought morosely, recalling Branwell's childhood nickname. Too bad you couldn't magically save yourself the way you once did old Napoleon and Alexander Percy and all your other imaginary heroes.

But Alex was not entirely without sympathy for Branwell. The story went that the cause of Branwell's final emotional collapse was the betrayal of a woman whom he loved deeply, a woman who ultimately chose financial security over Branwell's charms. Her name was Lydia

Robinson—*Mrs*. Lydia Robinson. She was the wife of his employer, and mother of the two boys he was hired to tutor.

When Branwell was abruptly dismissed from his job in the summer of 1846, he let it be known, especially around the Bull, that Mrs. Robinson was madly in love with him but wouldn't leave her husband because she couldn't stand the shame of divorce.

Scandalous as the idea was, everyone, including his family, believed his story, at least for a while. A short time later, however, Mr. Robinson died, leaving Lydia free to join her true love. Instead, she immediately dispatched an agent to Branwell, who bore the message that she never wanted to see him again.

Branwell met the messenger in a private parlor in the Black Bull, and after the man left, Branwell's friends found him writhing on the floor in a terrible fit. When he recovered, he told everyone that Mr. Robinson had changed his will, stipulating that if Lydia had anything to do with Branwell Brontë, she would be cut off without a penny. Since Branwell was in no position to support her, she had no choice but to opt for money over love.

Or so went his face-saving story.

Alex opened the door and stepped inside the pub. Whether Lydia Robinson loved Branwell, or whether he'd been dismissed for making a pass at his employer's wife, Alex didn't know. There was much conjecture among his colleagues on the matter, and it remained just one more unanswered question about this peculiar family. He did know that Branwell went into a tailspin after receiving this news, drinking heavily here in the Bull every night and taking laudanum to kill the pain of this and the many other failures in his life.

In less than two years he was dead.

Alex knew about that kind of pain. It was dark and deep and hopeless. It called for a drug to deaden all feeling just to make it possible to get through the day. His own drug had been called Jack Daniels, and for a time after his wife had taken off with her new lover, he'd gone to bed with Jack, awakened with Jack, taken Jack to lunch, until not only his career but his very health was at stake. At that time, his health had seemed unimportant, but the risk of losing his career finally brought him to his senses. His career was all he had left. With little more to sustain him than an angry determination not to allow the only other thing in life he cared about slip away, Alex forced himself back into the real world. It was, he'd learned later from a colleague, just in the nick of time, for the dean of Arts and Sciences had already drawn up his walking papers and was watching Alex closely for one more screw-up.

Alex had managed to clean up his act, but the pain remained, only a few shades lighter than before. He'd looked around for another anesthetic, and found it in the stream of one-nighters, which served to numb the pain but left no hangover or telltale whiskey breath to offend his students the morning after.

Bringing his attention back to the moment, Alex surveyed the ancient inn. The warmth of incandescent lighting reflecting on polished copper and brass filled the room with a cozy glow, dispelling the gloom of his melancholy thoughts. The manager appeared from the cellar.

"Hello!" He greeted Alex in a hearty voice, wiping his hands on a dingy white towel. "I'm David. What'll you have?"

Alex introduced himself and allowed the man to draw him a half pint of lager while he registered for his room.

"How many days will you be staying?" David asked.

"I don't know for sure. Two or three at least. I need to find an apartment as soon as I can. I plan to be in Haworth all summer."

"Is that so? You working on the Brontës?"

Alex supposed the innkeeper was used to visitors interested in the Brontës. Why else would anyone make the trek to this remote village, isolated as it was on the edge of the vast and looming moors?

"Yes. Yes, I am."

"Remarkable family, that," David commented, picking up Alex's heavy bag and heading for the stairway. Reaching the landing, he pointed to an old chair that sat next to a grandfather clock. "That there's Branwell's chair," he said. "He used to sit in that chair by the fireplace and drink ale and tell stories. A merry one he was."

Alex studied the chair for a moment. The seat, instead of fitting squarely between the four legs as most chair seats were positioned, was turned so that the corner was right in the middle, requiring the occupant to straddle it. Definitely a man's chair, he thought, amused, as he followed the manager to his room.

A stray shaft of late afternoon sunlight managed to pierce the clouds and stream through the shining windowpane in the tiny hotel room. Alex pulled the curtain back, and his eyes widened at the sight before him.

An ancient, overpopulated graveyard stretched from the rear wall of the Black Bull uphill to the edge of the Parsonage garden. Literally hundreds of moss-covered tombstones, as tall or taller than the human remains that lay beneath them, stood or leaned in row upon row like tired old soldiers. Other stones lay flat, covering graves that entombed entire families. Large trees that had grown up in the churchyard since the days when Patrick Brontë was curate here were home to a chorus of rooks, whose harsh cacophony added to the macabre atmosphere.

No wonder Emily was obsessed with death, Alex thought grimly. It had surrounded her.

Cold in the earth, and the deep snow piled above thee!
Far, far removed, cold in the dreary grave!
Have I forgot, my Only Love, to love thee,
Severed at last by Time's all-wearing wave?

Late afternoon was rapidly turning into early evening, and Alex was once again travel-weary, but he splashed cold water over his face and shook his head. It had taken him thirty-four years to get here. He had a lot to see and do. He could sleep when he, like those souls outside his window, was dead. Donning a heavy sweater under the mackintosh, he left the room.

Outside, a golden evening sun was successfully dispersing the earlier clouds. The air was clear and surprisingly unpolluted. From what Alex had read about the history of Haworth, he had envisioned a dingy, smog-filled town with factories belching heavy coal smoke into the air.

That was then and this is now, he reminded himself. Many of the textile mills in this valley had long since shut down.

Good for the air.

Bad for the economy.

He wondered what Haworth survived on now. Tourism? It hardly seemed possible. People like him who knew and loved the work of the Brontës came on literary pilgrimages, he figured. But in a world of television addicts, the percentage of any given population who even knew who the Brontës were had to be minuscule.

He mounted the steps that led to the church next to the Black Bull. Not fifty feet from his window at the inn, beneath the floor of this sanctuary, all of the Brontë family except Anne lay buried. Unfortunately, it was not the same church in which Patrick Brontë had held forth for almost four decades.

After his death, the new curate had wrought many changes in both the church and the Parsonage. The church, in fact, had been completely rebuilt in the late 1870s, a fact that Alex found appalling, considering the historical importance of the original building.

He entered the hushed and darkened chapel and walked down the aisle toward the altar. Above, a large stained-glass window let in most of the light that illuminated the gray stone walls and dark pews. Alex stood quietly, letting his eyes travel over the small church, as if seeking the spirits of those who had been the objects of his years of study. Somewhere they lay buried beneath this floor, only feet from where he stood.

Looking down, his gaze fell on a small, well-polished brass plaque set into the floor:

> In memory of
> Emily Jane Brontë
> Who died December 19, 1848
> And of Charlotte Brontë
> Born April 21, 1816
> Died March 31, 1855.

Alex discovered later that the graves were actually beneath the supporting concrete column to his right, supposedly sealed and forever inaccessible. It was as if the new curate had sought to wipe out all traces of his famous predecessor and leave his own jealous stamp on the curacy.

At the moment, Alex stood frozen to the spot. He noted that someone had placed a sprig of dried heather in a small vase on the brass plate. Someone who had loved Emily for as long and as well as he?

Alex exhaled a slow breath and sat down on the first pew, staring at the memorial. Emily Brontë was the love of his life right now, he thought morosely, maybe even the only woman he would ever love, safe as she was across time.

June 29, 1845

Tomorrow Anne and I depart for a short holiday in York. I must act as if I am anxious to go, when in truth I want nothing to do with York. Let Charlotte go instead! Then I would truly be free to spend my days upon the moors, for there is where my heart lies.

Never in all of Angria or Gondal have I found such a hero! He is dark, yes, and brooding, but when he laughs (rarely) his face lights up like a bright summer morn. He is like me, free in spirit, but unlike me, he is unhampered by life or convention. Oh, to be so free! My freedom lies in the world within, while he enjoys it there and in the world without as well.

But wait. There is more! Oh, dare I write it? This gipsie has touched me in a way I have not known until now. I must describe it honestly, for I want to relive those feelings again and again. I must never forget. He was standing, leaning against the rock that has been his only shelter for these many days. I brought him water from the beck, and wood for his fire. He said nothing, but he watched me as I busied myself in his behalf. And then he called my name. Emilie! It sounds so different in his tongue. Different and delicious. Emilie, he called. I turned, and in his eyes I read a command. As if in a trance, I moved toward him, my gaze never leaving his. He held out his hand, and I placed mine in his. It was as if lightning struck me at his touch. My skin turned feverish and my brow began to throb. What was he going to do? Would he hurt me? Instead he pulled me gently toward him. I could smell the dried sweat on his skin—not an unpleasant odor, but a manly smell I am not used to. Looking into his face, I sensed he wanted to say something, but no words came. Instead he very slowly leaned forward and placed his lips upon mine.

I feel myself burning as I write this. His kiss has set my soul on fire. I never before succumbed to such temptation, and I should feel ashamed. But this is not the case. Instead

I feel as if I am alive for the first time in my life. I thought I knew about the things that transpire between men and women, but I did not know about the feelings that accompany the act. Is this what is called love? Is this why Charlotte pines for Msgr. Heger? If it is so, I can no longer disdain her actions as regard to that gentleman. It would seem we may not be able to control those feelings that accompany such a state as this. Now I am truly afraid . . .

Selena's hand shook as she opened the tattered envelope. Her earlier efforts at breaking the spell that seemed to have a stranglehold on her work had left her weak and drained, but she was not surprised that they hadn't worked. She laughed at herself bitterly.

She scorned "Gypsy nonsense," but she'd just acted like some kind of possessed sorceress trying to break a curse she didn't even believe in. But she had to try everything, anything to get past this mental block, wherever it came from, and salvage her career. Curse or no curse, she must get on with other projects.

Turning the envelope upside down, she watched the contents flutter onto the low table that sat in front of the fireplace. Twenty-one bits of paper, each smaller than a silver pound coin, lay in front of her like so much innocuous confetti.

But Selena suspected they were far from harmless.

With resignation, she sat down and, with a large magnifying glass and a pair of tweezers, began to piece the confetti back together. Each piece was covered with tiny lettering, and she knew by heart where each one went.

Selena remembered vividly the day she'd torn the note to shreds. It was just more than a year ago when Matka had handed her this photocopy.

"'Tis time I passed this along," she'd said without emotion. "I know y' don't believe in t' curse, but y' must read this. I have made y' a copy. When I be gone, y' may have the original, but only if y' promise, as I promised my mother before me, not t' destroy it."

"I'll promise no such thing," Selena had replied tartly, crushing the copy into a ball. "This is just so much Gypsy rubbish, Gran, and you know it. It's ruled the lives of lots of ignorant people, but it's not going to rule mine!"

The old woman had only nodded. "I hope y'be right, daughter. But y' must read it. 'Tis your unfortunate heritage, whether y' accept it or not. Your lot was cast when your great-great-great-grandfather foreswore his Romany blood for a *Gorgio* woman, and by so doing, brought down a curse so strong it even caused his lover's death."

Selena had sighed deeply and sat down at the foot of Matka's bed. "Even if that's true, Gran, that was a long time ago. Don't you think it's time we give this all up? I mean, it has to stop somewhere."

"Unfortunately, girl, tha' can never be, not unless our line dies out." She eyed Selena shrewdly. "Which i'twill, unless y' have children."

Selena picked at the bedclothes. "Sounds to me like a good reason not to. Who wants to bring a cursed child into the world?"

The old woman ignored her logic. "Y' must hear the tale, Selena. In full."

Thirty minutes later, still seated at her grandmother's feet, Selena was so astounded she could hardly move. She had heard scraps of the story before, but she had no idea of the depth of the tale and the pain those lovers must have endured. Tears welled and spilled down her cheeks, not because she now believed in or feared the curse, but because the tale was immensely sad.

"Who was she, Gran?" Selena asked quietly at last.

"Nobody knows. Tha' be the difficult part. By our ancestor's decree, the curse could only be lifted if one o' the girl's family could grant forgiveness. But that is impossible, y' see. And so the curse continues . . ."

Selena pulled herself together and slid off the bed. "No, not unless we believe in it. Which I don't. But thanks for telling me the whole story." She kissed her grandmother good-bye lightly, not wanting to reveal her own shaken emotions. "I have to go now."

Later, back in her studio, Selena had taken the crumpled photocopy out of her purse and sat down by the fireplace, tempted to toss it unread into the embers and be done with it.

She wished now she had done just that. Instead she had read the tiny words, and in so doing, had seemingly transferred the message from the paper into her heart, where it had tormented her ever since. Perhaps her subconscious had known what she was in for, for after she'd read it, she had sat entranced, staring at the glowing coals and tearing the paper methodically into little pieces.

She'd left the tiny, odd-shaped scraps scattered on the table, but later that night she crawled off the sofa where she slept and went into the back room of the studio, drawn by an inexplicable urge to paint. She had begun the series then by picking up a single shard of the note which, by morning, was captured on canvas, alongside the other images that were to recur in different forms throughout all of her work for the next year.

Selena stretched. The late afternoon sun, wonderfully golden now that the clouds had dissipated, spilled through the north windows onto the table where she worked at piecing the puzzle together. At this time of year the sun would not set until almost half past ten, giving her plenty of daylight to pursue what she knew she must.

The pieces in place as best she could arrange them with their frayed, curling edges, Selena studied the letter as a whole for a long moment, feeling a deep sense of sadness envelope her. That poor, desperate woman, she thought. And that tragically tormented man.

Then she took the tweezers and removed the pieces she had already included on her canvases. There were only five remaining when she finished. She stared at them.

Five pieces left.

Only five.

And suddenly she knew the answer to her dilemma. She'd used the pieces of the letter to create a series. She had only to finish that series, painting these five remaining images onto canvas, to wrest herself from its possession.

Simple.

Logical.

If it worked.

Quickly, she selected one of the remaining bits of paper and replaced the rest in the envelope. It had to work!

She moved across the room to a window. Holding the slip of paper up to the light, she read:

> *In death my sh*
> *never to hurt*
> *forgiveness*
> *is of you a*
> *retributio*
> *no hell he*
> *the hell h*
> *I will miss*

With a racing pulse Selena went into her storage room and began selecting a canvas. Already the images were swirling in her brain.

It had to work. . . .

❧ *Chapter 5* ❧

In a high-ceilinged room in one of the finer neighborhoods of Leeds, an old woman in an expensive dressing gown sat before a flickering fire. She got cold even in summer these days, it seemed.

Along the walls, mementos and photos of various younger versions of herself told the story of her life. Her husband. Her only daughter. Her meeting with the queen. Her visits with Winston Churchill. Her many diplomas and service awards. All hung in an orderly array. Hers had been a rich and stimulating life.

And it wasn't over yet, she vowed with a mischievous grin.

With a steady hand she picked up the portable phone and pressed the numbers listed in the Oxford faculty directory. A woman's voice answered after only one ring.

"Dr. Flynn? Eleanor Bates here. Brontë Society."

"Ms. Bates!" Maggie was clearly surprised. "I hope you are well."

"Yes, yes, very well, thank you. I'm so looking forward to your debate at the end of August. But that's not what I'm calling about, dear. My daughter, Mrs. Hillary Durham, is hosting a *soiree* at Harrington House in a couple of weeks, and I thought it might be good for you to come and get acquainted with some of us Yorkshire folks. We're keen on your Brontë work, and there will be a number of Society members there. Do tell me you will come . . . on the seventeenth."

A slight pause. The sound of flipping pages. "I have my date book right here. Yes, I believe I can make it."

"Oh, wonderful! And oh, by the way, I had a chance encounter on the train the other day. Ran into that Dr. Hightower you are debating. My, but he's handsome! You are acquainted with him, I believe? I don't suppose you could convince him to come along with you for the evening, could you?"

A longer hesitation, then, "I think it is . . . unlikely. From what I . . . understand . . . he's not keen on formal affairs. But," Maggie added, "I'll ask him."

"Please do, and if he declines, invite someone else. I'll add your name and a guest to the invitation list. Look forward to seeing you there."

The clock on the mantel ticked loudly in the silence left by the absence of her voice, and Eleanor Bates settled back against the comfortable cushions of her divan, a small smile playing on her ancient lips. Maggie Flynn and Alexander Hightower. Now there was a pair! Both brilliant and good-looking. Both Brontë scholars. Eleanor had never been able to resist an attempt at matchmaking, especially when such eligible and obviously compatible candidates came her way. Maybe with a little creative manipulation, she thought, she could orchestrate more than a debate between them. Picking up a crossword, Eleanor Bates wondered when she'd become such a shameless romantic.

The library at the Brontë Parsonage Museum was housed on the ground floor of the new wing, which was added after Patrick Brontë's death. It was small, intimate, with room for only a few investigators to work at a time. Its size, however, was not indicative of its worth, for Alex discovered it held a literary cornucopia of bits and pieces of Brontëana he'd never seen before, much of which, to his surprise, came from the Brontë Society Transactions.

These treatises, submitted by scholars and members of the Society, provided him with a glimpse into the lives of the Brontës from a different, very British and sometimes possessive point of view. His estimation of Eleanor Bates and others like her who through the years had worked to preserve the Brontë heritage reached a new height.

Alex had been buried in the library for three days straight. The superbly professional and knowledgeable librarian had unearthed a mountain of materials for his study, and he had worked straight through each day, breaking only when the library closed for lunch.

He looked at his watch with bleary eyes. It was almost one o'clock. His stomach growled a Pavlovian response, and Alex closed the book in front of him.

"Think I'll take a break this afternoon," he said to the attractive librarian. He slipped into his windbreaker. "See you in the morning."

The library door opened directly onto the reconstructed Parsonage kitchen. It had been in the kitchen that Emily and Charlotte and Anne had created much of their work, and Alex paused after shutting the door behind him, trying to visualize the young women at work in a room very much like this one.

The Parsonage itself had been carefully and lovingly restored and contained some of the Brontë's furniture, including the couch on which Emily died. Above the library, in the new wing, items of Brontëana were attractively displayed.

Alex decided to take the long way out and mounted the steps that led into the display area. On the landing, he passed the tall, somber grandfather clock that had also been part of the Brontë household in Emily's day, and he could almost see the Reverend Patrick Brontë stopping to wind it every night on his way up to bed.

He made his way through what had once been a bedroom and into the new wing, where he let his eyes roam with the pleasure of a hungry man at a feast over the personal effects of the Brontës displayed in the lighted cabinets. He was especially fascinated by the intriguing miniature books created by the Brontës as children. Some of the pages were scarcely wider than a ten-pence coin. How, he wondered, could they have inscribed such minuscule words using the rough quill pens that were the writing instruments of their day?

Closing his eyes, Alex could almost hear the squeals of laughter and the whoops of the young Brontës at play in their small "children's study" upstairs. They were not a quiet bunch, at least as children. Nor could their childhood ever be described as conventional.

Brilliant and mature beyond their years, Charlotte, Branwell, Emily, and Anne learned their lessons from life and the books and magazines in their father's library, and that of the Keighley Mechanics Institute. When other children were playing blind man's bluff and chasing each other around the mulberry bush, the Brontë children's games often consisted of reenactments of actual historical events, embellished by a rich and vivid well of imagination. Once, Emily, dressed up as Bonny Prince Charles, effected the royal's escape by climbing out of her father's bedroom window and down his prize cherry tree, tearing a limb off in the process.

Before they were much more than infants the Brontë children knew death intimately, losing first their mother and then their two older sisters. The four remaining siblings turned to each other for solace in the face of this crushing emotional devastation. Their father, although loving, was stern and aloof, as was their aunt Branwell, their mother's spinster sister who, martyrlike, moved in with them to care for the children. Only Tabby, the old cook, showed them any kind of affection from an adult.

Their house, although adequate, was drafty and cold. Their meals were uninteresting and uninviting.

But one day, the Young Men came into their lives, changing them forever.

Returning from a convention of clergy in Leeds, Patrick Brontë brought gifts for his children, including a set of twelve wooden soldiers which, although intended for Branwell, captured the fancy of them all. Generously, Branwell shared with his sisters, and the toy soldiers became the Young Men. Later they were appointed to be the Duke of Wellington, Napoleon, Captain Edward Parry, Captain John Ross, and their loyal troops.

Using their not-infantile knowledge of the world derived from their reading of current newspapers and magazines, and stirring it up with the drama created by their favorite authors, including Milton, Bunyan, Scott, Coleridge, and especially Lord Byron, the four became the "Chief Genii" and conjured up fantasy worlds in which it never got cold and no one ever died.

Or if they did, they were instantly "made alive again" by the Genii, to wit, Tallii, Branii, Emmii, and Annii. Playacting, they traveled to far distant lands, fought wars, built empires, and in general escaped from Haworth.

The little magazines in front of Alex were part of that escape. Three years after the Young Men came alive in their imaginations, Charlotte and Branwell, who were older, began recording the history of their fictitious Glass Town Confederacy in the tiny books. They were supposedly modeled on *Blackwood*'s magazine, one of the children's favorites, which published tales of adventure, book reviews, and political commentary. Not exactly the nursery rhymes and fairy tales other children of their ages read.

Alex gazed at the little magazines for a long while. The handwriting was so tiny it was barely legible. He knew that had served a purpose for the children as well. Not only did the size of the books make them easy to conceal, the tiny print was difficult for adult eyes to read.

And secrecy was of utmost importance to the children. It was their only line of defense against adult intrusion, enabling them to safeguard their fantasies from prying grown-up eyes.

Glass Town later became Angria. Still later, Emily and Anne broke away and created Gondal. But by whatever name, the magical imaginary kingdoms created by the Brontë children set the stage for many other aspects of their lives—their writing, their storytelling abilities, and their penchant for escapism.

Charlotte, Branwell, and Anne eventually outgrew most of their childhood preoccupations with their fantasy worlds, but Emily never did. At least not according to history. Nor did she change her style of handwriting, except when teachers demanded. Then she proved she could write in a graceful cursive. Samples remained in the Parsonage Library from the time she was in the Pensionnat Heger in Brussels. But once away from the eyes of exacting schoolmasters, Emily reverted to the tiny, cramped, secretive handwriting she had used as a child.

Alex forced himself out of his reverie and made his way down the back stairs and out the door. On the way he passed the priceless collection of Brontëana that had been donated to the museum by an American collector, Henry H. Bonnell. Interesting, he thought, that it was an American who restored much of the Brontës' work to the museum.

Now it was up to him to dig through it all to find new information that might support his suicide theory.

Regardless of what he found, however, or the outcome of the debate, Alex knew his summer in Haworth would prove invaluable to his career. Here, the three sisters and their brother were taking on new dimensions. They were becoming more than just literary figures to him. They were like real people, old friends, and being in their surroundings was providing him with insight into their lives he could never have acquired from books studied in a far distant land.

July 3, 1845

Anne and I returned from York yesterday, and today Charlotte is off to visit Ellen at Hathersage. I am on fire to return to the moors, and yet I must bide my time. I do not want to appear overly eager to see my tormentor once again. He must have known when I took my leave of him last that my knees were weak, and I do not want him to think he can take advantage of my momentary delirium. But the truth is I have been unable to think of anything else since I left him. When I close my eyes, I see his dark visage looming there. I hear him call my name. I taste his kiss once again. It was almost humanly impossible not to speak of him to Anne on our journey, but I still dare not confide in anyone! I only survived these few days because I cast my longing onto the Gondals. And what adventures they had! Juliet and Ronald and the rest were never so alive as they made their escape from the palaces of instruction and went on to fight the Republicans! Anne and I played at Gondal almost incessantly while we were gone, and I remember little of York. Why should I care about a city that is just another pile of stones when my great adventure lies on the moor? Oh, my very soul aches to see his face again. I have never met a spirit so free. Would that I could leave behind this prison that is my life and follow him on the wings of the wind!

Heeding a second reminder from his stomach that he'd gone to work with no breakfast, Alex made his way to a nearby pub, where he indulged in what the locals called a "giant Yorkshire." The famous Yorkshire pudding resembled not at all the so-called "pudding" his mother had made from a package of Jell-O mix. It was, instead, a baked pastry, a hybrid that fell somewhere between a yeast roll and a biscuit. This one was as big as his plate, filled with savory beef stew, of which he consumed every bite.

He did so without guilt, knowing that after taking care of one small piece of business in the village, he planned to strike out across the moors to Top Withens. It was almost seven miles round-trip to the ruins of the farmhouse purported to be Emily's location for *Wuthering Heights*. He was a little out of shape, not having kept up with his usual workout regimen since he'd arrived in England, and he figured he would burn the Yorkshire, and hopefully a few additional calories, on the hike.

But first Alex made his way down the steep cobblestones of Main Street, seeking the address of a bed-and-breakfast that had been recommended by one of the staff at the Parsonage Museum as possible extended lodgings.

Although he liked the Black Bull, Alex was ready to find quieter quarters. Apparently, time stood still in Haworth, and in some respects little had changed since the days when Branwell hung out at the Bull. Although the place had been enlarged, the floor carpeted, and, to the horror of some of the local historical purists, video games installed, the Bull remained a popular watering hole for locals as well as tourists.

Alex personally thought Branwell would have taken immediately to the video games, seeking as he did any diversion that would take his mind off his own shortcomings. Whatever the history buffs thought, customers flocked to the pub each night, and the sounds of their revelries made sleep impossible until well after midnight.

As he walked he glanced into the windows of the shops that were shouldered against one another like giant stair steps down the steep hill. The bakery. The gift shop. The souvenir shop. A small art gallery. Alex froze, his gaze riveted on the painting displayed under a spotlight in the window. A painting he recognized instantly.

The background was the wash of gray and mauve that he'd seen in the gallery in London. The images were the same, yet different. Horses galloped across the mists, a red rose opened to reveal a white-hot flame, and the monkey was only a tiny figure seated on the shoulder of an old man in rags.

Alex's heartbeat quickened. Where was the scrap of the note? He jerked open the door of the gallery and went straight for the painting.

"C'n I help y', sir?" The large woman behind the counter looked up, startled.

"Yes, actually," he said. "Could I please have a closer look at this painting?"

"Cert'nly," she said, removing her bulk from the stool where she was perched and bringing it on slow, flat feet to the front of the shop. She turned the painting to face Alex. "It's a strange one, 'n't it?"

Alex murmured his agreement. He spotted what he was looking for and leaned over, peering closely at the letter. In this painting it was revealed beneath the hooves of one of the horses. The writing on it was so tiny he would have to come back with a magnifying glass to discern the content.

"Who painted this?"

"She's a woman artist, lives nearby. Name's Selena."

Alex stood up abruptly. "Nearby? Where?"

The woman, figuring she had a customer for a painting she'd never thought she could sell, was more than accommodating. "She left me her card when she put that work on consignment," she said, going back to her desk. "I know I've got it here somewhere. She's a strange little bird," she continued as she fumbled through a cluttered drawer. "Real private like. Her grandmum was friends with my mum. Told her fortune. Mum'd never make an important decision without consultin' old Matka."

At last she retrieved the card out of the disarray. "There's no phone number on't. Says here she's on Bridgeton Lane, over Stanbury way." She squinted, thinking. "Seems I remember she's livin' in one of 'em old farmhouses, up on t' far side of Haworth Moor, past Ponden Hall. Y' know wherit's at?"

"I can find it," Alex replied, his eyes never leaving the painting. That writing. That writing. His mind flashed back to the miniature books at the museum.

Finally he drew away and turned to find the shop-keeper staring at him expectantly. "Uh, what is the price on this?" he asked.

"She wants five hundr't pounds, plus our commission, which 'ud bring it t' six hundr't."

Alex translated that into American dollars and figured immediately it was not feasible to purchase the painting, which he didn't really want anyway. All he wanted was the opportunity to decipher the words on the scrap of paper painted there. At that price it would be a very expensive pastime.

"Well, thanks very much," he said, then indicated with a nod Selena's card, which the woman still held in her hand. "Could I have that?"

The woman looked at it, hesitated, then shrugged her shoulders and handed it to him.

Alex slipped it into the pocket of his jeans. "Thanks," he said again, and left before she had a chance to attempt to offer him a better price on the painting.

Back in the street, Alex inhaled deeply of the moisture-laden air. What was it about those crazy paintings that seemed to punch his buttons? Was it the handwriting? It did indeed resemble Emily's childish scratchings.

That was part of it, he felt sure. But there was something else.

Something that had to do with blue-black hair and dark, exotic eyes.

July 5, 1845

I could contain my eagerness no longer, and so today I escaped from Anne and made my way to the back ravine, only to find Mikel asleep beneath the noontime sun. I did not awaken him, but sat on a rock and watched him in his slumber. Just the sight of his handsome face was enough to unleash those feelings that are so new (and delicious!) to me. I wondered what he dreamt. Was it of me? Do I dare let such thoughts enter my head? It strangely excited me to look upon him when he wasn't aware of my presence. I could study the length of his body without embarrassment, and I did so, feeling all the while that indescribable yearning building deep inside until I was almost in pain. I wondered what it would be like if I lay down beside him and he encircled me in those strong arms. What would happen if I did? My head swims to think of it even now. He awoke and caught me staring at him, and my face blazed with shame. But he only laughed, as if the idea that I had been spying on him pleased him greatly. We talked together for the longest we ever have, and it was all I could manage to keep my attention on what I was saying. I told him about our trip and about the Gondals. I've never told anyone about the Gondals, but I let slip a mention of them, and he was eager to hear all about their adventures. The afternoon slipped away, and at last I had to leave. I did not touch him today, nor did he touch me, and even though I know it is for the best, my very soul cries out for his kiss again. What, oh, what is this madness?

❧ *Chapter 6* ❧

The image of Selena's raven hair and obsidian eyes stayed with Alex as, a short while after leaving the gallery, he turned his feet down the well-beaten path that led away from the Parsonage in the direction of the Brontë Falls and, farther on, to Top Withens. The day was warm and bright, with no hint of the mauve-gray mist he'd observed from the train window and which, he now believed, provided the background for Selena's paintings.

He wondered where the rest of the imagery came from. Certainly not from anything he'd seen around here so far. But then, he was still very much a newcomer. Maybe there was a circus or carnival in the area at the time she'd created that particular work, he thought.

The scrap of letter fluttered across his mind as well, but he let it float on out of his consciousness, for at that moment he crested a hill and what he saw took his breath away.

Below him the moors spread out and rolled away into forever, an infinite sea of tall golden grasses billowing in the westerly wind. The breeze bore the call of a bird he couldn't name and the occasional bleat of a sheep grazing on the rough pastureland. Above him fluffy white clouds played chase against an azure sky.

He'd seen this place before, he thought with a smile of deep satisfaction. At least in his mind, when Emily's character, the spirited young Cathy, described it in *Wuthering Heights* as being her dream of Paradise.

> *. . . rocking in a rustling green tree, with a west wind blowing, and bright, white clouds flitting rapidly above; and not only larks, but throstles, and blackbirds, and linnets, and cuckoos pouring out music on every side, and the moors seen at a distance, broken into cool dusky dells; but close by, great swells of long grass undulating in waves to the breeze . . .*

Alex walked on, whistling softly, feeling ever more connected to the writer of this sylvan reflection. Although much of her work was gloomy and haunting, she had these brilliant moments when she seemed so alive, she virtually sparkled in her imagery.

He suddenly felt more alive than he had in years, and his spirits surged upward, stretching, seeking the outer limits of this limitless landscape. No wonder Emily escaped to the moors at every opportunity, he thought, especially on days like today. Here, she found the freedom to roam, or write, as she wished, rather than the drudgery of housekeeping, the needlework she hated, Aunt Branwell's stern eye.

Here she left behind the stench of Haworth's putrid, disease-infested streets, embracing instead fresh, clean-scented air and healthy sunshine. He filled his lungs with the sweet fragrance of summer, much as she must have done when she and her large yellow mastiff, Keeper, trounced along this same path when Queen Victoria was still a child.

Alex reached the tumbling waters of the beck that had

been labeled "Brontë Falls" and sat for a moment on the "Brontë Bridge." Above his head was a signpost, carved in both English and Japanese, pointing to the "Brontë Way." He frowned, feeling that Emily's private territory had become terribly commercialized.

Still, it was remarkable how many people traveled to Haworth to pay their respects to Emily and her siblings, or, as he had, to try to capture some of the romance and spirit of this talented family.

He stood and looked up the hill that rose starkly in front of him. In the distance he could see a tiny black smudge against the golden slope, and knew he still had a long walk ahead of him. He resumed his trek, letting his mind roam as he made his way up the steep incline. He was deep in the heart of Emily's realm, and he tried to resonate with her spirit, as best he understood it.

Many adjectives had been used to describe Emily Brontë. Free-spirited. Strong-willed. Talented. Intelligent.

But rarely "suicidal."

He alone seemed to have come up with that one. What could she have been thinking when she deliberately refused medical help that early wintertime so long ago? Did she just not like doctors? Had she misjudged the seriousness of her illness? Hadn't it occurred to her that unless she got well, she might not be able ever to return to this wondrous piece of geography that she loved so fiercely?

For half an hour more these and other troublesome thoughts and questions tumbled about Alex's mind while sharp air filled his lungs during the strenuous climb. By the time he reached the crest of the hill, he was slightly light-headed from the increased oxygen in his system, and when he looked up, he thought he was hallucinating to see a man on a bicycle speeding toward him down the steep incline. The cyclist rode with his head down, intent on avoiding bumps in the path, and he looked up scarcely in time to prevent a collison with the astounded hiker. He braked and skidded, sending a shower of small stones down the hillside.

"Sorry, old chap," the cyclist said, recovering from the swerve and dismounting the bicycle. He was lean, spare as the thin machine he rode.

Alex stared, still thinking this person was some sort of bizarre apparition. Surely no one in his right mind would try to ride a bicycle in this terrain. "Do you ride this way often?" he asked incredulously.

The biker laughed. "Every day. Live down there in Stanbury. I'm in training for the Tour de France." He looked out over the vista in front of him. "Quite a view, i'n't it?" he said. "I've lived here all my life, and I never tire of 't."

"All your life?" Alex considered that a moment, then added, "I don't suppose you know a woman named Selena. I understand she's an artist. Lives somewhere nearby."

The thin young man furrowed his brow. "Selena, eh? I went to school wi' a girl named Selena. Wha's the last name?"

Alex shrugged. "I don't know. Her paintings are signed with only one name."

"The girl I knew was Selena Wood. A bit of a mystery to me she was. I didn't know her well. They said she was a Gypsy. I don't know if tha's true, but I know she was real standoffish. Didn't have much to do wi' us regular kids."

"A Gypsy!" Alex's mind flashed to Selena's images of the organ grinder with his monkey and the black horse rearing before the campfire. He recalled the woman in the art gallery mumbling something about fortune-tellers. "I didn't know there were . . . such people, at least not in this day and age."

"Oh, they've lived 'round here for years, but y' know, they come and go. I can't recall seein' any in these parts for a long time. And I don't think Selena was a real Gypsy. She lived in a house, just like all the rest of us."

Alex tried to conceal his astonishment. He reached into his pocket and retrieved the card the shopkeeper had given him. "Do you know where this is?" he asked, handing it to the man.

"Bridgeton Lane? Sure. It's just there, down the hillside." He pointed to the northwest. "See tha' house, way down the valley there? Tha'd likely be it. Why?"

"That's where she has her studio, I think."

"Y' don't say. Selena Wood turned out to be an artist, eh? Doesn't surprise me none. She was always drawin' things on her work. She was pretty good, too, now't I think of it. Well, I'd best be off." He gave the card back to Alex. "Nice chattin' with you. And sorry about the scare."

"No harm done." Alex stared after the figure of the bike rider, watching the fragile-looking cycle, incongruous in its surroundings, bounce over the rough pathway.

Alex turned and resumed his hike up the path, which at this point had been paved with large slabs of the local sandstone to protect against erosion and further destruction caused by hikers like himself. Gray clouds had begun to overpower the earlier white ones, and a brisk breeze brushed against his face. By the time he reached the ruin at Top Withens, the golden day had turned into a damp shroud of mist and fog, and clouds had slunk into the valley below, obscuring the farmhouse.

He hoisted himself onto a stone wall, opting to ignore the deteriorating weather at least for a little while. The climb had been exhilarating, and for the first time since he'd arrived in England, he felt as if he'd had a good workout. He wanted to allow his muscles a brief respite, then he'd give them another round as he headed back toward town.

Alex peered into the gathering gloom, his curiosity wending down the hill and into the valley below. The woman who lived there was as enshrouded in mystery as her house was in mist. He was alarmed that he seemed to be so drawn to her, for he sensed she was exactly the kind of female he wanted to avoid. Although he knew little about her, he perceived from her artwork and the success of her showing in London that she was a woman with passion in her heart and depth to her soul. She was obviously intelligent and talented as well as beautiful, and when she'd entered the gallery, he'd noted she strode past him with an air of self-confidence and independence. She was the kind of woman he was attracted to, and the kind who could destroy him. The kind who, like his ex-wife, could walk up to him after six years of marriage and say, "I've had enough. I'm tired of taking second place in your life, especially behind a bunch of dead poets. I've found someone who will put me first, and I'm leaving you."

Alex realized he was sweating. He brushed a sheen of dampness from his brow and jumped to the ground, heading through the mist in the direction of Haworth. It seemed there was more that he found familiar about Selena than long, dark hair.

July 7, 1845

Today Mikel attempted to take a few steps, and although it looks as if his leg is mending well, it will be a few more weeks before he will be able to put his weight fully upon it. Until then I shall be his strength. I will gladly bear the weight of his body as I did today when he put his arm across my shoulder for support. I feared my heart would burst with this unknown feeling of tenderness I have for him. Is this love? Could it be? My inexperienced heart does not know.

All I know is that I want to care for him and protect him until he is well enough once again to be on his own. I also know that there are times when I am with him (nay, even times when I am not!) that my entire body feels as if it is deprived of something precious that only he could grant. I am unsure exactly what this is, but it must be the most important thing in the world! Important, and frightening, for I feel overpowered and out of control when I am with him. I want him to get well, and at the same time I dread the day when he no longer needs me, but I know it would be best if he left. I have so far managed to bring him sufficient food without arousing the suspicion of the others, but I do not know how long I will be able to protect my secret. My sisters have noticed a change in my being, they tell me, saying that I seem to look healthier and prettier than I used to. Do they suspect the reason for my long and private tours on the moors? I long to share my happiness with them, but what would they say? I wish I could read the future, for a part of me is terrified of losing Mikel, and another part is terrified of exposure of our liaison. At times I feel almost sick with anxiety. Whatever will become of all of this?

It was past midnight when Selena finally turned out the light in her studio and descended the stairs seeking a bite to eat, glad to leave the brushes and the frustration behind for a while. The fresh white canvas that had beckoned earlier that afternoon had, by evening, been filled with the beginning of still another painting, much like the others, this one different only in that the figures were twisted, as if revealing her inner torment.

The rider was in the act of being thrown from his horse, the rose hung wilted from its stem, the monkey cried. In all, it was hugely depressing, and Selena vowed to trash it tomorrow.

❧ *Chapter 7* ❧

July 10, 1845

    What a feckless fool I have been, pining away for this stranger who has taken his leave with not even so much as a faretheewell. Yesterday we laughed together and he taught me a gipsie song, and today he is gone. My face burns with shame when I think of how I hastened into the sunshine this morning, my heart bursting with my desire to see him. I even spoke harshly to poor Anne, who only asked if she could go with me. But when I reached his camp, I knew at once he was gone. The fire was cold and he was nowhere in sight. At first I was worried that he might have fallen into the ravine, but a search quickly proved me wrong. Then I wondered if someone found him, or if he met with foul play. But in my heart I know he has left for good, to return to Wales and his family, although I do not know how he managed, for his leg was still lame. I don't blame him for going. I knew he would leave when he was healed. If only he had left a note or some short message of good-bye. Instead he just disappeared. A crude farewell, but one I should have expected. He is, after all, just a gipsie. But his kiss burns still on my lips, alas a lasting impression, I fear. It is just as well he is gone, for my weakness and my foolish romantic notions would surely have led me astray. Let me learn from

*this. In Gondal only shall I allow myself to feel the passions
of the flesh, for there, in words, I can assure a safe passage
for my unwanted but insistent desire.*

Alex stepped down from the bus at the end of the line,
just short of the Old Silent Inn on the far side of Stanbury. It was Saturday, and he was too restless to face
another day in the library, so he'd donned his hiking gear
and set out for Ponden Hall, an old manor house many
believed to be Emily's model for Thrushcross Grange in
Wuthering Heights. Now a privately owned inn, the old
country home was nestled in the valley on the lower
slope of Haworth Moor, just above the reservoir. If the
weather held, he planned to climb the moor behind the
inn and reach Ponden Kirk, a high outcropping of rock
known to Emily's readers as Penistone Crag, a favorite
trysting place of Heathcliff and Cathy.

Or . . .

Standing alone in the tranquil morning after the noisy
bus disappeared around the bend on its return trip to
Haworth, Alex reached into the pocket of his jeans and
retrieved the slightly crumpled card he'd brought along,
the one the woman at the local gallery had given him.
Selena. Bridgeton Lane. Stanbury. A quick look at a map
had let him know that Bridgeton Lane was scarcely two
miles past the entrance to Ponden Hall. He thought of
the paintings and the tiny Brontëlike handwritten messages. He thought of the artist in black and magenta.

He thought, pocketing the card once again, of the options for the day.

Around him the Yorkshire landscape rose and fell in
acres of green. The clouds and wind played with the sun,
which was high in the sky by now, casting cloud shadows
that raced across the pastures, creating an ever-changing
scene before his eyes. He set off at a brisk pace, wondering how Selena would react if he just showed up at her

doorstep. What reason would he give for being there? To learn more about the fragments of a letter painted onto her canvases? True, he was curious about them, but he was aware that his interest likely amounted to nothing more than an excuse for meeting up with the artist who'd painted them. What was he thinking! He knew better than to pursue a woman like Selena, for all the reasons that he'd gone over a million times in his head. And yet, when he reached the entrance to the Ponden Mill store and the turnoff to Ponden Hall, he hesitated only briefly, then kept to the main roadway.

About a mile farther on he came to an intersection where a small, unpaved lane crossed the highway. The signpost read Bridgeton Lane.

The clouds thickened, and a few cold raindrops struck his cheek. Damn it, he'd thought he was prepared for the changeable weather, but he'd forgotten the umbrella. He pulled his collar up but turned into the lane undaunted.

Alex had walked about three-quarters of a mile from the intersection when he came upon an old farmhouse, but it was so dilapidated, he decided he'd taken the wrong road. The house appeared deserted. Like many of the other old farmhouses he'd seen on the moors, the wind and rain had taken their toll on this structure. Slates were missing from the roof, and the panes in several of the narrow windows were cracked. The house was not large, but because it was built on a steep slope, the front half was two-storied.

He approached the wall that once prevented sheep from wandering into the garden but now had crumbled into piles of scattered rocks, and he saw that behind the house there was a barn. Oddly, the barn appeared to be in better shape than the house. New windows lined the north side on the second floor, and the roof had been retiled. It had, Alex thought, the yuppie look of those restored agrarian buildings seen in American homes and gardens magazines. An old blue Land Rover was parked next to the barn.

Suddenly, the fierce frenzy of a dog's barking shattered the hushed silence of the mist-veiled scene. Adrenaline surged through him as a black and white dog bolted out of a doorway on the left side of the barn. Alex scrambled onto a heap of rubble from the stone fence, then realized that although the animal was yelping excitedly, it wasn't baring its teeth or showing an intent of actually attacking him.

"Here. Here boy. It's okay," he said, coaxing the animal to calm down.

Alex heard the sound of metal scraping against metal, and he looked up to see a figure flinging open one of the windows of the upper floor of the barn.

"Domino! Stop it! Domino! Come here!" The voice was strong, commanding, but at the same time feminine. It belonged to a woman with hair as black as a raven's wings, and Alex wasn't surprised to find himself staring at the alluring artist he'd seen at the gallery in London.

But it was certain from her expression that she was surprised to see him, or anyone, in her drive. The dog obeyed its mistress inasmuch as it stopped barking, but it continued to eye Alex with distrust.

The woman's voice was no less trusting. "What do you want?"

Alex brushed beads of rain from the sleeves of his windbreaker. "I'm here to see Selena Wood," he called up to her.

The woman gazed at him steadily. "Who are you?"

"The name's Hightower. Alexander Hightower. Look," he said, pointing to the dog. "Can we talk? I mean, can you—"

His question was answered with a shrill whistle, and it was a command that meant something to the animal. It turned tail and edged toward the barn, not going back into the doorway from which it came.

"What do you want?" the woman called again from the window.

"I came to . . . to discuss some paintings of yours which I've seen. You see, I . . . represent an interested party . . . from the States." Alex was surprised at his instantaneous ingenuity. Of course she'd see him, if she thought he was here to buy some of her work. He hadn't really meant to mislead her, but somehow the words just sort of took care of themselves.

It was immaterial, however, because his words were cut off with the metallic slam of the upstairs window. Alex continued to look up at the now-vacant window for a moment. So he'd been wrong. She obviously wasn't interested in a drop-in buyer, and it had been a mistake to come. He shrugged and was about to leave when the door opened and she stood framed in the dark shadows behind her.

She wore a high-necked tunic of rich amethyst, which reached to just above her knees. Her legs were clad in black leggings, like before. Despite the chill, she appeared to be wearing only heavy black socks on her feet. Over the sweater, a loose smock flowed the length of her slender figure, stained with paint of every color.

Her face appeared strained and her hair was in disarray, but Alex was transfixed by her dark, exotic beauty. It was natural and untamed, as wild and free as the images she painted. He tried to neutralize the effect her loveliness had on him by reminding himself that it was Maggie's flaming good looks that had gotten him into trouble the last time.

But his body, he realized, wasn't listening.

She looked at him for a long moment, frowning, suspicious caution in her eyes. Then she said, "Come in. It's raining."

Alex gratefully followed her up the narrow stairs. At least he'd have the chance to warm up a little, and if necessary, he could explain that the interested party he represented was himself. He watched the shapely legs ahead of him, ascending the stairs just at his eye level.

Oh, sweet Jesus!

At the landing, a window on the left looked out upon the driveway and the Land Rover. On the right was an open door with glass panes in the top half. She motioned him through the door and shut it behind him quickly in an attempt to hold the chill weather at bay.

Alex entered a large open room with windows extending the length of the north side. The other three walls rose to the rafters and were hung with paintings, all of which resembled one another in style and imagery, imagery he was becoming increasingly intrigued with. A fire crackled in a grate to his left, and two cats eyed him with disinterest.

He turned to face Selena. She had taken off her smock and was staring at him expectantly, obviously awaiting an explanation for this unannounced intrusion.

"Nice place," he managed at last, running his fingers through his damp, disheveled hair. "Sorry for the mess," he said, looking down at his wet jeans and muddy boots, thinking how ridiculous it was for him to expect her to believe he was some kind of art collector's representative. What kind of agent paid a call dressed like this?

"You are an American, I take it?" She handed him a small towel, and Alex noted that her hands were shaking. He realized suddenly and with regret that he must have frightened her.

Alex wiped the rain from his face and grinned, hoping to dispel her fear. "I guess my accent kind of stands out around here, doesn't it? My name's Alexander Hightower." He extended his hand, but she kept her distance, motioning to a straight-backed chair.

"You can hang your coat over there if you'd like. You look cold. Would you care for tea?"

Happy to have something for his extended hand to do, Alex took off his windbreaker and hung it up to dry. "Yes, thank you very much," he replied to her offer of tea. He turned and watched as she went to a small hot plate in the corner of the kitchenette and poured bottled water into a tea kettle. She reached into the cupboard for mugs, stretching her arms over her head, and the deep purple tunic rose just to the curve of her rounded bottom. Alex let his eyes follow the soft fabric upward to where it fell against the full curve of her breasts. Her long dark hair shone in the warmth of the lamplight, and despite her air of aloof independence, she appeared softly feminine, vulnerable.

The kettle whistled, and Selena poured a little of the hot water into the pot to warm it. "Do you take milk?"

Alex had to bring himself back into the moment. "No. No thanks." He was disturbed by the overwhelming urge he felt to protect her, but then he laughed silently, realizing the only thing she needed protection from was himself.

She emptied the pot again, opened a box of Darjeeling and placed two tea bags in the warmed vessel, then refilled it with hot water. It was a simple thing, sharing tea together, but intimate nonetheless. Alex was reminded unexpectedly of another kitchen, another dark-haired woman, another lifetime. A frown furrowed his brow. He mustn't let that happen again.

But when Selena spoke, her voice resonated somewhere dangerously close to his heart.

"I don't get many business callers out here, Mr. Hightower," she said, cocking her head skeptically to one side. "I work strictly through my dealer in London, Tom Perkins."

"I'm aware of that. I saw your exhibit at the Perkins

Galleries in London," he said, thinking fast. "Or at least the last of it. I didn't have much time to get a good look at your work, however, because you were already taking it down." Alex thought he saw the woman's eyes narrow ever so slightly.

"You were with the red-haired woman."

The comment caught him squarely in the solar plexus. "Uh, yes. That was my . . . colleague, Maggie Flynn."

He could tell by her expression that she didn't believe for a moment that Maggie was a "colleague," but she didn't ask further. "How did you find me?"

"I'm staying in Haworth. I saw one of your works in a gallery there. They gave me your address."

At that, Selena seemed to relax a little. She even gave him a small smile. "The woman whose daughter owns that gallery is a friend of my grandmother's," she said. "Tom doesn't like it that I've put a painting on consignment there, but that's his problem."

Selena poured them each a full mug of tea, then motioned for him to sit on the sofa by the fire. She perched on a nearby stool. "So tell me about your client."

"My client? Oh, yes . . ." That. Behind Selena the paintings beckoned enticingly from the wall. His interest in them was innocent and quite academic. Perhaps if she believed he had a client, she'd let him look at the paintings, his curiosity would be satisfied, and he'd be on his way. No harm done.

"Well, he is an historian of sorts, and he's very interested in . . . unusual artwork."

Selena considered that a moment. "I suppose my work could be classified as 'unusual.' What other artists' work has he collected?"

Alex burned his tongue on a too-hot sip of tea. "Good question," he replied, flashing her another grin, knowing other women thought it sexy the way his cheeks dimpled when he curved his lips up in a certain manner. Since he knew virtually nothing about the world of art, he would have to rely on his charm to get him through this one. "I honestly don't know. My client is interested specifically in you, I mean your work, and when he heard I was coming to the U.K., he asked me to look you up. It was a convenient coincidence to find you so close by."

"Then you are not a dealer?"

Alex let out a deep breath. "No, not exactly. I'm an historian. His is just a . . . special project."

"How did he hear about my work?"

"Uh, well, you know, the usual."

Selena did not answer, but only raised one eyebrow. Alex continued, pedaling fast down Deception Lane. "Well, you know, word of mouth. He heard your exhibition at the gallery in London was all the rage." He tried to think of how Maggie had described it. "He told me that everyone was . . . hot for your work."

Selena laughed. "Hot for my work? Is that what he said?" Then she paused and looked amused. "I suppose I should be flattered."

Alex finished his tea and set the mug on the table, determined to accomplish what he'd supposedly come here for and then get the hell out. Selena was far too trusting . . . and far too beautiful. "Well," he said, clearing his throat, "may I take a look around?"

"I suppose." Selena led him to the first in the series. "This was the earliest one. I painted it about a year ago."

Alex attempted to ignore her closeness, but the essence of the woman threatened to overwhelm him. Mingling with the plastic smell of acrylic paint was a heady woman scent, a disturbing musky, spicy fragrance. Distracted, he had to force his attention to the canvas she was showing him.

The painting looked more like a cartoon than the ones he had seen in London and Haworth. A muscular man in a torn shirt strode up a hillside, looking back over his shoulder. The monkey was comical, laughing with his upper lip raised to expose his large teeth. The roses grew in a neatly tended garden, and the fire was contained in a hearth. In all, it didn't have the enchantment of the others, but he wasn't about to say so. For the part of the painting he was most interested in, the letter, was larger than in the others, and easier to read.

"What gave you the inspiration for this work?"

She didn't reply for a long while, and when she did, her answer was short, almost angry.

"Who knows where any artist's ideas spring from? I suppose the background comes from the moors. It looks like that much of the time around here."

"I've noticed." Why did she seem so defensive?

She continued, twisting a strand of hair absently with her fingers. "The other images I guess came from my grandmother. She . . . she is a Gypsy. One of the last in England to actually travel in a caravan. She has told me lots of stories about her adventures."

So the cyclist had been right, he thought, studying the Gypsy images. Then he stepped closer to the canvas and peered at the piece of the letter. "And this?"

Selena regarded him now with open antipathy. "What?"

"There seems to be something like this," Alex continued, pushing his luck, "a scrap of paper, like a letter, in all the paintings I've seen."

"So?"

Alex could tell his welcome was wearing thin. "Where did it come from? Does it mean anything?"

"It's . . . just something I made up."

Alex perceived she wasn't telling the truth and wondered why. What was the truth, and why would she want to hide it? He said nothing, but moved to study the painted message up close. This one he could plainly read:

and
s o'er, I weary
ere we were
all meet our
ffering
to

"Sounds like part of a poem. Do you write poetry?" he asked, his eyes riveted to the word puzzle.

"No. No, I don't. I . . . I may have gotten some of this stuff out of books. I don't recall. It's really not important."

Alex began to suspect that wherever she had conjured it up, the content of the letter was likely the most important aspect of her work. And for her, disturbing. Curious . . .

"I'm really very busy this afternoon, Mr. Hightower," she said at last, a discernible edge in her voice, as if he were making her very uncomfortable. "Perhaps you could make an appointment with Tom Perkins . . ."

"But the paintings are here, not in London," he pointed out, not wanting to miss the chance to see the rest. That handwriting . . . "If I could only take a quick look at them all, I'll be on my way."

She stepped out of his way, and he moved swiftly to the next painting. Although more sophisticated than the first, it still showed an artist experimenting, flexing her creative muscles. In it the scrap of paper was caught by the wind and appeared to be blowing away. The lines were neatly painted, in that odd handwriting. This one read:

fully, sh
wish only
put an end

brought upon
ust pay for
y foolish and
ear not death
in death I shal

"It sounds rather morose," Alex commented.

"Maybe I was in a bad mood when I wrote it."

"Where did you get the handwriting style?"

He saw Selena's back straighten, and he knew he'd pushed his queries past the limit.

"Handwriting is handwriting."

His time was running out, and Alex knew it was unlikely he would have such an opportunity again. Still, he must find a way to see each bit of the puzzle.

"I know you are very busy, but my client is extremely interested," he said, wondering if technically a person can be his own client. "Would it be possible for me to take some photos of these to send him?"

Selena seemed to vacillate for a moment, then said, "I suppose that would be all right. What was your client's name again?"

Alex felt his stomach lurch. Deception Lane had ended at the edge of a cliff, and he carelessly pedaled right over the precipice. It was too late to save himself.

"Bonnell," he replied with the only name that came quickly to mind. "Henry H. Bonnell."

❧ *Chapter 8* ❧

July 25, 1845

   Shock seems to fall upon shock this summer. Branwell has returned from his post with the Robinsons, and on his heels was a most disastrous letter from his employer, dismissing him and threatening him direly. Branii tells us that he has been carrying on an adulterous affair with Mrs. Robinson, who, he claims, had tempted him into her arms when he in fact tried to resist. Charlotte and Papa are scandalized, but I less so. Who am I to fault Branwell when I myself have known the temptations of a seducer?

July 31, 1845

   Yesterday was my birthday, and today Anne and I opened our diary papers which we wrote four years ago. How life changes with time! Our scheme to open the Misses Brontë's Establishment has vanished, and along with it, Charlotte's dream for our security. (It was never my dream, to be sure!) I am immersed in my writing, which gives me great solace, for although I wrote in my other diary paper—the one we will open three years hence—that I was comfortable and undesponding, this is not an accurate picture of my state of mind. I am, in fact, quite desponding, but I must not let the others know. We have enough trouble in this house with

Branwell's madness. I sometimes think if I didn't have this diary to turn to, I would go mad myself. It helps to put my thoughts on paper so I can sort them out, for many times I find myself confused and betrayed by my own feelings. I turned twenty-seven today. I feel old and I am filled with a desperate, foolish yearning. I should be content. I have my life in order, the way I want it. I no longer have to worry about leaving the Parsonage. I am happy here keeping house and writing. I am free to walk upon the moors as often and as long as I wish. But since Mikel left, the hills seem lonely and desolate. I ache for him to return, although I know he will not, and I am wrong to wish it. Mikel is free, like the wind itself. I knew he must go sometime. If only he had waited long enough to say good-bye. Then I would know that he cared for me and didn't just take advantage of my sympathies. I waver between grief and anger, and all for what? It is nonsense.

I know not what will become of us. Branwell is like a madman since his disgraceful dismissal and has taken to drink and laudanum to ease his pain. I wish I could find some way to ease mine . . .

Selena watched from the upper window as the figure of the man disappeared into the mists. What an odd encounter, she thought.

Odd, and troubling.

She went down the stairs and called to Domino, who, eager to be reinstated into his mistress's favor, came happily awag. Together they clambered back up to the studio, Domino intent on drying himself by the fire, Selena on quieting her thoughts.

There was something wrong, something that disturbed her about Alexander Hightower. Perhaps the way he had just appeared at her doorstep out of nowhere. The Yanks were a presumptuous lot, she thought. No legitimate British art dealer would have approached her like that.

But then, he'd told her he wasn't really a dealer, just a personal representative of someone named . . . what was it? Bardwell? Bonhill? No, Bonnell. Henry H. Bonnell. She wrote it on a notepad so she wouldn't forget it.

Selena also made a mental note to mention the incident to Tom Perkins. She had agreed to give Tom the exclusive rights to market her work, except for that one painting in Haworth, because Tom was the best and she needed his help. She didn't want to risk a misunderstanding that she was trying to sell behind his back.

Selena went to the fireplace and added a stick of wood to the dwindling flame, her mind still on her mysterious American visitor. How had he known her last name? She should have asked him. She had not used it in years, in fact, not since she'd returned to England from Paris. Wood was her ancestral name, Anglicized from the Welsh Wd. She used it only when a surname was required, such as when she'd enrolled at the École des Beaux Arts.

When she had become a professional artist, she'd decided to use only her given name, Selena. Tom had liked the idea. Said it added to her mystique. She liked it because it distanced her from memories of her father and the horror of her childhood.

Something else about the man who called himself Alex Hightower unsettled Selena as well, but it was not easy to isolate. It was his presence, perhaps, the strong sense of his maleness, something she wasn't used to in her isolated life. While he was taking pictures of her paintings, she had leaned back against the windows, watching him move and bend to get the right camera angle. Even beneath the thick sweater he wore, she could tell that his broad, muscled shoulders tapered to a trim waistline. He crouched to get a certain shot, balancing on his scuffed western-style boots, and she saw his faded jeans stretch snugly across his muscular legs and firm backside. He'd

said he was an historian, but he looked more like a cow-
boy. To her amazement, Selena had caught herself wondering what he looked like in the nude. Disconcerted,
she was glad when he finally finished his picture-taking
and took his leave.

Was he really someone's representative, interested in
her art? She had no reason to believe otherwise. Yet his
overt curiosity about the letter made her uncomfortable.
Was that what his client found so unusual about her
work? If so, she thought cynically, she wished he'd buy
the whole damned bunch so she wouldn't have to look at
them again.

She'd even throw in the letter!

She would, that is, if she had it. The torn pieces would
have to do. And at that thought, those torn pieces re-
claimed her, and she returned to the smaller room of the
studio where a half-finished painting awaited her. She
attempted to pick up where she left off when she'd heard
Domino's demanding alarum, but instead of finishing the
image of the roses, she began to draw the figure of a
man.

August 21, 1845

*I am writing today as I sit upon the moors, here where I
come so often of late, to the ravine along the back hill. I
know in my mind it is foolish to torture myself so, but I
cannot seem to stay away. It is beautiful here, and peaceful.
And free. I like to sit on the large rock by the beck and just
think about what it means to be free—truly free, like Mikel.
Earlier I spotted a lone hawk soaring high above me. To fly
must be the greatest freedom of all. While I watched, I saw
the creature suddenly fold its wings and dive headlong
toward the earth, then stop in time to regain control, snatch
its prey, and climb once again. That freedom! That control!
Would that they were mine in my own life.*

Freedom and control. They must go together, for one

without the other can spell disaster. I think of poor Hero, a hawk like this other, who somehow lost control and injured his wing. I found him and saved his life, but he could never fly freely again. I suppose Mikel was injured because he lost control, too, when the horse threw him off. The difference is that Mikel was able to regain his freedom where Hero could not.

And what about me? Wherein lies my freedom? I am filled with control—I scarcely know anything else. I am controlled by my station in life, the limitations of being a woman, my lack of money. And yet, I am not without freedom. I am free when I walk alone here on the moors. I am free when I think and when I write. I am free because I share my soul with only a few, and then not all of it. I suppose I must be content with inner freedom, for it would appear that outer controls will prevent me from having the kind of freedom Mikel knows.

How I long for it, though! How I long to release these bonds and fly free as the hawk. And if I could, I would soar across the Welsh mountains and search far and wide until I found Mikel again. I would never give up until I was with him once more. But then—what would that bring? If he loved me, perhaps a fleeting happiness. But if this were so, he would not have deserted me the way he did. And so there would only be disappointment if I found him again. (He has left me the same as Fernando left his sweetheart. Did Mikel have an Augusta waiting for him?)

I must take heart in this. It is far sweeter—the anticipation of what might be—than the fulfillment of the dream. The idea is the freedom, while the attainment is the control.

The phone in the Parsonage Library rang shrilly, shattering the contented quietness of the room. Alex jumped. He heard the librarian speak softly into the receiver, and then, to his surprise, call him to the phone.

"Hello?"

"Hello, love. It's Maggie. How is your project coming along?"

Alex rolled his eyes. Until this moment he had successfully banished all thoughts of Maggie Flynn for days. "Fine. Just fine," he answered, irritated. "What's up?"

"You won't believe this. The other day I got a call from Eleanor Bates. You might not remember her, but she is the elderly woman you met on the train."

"How did you know about that?"

"She told me. She's very excited about our debate, you know."

"So she said. Who is she anyway?"

"Only one of the most important philanthropists in all of England. Her husband left her quite a bit of money, and rumor has it she's a whiz at investments. She endowed a chair in English Literature at the University of Leeds and is an absolute Brontë fanatic. Quite a colorful old lady. I heard that she was a spy during the war."

Somehow this didn't surprise Alex. Eleanor Bates, it appeared, was a woman of many talents. He made no comment, however, but waited for Maggie to continue, which she did after a moment of silence on the line.

"The reason she called me was to invite me to a party her daughter and son-in-law are giving at Harrington House on the seventeenth. Apparently her daughter married quite well. Her husband is a member of Parliament, and Elizabeth, that's her name, has her own business. Trades in art and antiques and the like."

Like Henry H. Bonnell? Alex thought sardonically.

Maggie continued. "They are entertaining a variety of people that night apparently. Business associates, personal friends, even some celebrities. Which I guess in a way is where we fit in. In her circle at the university, we seem to be the main event later this summer. Anyway, she wanted me to call and invite you to come with me."

Here she faltered. Then, after a telling pause, her

voice not so strong as before, she asked, "Would you like to do that?"

Alex ran his fingers through his hair. It was the last thing he wanted to do. He hated formal occasions. He didn't want to be put on display by Eleanor Bates or anyone else. And he had no intention of being Maggie's date anywhere, anytime, ever again.

"Look Maggie, I'm sorry, but I think I'm busy that evening. But thanks anyway. And please tell Mrs. Bates thanks for the invitation."

"Oh, come on, Alex. Look, I know things aren't the same between us as they used to be. But we're still friends, aren't we? I don't know exactly what went wrong, but whatever it was, I'm willing to forgive and forget if you are."

Maggie's attempt at reconciliation was almost wheedling, and Alex suddenly wished she hadn't tried. It was weak, out of character, unless, he considered, it was just another of her manipulative ploys.

Either way, he found he just didn't care.

"That's fine, Maggie. But I still can't make the event."

"You're making a mistake, Alex. She could be a great help to your career. She's a good ally."

"I'm sure. Look, I'll give her a call myself and decline. I'm sure she'll understand. Do you have her number handy?"

Maggie read it off to him, and they said a formal good-bye. Hanging up the phone, Alex drew in a deep breath and let it out in a long slow sigh.

The following Tuesday morning, Alex noted an unusual number of visitors roaming the Parsonage. Not just the usual tourists. These people seemed to be at ease here. They acted, in fact, as if they owned the place.

Which later he found out they did.

Members of the Brontë Society were gathering from

around the world for their AGM, as Eleanor Bates had called it. The Annual General Meeting. Teachers and housewives. Professionals and hobbyists. Men and women. Old and young. Rich and not so rich. They shared one thing in common. A passion for the work of the Brontës. Many of them, he learned, saved all their vacation time and money to come here once a year.

He'd thought his obsession with the Brontës was abnormal, but in comparison to some of these people, he looked like an amateur.

His work began to be interrupted frequently by staff members at the Parsonage who took it upon themselves to introduce him to various Society members. He found to his consternation they all knew who he was and what he was trying to prove. Some were open to his theory; others were openly hostile. Still, it was obvious that he was something of a celebrity among them.

He couldn't concentrate with all that was going on around him, so he closed his books, returned the files to the librarian, and decided to take a hiatus in his academic work until the AGM was over. He was headed for the back door when he heard a woman's voice call his name.

"Dr. Hightower! Hello there."

He turned, not totally surprised to see Eleanor Bates hailing him from across the lobby.

"Ms. Bates. What a nice surprise. I've been meaning to call you."

"Maggie told me. I'm terribly disappointed that you can't come to the party at Harrington House. Are you sure you won't change your mind? The place itself is worth the trip. A marvelous example of mid-eighteenth century architecture. Designed by John Carr of York. A masterpiece!"

"This is your daughter's home?"

"Oh, good lord no. They live in Leeds. Harrington is

open to the public. But it's available for parties and special occasions. They've hired the best chamber orchestra in England for the evening. They'll be playing in the gallery early on, and then later there will be a dance band. Oh, do say you'll come."

Alex had not one good reason to decline, except Maggie Flynn. He decided to be honest.

"Ms. Bates—"

"Please, call me Eleanor."

"Uh, Eleanor, you of all people understand the importance of the debate in which Dr. Flynn and I will be engaged later this summer."

"Of course."

"And we are diametrically opposed to one another on the issue."

"Undoubtedly."

"Would it sound unkind if I said I would rather not encounter her until after the debate? Nothing personal, you understand. I just wouldn't want to unwittingly give away any secrets."

Eleanor Bates's eyes widened. "Have you discovered something?"

He didn't want to tell her that so far he'd turned up nothing of any great significance. Just a few new facts he might be able to use. Intrigue was part of the game when it came to debates. It was like poker. And he wasn't about to tip his hand, especially since he held no good cards.

"I don't know yet. It's early. But promising."

"Oh, dear. How exciting. Of course, I understand. But if it's Dr. Flynn you're worried about, she said she probably would be unable to make it as well."

Alex thought quickly. "I didn't bring a tuxedo."

Eleanor stood back from him and surveyed his form. "My son-in-law has a closet full of evening wear. You

look to be the same size. I'll send something over for you
to try."

"I don't have a car, and I imagine it would be too far to
take a cab, wouldn't it?"

"How silly of me. Of course it would. You can borrow
one of my cars. Dr. Hightower, do say you will come. I
promise it will be an important evening for you. I can
introduce you to a lot of people you ought to know.
Including the chancellor of the university. Now tell me
you will change your mind."

And he'd thought Maggie Flynn was stubborn. "What
night did you say it was again?"

"The seventeenth. A week from Saturday. Then it's
set?"

Alex finally gave up and smiled into her blue eyes. "I
would be honored," he said at last, hoping down to his
bones Maggie never found out.

Leaving the library, Alex decided to take the bus into
Keighley. He'd dropped the roll of film he'd shot at Selena's studio at the photo lab there, and the pictures
were supposed to be ready this afternoon. He was anxious to see what he'd been able to capture on film.

An hour later he stood at the counter of the lab, shuf-
fling through the prints with growing disappointment.
Even using his strongest magnifying glass, he could make
out almost nothing of the letter fragments. Only in the
first painting, the one with the largest lettering, was it
legible.

"Is there something you can do to enlarge these?" he
asked the technician.

"Certainly. We can blow up the whole thing as large as
you want. Well, within reason, of course."

Alex took out his pen and carefully circled the letter in
one of the prints. "Can you blow up just this piece?
That's what I'm really after."

The man looked at the print through an eyepiece. "I can try," he replied at last. "But I can't promise you'll be able to read it even enlarged. This is a snapshot, and the lighting is, well . . ."

"Amateurish," Alex finished for him.

The lab tech smiled apologetically. "I'll do the best I can, sir."

Alex thanked him and left the small shop, greatly disappointed. He would have to wait another week to see if the enlargements were legible, but he didn't hold out a lot of hope. How, he wondered, could he arrange to get another look at all of Selena's paintings again? Tell her he'd come to pick one out for Henry Bonnell?

Outside, the earlier drizzle had turned to a downpour, and Alex was soaked by the time he returned to the small flat he'd rented for the summer. The Parsonage was packed with Brontë Society members. The weather precluded a walk on the moors. Alex didn't feel like reading a book or watching television. But it was only four o'clock in the afternoon. Too early for a beer at the Bull.

Alex paced the floor, knowing what he wanted to do and hating himself for wanting it. He had no business wanting to sit in front of the fireplace in Selena's studio. Wanting to hear her softly accented words, to watch her paint, drink tea with her . . .

No, he acknowledged, he wanted more than that. What he really wanted was to touch her hair, inhale her perfume, feel the softness of her skin as he held her body close to his own. With a groan, he leaned with both arms against the windowsill, looking out into the gloom. He'd been right. She was the kind of woman he should scrupulously avoid. But had he flown too close to the flame?

In the streets below, the lights from the shops struggled to dispel the inclement weather. He could just see the art gallery if he pressed his face very close to the glass.

The art gallery.

He couldn't go to Selena's, and he might have to wait a week to see the photos of her paintings, but he knew one place he could encounter her spirit on this rainy afternoon. Gathering his strongest magnifying glass and a small writing tablet, he put on his raincoat and took the umbrella down from where it hung at the top of the stairs.

The woman in the gallery recognized him right away. "Did y' come for your paintin'?" she asked hopefully.

He smiled. "I'm still thinking about it. Could I take a closer look, do you think? There's something about that painting that intrigues me, but I want to make sure about it before I make up my mind."

She looked at him doubtfully, but shrugged. "Suit yourself. Your the one's go'n t' be lookin' at it."

He carefully surveyed the picture as a whole, waiting until the proprietress had shuffled back to her stool at the rear of the store. The work was good, even to his untrained eye. There was a pleasing balance of light and color that offset the startling surrealistic images.

Taking the magnifying glass out of his pocket, Alex captured what he'd come for. On the pad, he carefully copied the word fragments that were clearly legible in this painting:

no
its
Time's wi
at land divi
n, where you a
arest when we d

The exercise took only a few minutes. When he was finished, Alex lowered the looking glass and ran his hands through his hair. He frowned. Something about these word shards seemed familiar. Or was it just the cramped handwriting which he fancied to be like Emily's? He was struck again by the evidently poetic nature of the language, despite its brevity.

Remembering Selena's reticent reaction when he'd questioned her about the content of the message, he wondered if it might be a poem she had written. Maybe a deeply personal piece she didn't want to share with anyone else. But that didn't make sense. After all, she'd painted pieces of the whatever-it-was onto every canvas he'd seen so far.

Alex thanked the proprietress, promising to get back to her, and stepped out into the darkening storm. The word puzzle fascinated him, but he found the woman behind it an even more perplexing and enticing mystery. Turning up the lane for home, he was unaware of the traffic in the streets or the steady drizzle that ran off his jacket. His mind saw only the outline of Selena in her doorway, the soft roundness of her hips when she reached for the tea mug, the coal-black eyes that looked up at him, trusting.

Raw sexual desire shot through him.

Later, he stood in the shower, feeling the warmth of the water sting against his skin. Forget the woman, he commanded himself silently over and over. You've blown one marriage, aborted another love affair. You're no damn good at that kind of stuff. Leave it alone. And besides, the pain . . .

The pain.

But much later, half a bottle of brandy to be exact, the image of the woman was still very much with him. Alex lay back against the pillows on his bed. Outside, the "wuthering" continued unabated, with winds lashing the branches of trees and rain battering their leaves. Trying to get his mind off Selena, he picked up the copy of the issue of the Brontë Society Transactions he had intended to study before Selena had crept into his thoughts and seduced him so remorselessly. He glanced at the front page, and the title of one of the articles jumped out at ·him.

"Emily's Lover."

He studied the small booklet with brandy-blurred vi-sion. Whether Emily Brontë had a lover was one of those perennial questions addressed by scholars of her work. He rolled the idea over in his mind. Was a love affair gone sour the cause of her distress that cold winter so long ago? Had she, too, felt the pain and confusion that was raging through him at the moment? Had it caused her to take her life? Alex laughed bitterly at the direction his drunken thoughts were taking him.

"Love sucks, Emily," he said out loud, slurring the words. "Lucky you knew better."

☙ *Chapter 9* ☙

His land may burst the galling chain,
His people may be free again,
For them a thousand hopes remain,
But hope is dead for him.
Soft falls the moonlight on the sea
Whose wild waves play at liberty,
And Gondal's wind sings solemnly
Its native midnight hymn.

Around his prison walls it sings,
His heart is stirred through all its strings,
Because that sound remembrance brings
Of scenes that once have been.
His soul has left the storm below,
And reached a realm of sunless snow,
The region of unchanging woe,
Made voiceless by despair.

And Gerald's land may burst its chain,
His subjects may be free again;
For them a thousand hopes remain,
But hope is dead for him.
Set is his sun of liberty;
Fixed is his earthly destiny;

A few years of captivity,
And then a captive's tomb.

—Emily Brontë

Darkness surrounded Alex, a cold, dank, stone-hard darkness. He could feel the icy roughness of a wall against his face and hands. The air was stale, suffocating. Terror left a sheen of clammy perspiration on his skin, chilling him to the marrow. His fingers groped along the wall in the inky blackness, seeking in vain for a door latch. He tried to call for help, but found himself voiceless.

The night was soul-deep, and he was alone.

Escape. There must be a way out, his mind told him logically. But there seemed to be no exit. He turned his back to the wall and faced the infinite void. What lay in wait there? Dread poured through his bloodstream and settled heavily in his stomach. He was trapped, he knew, but he was also aware that it was his own fear that held him captive. His choices were suddenly clear. Stay here and die, or wrestle with whatever devils awaited him in the eternal night.

Whatever might befall him, nothing could be worse, he decided, than the hellhole of his present existence. Summoning all of his courage, Alex took one step into the void, and then another and another.

And then he was running, fast as the wind, down a path that led away from the darkness. Behind him a soot-stained church guarded the souls of the dead and the undead. Ahead of him lay the open moors . . . and freedom.

Sharp, cold air filled his nostrils, and his heart beat hard. But he kept on running until he knew he was safely away from the terrifying darkness. Only then did he stop to catch his breath.

He found himself deep in the high moorland, surrounded only by the wind and the wide, wide sky. Far below him, villages lined the valley where once a river ran. Derelict farmhouses were scattered like so much windblown debris across the vast expanses of the moors on either side.

But here there was no darkness. Here, freedom was borne on the wind, and he raised his face to it.

He inhaled the animal smells, the scent of the sodden undergrowth. From a distant hillside he heard a sheep bleating into the wind and, from still farther on, the plaintive answer of another. His terror subsided, giving way to a sense of accomplishment and relief. Strangely, out here in the open, he felt safe, protected. Around him, tall gray-brown grass rustled in the breeze.

And then he heard a whisper. "It's here," it said.

Startled, he turned to see if someone had followed him. But there was no one. Must've been the wind singing in the reedy grass, he thought, and began walking down the path. Sunshine and shadow played chase across the barren land.

"Look. Look. It's here." He heard the whisper again.

He stopped. "What's here?" he called out, but there was no reply. He listened intently, but the earth was silent save for the sighing of the wind as it hurried past.

Then, from far away, came an animal's keening howl. Alex looked in the direction of the mournful cry and saw a large, yellow object. His earlier terror returned when he saw it move. A wolf? Were there wolves in these parts? He began to walk briskly down the path, away from the animal. Were there such things as yellow wolves?

Looking back over his shoulder, he saw the beast pursuing him at a run. It wasn't a wolf, but rather a large dog, a mastiff mixed breed of some sort. He looked around for a stick or a rock, just in case, but found nothing with which to arm himself.

When he looked up again, the creature was almost upon him. But before he could cry out, the dog brushed past his legs as if he didn't exist and ran on ahead, its gaze focused on the distant horizon. Alex turned and continued to watch in amazement.

High above on the hillside across a ravine, Alex discerned another figure. A woman wearing a long, old-fashioned dark brown dress stood watching the dog unerringly make its way toward her across the matted heather. She was tall, slender, with dark hair wisping from beneath a plain bonnet. Her skirts blew loosely in the wind.

And Alex knew her.

"Emily." He breathed her name in disbelief. He tried to follow after the dog, but suddenly the path down which he had been traveling disappeared. The grasses and heather tangled in wild array around his boots, clinging to him, forbidding him to go on. But still he struggled with all his might to get over the hill. The effort left him gasping painfully for breath.

The sky grew dark, and large drops of cold rain began to splash against his face. "Emily?" he called again, louder, stumbling through a patch of low scrub. A heavy, misty rain began to fall, obscuring his view momentarily. His eyes searched the hillside opposite the ravine, straining for a glimpse of the figure.

His heart leapt as he saw the dog. It had reached the woman's side and was happily wagging its tail and licking her in greeting. She bent to pet the brute's head. She was close. So close. Could he catch her?

"Emily!" he cried into the wind.

If she heard, she paid no attention, but rather turned and began to climb the steep hill, moving away from Alex. "Wait!" he called. "Wait. I must talk to you."

The woman in brown muslin climbed surefootedly, without hurry. It was as if she floated above the grass and the wiry black heather that snagged Alex's every move. I must reach her, he thought desperately.

To save time, he leapt across the ravine, finding it surprisingly easy to gain the far side. He simply stepped off the side of the crevice. The wind supported him, and he landed lightly on the soft grass on the other side, where the figure had stood petting the dog. But she had moved on. He looked up to see her silhouette against the sky at the top of the slope.

"Wait!" he called. "Wait for me!"

This time she didn't move, but observed him from her lofty crest. He climbed quickly now, and he grew tired from the exertion. "Wait. Don't go," he panted. "I'm almost there." But when he got there, she was gone. At the top of the craggy hillside he saw only more craggy hillside covered with brown grass and dark heather.

Looking across the moors, he could make out the dark shape of Top Withens. Roofless, the gray stone walls of the ruin offered only partial protection from the wind, but the storm was growing menacing, and Alex decided to make for the only shelter in sight. Beneath his feet there appeared large slabs of the local sandstone, suddenly paving the way toward his destination. In only moments he was standing next to the ruin, wondering how he got there so quickly. It had taken hours when he'd hiked here before.

The figure of the woman stood on the other side of the wall, next to the bent and twisted skeleton of a tree. "There you are," he said, as if he'd caught up with an old friend.

"Leave me in peace." The words were soft, feminine, and yet the command was imperative.

"But you know I can't do that."

"You must," the voice said, the head never turning to face him.

Alex took a step closer, and the figure vanished. "Who are you?" he whispered.

From behind him came a surprising reply. "I am who you want me to be."

Alex spun around, and there she stood, half hidden behind one wall of the old farmhouse. "Are you Emily?"

"I am who you want me to be," she repeated. "But you must go now."

"No. I can't go. I must talk to you. I have questions. I have so many questions."

"Only you can answer your questions."

"I can't let you go."

"Why not?"

Alex's chest contracted painfully. Blood raced through his veins, making him dizzy. "Because . . ." He searched for a reason that would convince her to stay. "Because," he said at last, taking a deep breath to steady himself, "I love you."

The rush of the storm's wind filled the silence that fell between them. Then the figure stepped from behind the wall. The plain brown garment was transformed into a flowing blue gown that floated like gossamer in the breeze. The woman removed the bonnet, letting loose a mass of blue-black hair to dance in the wind. She looked up and smiled at him through obsidian eyes. And then she vanished into the mists.

"Don't go! Wait!" Alex called out again. "You can't go. I love you. I love you . . .

". . . I love you."

The sound of his own voice awakened him, and Alex bolted upright in his bed, in the small flat overlooking Main Street, in Haworth, West Yorkshire, England, Planet Earth. His skin was clammy, and his hands trembled. Beside him on the nightstand was a half-empty bottle of brandy, and on the still-made bed lay the copy of the Brontë Society Transactions he had been studying before he nodded off.

He swung his feet to the floor and rubbed his eyes, breathing hard, feeling as if he had actually chased Emily to Top Withens.

Emily.

Was that what the dream was all about? Was his subconscious telling him he should give up his search for clues about her death? But even as the fragile details of the dream began to disintegrate in his memory, he knew there was more, much more to it than that. Alex switched off the small lamp by the bed and lay back against the pillows.

Outside, the wind shrieked in the midnight darkness.

October 16, 1845

My hands shake with rage as I write this. In all likelihood, it will prove unreadable. And just as well so! For snooping eyes won't be able to repeat their invasion of my private thoughts as Charlotte has so wantonly done on this day. It is my fault, I suppose, for I carelessly left my desk open on the dining room table. But my sister knows better than to peruse uninvited any material there.

My poems have been desecrated by her thoughtless rummaging! My most private moments captured from the world within have been exposed to her prying eyes. (Thank God she did not find this diary as well. I must burn it soon.)

Not only did she read my words, she had the audacity to comment upon them! Hers were words of high praise, but I question their sincerity. She might have spoken only to quell my flaming anger. I begged her to be still, but she would not, and now she is raving on about some fool scheme to publish these and other poems she and Anne have written. Charlotte has such grandiose ideas! First the Misses Brontës Establishment, and now this. As if any reader would buy

*words penned by women. It matters not. My words are not
for sale.*

Faint rays of early morning sun struggled through the
thick glass in Selena's rustic kitchen window. Outside,
the wind blew the tall spires of grass on the hillside like
waves upon a brown sea.

Restless. Restless.

Going to the stove, she poured herself a third cup of
coffee, knowing as she did it would unsteady her hand for
work. What did it matter? she thought sullenly. She no
longer cared if what she painted was any good. She just
had to get through it. Four more. Then she would have
captured that poor woman's entire wretched note on
canvas. Perhaps then it would be over and she could
move on with her work and her career.

But this morning her career was not the cause of her
ennui.

Selena pulled the heavy woolen shawl closer around
her shoulders and warmed her fingers on the hot coffee
mug. She sat down heavily in one of two creaky chairs at
the rough wooden table. Only then did she pick up the
invitation again. She ran her slender fingers across the
creamy and very proper stationery, embossed with a
crest.

Another invitation to an elite social affair.

Why? What was with these people? They didn't know
her; they only knew *of* her. It was the third invitation of
this kind she'd received since her opening at the Perkins
Galleries. The first she had accepted and had attended—
that dreadful ordeal at Moorehead. The second was in
Cornwall, an easy one to decline because of the distance.
But this one . . . this one was virtually in her dooryard.
At Harrington House, just north of Leeds.

She knew Tom meant well when he urged his well-to-
do friends to include her on their invitation lists. He ran

with all the right people, and he was determined to use his connections to advance her career, to their mutual profit. But she wished he'd leave her out of the social scene. She wasn't good at it. The thought of entering a room filled with gushing, bejeweled women and prurient, predatory men filled her with dread. The only face she would know among hundreds would be Tom's.

And that left her with another problem.

She knew Tom Perkins had more on his mind than her career when he wangled these invitations for her. At first she'd thought nothing of it when he offered to escort her to the affair at Moorehead. And he'd been the perfect gentleman there, going about his role as her agent, steering her from one wealthy potential client to another.

But later, when he was supposed to take her back to her hotel, he'd driven instead to his town house in one of London's more affluent neighborhoods, insisting she come in for a nightcap. She'd been genuinely about to collapse from exhaustion after playing the part of budding-star-artist all evening, and only because she felt so miserable had she been able to convince him to take her home without offending him with a turndown of sexual favors.

It was a fine and most uncomfortable line she had to draw with Tom. She had the talent to become a world-class artist, or so he had told her. And he'd also told her she needed him to make it happen.

Now, she was beginning to doubt him on both scores. Would her "talent" disappear when she finally forced the series from hell out of her life? Did she really have talent to begin with, or was Tom just using that to try to seduce her? She suddenly wondered how many other young female artists he had made the same promise to, and she felt slightly nauseous.

Selena picked up the other letter that lay on the table, the one that had accompanied the formal invitation.

Both had arrived inside a brown shipping box which was also in front of her. Tom wrote:

> I know you are not keen on these affairs, but darling, you really must attend this one with me. Simply everyone will be there, and I needn't remind you of the sales we generated from our last *soiree*. Just so you will have no excuses, I took the liberty of buying you the perfect dress for the occasion. You will turn every head, trust me. You will be stunning, but then, you always are.
>
> I plan to arrive in Stanbury no later than noon on Saturday, and I will come for you directly. We have several matters to discuss, and it would be my privilege to take you to lunch. Please do be a love and make arrangements for me for that night. Nothing fancy needed. In fact, a blanket on your sofa would do.
>
> And now I must get back to work. See you on the seventeenth.
>
> Much love, Tom.
> P.S. How is your work progressing? I do hope you will have some new, exciting things to show me when I am there.
> P.P.S. When are you going to install a telephone? I would find it immensely easier to communicate if I could ring you. Hugs. T.P.

Selena cringed. A blanket on her sofa indeed. Tom hadn't been to the farmhouse yet. He didn't know that a blanket on the sofa was *her* bed. If he wanted to stay over, he'd have to take the bed in the house. There was no hot water in the house, and the window in the bedroom was cracked, making it rather breezy for sleeping. She would find him lodging in town. *If* she decided to go to the affair with him.

Reluctantly, she removed the dress from the package. If nothing else, Tom had impeccable taste. It was a statement of simple elegance, a full-length gown of rich sapphire silk, a color Selena favored and that enhanced the highlights in her hair. It was unadorned, letting the sumptuous fabric take center stage.

In short, it was exquisite.

Damn it, she thought, wishing he'd sent something really ugly that would be easier to turn down. When she looked inside to check the size, the designer label did not escape her notice. The dress must have cost hundreds.

Holding the garment against her, she went into the bedroom and laid it carefully on the bed. Shivering in the chill of early morning which blew in freely through the cracked windowpane, she removed the shawl and the warm flannel nightshirt she wore. Without wasting time with undergarments, she slipped the dress over her head, hoping it wouldn't fit.

But it did. Perfectly. And it felt wonderful.

She moved across the bedroom to the faded full-length framed mirror that stood on carved wooden claws in one corner. Tom was right, she thought, not vainly, but seeing herself through objective eyes. She was stunning. Or at least the dress was. The neckline was cut low in front, and square, and it revealed just enough of the softly rounded tops of her breasts to show them off enticingly to the leering eyes of any prospective male clients Tom might steer her way. Her nipples, standing erect in the cold room, added another erotic feature beneath the silken fabric. The bodice fit snugly, too snugly, she realized, to accommodate underwear should she want to wear it. It showed off her slender waistline, then fell into a flowing bias-cut skirt which clung to her thighs when she walked.

She turned around and peered at herself over her shoulder, only to find the back as suggestive as the front.

Although it fastened across the top of her shoulders, the rest was cut out in an elongated rectangle that dropped from shoulder to waist to reveal the smooth skin of her entire back. The designer, she noted, had succeeded in draping the fabric to display the wearer's *derriere* most appealingly. Yes, Tom was right. She would turn every head, which was exactly what he wanted. She was, after all, his merchandise, and he aimed to show it off to his advantage.

The wave of nausea she'd felt earlier surged again.

The dress was lovely, but it wasn't her. She didn't want to accept it. She didn't want to wear it. She didn't even want to go to the damned affair. Wishing she had never become so enmeshed in the sale of her art that she found herself in this predicament, Selena removed the dress and laid it gently back on the bed. She would box it up and return it to Tom this afternoon. Keeping it would only encourage him in his misguided quest after her body. She'd simply have to find something else to wear.

Hastily she donned an old pair of denims and a sweater and hurried back to the kitchen, where she warmed her now-frigid coffee in the small microwave. She picked up the box to take it into the bedroom and felt something shift inside it. Opening one flap, she discovered a small but heavy parcel wrapped in white tissue. She removed the tape holding it together and drew her breath in sharply when she unwrapped the golden necklace within.

Laying it flat on the palm of her hand, Selena was spellbound by the sheer beauty of the piece. The golden filigree was laced daintily into a triangular-shaped pattern and sparkled with brilliant rubies and sapphires. In a second packet she found earrings to match, along with a card from the Perkins Galleries on which the sender had written: "The pièce de résistance."

Selena softened a bit in her attitude toward Tom. She

knew he must have remembered how out of place she felt at Moorehead, Selena the starving artist in her plain Jane dress and no glitter, and she appreciated his attempt to groom her, Pygmalion-style, for the next event. But that still didn't mean she would keep his gift.

Rewrapping the jewelry and putting it back in the box, she took her hot coffee and returned to the bedroom. There, she opened the doors to the old armoire that held what could scarcely be called a wardrobe. Until recently she hadn't needed dressy clothing, and she wore mostly knitted tops and leggings or denims to work in. She had a single dress that at one time she might have thought appropriate for the occasion, but it was the same one she'd worn to Moorehead, only to feel shabby against the opulence of the other guests.

She sighed and sat down heavily on the bed, weighing her options. She could keep the dress, go to the party, and deal with Tom's advances later; or return the dress, decline the invitation, and face the possibility that Tom Perkins, the most influential art dealer in London, would refuse to promote her work further.

Either way, she thought gloomily, she would probably destroy her future with the Perkins Galleries. Her gloom changed to anger at the thought. No male artist would find himself so compromised. Perhaps that's why so few female artists made it to the top. Maybe they didn't want to sleep their way up.

Well, she wasn't going to sleep with Tom Perkins or anyone else. She'd find another dealer, someone who wanted her work more than her body. Maybe that American who'd showed up on her doorstep so unexpectedly.

What had become of him? she wondered. Had his client in the States seen the photos he'd taken? Did he like her work? Maybe she ought to drive into Haworth and try to locate him. What did he say his name was? Alex something. She wished she wasn't so bad with names. Hickton. Highton. Damn, she didn't even get his card. It didn't matter. Haworth was a little town. She'd find him.

With a slow smile, Selena picked up the shimmering blue dress, folded it carefully, and repacked it for shipping.

There were always options, Tom.

Always.

❧ *Chapter 10* ❧

Harrington House glowed in the late evening sun like an ornate, golden treasure chest hidden by some wealthy giant amidst lush parklands, gardens, and woods. The road wound toward it through fields so green that if they were faithfully reproduced on canvas at the hands of an artist, the work would be criticized as being unrealistically verdant. The sky was laced with high white clouds blushed with tints of rose and amber, and the air was heavy and sweet with the smells of summer in full bloom.

Alex downshifted the powerful sports car as he rounded the last curve and entered the gates to the Harrington estate. When he'd accepted Eleanor Bates's offer of the use of one of her cars for the duration of his stay in England, he didn't realize she meant a vintage Jaguar XK140. The sleek black convertible had belonged to her husband, who had purchased it shortly before his death. It had been specially made for him with a red leather interior, and when he'd died, Eleanor had been unable to bring herself to sell it, but instead kept it covered in the garage, driving it only to have its engine checked once a year. It was in mint condition. "It needs to be driven," she'd insisted. "You would be doing me a great favor."

Alex knew who was doing a favor for whom, but he

didn't argue the point as he slid into the rich leather seat and ran his fingers over the steering wheel. He'd been nervous at first to be responsible for such a vehicle, but it had taken only an afternoon on the roads around Haworth for him to get used to driving on the left-hand side with a gearshift that was the exact opposite of those on American cars. He'd found the challenge exhilarating.

The only thing missing was a beautiful woman in the seat beside him.

He'd driven past Bridgeton Lane several times, considering the possibilities, but when he'd finally turned down the small road, he'd seen that the Land Rover wasn't in the driveway and the dog was on the doorstep, so he hadn't stopped.

Approaching Harrington House, he drove slowly up the pristinely manicured lane, having difficulty conceiving that this once was a single-family dwelling. It looked like an enormous, elegant hotel, a relic of bygone splendor. But Eleanor had told him that the fifth Earl of Harrington and his wife had lived here until his death in 1966. Today, she'd explained, it was operated by a trust as one of England's "treasure houses," and from Alex's perspective, it certainly fit the description.

Handing the Jag over to the parking attendant, Alex determined to make the best of the situation in which he found himself. Even though he hated affairs such as this, the drive over the rolling hills of Yorkshire had been worth the boredom he expected over the next several hours while he made small talk with the county's finest. But if Eleanor was telling him the truth, that many of these socialites were also scholars and Brontë Society members who would be attending the debate, it wouldn't hurt, he decided, to turn on the charm.

He could use some fans in his corner.

He took a deep breath, straightened his bow tie and ran his fingers through his hair. Before his eyes, a queue of Rolls Royces, Mercedes, BMWs, and Jaguars discharged gentlemen in formal attire and ladies dressed in flowing gowns and jewels. He knew no one, although several people, particularly women, smiled at him warmly as they passed him on their way up the front steps. He was about to join the throng moving inside when a flash of copper caught his eye.

Appalled, he watched Maggie Flynn emerge from the passenger side of a black Mercedes. She smoothed her hair, waiting for the man she was with to speak to the attendant. It took him only an instant to figure he'd been set up. But by whom?

Maggie could be an incorrigible manipulator, but this was astonishing. Had she deliberately lied to Eleanor Bates that she was not coming? Surely she would never commit such a social *faux pas*. And it was embarrassingly egotistical to think she would go to such extremes to get him there, Alex thought.

Or had the two of them, Maggie and Eleanor, conspired to get him to change his mind about coming? Was Eleanor trying to orchestrate some predebate drama at this shindig?

Whatever had transpired, Alex was seething. He stood like a stone and watched as the tall redhead approached, not yet seeing him. She wore a black dress, long and tightly fitted, with a slit up one leg. High up. She would be the envy of all the women and capture the eye of every man, no doubt.

Not until she reached the first step did Maggie look up. She was smiling and talking animatedly to the man who escorted her. But when she saw Alex, the smile froze solidly on her lips. Green eyes widened momentarily in genuine surprise at seeing him there, then flashed in anger.

"Good evening, Alex," she said curtly.

He could almost see her lip curl as she brushed past him in a cloud of familiar perfume.

Alex nodded mechanically, trying to understand how this could have happened. Had Maggie, like himself, simply changed her mind? Or had she been manipulated as well by Eleanor Bates? What was the old woman up to? Dismayed, Alex was ready to turn around and head back to Haworth and the comfort of his bed and a good book when Eleanor Bates's voice resounded in his ear.

"There you are, my dear man. Are you getting along with the car? Come. Come in. I have so many people waiting to meet you."

"Ms. Bates, I think—"

"I've asked you to call me Eleanor. Please. Now do come."

"You told me Maggie Flynn had declined the invitation." His voice was coldly accusing.

"Did I? Oh, dear. No, no, she was looking forward to coming. I must be getting forgetful in my old age." She turned a wrinkled but sunny smile on him. "Do say you will forgive me. I'm sure you will not have to engage her in conversation unless you choose to. There are hundreds of people here, after all."

Alex glared at her, but she ignored him. Slipping her hand under his elbow, she maneuvered him skillfully up the crowded steps and into the grand entranceway. Around him, ladies in silks and satins, taffetas and lace, engaged in lively conversations with one another or with their stiffly suited male counterparts. The great hall and all within exuded opulence, and Alex felt out of place as well as out of sorts. He hated conniving women, no matter what age.

"This is my daughter, Elizabeth," Eleanor said as she began his formal introduction down the receiving line. "And my son-in-law, Sir Hillary Durham."

Alex nodded and smiled mechanically, but his pulse

beat heavily against the constricting fabric of his shirt. Damn Eleanor Bates, he thought as he shook hands with her daughter. Damn Maggie Flynn. Damn them all. I'm out of here.

But there was to be no such escape. After the receiving line, an endless stream of Eleanor's cronies from the Brontë Society poured around him, anxious to share their own theories with the American professor they'd all heard about.

"How will you prove she committed suicide?" "Have you found any new evidence?" "Personally, I agree with you, but you'll have a hard time getting past Dr. Flynn's arguments, I'm afraid." "Dr. Flynn says . . ." "Dr. Flynn is such a darling woman. Have you met her? I believe she's here . . ."

She was nowhere in sight, but Maggie Flynn was ubiquitous at this gathering. Was there no escaping this woman?

A chamber orchestra played, and waiters served champagne in long-stemmed flutes. The gallery of Harrington House gleamed in rich red and gold, and a few dancers waltzed on the highly polished wooden floors. Delicacies on silver trays were passed among the guests who attempted, mostly unsuccessfully, to gracefully talk and munch at the same time. Alex wondered cynically why eating ever became a social custom. He passed up the tidbits, sticking with champagne. He would be leaving shortly, as soon as he could make an inconspicuous exit. He could stop for a bite at a nearby pub.

His gaze traveled the room, scanning for the dragon lady. If he could locate her, perhaps he could also avoid her. Instead his attention fell upon the figure of a slender, dark-haired woman on the other side of the gallery.

Her back was to him, and she was surrounded by tuxedoed men, like so many penguins. She was dressed in a stunning blue gown, cut out in back, exposing smooth olive skin beneath the luxurious billows of slate-black hair that played freely along her shoulders. Alex's heart almost stopped.

Selena!

What was she doing here? Not in his wildest imagination would he have expected to see the artist who lived like a recluse on a derelict farm at an event such as this. Suddenly the evening became much more interesting.

But his initial pleasure at discovering Selena at the affair was quickly replaced by panic. What, he thought suddenly, if he was introduced to her and the name of his "client" slipped out in front of someone like Eleanor Bates? His integrity as a scholar would be severely jeopardized.

With a scowl, he reached for another glass of champagne from a passing waiter. Now there were two women to watch out for tonight.

Selena excused herself from the company of the rich old men Tom had set her up with, pleading a need to powder her nose. She was wretchedly angry with herself for having let Tom manipulate her like this. She had been working in the studio earlier in the day when she'd heard a car door slam, and had been mortified to see Tom Perkins standing on the drive below.

"Selena!" He'd shouted loudly enough to be heard the next farm over, which sent Domino into a frenzy. She should have known Tom wouldn't give up so easily, she thought, wiping her hands on a soft towel and going downstairs.

"Domino! Quiet!" She placed two fingers in her mouth and emitted a most unfeminine whistle. The dog shut up. Then she turned to face the sandy-haired man who stood gazing at the dog uncertainly. "Hello, Tom." She tried to sound surprised, uninterested. "What brings you here?"

His blue eyes gleamed in his ruddy face when he saw her, and he hurried over to her and gave her a wet kiss. He aimed it at her lips but, because she turned her head in time, planted it on her cheek.

"Now, what's the matter, love?" He put a hand on each of her shoulders and stood back, looking into her face. "Was it something I said, or do you just not like blue?"

"I'm not going to the party tonight, Tom."

"But darling, you simply must. I have set you up with at least two buyers I think are just right there, ready to make multiple purchases. I've worked hard on this pre-sell," he added, his voice revealing a harder edge than before. "I need you to be there to close the deals."

"I thought that was your job." Selena had decided to cut him no slack. She was the artist, he was the dealer. There was nothing between them other than a business arrangement, and she wasn't interested in his techniques for closing deals. Techniques that involved lecherous men eyeballing her breasts.

"It takes teamwork, love," he said, the smile disappearing. "That's what we are, a team."

"Sorry," she said, wriggling out of his grasp and walking away, signaling for Domino to follow her. "I have a lot of work to do."

Tom was hot on her trail. "Well, that's what else I came for. I wanted to see your new work."

Selena stopped so quickly and unexpectedly that Tom, hurrying behind, almost ran into her. "I thought you wanted more of the letter series," she said slowly, turning and leaning back against the sill of the doorway.

"I do. I do." Tom hedged a moment. "But, you know, Selena, you can't go on just doing this one treatment. I mean, get real. The more you paint like this, the less value they will ultimately have. Sort of like having too large of a print run on your signed lithographs."

His words struck a raw nerve, but she tried to show no reaction. "I have another in the series almost completed," she said. "I plan four more after that, and then I'll go on to something else. You do realize there is a reason why I must complete these, don't you?"

Tom looked perplexed. "What would that be, love?"

"The letter. There are twenty-one pieces altogether. Don't you think the series would be more valuable, have more of a collector's interest, if bidders knew the pieces put together meant something?"

The words were out of her mouth before she could stop them. The thought had actually never occurred to her before that anyone might view the entire series as a puzzle and wish to collect them all. This was not the reason she felt compelled to paint all of the images of the scraps of the letter, but it was one Tom Perkins could accept, and she could see the wheels starting to turn in his mind.

"Yes," he said at last. "That makes sense. I just never knew they were anything other than part of your, uh, imagery. Twenty-one, eh? Where did you get that number?"

"That's how many pieces I tore the letter into."

"Is it a real letter? What does it say?"

"It's nothing. Just a lover's farewell note I . . . made up on a whim."

Tom looked at her knowingly. "A lover's farewell? Someone you knew?"

"No. It's just a piece of fiction. Romantic. That's all. I thought it would work in well with the other images." Selena wished she hadn't described the contents accurately. She could see she had impelled Tom's imagination in the wrong direction.

"Could I see it? The letter, I mean. The whole thing."

Selena shrugged and went up the stairs. Without

speaking, she took the grubby envelope from the drawer where she kept it and turned to face Tom.

"Hold out your hands."

He did, and she shook twenty tiny white pieces of paper into them. The other was still in her studio. She watched with amusement as he examined them.

"How can you read this stuff?" he said at last. "Are you sure it means anything?"

"I told you, it's just something I made up."

"Don't you think you could have written it a little larger? Why the miniprint?"

"I'm an artist, and like I said, it was a whim."

Without further questions, Tom carefully replaced the pieces into the envelope and gave it back to her. "I'll take your word for it, darling. But it is an interesting idea. I'll have to add that aspect to my spiel. Which brings me back to the main reason for my being here . . ."

He'd brought the dress and jewelry with him, along with an ironclad intent that she would go with him to the gala after all. Throughout the afternoon, listening to his tirade designed to change her mind, Selena wished she'd had a phone installed so Tom Perkins would not have had the excuse to show up at her studio. Budget or not, she vowed silently to have one put in next week. In the meantime, little by little, Tom had worn her down, until finally she'd agreed to attend the event at Harrington House with him.

On one condition.

That he'd never, ever ask her to do it again.

It was all that was getting her through the evening.

Once out of the line of vision of her admirers at the far end of the gallery, Selena accepted a flute of champagne from a young waiter whose eyes admired her openly, and she rewarded him with a smile. It was an empty smile, however, practice for the evening.

She wondered if she practiced enough, would she be

able to turn it into a genuine smile, with warmth and depth, and the ability to attract friends?

Growing up, she was always the outsider. She had made few friends in school. She was afraid to bring anyone home to witness her shame. Avoiding her parents, Selena had felt an outsider even in her own home. Only at the École des Beaux Arts had she experienced a few friendships that made her feel like she belonged, relationships with other young artists who felt equally out of place in the new world of higher education into which they found themselves thrust.

Slowly, Selena made her way along one wall of the gallery, smiling occasionally at other guests here and there, but not with the warmth that would encourage anyone to engage her in a conversation. She wanted to stretch her reprieve for as long as possible. She felt sure Tom would realize she'd left the group he'd carefully gathered for her to entertain, and he'd be on the prowl to find her again soon.

Around her, from floor to ceiling, portraits and soft landscapes hung in gilded frames. Selena recognized many of the works. British artists Thomas Gainsborough, George Romney, and Sir Joshua Reynolds had captured individuals and families of the gentry of the eighteenth and nineteenth centuries in portraits commissioned by the subjects.

She studied one family group, absently entwining a strand of hair with her fingers. Aristocratic father figure. Softly feminine mother. Cherry-mouthed children in high fashion. What were they like? she wondered. In real life. Did the father love the mother? Or did he secretly abuse her when the portrait artist wasn't around? And those rosy-cheeked children. Were they happy? Their eyes looked sadly empty, or was that only her imagination?

Why did she think every family was as unhappy as her

own had been? Couldn't it be that some men and women could share a loving, long-term relationship? A deep, silent pain ached within her. Would she ever share such a bond? Or was she destined to always be alone? Was Matka right? Was this the curse in action in her own life?

She moved on. Landscapes by Turner and Girtin showcased their considerable talents. Would she ever paint a realistic landscape like that? Or was she imprisoned forever in surrealism? Would she ever be able to paint angels and cherubs? she asked herself, looking at those by Renaissance masters Bellini, El Greco, Tintoretto, Titian, and Veronese, whose works hung here as well.

Selena decided she was worse company than the men she'd been speaking with earlier, and she made her way through the throng of guests back toward the group. With them, she could at least escape her own morbid thoughts. In moments she found herself surrounded once again by men of varying ages, all dressed alike. She concentrated on remembering their names as she was introduced, but she had the sudden impression that she was surrounded not by individuals, but rather by clones. Not only did they look alike, they sounded alike. They smelled alike. Selena fought back a frightening sensation that she had somehow gotten lost in an alien, surrealistic world.

One in which, once again, she did not belong.

What would it be like, she wondered as she pretended to listen to one of them pontificate on the merits of art as an investment, to find a man who wasn't like all the rest? Didn't look or act or think like these sexually-driven, cookie-cutter reproductions. Or Tom Perkins. Or her father.

Did such a man exist? She suddenly longed to meet just one man who stood out from the crowd. A man who didn't try to impress her, as these were so obviously working hard to do. Someone who could just be himself, and let her be herself. Someone she could trust, who would hold her and understand her and make her feel as if she belonged, after all, to the human race.

Then she heard the cautious whisper of Matka's ancient advice, "Be careful what you ask for, child. You just might get it."

Then another thought sent her spirits to new depths. What if she did get what she was asking for? Would she be able to let such a man into her life? Or would the curse prevent her from becoming involved, demanding its atonement from her as it had her ancestors?

Selena caught herself before this ridiculous inner conversation could go further. With her most charming demeanor, she turned to the gentleman who had been speaking. "I agree that art makes an excellent investment," she said. "Especially if you find an up-and-coming talent and can buy at a good price." Then she smiled her brightest. "I will be showing again this autumn in London," she solicited unabashedly. "In case you're interested." She caught sight of Tom Perkins headed her way, and added, "But if you'd like to see my work before then, I could arrange something through my agent. In fact, there he is now."

Thank you, God, Selena thought, relieved that Tom was there to take over the hustle. Never again, she promised herself, never again will I attend one of these dreadful affairs. My career be damned!

November 20, 1845

I live with rage these days. Mine is a quiet rage, and most of the time the others do not suspect. Charlotte thinks I have softened in my attitude toward the publication of our poems, but in fact, the opposite is true. I think it infinite folly, and the only reason I have acquiesced is to quiet her constant harangue. She has almost driven me insane on the matter, and Anne with her, until I have no will to fight them further. Let them do as they may. But I will give them only what I choose, and so I am working to bring my words into a state I deem presentable. I dread the reviews, but then, no one should know the source of the foolishness, as we have come upon a plan to publish veiled under pseudonyms. It is the one sound thought Charlotte has had since raiding my privacy.

She is to be Currer Bell. I am Ellis Bell, and Anne will be Acton Bell. We have chosen Bell as a joke. The new curate, whom we all find tedious and far less interesting than jovial Willie Weightman, God rest his soul, is Arthur Bell Nicholls. Little will he know his name is so used.

It is not the poems that distress me, however. It is the intense feelings of hatred and despair that engulf me in moments most unexpected. They arise always from the specter of Mikel's face, which stalks me at every turn. I can be making bread, and suddenly his face, that beautiful demon face, confronts me as if it were real. It might waylay me on the stair, or rattle my bed in the dark morning hours. I am haunted, haunted, by this unrelenting ghost! I fear for my sanity, and yet I can tell no one. I must find a way to rid myself of these despairing apparitions.

December 11, 1845

Tonight as Anne and Charlotte and I sat by the fire, as we always do after Papa goes to bed, our talk turned to writing and of Branwell's mad attempt at writing a novel. He calls his work "And the Weary Are at Rest." I have not seen it, but he has informed Charlotte that it is a tale not unlike his own unfortunate affair with the Robinson woman, and that he plans to write it quickly and sell it for a tidy sum.

Charlotte doubts, as I do, that we will see him succeed in this venture, although we all would pray it so. Poor Branii. He will never finish it, I fear, for his thinking is too muddled from drink and laudanum. But his efforts have raised Charlotte's ambition far higher than merely publishing our po-

etry. Now she wants us all to work at writing a novel! Who is the more mad—Branwell or Charlotte?

I told Charlotte that I was loath to force words for commerce. The poems I have written sprang from my heart, and to write for the mere possibility of earning a living seems impossible to me. Whereupon I made this statement, Anne surprised us both by revealing that while still at Thorp Green she had started a novel she hopes to sell. Charlotte was delighted, and then went on to outline an idea of her own. She will call her novel "The Professor." It is, she says, her tribute to Msgr. Heger, although Anne and I both deplore her continuing obsession with that dreadful man. Still, as I listened, some thoughts of my own were set into motion.

To wit: If Branwell can successfully overcome his grief over losing Mrs. Robinson, and if Charlotte can rid herself of the possession of Msgr. Heger through the writing of their stories, perhaps it is a way that I, too, can rid myself of Mikel's ghost. Already the thoughts and ideas tumble about. I will make him a madman. A dark and hateful personage no sane person could love. And I will betray his love. Yes, I will destroy his sanity, on paper, the way Mikel has destroyed mine in the flesh!

December 26, 1845

Christmas passed quietly yesterday, the day being little different from any other Christmas day. We attended church services to please Papa, and I supervised the roasting of a fine fat hen. Our meager financial resources precluded the giving of gifts, other than of the handmade variety. A small, uneventful holiday, to be sure, but one, I would avow, far preferable to that of a gipsie camped out in a snowstorm.

Charlotte and Anne and I continue to talk of writing our novels, but we have decided to keep these efforts to ourselves. Branwell, as expected, is making little progress in his writing, and should by some miracle we be successful in our own, it would only painfully underscore his failure once again. We love him too much for that, and so we remain silent, except in the quiet hours late at night when he is not at home.

Outside, the snow lies deep and silent, with more promised by the look of the clouds. I cannot walk upon the moors today, although I long for the solace I find there. My soul remains rent into warring factions over my continuing weakness as concerns Mikel, and I long for the peace within that once was mine. I long to regain my strength and courage and become once again the soul without doubt that I was before the events of the past summer slew my reason.

Ideas for my story surge through me, but I cannot seem to begin writing on a novel, although Charlotte and Anne are busy with theirs each night. My thoughts are still too confused and painful. I must gain control over them first, for I can only purge what I can control. I must find my courage once again before I can find my way out.

❧ *Chapter 11* ❧

Alex had failed to escape the clutches of Eleanor Bates, who had, true to her word, introduced him to many important figures in the academic world, including the chancellor of the University of Leeds. He had spent the last thirty minutes with the scholar, who turned out to be an adroit conversationalist as well as a Brontë lover. Alex began to relax a little, and decided, as he headed toward the men's room, that he might as well stay awhile. So far, he had managed to avoid both Maggie and Selena, although the latter had never strayed far from his thoughts.

Harrington House was open for viewing by the guests, and Alex took advantage of the break to look around. Everywhere, there was beauty. Paintings. Sculpture. Eighteenth century furniture made especially for the estate by Thomas Chippendale. Fine Chinese porcelain and exquisite pieces of Sevres and Crown Derby china. A treasure house, filled to the brim.

Alex wandered aimlessly from room to room, enjoying a solitary interlude, away from the pressure of attempting to be something he wasn't—a social animal. Entering a carefully preserved bedroom, he surveyed the opulent contents. The ornately carved bed, high enough off the floor to require a small step stool to mount the mattress.

A chiseled and polished marble mantel and hearth. A mahogany chaise covered in luxurious white damask.

As an historian, Alex knew intellectually that these overstated furnishings and surroundings were part of the everyday life of those born to the upper classes in nineteenth century England. But to a boy born into middle-class America, it was a reach of the imagination to conceive of such a lifestyle.

On a whim, he decided to give it a try.

He looked around to make sure he was unobserved. Then, with a theatrical flair, he strode to stand in front of the fireplace. As lord of the manor, he commanded his servant: *Draw my bath now, James, and lay out my riding clothes. It looks to be a suitable day for a round about the place. A spot of port, if you will. And what is m'lady about this cheery morning?*

In the theater of his mind, he cast a leading lady, a dark-haired beauty in blue silk who stretched lazily on the snowy white chaise, her long legs bare, one knee bent. She smiled up at him and beckoned him into her arms.

Rock-hard desire suddenly slammed through him, and Alex knew he had to see Selena again.

Here.

Tonight.

In the flesh.

He could explain the Bonnell thing to her. It wasn't a big deal, but he needed to tell her the truth before somebody else did. Hurrying back to the gallery, deep in debate with himself, Alex didn't see the redhead until it was too late.

She was just coming out of the ladies' room, lips freshly reddened, hair gleaming. "So, Alex, dear," she said, walking straight for him, her green eyes wide with anger. "I *am* surprised to see you. I thought you weren't coming tonight."

Caught off guard, Alex reflexively went on the defensive. "It isn't what you think, Maggie. I hadn't planned to come. You know how I hate these affairs."

"So you've told me." She surveyed him slowly from head to toe. "So why *are* you here?"

Her tone was imperious, as if she were the lady of the manor and he only a minion with no right to be in the presence of the peerage. And suddenly Alex got it, that in her mind, he had held that status all along. She had claimed she loved him, but she hadn't. She wanted to own him. Own him and control him, like she did everything else in her life.

Anger flared through him but quickly turned to disgust. Maggie Flynn was a despicable woman who did not deserve one moment more of his time or energy. Alex planted his feet firmly and squared his shoulders, crossing his arms in front of him. He studied those blazing eyes intently, without blinking. When at last he spoke, his voice was flat, calm, emotionless. "I didn't want to come, but I changed my mind, Maggie. As I am sure you have learned, Eleanor can be most convincing."

Maggie glared at him, and Alex could see the pulse pounding in the hollow at the base of her neck. "It wasn't that you didn't want to come, Alex," she hissed. "If that were the case, you wouldn't be here. It's that you didn't want to come with *me.* Why didn't you just say so from the start? You didn't have to lie."

"I wasn't lying."

"You were lying then, and you're lying now. The *truth* is, we're not friends anymore, Dr. Hightower. And you needn't worry about going anywhere with me ever again." She paused, her face flushed, then lowered her voice and continued. "I won't bother you further, Alex. At least in your personal life. But I intend to bother you a lot in August.

"In fact, I intend to destroy you."

* * *

Selena's feet hurt, and she was exhausted from being on display. All evening, Tom had dragged her from one group to another, showing her off to all the right people, his hand rarely leaving the curve at the back of her waist, where, to her repugnance, it rested lightly against her exposed skin. She had discreetly removed it more than once, but she detected a perverted pleasure on Tom's part when she did so. It was as if by touching her when he knew she objected, he was asserting an unspoken dominance over her.

Just getting through the evening, and the scene with Tom that she knew would be unavoidable later, was Selena's main goal in life at the moment.

She had managed to free herself, even if only momentarily, from Tom's jealous monopoly, and stepped outside onto the terrace, which overlooked lush Italian gardens and a small, serene lake. The sun had disappeared behind the surrounding hillsides, but the sky retained a brilliant luminescence.

Going to the balustrade, Selena leaned against it, delighting in the display of the late night sunset. In the distance the surface of the lake was like a looking glass, a slate-blue mirror reflecting the resplendent sky overhead. A night bird called plaintively from the wood. She breathed deeply of the sweet summer air and for the first time that evening began to relax.

Selena sensed more than saw a man approaching her, and her reverie was shattered. She tensed, preparing to confront Tom Perkins. Instead she turned to find the tall, good-looking American heading straight for her. Their eyes locked, and although she'd been wanting to talk to him about his client's interest in her work, seeing him tonight spawned an entirely new and disturbing agenda within her.

He looked different tonight. Perhaps it was the clothes

he wore. He filled out the formal jacket better than most, she couldn't help noticing. And he wore it easily, with an air of nonchalance, as if he'd rather be in jeans.

His face was solemn at first, then the corners of his mouth turned up into that same sexy smile he'd given her when he'd shown up at the farmhouse. His smile moved upward into his gray eyes, which were riveted on her own. Selena's heart skipped several beats. She hadn't remembered him being this handsome. She swallowed, watching him stride purposefully toward her, and the rest of the world seemed to dissolve around her.

"May I join you?" he asked.

She liked his distinctly American accent, with its hint of a southern drawl. Her own voice seemed lodged on an unfamiliar emotion that constricted her throat. "On one condition," she said at last.

"And that is?"

"We don't talk about my work."

Selena saw what could only be described as relief flash briefly across his expression, and she suspected the reason she hadn't heard from him was that Henry Bonnell had decided against acquiring her paintings. If that was the case, she didn't want to know it at the moment anyway.

"It's better not to mix business with pleasure, don't you think?" he replied, and Selena nodded, wishing certain other business people held the same view.

"Quite an affair, isn't it?" she said, motioning to the tall doors which barely contained the noise of the party beyond, searching for some common ground between them other than her work.

"I suppose it is. But it's not exactly my cup of tea."

Selena raised an eyebrow, surprised. "How so?"

His grin was engaging. "I just don't like formal affairs."

Well, at least they had one thing in common, she

thought, and his easy smile worked its way steadily into her heart. "Neither do I."

He looked deeply into her eyes. The grin vanished, and he spoke in a low, husky voice. "But here we are. We might as well make the most of it, don't you agree? Would you care to dance?"

Alex took Selena's slender hand in his and led her through the doorway and onto the dance floor. Her skin was cool, electric, like the blue of her gown. He allowed himself momentarily to get lost in the dark depths of her eyes. Around them, the opulence of the glittering gallery suggested the grandeur of a gilded make-believe castle. The music spiraled magically throughout the ballroom. And in his arms he held a beautiful princess.

For a fleeting moment Alex almost regretted having sought her out. What was the point if she, like that other fabled princess, left him, if not at the stroke of midnight, then at some other time, leaving him bereft once again?

But the thought faded as quickly as it had appeared, for Alex could scarcely think about anything but the woman in his arms. He breathed in the scent that suffused her being, a heady, exotic fragrance, like spices growing wild in the rich earth. He closed his eyes, wanting to bury himself in that earth. He felt the skin of her bare back where his hand rested at her waistline, and allowed private fantasies to move his touch lower still. He held her formally, slightly away from him, fighting the urge to pull her against him too tightly as they danced, lest his growing desire for her become embarrassingly apparent.

He looked into her face once again, anxious for some sign that she might desire him as well. Her cheeks were flushed, but when his eyes met hers, she smiled hesitantly, then looked away.

Too soon, the slow number ended, and the band

moved into a rock and roll oldie. Alex cocked his head slightly and shrugged.

"I never was very good at rock and roll. Would you like some champagne?"

Selena's dazzling smile threatened to burn into his soul. "Yes, actually, that would be quite nice," she said. They made their way to the bar and then back outside to the terrace.

The cool air restored his senses somewhat, which only served to heighten his anxiety. There was so much he wanted to know about her, had to know, before he could allow himself to take one more step along the dangerous course he was traveling; headed, he felt sure, for another emotional disaster. But try as he might, he seemed unable to steer in another direction.

Alex seldom felt clumsy with words, but at the moment he didn't know how to phrase the question he was burning to ask without sounding stupid. He opted for a direct approach.

"Are you with someone tonight?" he asked. "Like a husband, for instance, who might decide to break my nose if he found me drinking champagne on the terrace with his wife?"

She laughed, and the sound sparkled in his ears. "Oh, good lord no. I'm not married. I came tonight with Tom Perkins. You know, my agent in London."

Alex frowned, recalling the gallery owner's too-affectionate greeting when Selena had arrived to pick up her paintings. She might not be married, but obviously there was more between them than a client-agent relationship.

"Is he your boyfriend?"

She shot him a quick glance that said he was out of line. "I came because Tom insisted it was terribly important for business." Her voice was taut, but then it softened, and she laughed softly. "But as I said, I despise these affairs. I managed to escape him a little while ago, but he's bound to be on the roam for me."

Alex stiffened. Whether Perkins had designs on Selena or not, he had no desire to run into the art dealer and be forced to maintain the farce of his little masquerade in the presence of the genuine article.

But he was even less inclined to take his leave of Selena prematurely. Perhaps if they remained outside for a while and kept to the shadows, Tom Perkins wouldn't interfere.

"I understand you grew up in Stanbury," he said at last, and he noted the look of surprise on her face.

"How did you know that? And how did you know my surname name is Wood? I don't use my last name anymore." Her voice held an edge of suspicion.

He laughed casually, using every ounce of his will to refrain from reaching out to touch her. His fingers longed to stroke her graceful, slender arms, the curve of her neck, the lovely fullness exposed between the jeweled necklace and the low-cut bodice of her dress. "Let's just say I ran into a mutual friend."

She looked at him queerly, as if he'd taken leave of his senses. "I have no friends."

Startled, Alex replied, "Don't be silly, everyone has friends." Abruptly, Selena turned away from him, looking out into the night, but not before Alex caught the melancholy look that stole into her dark eyes. He would have bitten off his tongue to be able to retract his casual remark. But what a strange and unbelievable comment coming from such a talented and beautiful woman.

An extended silence stretched between them. Then Alex answered her questions.

"I met a fellow, quite by accident, up on the moors. It was before I came to your place. He said he was from Stanbury, and I'd just come from the gallery in Haworth where they told me you lived near Stanbury. So I asked if he knew an artist named Selena. He said he'd gone to school with a girl named Selena Wood."

He paused, hoping she would comment, but she didn't, so he went on. "He said she was a Gypsy. The images in your paintings immediately came to mind, and I figured you must be that girl."

When she didn't respond, he touched her shoulders gently and turned her to face him. "Selena?" Her eyes seemed even larger than usual, and brighter, and Alex realized with a start it was because they were brimming with tears. "Selena, what's the matter? I'm sorry, I didn't mean to—"

Before he knew what he was doing, Alex pulled her into his arms and kissed her, gently at first, and then with a desire he had held in check for a long, long time. He wanted to kiss away her tears, and her loneliness, and whatever other demons haunted her soul. He felt the smooth skin of her bare back beneath his touch, and he deepened his kiss, as if he could drive her devils away by the very force of his passion.

Selena didn't resist, but instead put her arms around him and leaned into him, as if she sought shelter in his embrace. Her lips parted beneath his demanding kiss as naturally as if they'd been lovers always. Holding her tightly against his chest, he could feel the curve of her breasts and the beat of her heart, which seemed to match his own heart's wild cadence.

And then suddenly she pulled away from him and stepped back, looking at him with a mixture of astonishment and dismay. Neither spoke for a long moment, and it seemed to Alex as if the universe held its breath.

At last Selena broke the silence. "Please forgive me," she said, her voice husky and breathless. "I . . . I must have lost my senses. I don't know what came over me."

Alex couldn't bear the emptiness in his arms. Without

thinking, he reached for her hand, but she drew it away and turned to go.

"Selena!" he called out, fearing the princess was about to flee. "Don't. Wait a moment."

She stopped, but did not turn around. Her back was stiff. "I don't usually act like such a fool."

Alex stepped closer, not daring to touch her, although the silken skin of her exposed back tempted him only inches from his fingertips.

"There's nothing foolish about needing a friend," he said.

"Who said I needed a friend?"

Alex felt her unspoken pain. "Do you?"

She turned to face him, smoothing her voluminous hair away from her face with both hands. Her eyes searched his, then she looked away. "I'd better go back inside. Tom will be livid."

"Do you care?"

She hesitated, then replied with a hint of a smile edging her lips upward, "No. I guess I don't."

"Then stay."

He saw her body relax, and she leaned against the balustrade once again. "You want to know the truth?"

"Sure."

"I'm so exhausted I can barely stand up. I need to find Tom and get out of here."

"Can I drive you home?"

Selena looked at the sky. A slender crescent moon peeked over the roofline, shedding its pale light upon them. "No," she replied simply. "I have to go with him. Otherwise, he might not find his way home."

Home. Was Tom Perkins going home with her? The very thought enraged Alex. Forgetting his own emotional prohibitions against getting involved with a woman like Selena, he took her hand once again. "Can I call you?"

This time she did not take her hand away. "No, you can't call me, Alex. I don't have a telephone."

Alex was determined not to let her slip away, even though he knew it would likely be the safest thing for the protection of his heart. "Then you call me. Use a public phone."

She considered his suggestion for a moment. "Give me your number," she said at last with a sigh, leaving Alex convinced it was just to get rid of him.

Whatever her reason, he wasn't going to give her the chance to change her mind. He took a soggy napkin from beneath an empty champagne flute on a nearby table.

"Got a pen?" he asked, frisking himself in vain for a writing instrument.

She produced a lipstick from her handbag and held it up, raising her shoulders in query.

"That ought to work." Taking care not to press down too hard or break the colored matter that might well be the only link between them, Alex traced his own telephone number on the napkin. "I'm across from the apothecary shop in Haworth," he said, returning the slender tube to her along with the napkin. "In case you lose this."

He was rewarded for his efforts with a smile that filled her ample lips, a smile that sent an arrow of fear through his heart. She was going to leave him.

"I must go now," she said.

Alex knew he'd lost, but he nodded and followed Selena down the long terrace. They were almost at the entrance to the gallery when the door opened and Tom Perkins, followed closely by Eleanor Bates, burst through.

"There you are," Tom cried, exasperation overcoming any hint of worry in his voice. "You've been gone so long, I was terribly worried. I even called on our hostess here to help me find you."

Selena stared at him aghast. "What terrible fate did you think might have befallen me, Tom?" she asked, her voice dripping with sarcasm. "I'm not exactly in some back alleyway in London."

Alex wanted to be anywhere other than the spot he was in at that moment. He glanced at Eleanor, who seemed to be enjoying the whole scene immensely.

Then Tom spied Alex and realized he wasn't just a bystander, but rather seemed to be with Selena. "Who's he?"

Selena turned and looked up at Alex. "Someone I've been wanting to introduce you to, Tom. This is Alexander Hightower. He's the personal representative of a private collector in the United States. Someone who, I think, is showing some interest in my work. Am I right, Alex?"

Alex hoped he would die that very second. If Selena dropped the name of Henry Bonnell, it was all over, at least as far as his credibility with Eleanor Bates was concerned. He looked across Tom's short, round figure and into the eyes of the old woman, whose expression at the moment was entirely unreadable. And then she smiled.

"Personal representative of an art collector?" she said without missing a beat. "How very interesting."

Eleanor Bates's face seemed to blur suddenly into that English teacher once again. But she seemed, miraculously, willing to play along. At least for the moment. He decided to push his luck.

"I have a friend, you see, who is very interested in Selena's work. Unfortunately," he added, "he has been ill . . . a slight mental derangement . . . and I'm afraid all acquisitions have been put on hold."

Tom scowled doubtfully at Alex. "You do know that I have an exclusive on her?"

Alex glowered at the agent in return. "On her work, you mean?" he replied pointedly. "Yes. She's told me you're the man."

With that, Perkins backed off somewhat. "Well, then, we must get together sometime. Whenever your, uh, friend gets well again." He turned to Selena. "Come along, my dear. You look tired."

Alex watched them return to the gallery and felt a familiar emptiness engulf him. Then he turned to Eleanor Bates.

"It's not what you think—" he started, but she laughed and put her arm through his.

"I don't know what you're up to, Dr. Hightower," she said, her eyes twinkling. "And I don't really care, because it's none of my business. But it looks for all the world like you've fallen for a certain . . . artistic type, shall we say?"

Alex started to object, but Eleanor continued.

"She's a beauty, Alex. Where'd you find her?"

Alex turned and looked directly into the old woman's eyes. "Maggie Flynn introduced us," he said, a mischievous grin letting her know her own efforts at matchmaking had failed utterly. "Would you care to dance?"

❧ *Chapter 12* ❧

January 2, 1846

> *No coward soul is mine*
> *No trembler in the world's storm-troubled sphere*
> *I see Heaven's glories shine*
> *And Faith shines equal arming me from Fear*
>
> *O God within my breast*
> *Almighty ever-present Deity*
> *Life, that in me hast rest*
> *As I Undying Life, have power in Thee*
>
> *Vain are the thousand creeds*
> *That move men's hearts, unutterably vain,*
> *Worthless as withered weeds*
> *Or idlest froth amid the boundless main*
>
> *To waken doubt in one*
> *Holding so fast by thy infinity*
> *So surely anchored on*
> *The steadfast rock of Immortality*
>
> *With wide-embracing love*
> *Thy spirit animates eternal years*

Pervades and broods above,
Changes, sustains, dissolves, creates and rears

Though Earth and moon were gone
And suns and universes ceased to be
And thou wert left alone
Every Existence would exist in thee

There is not room for Death
Nor atom that his might could render void
Since thou art Being and Breath
And what thou art may never be destroyed.
                                        —Emily Brontë

January 28, 1846

Today Charlotte has sent by post the collection of our poems to a publishing firm, a foolish enterprise, I fear. It will cost us money, and our hope of seeing any financial return is slim. It is done, however, and the endeavor makes her happy. In the meantime, I have invested what remains of our slim legacy from Aunt Branwell into something more solid than Charlotte's dreams of authorship will provide. The York and Midland line will survive this temporary panic and, despite Charlotte's fears, I remain steadfast in my decision about the investment. We will see whose judgment will prove the better.

I have at last begun work in earnest on my novel. If Charlotte's ravings have produced nothing more than this fresh start in writing, then they shall not have been for naught. It has taken nigh unto one month of struggling with my soul to pull my courage together once more and quit pining for what might have been. I am disgusted with my own weakness in this matter of Mikel, for it was only a passing fancy. Still, I must write the truth here for only my eyes to see. There are nights when I lay alone upon this cot and look out on the stars, I wonder if he is looking on the same stars. I wonder if he ever thinks of me, and if I will *ever see him again. I sincerely doubt the latter two, but my restless mind will not let go of the idea. Nor will it let go of those sensations that creep back to me in dreams from time to time. Sometimes they are so strong they frighten me, and I have no one to ask about them. It is as if my body is on fire, wanting something I cannot even name, for I do not know what it is. But there is a pain in my lower regions that is real and is only lessened when I contract the area tightly. These dreams did not visit me until after Mikel touched me and kissed me upon the moors. How I rue that day! I am hoping that somehow, through this novel-writing project, I can command these dreams to quit me at night, for now I can feel that same energy flowing from my pen as I sit writing with Charlotte and Anne. I began the novel thusly:*

1801—I have just returned from a visit to my landlord —the solitary neighbour that I shall be troubled with. This is certainly a beautiful country! In all England, I do not believe that I could have fixed on a situation so completely removed from the stir of society. A perfect misanthropist's heaven: and Mr. Heathcliff and I are such a suitable pair to divide the desolation between us. A capital fellow! He little imagined how my heart warmed towards him when I beheld his black eyes withdraw so suspiciously under their brows, as I rode up, and when his fingers sheltered themselves, with a jealous resolution, still further in his waistcoat, as I announced my name.

"Mr. Heathcliff?" I said.

A nod was the answer.

"Mr. Lockwood, your new tenant, sir. I do myself the honour of calling as soon as possible after my arrival, to express the hope that I have not inconvenienced you by my perseverance in soliciting the occupation of Thrushcross Grange; I heard yesterday you had had some thoughts—"

"Thrushcross Grange is my own, sir," he interrupted, wincing. *"I should not allow anyone to incon-
venience me, if I could hinder it—walk in!"*

The *"walk in"* was uttered with closed teeth, and
expressed the sentiment, *"Go to the Deuce"* . . .

February 2, 1846

*I have just come up to bed after reading a few opening
pages of "Wuthering Heights" to Charlotte and Anne. How
delicious it was to see their faces, for it was clear they were
quite shocked by the direction of my writing. They were too
polite to say anything directly of course. Charlotte expressed
that she found it "daring" to introduce such a malignant
person as Heathcliff on page one, but I know what she
wanted was to understand from whence such a devil was
derived in her own sister's mind! I told her what I could
impart without revealing the true source of that dark personage.*

*I told them his name was an obvious offspring of the
nature of the moors on which he is to live in this world of
ink on paper. To tell the full truth, I chose his name for the
place where I found Mikel, where the heath grows to the
base of the cliff in the back ravine. It is a simple medley of
two ordinary features of the moors, but hopefully it will also
capture the fierceness of the wild landscape. Top Withens I
chose to become Wuthering Heights, for no more wild and
austere a farmstead could be found throughout all of Yorkshire, I suppose. Unfriendly and unwelcoming, it perches
like a black vulture at the crest of the moor, peering malevo-
lently into the valley below, as if waiting to pick apart the
remains of the more civilized establishment there.*

*And so will be the theme of my story. A vulture this
Heathcliff becomes, turned so by betrayal and shame. It is
an exaggerated pain of which I write, for I am infusing this
wretched character not only with his pain, but my own as
well. I must direct my smoldering desire and foolish emo-*

tions strongly into my story, and in so doing, attain release from my almost nightly torment.

I continue my narrative:

> *Her affection tired very soon, however, and when she grew peevish, Hindley became tyrannical. A few words from her, evincing a dislike to Heathcliff, were enough to rouse in him all his old hatred of the boy. He drove him from their company to the servants, deprived him of the instructions of the curate, and insisted that he should labor out of doors instead, compelling him to do so as hard as any other lad on the farm.*

> *He bore his degradation pretty well at first, because Cathy taught him what she learnt, and worked or played with him in the fields. They both promised to grow up as rude as savages, the young master being entirely negligent how they behaved, and what they did, so they kept clear of him . . .*

February 15, 1846
Heathcliff is consumed by his need for the love and affection of that petulant girl, Catherine, for she is the only source of it in his miserable life. Cathy's passion rides high, and she delights in tormenting him, although she does indeed love him. She gives her love, then takes it away again with her scolding until the boy is nearly crazed! He is nothing, a lowly gipsie brat, an orphan befriended. She is the spoiled and petted daughter of his benefactor, who has just died a few pages past. And tonight, I "made alive again" her brother, Hindley, who hates Heathcliff and who, as the new master, will treat him, and Catherine as well, severely unkindly in a short time.

I find I am increasingly intrigued by this exercise of writing in the form of a novel. I can, as I did in Glasstown and Gondal, create and destroy my characters as I will, but in this form, I find I must paint a deeper picture of their lives than I have before. I must show what drives them to the actions they take, give them reasons for what they do. It is an intellectual challenge, but at the same time easy, since I know well my own reason for cursing Heathcliff with unfulfilled love and lifelong pain, as I fear I am also cursed.

"I was only going to say that heaven did not seem to be my home, and I broke my heart with weeping to come back to earth; and the angels were so angry that they flung me out into the middle of the heath on the top of Wuthering Heights, where I woke sobbing for joy. That will do to explain my secret, as well as the other. I've no more business to marry Edgar Linton than I have to be in heaven; and if the wicked man in there had not brought Heathcliff so low, I shouldn't have thought of it. It would degrade me to marry Heathcliff now; so he shall never know how I love him; and that, not because he's handsome, Nelly, but because he's more myself than I am. Whatever our souls are made of, his and mine are the same; and Linton's is as different as a moonbeam from lightning, or frost from fire."

Ere this speech ended, I became sensible of Heathcliff's presence. Having noticed a slight movement, I turned my head, and saw him rise from the bench, and steal out noiselessly. He had listened till he heard Catherine say it would degrade her to marry him, and then he stayed to hear no farther.

March 12, 1846

I have done it! I have torn his heart out and flung it to the mad dogs that growl and lurk in the shadows. Heathcliff, lurking as well in the shadows, hears his love, Cathy, declare that it would degrade her to marry him! He is a low cur himself, stooping to eavesdropping behind the settle but

*staying only long enough to learn a part of the truth. He is a
fool and ignorant of the fact of Cathy's deep love which
would redeem him, and he, like Mikel, slips away without
adieu.*

*But I find even as I take my revenge on this dark gipsie
and seek through his character to settle affairs with my own
tormentor, I have sympathies with him as well. I have come
to know him in our days together since the outset of this
novel, and though it was my heart's desire to inflict on him
the deepest pain of a lover's betrayal, now that the arrow
has been flung, I feel remorse at what I have done. His pain
is my pain, and my heart aches tonight for us both.*

*But what talk is this? I write this as if Heathcliff were
really a person and not just a figure out of my imagination.
But in ways I cannot explain, he is real to me. Like Cathy, I
am Heathcliff! I have created his miserable world as a par-
allel to my own. I have given him an untrustworthy being to
love and made him love her to the point of distraction, and
then caused her to destroy what little self-regard he had
remaining. She will destroy him in the end. Is this to be my
fate as well?*

*I read aloud this scene to my sisters tonight, and although
they encourage me to continue, I can feel a sense of unspoken disapproval at the ruthlessness of my tale. I care not, for
I do not need approval. It is not for approval, nor publication, that "Wuthering Heights" came into being.*

*Something stirred in the porch, and, moving nearer,
I distinguished a tall man dressed in dark clothes,
with dark face and hair . . .*

*"What!" I cried, uncertain whether to regard him
as a worldly visitor, and I raised my hands in amazement. "What! You come back? Is it really you? Is it?"*

*"Yes, Heathcliff," he replied, glancing from me up
to the windows, which reflected a score of glittering
moons, but showed no lights from within. "Are they at*

home? Where is she? Nelly, you are not glad! You needn't be so disturbed. Is she here? Speak! I want to have one word with her—your mistress. Go, and say some person from Gimmerton desires to see her."

"How will she take it?" I exclaimed. "What will she do? The surprise bewilders me—it will put her out of her head! And are you Heathcliff? But altered! Nay, there's no comprehending it. Have you been for a soldier?"

"Go and carry my message," he interrupted impatiently. "I'm in hell till you do!"

March 31, 1846

Not knowing what else to do with him, I sent Heathcliff away. It was a device, nothing more, to make sure his fate, as regards Miss Catherine Earnshaw, was sealed. For with Heathcliff's disappearance, Catherine had no more excuse to refuse to wed the limp-wristed Linton. But now Heathcliff is back, full-grown, but tormented as ever by Catherine. Will he win her back? Nay, she is now a lady, Mrs. Edgar Linton. It is too late, Heathcliff! Too late.

It is too late for me as well, too late to regain my senses as regards Mikel. When I wrote of Heathcliff's return, I felt a fire ignite in those mysterious parts of my body that cry out to me in my dreams. Oh, how I longed for Mikel to come back, as Heathcliff did, to claim my love. How tortured I feel and so I have tortured Heathcliff in return.

I could not bear to keep Heathcliff too long away from my story, for even his snarling countenance brings me some measure of comfort. I will not send him away again, but will make him endure my own pain until, perhaps in time, we will both be free.

I wonder what I would do if Mikel did in truth return?

In her eagerness she rose and supported herself on the arm of the chair. At that earnest appeal he turned to her, looking absolutely desperate. His eyes wide, and wet at last, flashed fiercely on her; his breast heaved convulsively. An instant they held asunder, and then how they met I hardly saw, but Catherine made a spring, and he caught her, and they were locked in an embrace from which I thought my mistress would never be released alive—

"Let me alone. Let me alone," sobbed Catherine. "If I've done wrong, I'm dying for it. It is enough! You left me too—but I won't upbraid you! I forgive you! Forgive me!"

"It is hard to forgive, and to look at those eyes, and feel those wasted hands," he answered. "Kiss me again; and don't let me see your eyes! I forgive what you have done to me. I love my murderer—but yours! How can I? . . ."

About twelve o'clock, that night, was born the Catherine you saw at Wuthering Heights; a puny, seven months' child; and two hours after the mother died, having never recovered sufficient consciousness to miss Heathcliff, or know Edgar.

April 2, 1846

I have devised the greatest torture yet for my hero villain. I have taken his love away with absolute finality. I have killed her, and buried her at the edge of the churchyard. And she has died bearing another's child. It is the ultimate betrayal. No longer can he see her, even if from a distance and as another's wife. No longer can he hold out hope for their reunion. She can be no more to him now than a ghost, haunting his every moment as the ghost of Mikel haunts me still. What will we do now, Heathcliff? What must we do with our ghosts? Is there naught but suffering ahead? Haven't we suffered enough? Where I will take my story from here my muse may know, but I do not.

April 29, 1846

The dreams have ceased. Even as I write each page, I can feel that energy losing its power. Heathcliff's fury-fueled and deliberate plans for revenge against those whom he blames for the loss of his love have evolved into a determination to be together with her again. Believing as I do in all things being Eternal, I am beginning to form an idea for the resolution to his torment, and my own.

May 16, 1846

As my story wends to a close, I feel a sense of peace returning to my heart and I can no longer sustain the bitterness I have felt against Mikel. Perhaps I am just tired of the strife, or maybe the writing has completed its work and has, as I wished, removed the tribulation from my soul. Perhaps that is Heathcliff's redemption, that he has freed my spirit from the torment I suffered. I must thank him for this gift. I must reunite him with his love even if, as it must be by the evolution of this story, in death. I can tame his wickedness, fulfill his obsession. I can, and will. But how shall I do the deed? Not by murder, surely, although there are many in the farmhouse who would happily help in the effort. Not by accident. That would be too contrived an ending. I rather think I will do it more subtly. He will end his own life by simply losing the will to live. He will quit struggling against a life he despises. He will enter into a strange peace of mind, where time and nourishment matter not. He will see the blessed shore on the other side and Catherine will be waiting there for him. I have contemplated such an end to my own misery this last year, but now there is no need. I can once again let Heathcliff do the work for me. When he is in peace and reunited with Cathy, I too will find my peace.

May 26, 1846

Two entries of significance tonight. First, our poems, to Charlotte's delight, have finally reached publication. It is *strange to see our words and thoughts bound in volumes for all to read. Not that we need worry on that account. For who would buy such poems as these? No reader in England has any knowledge of the poets, Currer, Ellis, and Acton Bell. We shall try, nonetheless.*

What is more important to me is that I have written the last line of "Wuthering Heights." The story is told. All that remains is to review it and clean up the manuscript, for Charlotte, as she did with the poems, has convinced me our three novels should be submitted for publication. It feels strange to let Heathcliff die and to let all the others go now into a world I will no longer attend to. Young Cathy and Hareton have found the happiness which escaped the rest, Nelly Dean will find some peace at last, and Mr. Lockwood, lingering round the three graves in the old churchyard, will never know that the bodies of the lovers lie in ghoulish consummation beneath his feet. The ghosts of Catherine and Heathcliff, no doubt will walk the moors forever.

As for my own ghosts, I believe they too are now at rest.

❧ *Chapter 13* ❧

*F*rom high atop the rock formation known locally as Ponden Kirk, Alex could just make out the old farmhouse in the valley below where Selena lived. The precipice on which he stood was called Penistone Crag in *Wuthering Heights*, the place where Emily Brontë had allowed Heathcliff and Catherine to escape from their tormented lives and into each other's arms.

Staring across the expanse of gorse and heather that stretched between him and the farmhouse below, Alex hungered to see Selena's slender figure running up the hillside toward him, as Catherine had run to Heathcliff.

But the hard reality was, he hadn't seen her or heard from her in the week that had passed since the evening at Harrington.

He knew he should be relieved, because he was moving into dangerous territory in pursuing her. When he was near her, he seemed to lose focus of the fact that he didn't want or need the aggravation involved in a committed relationship, and he was unwilling to risk the pain when things fell apart. It had taken some time, but he had his life sorted out. It wasn't great, but it wasn't bad either. He had only himself to answer to, and if he wanted to drown himself in his work, there was no one else he had to consider.

But in spite of all that, he was driven by an irrational urge to see Selena again. Since the party, he had been distracted, edgy, unable to concentrate. He was consumed with thoughts of the beautiful woman in the blue silk dress that revealed her soft breasts and clung to her thighs as she walked. The scent of her perfume lingered in his memory, and lying alone in his bed, he ached to hold her again in his arms, to taste the sweetness of her lips.

He frowned, wondering what she was doing down there in that house right now, while he stood on this jagged crest, unable to get her off his mind. Why hadn't she called? Was she too busy working?

Or did she simply not want to call?

Unhappily, he settled back against a soft clump of grass where he could still spy on her dwelling. Perhaps if she stepped outside he would catch a glimpse of her. Small satisfaction for his hungry heart, but safer than going there and knocking on her front door again.

With an effort, he forced himself to concentrate on the reason he was here, high on Haworth Moor, the reason he'd come to England in the first place—the debate.

The clock was ticking.

Alex had climbed to this particular place on the moors today to seek an answer to the riddle of Emily's death amidst those things she loved most in her life.

Heather and sandstone.

Wind and sky.

It was here, perhaps on this very spot, that Emily had found her greatest happiness in life. It was to these moors that she fled to find the only freedom she knew in the "outside" world.

Otherwise, her freedom came solely from the world "within," that intensely private, personal domain that was the source of her powerful poetry and passionate single novel. From his studies, Alex knew that Emily's inner world was her very life, but he wondered how much that inner world depended for its survival upon this outer world, the moorlands she loved so fiercely.

If she had indeed taken her own life, was it because of something that happened in this outer world, which threatened to destroy the inner?

Alex tried to stretch his imagination to encompass a problem she might have encountered here on the moors intense enough to drive her to suicide, but his mind couldn't reach that far.

Around him the hillsides were verdant, as it was too early for the heather to paint them purple. The summer sunlight was strong and warm. The wind was light, and there was not a hint of a cloud overhead. All was peaceful, as it must have been in early June of 1845, when she wrote one of her most famous poems:

> *How beautiful the Earth is still*
> *To thee—how full of Happiness; . . .*

Alex took out a battered copy of her poems and read the entire text, even though he knew it by heart. It was a masterful piece, admired by her sister, Charlotte, who had notated Emily's manuscript with "Never was better stuff penned." It was a pleasant enough poem in which the speaker, somewhat smugly, advances her own philosophy that it is preferable to anticipate "what is to be" rather than destroy one's illusions by pursuing their fulfillment and ultimately being disappointed.

Sound familiar, Hightower?

Emily knew better than he how to cope with love, he thought bitterly, remaining aloof as she did, above those *"Poor slaves, subdued by passions strong, A weak and helpless prey!"*

Was she referring here to her own siblings' pathetic longing for their respective unrequited loves . . . Charlotte for her former teacher, Monsieur Heger, and Branwell for Lydia Robinson? Or was this philosophy her own emotional wall that enabled her to remain happily isolated from most of the rest of the human race, as history depicted?

Or could it be that Emily had been emotionally hurt at some point, and that this poem reflected her strategy for avoiding any relationship that might result in more pain?

He could relate.

Avoiding involvement had a certain security. But the cost was high in terms of loneliness, he'd discovered. It was easy to vacillate in one's determination to remain uninvolved, when the lonely nights threatened to eat you alive and normal hormones screamed for satisfaction. He'd tried to escape that lonely hell with the string of one-nighters, and later with Maggie.

But in the end, the result was still more pain. ·

Followed by more lonely nights.

Alex glanced down the mountainside at Selena's house. Was that what his attraction to Selena was all about? A need to assuage his loneliness and satisfy his sexual drive? It was a simple answer. Rational. But a closer examination of his feelings told him Selena's special allure was more than just her beauty and sex appeal. It included fascination, respect, and something more. . . .

Love?

The thought terrified him. Besides, he didn't know how that could be possible. They were virtually strangers.

And yet . . .

No! Whether he loved her or just felt a fleeting infatuation, he must let it drop now. Stop it before it ever got started. Like Emily's poetic speaker, he preferred the safety of anticipating what might have been and not putting his heart on the line again.

Love, Alex knew, was something he wasn't very good at.

He looked back at the book in his hand and the puzzle of Emily Enigmatic Brontë. Had she ever known love, or were her lines written as so many scholars believed, in an emotional vacuum? There was no biographical evidence that she'd ever had, or even wanted, a love in her life, although it remained a popular topic of conjecture. Most scholars accepted the traditional image of Emily as being a strong-willed, philosophic, sometimes mystical poet, reclusive, celibate, and idealistic.

And based on these and many other lines and images in her work, it was a believable portrait.

Alex supposed Emily could have looked around at the plights of Charlotte and Branwell and congratulated herself on her wise decision to always anticipate rather than consummate. Or, he supposed, she could have just made it all up from her obviously fanciful imagination.

But in January 1846 this same detached, lofty philosopher embarked on her first and only novel, *Wuthering Heights,* and produced a work so dark and disturbing that Alex couldn't begin to conceive that its source lay solely in the author's imagination. That an isolated spinster holed up in her father's Parsonage on the edge of the wild Yorkshire moors could have conjured up purely from her imagination a work so filled with passion, vengeance, anger, cruelty, and manipulation was beyond Alex's comprehension. Her dark hero, Heathcliff, despotic and driven by pain and passion, was so strongly drawn that he remained one of the romantic giants of English literature a hundred fifty years later.

Such heroes are not created in a vacuum.

And yet the author of *Wuthering Heights* was the same person who had written *"Anticipation"* and other equally sublime lyrics. What happened to her between June 2, 1845, and January 1846 to alter her writing so drastically?

He scribbled the question on his notepad.

Then he added a second question, one that was not unfamiliar to most Brontë scholars: From what part of Emily's imagination did Heathcliff spring?

And to that, a third: Was Heathcliff an imaginary figure, or was there a model for his character, as there seemed to be for so many other people and places in the book?

And from that followed another and another: If Heathcliff was based on a real person, was it someone Emily loved and lost? Could it have been a lover's betrayal that drove her to despair?

Alex knew he was reaching, but his research down traditional pathways had led to nothing he could use in the debate. His suicide theory was certainly not traditional, and to prove it, he now felt compelled to turn tradition on its ear.

What if . . .

What if Emily had a lover? A secret lover she'd managed to hide even from her sisters? What if that lover was the model for Heathcliff? Alex ran his fingers through his hair. Where in the world would she have met such a character in real life?

Certainly it seemed doubtful that Emily ever encountered such a personality, cloistered as she remained most of her life behind the walls of the Parsonage. Alex chewed on the end of his pencil, his imagination traveling back in time to visualize a young Victorian woman who shunned the presence of others to the point of rudeness, who chose solitude over the companionship of others, the only exceptions being her siblings. It was inconceivable that she had ever actually met such a ruffian as Heathcliff.

Or anyone so tormented by love for another. Perhaps

Branwell could have provided part of that drama in his grief over losing Lydia Robinson, but short, paunchy, carrot-topped Branwell was no Heathcliff.

No, Alex felt sure Emily had never met anyone like Heathcliff. She was a preacher's daughter, and even though she didn't buy into the dogma her father spouted from the pulpit, neither did she associate with the vulgar elements of society, with the possible exception of the times she and her sisters were called upon, as the curate's daughters, to nurse the sick in the village.

What caused her to create this monster, Heathcliff, who, for vengeance against Catherine's betrayal of his love, seduced her innocent sister-in-law and then violently, physically and emotionally abused her? Heathcliff, a villainous hero who came to Wuthering Heights as a befriended Gypsy orphan at the beginning of the book, and who, before it was two-thirds finished, managed to steal his benefactor's property:

> The guest was now the master of Wuthering Heights: he held firm possession, and proved to the attorney—who, in his turn, proved it to Mr. Linton—that Earnshaw had mortgaged every yard of land he owned, for cash to supply his mania for gaming; and he, Heathcliff, was the mortgagee.

Was Heathcliff a figment of an angry imagination, created to compensate for Emily's own lonely, loveless existence? And what about the other side of Heathcliff—the man who loved Catherine so completely and passionately that he will commit any crime, endure any pain, even welcome death, to rejoin her in the hereafter? Where did Emily learn of such passion?

And what dark emotions drove Emily Brontë to fill her novel with snarling dogs, derelicts, child abusers, and other such fellow travelers? In 1847, when *Wuthering*

Heights was first published, a literary review found it abhorrent:

> . . . people like Cathy and Heathcliff are too odiously and abominably pagan to suit the tastes of even the most shameless class of English readers.

Even by today's standards, the book would have to be considered one of the world's all-time frightful tales, the "grandmother of all shockers," as Eleanor Bates had so aptly described it.

Where in hell did it all come from?

Alex's line of interrogation produced one possible hypothesis for Emily's suicide: that this type of strongly negative review caused her such despair that she gave up on writing, her mainstay in life, and simply lost the will to live.

But he had some problems with this idea. First, some reviews were not so negative, and in fact had pointed out the strength and mastery of the work. Also, *Wuthering Heights* sold well, as did *Jane Eyre*. And even though neither Charlotte nor Emily believed they had created any great works of art, both took satisfaction in the fact they had published books that stood on shelves alongside authors such as Scott and Shelley, whose works they had admired since they were children.

His biggest problem with the theory, however, was that Alex did not think Emily Brontë really gave a damn what anyone thought about her work. She wrote because writing was in her blood. It *was* her. And she hadn't stopped writing, undone by the negative reviews, because as late as the spring of 1848, she was working on a second novel.

He had come here for answers, but it seemed the longer Alex sat and brooded, the more questions he raised. He looked at his watch. He'd been lost in his musings for over an hour. He stood up and stretched, noting with a frown that the blue Land Rover was no longer parked in the driveway below.

Selena slung her paintbrush at the canvas, splattering acrylic pigment across the images she had been fighting for hours. She watched a globule of orange drip like rusty blood to the base of the taut fabric and seep onto the easel. Frustration raged through her, and she felt as if she wanted to bite somebody.

She wiped her hands and took off her smock. She had to get out of here. The walls were closing in, and she felt trapped: trapped by her need to earn a living with the only talent and skill she knew, and trapped by another, perhaps greater need, to exorcise the artistic devils from her work.

But damn it if those devils didn't sell!

She'd heard from Tom Perkins only three days after the affair at Harrington that he had a buyer who wanted four paintings, but of specific sizes, none of which she had in her inventory. The price offered was enough to support her for many months.

At first it seemed like the perfect opportunity to accomplish two goals at once. She had four fragments of the letter left in the envelope, and she hoped, even expected, once they were on canvas she would be freed from the grip of the cursed, repetitive imagery. The client wanted four companion pieces using this theme, so it appeared an ideal conclusion to the ordeal.

But when she started on the first of the commissioned work, there was no life to what appeared on the canvas. The images seemed mechanical, unanimated, dull. She had demanded they let her go, and now, when she needed them most, it would seem they were slipping away like phantoms.

"Be careful what you ask for . . ."

And then there was that other matter, the one that disturbed her even more.

The one named Alex Hightower.

Selena took off the smudged painting smock and covered her shoulders with her woolen shawl. She filled the teakettle with water and placed it on the burner. Then she stirred the coals in the hearth and added another log. Doing simple, normal things to make her feel normal, but she was only partly successful.

The fact remained, she'd never felt normal in her life. What made her think she could start now? Except oddly, when she was with Alex Hightower at the party, when she'd let herself be comforted in his arms, she felt more normal than at any time she could recall.

Like she belonged there.

Like she could have a life after all.

The kettle whistled, and Selena poured hot water into the pot, half wishing a rain-soaked hiker named Alex Hightower would show up at her door again in time for tea.

But he wouldn't show up, not unless she called him. Which she had avoided for an entire week, even though she had a telephone in the studio now. Why?

She poured herself a large mug of tea and settled into the comfort of the shabby old sofa by the fire. Domino came to beg, but seeing she had no biscuit or other tidbit, he nestled at her feet. Peaches jumped onto the sofa and purred her way into Selena's lap. Hizzonor stood a stoic watch on the windowsill. All was peaceful and content.

Except for Selena's troubled thoughts. She stared into the flames, trying to understand what bothered her so about the tall, good-looking American. He had been gentle and tender with her when he'd held her in his arms and kissed her. She had felt great security and compassion in his arms. On the dance floor, he'd held her at a respectable distance, not like the other leering, lecherous partners she'd danced with that evening. There was nothing tawdry in his attentions, nothing like the slimy drunken passes Tom had made toward her after they left the party.

Selena shuddered, remembering the ugly scene that had erupted when she, as the designated driver since Tom had indulged in too much champagne, had pulled up in front of an inn in Stanbury and insisted that Tom stay there, instead of in her bed. He'd entreated her, pleaded with her, even threatened her with ruin, but finally, when the innkeeper offered to call the police, he'd acquiesced to her wishes.

When his car was gone from her driveway, and she woke up the next day, Selena figured her career was over. But when she placed a call to the Perkins Galleries later in the week to let him know she had a phone, Tom behaved as if nothing had ever happened. In fact, he said he was glad she'd called, and told her about the commissioned work she now struggled with.

Tom was not one to let his ego get in the way of filling his pocketbook.

Tom Perkins no longer mattered to Selena, one way or another, however. There were other dealers in London and elsewhere. Her career, she believed now, could go on without him.

But Alex Hightower was another concern altogether.

Selena sipped her tea, thinking about the way he looked the first time she'd seen him. She smiled, remembering broad shoulders and tight jeans and dark, rain-damp hair. From the night on the terrace at Harrington, she remembered full, sensuous lips, and arms that welcomed her into their strong protection.

And she remembered how easily she had fallen into them.

And that was what bothered her about Alexander Hightower.

She was fiercely attracted to him. Dangerously, intensely attracted.

Alex made her skin tingle, her heart race. He encouraged her laughter, and he freed her tears. He touched her somewhere deep in her soul.

And with him, she was vulnerable.

That was a place she'd sworn she'd never be with a man.

With another taste of the hot, soothing brew, Selena closed her eyes and thought back to the other times she'd been attracted to men, although those memories paled in comparison to what she felt now for Alex.

She recalled in particular one man. . . . Could she really call him a man? He had been no older than she, a fellow student in Paris, grappling as she had been with the realities of becoming an adult. He had been sweet, attentive, in love with her, or at least in love with the idea of being in love in Paris. Maybe that was what had attracted her as well. The idea of being in love.

But she hadn't been in love, nor was she interested in such a major distraction from her career training. A career to Selena meant she would never have to depend upon a man for financial support. Nor would she have to stand for any abuse, the way her mother had. Consequently, her first sexual relationship, although intense and passionate, was also very short.

Over the ensuing few years, she had dated other men but had never allowed herself to get to know them well enough for there to be a possibility of a future together. Her art was her future. It was her freedom. It was the only love she needed or wanted.

Until now.

Selena sat up with a start. Was she in love with Alex Hightower? How could she know? She didn't have a clue what being in love meant. And she'd only been in his company twice, both times just briefly.

But what other explanation could there be for the electric attraction that charged through her whenever she thought about him? That certainly hadn't happened in Paris. What else could explain her seeming inability to quit thinking about the man? He'd reigned supreme in her dreams each night, as well as her thoughts by day.

She didn't need this. Her life was crazy enough without this sort of complication. Her thoughts were in a muddle, like the paint splotched on the canvas in the next room.

What she needed right now was clarity.

Clarity. And freedom.

Freedom from thoughts of the handsome American. And from the disturbing and unbidden desire that accompanied those thoughts.

She needed freedom from the cursed images that were the nemesis of her career at the moment. She needed to finish those four paintings and sell them, then develop the new series or style that would mark the next phase of her career.

She hoped.

The thought of such freedom suddenly energized her. Like a housewife fired up for spring cleaning, Selena threw off the cumbersome shawl and bolted from the sofa, sending Peaches with a squall to the floor. Going to the armoire in the corner, she put on her boots and picked up a light cardigan.

She tucked her handbag under her arm and fairly ran down the stairs and out of the door, where crisp, clean air struck her full across the face. With determination to clear away the cobwebs in her mind, she got into the Land Rover, which surprisingly started on only the third try.

Selena sped toward town as fast as she dared. The wind brushed her skin, and she inhaled deeply, allowing the clean fresh air to sweep away the residue of obsessions that threatened the freedom she fought so fiercely to attain.

Obsessions like wild horses and Gypsy campfires and torn bits of a letter.

Obsessions like Alexander Hightower.

❧ *Chapter 14* ❧

June 6, 1846

My hands shake so that I can scarcely write this, but I must. Oh, I must! My heart is singing, and yet I am more afraid now than ever. Mikel has returned! Just as I managed to ease him from my mind, without warning I find him there again as large, nay, larger than life. He is no ghost, no spirit of my bedeviled imagination. He is flesh and blood, come back, he told me, to thank me once again for saving his life. But I must write it as it happened today . . .

Keeper and I left shortly after dinner for a long walk upon the moors. The day was filled with sweet warm air and sunshine, and I longed to be out there. As I have done so many times in this past year, I chose the path leading to the ravine at the back of the hill, never thinking, not even wanting, to find Mikel waiting for me there. I had completely erased the torment of my memories by letting Heathcliff suffer for me, and now it seems as if the poor man's fate was for naught, for the moment I laid eyes upon Mikel's dark, handsome face, everything I have striven to control fled in an instant.

I was almost upon him before I saw him, although Keeper raced ahead of me, barking and wagging his tail as if greeting an old friend. He was sitting by the beck, tossing stones into the stream. His black horse was tethered nearby. I feared my heart would stop, and I thought immediately to turn and run, but he saw me first and came toward me, calling my name in that wild and beautiful tongue. I was so stunned I could not speak. If I were a weaker soul, I fear I would have fainted, but I held steadfast and hid my feelings. Indeed, my feelings were and are in chaos once again. Seeing him unleashed my abated anger, and I fear my buried licentious desire as well.

He came to where I stood as if frozen to the spot and held out his hand. His smile was so beautiful to my eyes, I could scarcely take my gaze from his face. I wanted to smile in return, but I dared not. I can no longer trust my will where this man is concerned. Instead, I asked him what he wanted of me. He said he missed me and had thought about me all winter when he was home in Wales. I countered that I doubted his words very much, since he had left me without warning and without saying good-bye. It was then he told me what happened last summer.

His brother had been sent to find him, as his father lay dying and wanted his eldest son to be at his side. When I learned of this, I felt foolish and selfish for harbouring such anger toward him. Still, I replied, you could have left a message, somewhere or with somebody. He quietly reminded me that we had agreed to keep our acquaintance just between the two of us. And when I asked why he did not leave a note of some kind, he replied simply by saying, "Emilie, I cannot read nor write."

What am I to do? What will come of all this? Fear freezes my heart even as fire flames its passions. Control. I must maintain control. I have a strong will, and I must use it now. I cannot succumb to his attentions, albeit today he was formal and polite. It is not him I fear. It is my own weakness of character, my own feminine reactions to his physical presence. What is wrong with me? Why does my heart race even as I write this, thinking of this wild creature

*of the moors? His very countenance exudes the freedom
that eludes me. Perhaps therein lies my attraction. His skin
is tanned from the sun, and his hair is long and freely
flowing in the wind. His eyes are dark as midnight. They
burn like hot coals into my very soul. His lips are full, and
now that his pain is gone, he laughs often in a carefree
manner.*

*He says he will be nearby all summer, for there are many
wild ponies in the area. He mentioned that the encampment
there at the ravine would serve as his home for the summer,
since he was already used to the place. But then, he added
what my poor heart wanted so desperately to hear, that it
wasn't the place that drew him to return, but rather it was
me. Dare I believe he spoke the truth in saying that he
missed me? I want so to believe it, and yet it is not my
nature to presuppose such friendship. I am unused to the
attentions of a man, other than Branwell and Papa, and
this man's attentions do not fall into the same category. I
am afraid, for when I am with Mikel, the control that is my
mainstay vanishes into the air. Yes, I am afraid, and yet, the
danger of my dark desire draws me as a moth to the candle.*

*It is past midnight, and the wind is hushed and still. The
sky is clear and the stars are bright. I huddle here in my
miserable room, scratching like a madwoman in this diary,
while out there, Mikel sleeps in the cradle of the moors.
When I at last lay down upon my bed, I will dream that I,
too, sleep encompassed in that vast freedom.*

A week, then ten days passed since the party at Harrington House, and still there had been no word from
Selena. Alex had tried in vain to cast her dark-eyed image from his mind, burying himself in work, taking long
hikes on the moors, reading until the wee hours every
night.

But her grip on his heart appeared stronger than ever.

Alex could stand it no longer. Unlike Emily Brontë, it

seemed he could not settle only for anticipation. He had to see her, and let the chips fall as they may. Anything was better than the restless anxiety in which he'd dwelt for a fortnight.

He strode up the cobblestone street to the parking lot where Eleanor Bates's elegant antique Jaguar held court over the lesser vehicles parked nearby. The top was up, but since the day was gray, Alex decided to leave it there. The engine roared to life at the flip of the switch, almost as if it were new. Alex grinned and ran his hands over the red leather dash. He would have to come up with some very creative thank-you present before he left.

Winning the debate would help.

He made his way to Selena's farmhouse with the accuracy of a homing pigeon. A light drizzle slickened the roadway and turned Bridgeton Lane to sandy slime. The Jag approached the driveway, and his pulse quickened when he saw Selena standing in front of the Land Rover. Her long floral-printed skirt billowed in the wind beneath the magenta cape she'd worn the first time he saw her. The hood of the vehicle was propped open, and she was glaring at the engine, her fists clenched at her waist.

Alex frowned and reached for his umbrella as he switched off the ignition. "What's wrong?" he asked, popping the umbrella and going quickly to her side. He held its protection over them both, trying to ignore the way his heart was racing, as well as the barking dog that ran to meet him.

Selena transferred her glare to Alex. Then her face softened and she shook her head. "I don't understand it. I drove it to town just this morning, and now the stupid thing won't start." She leaned over and inspected the silent engine. "I've been having a lot of trouble with it lately, but I guess I've waited too long to have it looked at. I think it's a dead duck."

"Let me take a look." Handing her the umbrella, he

got into the vehicle and turned the ignition. It ground grumpily for a moment, then died with a metallic whine. Another turn. A low mechanical growl. And then nothing.

Something tickled the back of Alex's head, and he reached up to brush it away. His fingers encountered a soft, rubbery object that bounced away at his touch. Startled, he turned to find the entire backseat filled with balloons. Next to him on the passenger seat was a cake. A birthday cake. And a large, gaily wrapped package.

Curious, he returned to where Selena stood in the rain, her face as gloomy as the weather. "I'm sorry," he said. "It sounds like your battery is gone."

"I just bought a new one last month."

"Then something's probably wrong with the electrical system. You're going to need a mechanic. What's with the balloons?"

He saw Selena swallow, fighting tears that shimmered in her eyes. "It's my grandmother's birthday," she told him. "I've planned a surprise party for her at the nursing home. I'm supposed to be in Leeds in a little more than an hour."

Alex hesitated for less than a heartbeat. Although spending the afternoon in a nursing home wasn't exactly what he'd had in mind for the day, the time together in the car would give them a chance to get to know one another better.

"You get the cake," he directed. "I'll get the balloons. We'll take my car."

"I . . . I couldn't. I mean, I couldn't ask you to—"

"I love birthday parties." With that, he opened the back door to the Land Rover and secured the balloons, wrapping the ribbons around his fingers. They were filled with helium and bobbed gently in the wind. A bright yellow one managed to bounce loose and slipped from his grasp.

"Oh, no!" He reached for the tail of the ribbon, but it eluded him, and the balloon ascended happily into the misty skies above.

They watched it in silence. Then Selena shrugged. "Never mind. Maybe that yellow balloon will bring a little sunshine into this cloudy old day."

Alex turned to face her and felt his heart swell in his chest. Her large dark eyes looked childlike as they followed the balloon until it disappeared into the clouds. The mist hung in tiny diamond drops in her hair. Her lips held a pout, but only for a moment, then she turned to him and smiled.

"Are you sure you want to do this? I mean, I can—"

"What? Call a cab? Do you know what the fare to Leeds would be? Come on. Get the cake. We don't want to be late."

Alex was encouraged that Selena had seemed genuinely glad to see him, although he conceded that might be because he'd rescued her from a dilemma. He was determined to remain cool and let this unexpected turn of events unfold slowly. But as they turned out onto the main roadway, his long suppressed anxiety betrayed him. "Did you lose my phone number?"

Selena glanced at him out of the corner of her eye, then turned to him, sitting sideways in her seat. His eyes took in soft curves outlined by a close-fitting white knit top beneath the bright fabric of the cape.

"I . . . I've been busy," she said. "I received orders for four paintings after that party at Harrington."

"Four? Really? That's great."

"It is, and it isn't."

"What do you mean?"

"They are commissions. I have to paint them before I can sell them."

"What are they going to be of?"

Selena hesitated slightly before she answered. "The rest of the series."

"The rest? You mean you don't plan to do more along the same theme?"

"More? I've already done more than I ever wanted—" She broke off abruptly, leaving Alex perplexed.

"I don't understand. I thought artists painted whatever they wanted."

Selena didn't answer. Instead she turned away, toward the windshield, and stared out.

Alex sensed the deliberate distance she'd put between them, so he didn't pursue the issue. It was none of his business anyway, except he would like to know if she was going to paint more of the scrap of the letter in these final pieces.

"Tell me about your grandmother," he said after several miles. "What's her name?"

"Matka."

"Spelled . . . ?" he asked, not understanding such an unusual name.

"M-A-T-K-A. It's Romany."

"Romany? What language is that?"

Selena twisted a strand of hair. "It's not a language, really. It's more of a tradition. Gypsy tradition."

"Is your grandmother from around here?"

"She's from Wales. She claims she's a descendant of an ancient line of Welsh Gypsies that goes all the way back to the seventeenth century to a Gypsy king named Abram Wd."

Alex thought he heard a note of cynicism in her words and wondered why she seemed to be so sensitive about her background. Did Gypsies in England suffer from discrimination as minorities did in the U.S.? He personally knew nothing about Gypsies except that he somehow related them to circus people in the United States. They were the only folk he knew of in his own country who sometimes lived on the road. But as a people with a culture of their own, he was in the dark. To his American mind, Gypsies were not much more than mythical beings one read about in fairy tales or adventure stories.

He decided not to pursue the issue, at least not at the moment, although he was curious. Instead he glanced at her with a smile. "I guess that means I'm in the company of royalty."

Selena did not smile in return. "I suppose. By the way," she said, abruptly turning the conversation in another direction, "have you heard anything from your client, what's his name, Bonnell? Is he feeling any better?"

It took Alex a moment to grapple with her question. Do it! Explain it now and get it over with, he told himself.

A balloon bounced against the back of his head. Not yet, he advised himself. Not this afternoon. He didn't want anything to ruin the trip and the celebration she'd planned for her grandmother's birthday.

"I don't know," he replied noncommittally. "I haven't been able to get in touch with him lately." He felt rotten when he saw the disappointment mirrored on Selena's face, but it was better than the anger he'd likely see when he told her the truth about Bonnell.

"Did the photographs come out okay?" she asked. "I'd like to see them."

Alex had completely forgotten about the enlargements he'd ordered from the photo lab. How could he have let such a thing slip? "I'll have a set made for you." He was anxious to change the subject. "Actually, Bonnell is not the reason I showed up at your place today." Selena didn't respond, and a long silence ensued, making it even more difficult for Alex to proceed.

"I came because . . . I wanted to see you again. And I was curious why you hadn't called."

Selena's cheeks grew red, and Alex braced himself for

an answer he didn't want to hear. Instead, her words surprised him.

"I . . . I guess I was afraid to call," she said.

"Afraid? Of me?" he thought, deciding that kissing her had been a mistake.

"No. Of me."

This came as an even bigger surprise. "Want to explain that?"

She looked away from him. "No," she said at last. "I can't explain it. I don't exactly understand it myself." She turned back. "Look, can we not talk about this right now? I'm not very good at this kind of thing. . . ."

That makes two of us, Alex thought. He reached out and took her hand. It felt small and cool in his. Delicate. Fragile. He wanted only to hold it and warm it with his own body heat. Talk didn't matter.

"Sure." He paused. "Tell me a little more about your work. When did you start painting?" Alex hoped he was on safe ground. It was hard to tell with Selena, whose feelings seemed to be so fragile they were almost brittle.

"I've painted all my life. Ever since I was a little girl," she said with a wistful smile. "When Matka came to live with us, she saw I needed to draw and paint. I used to steal my mother's makeup pencils if I couldn't find something to work with, which as you can imagine got me into all kinds of hot water. Well, one day Matka took me to the market and bought me a pad of paper, and some colored pencils, and watercolors and crayons."

Alex heard her voice crack, but he remained silent as she composed herself and went on.

"I thought I was in heaven." She smiled. "I used those supplies to take me anywhere I wanted to go. I drew carousels and fairies and beautiful flowers and clouds and mountains and—" She stopped with an uncertain laugh. "Why am I telling you all this?"

"Because I asked," Alex replied, squeezing her hand

gently. "I want to know all about . . . you. Please, go on. How old were you when your grandmother came to live with you?"

Selena thought for a moment. "Seven or eight, I guess."

"Where did she come from? Did she live near you before?" Alex heard a deep sigh from the woman sitting next to him and realized she might think he was giving her the third degree.

"I told you Matka was a Gypsy," she answered, resignation in her voice. "She was born just after the turn of the century, and she lived most of her life in her family's caravan. They traveled all over Wales and northern England, sometimes into Scotland. When my grandfather died, Matka came to live with my family. My father—"

She broke off for a moment, and Alex sensed she was struggling with deep emotional pain. At last she cleared her throat and continued. "My father and mother, well, they had a lot of problems between them, and sometimes," she paused, drawing in a deep breath, "they took it out on me." Another long hesitation interrupted her story. "When Matka came to live with us, she became my best friend." She looked out at the passing scenery, then added pensively, "She still is, I guess."

Alex could only guess at what caused the anguish behind Selena's words. He remembered the bleak statement she'd made on the terrace at Harrington House: "I have no friends." He decided not to probe further, surmising Selena carried scars, deep, painful scars, from her childhood. Instead he squeezed her hand again.

"Lucky Matka," he said quietly.

It wasn't until they pulled into the parking lot at the nursing home that either of them broached a personal subject again. Then Selena said bluntly, "Matka may surprise you with some of her Gypsy mumbo-jumbo."

Alex laughed. "What's that?"

Selena twisted her hair, letting Alex know she was again entering painful territory. "She . . . she seems to believe that our family is under some kind of curse, and she doesn't mind talking about it when it suits her fancy."

"Is she . . . in her right mind?"

"Oh, yes. You'll find she is very sharp-witted. She's carried this delusion with her for her entire life."

"What kind of curse—?" Alex started to ask, intrigued.

"It's . . . it's nothing. Just something she heard around a campfire long ago. Don't put any credence to it whatsoever. Just play along, for her sake. She's so old, I never try to argue with her about it anymore."

Selena's words were detached, but she didn't quite succeed in covering the emotions that lurked behind them. Alex had realized before that talk of her Gypsy heritage made Selena uncomfortable, but he perceived it was more than her Gypsy background that seemed to be gnawing at her.

"I'll try to stick to birthday party conversation," he promised, taking the balloons out of the car.

Selena balanced the cake tray in one hand and pulled her purse over the opposite shoulder, then picked up the brightly wrapped gift. "If Matka decides to talk about it, you won't have much choice, I'm afraid." She smiled ruefully. "Hurry now. We're a little late."

❧ *Chapter 15* ❧

A young woman greeted them at the door. She wore a volunteer badge with her name, Margaret, printed on it. "We've been expecting you," she said with a smile, but Alex detected a note of relief in her voice. "We have the residents gathered in the Community Room, all except your grandmother, of course. She has no idea about the party."

Selena put the cake on the table, which was already laid with plates and napkins, forks and tea cups. Then she slipped out of the cape, revealing the slender yet curvaceous figure Alex had dreamed of for nights on end. He watched with growing desire as she moved gracefully about her party preparations. Careful, Hightower, he warned himself.

She separated three balloons from the rest of the bunch. "Tie these on the back of this chair," she directed Alex. "We'll transfer them to Gran's wheelchair when she gets here." She took the rest and gave each party guest a balloon, tying the bright, bobbing objects to wrists, wheelchairs, and walkers. She chatted and laughed with each resident, and he could tell she was no stranger to this place. Despite his conscious effort to control his feelings, Alex felt himself being swept along in a torrent of unbridled emotion.

"I think we're ready, Margaret," Selena said to the young woman.

The volunteer laughed. "If this wasn't a surprise, I'd send you in after her. She's bound to be hopping mad by now that I haven't brought her to sit by the fireplace to read her paper."

The others laughed knowingly. Even though it was the middle of summer, the nursing home kept a small fire going in the corner fireplace, and it was a favorite gathering place for residents, especially Selena's grandmother. Matka was a favorite among those who lived in this restricted world, for often of a winter's evening, she would sit by the fire and weave her storytelling magic as she once had beside the campfire when she was younger.

Selena grinned at Alex. "My grandmother is a true creature of habit. She always comes here at exactly the same time to read her newspaper, and she has a fit if she's late."

"You can blame it on me," he answered.

Selena came to his side. "She's going to love you," she whispered. "She's an incorrigible matchmaker. Don't take that seriously, either."

He placed his hand lightly in the small of her back. "Why not?"

At that moment the door swung open and Margaret wheeled Matka into the room. The woman looked like a miniature human being, so bent and gnarled was her body in the large wheelchair. "Surprise!" Selena cried, and the greeting was echoed by a chorus of elderly voices. The old woman, who had obviously been grumbling all the way down the hall, looked up in consternation.

"Now wha's all this? Selena, is't you?"

Selena ran to her grandmother and kissed her forehead. "Happy birthday, Gran!"

For a moment Matka said nothing. She looked around and saw the balloons and the cake and gifts on the table. Then she looked up at Selena.

"I thought y'd forgot," she said gruffly, but her eyes glistened.

"Forgot? Never in a thousand years."

"Don't want t'live tha' long," Matka said, a grin creeping in to replace her earlier frown. Then her gaze lit on Alex. "Who'd tha' be?"

"He's a new friend, Gran. His name is Alex." She took the chair and wheeled the crone over to where Alex stood by the table. "Alex, meet my grandmother, Matka."

Alex looked into eyes that once must have been as black as Selena's but were now faded and partially covered with cataracts. Still, they were mesmerizing eyes, and he felt almost as if he *were* in the presence of royalty. He took one of Matka's contorted hands in both of his, bent toward her and kissed the back of it.

"Happy birthday, Matka."

A rustle of approval went around the room, and Matka smiled a thousand wrinkles. "Y' know y'll be the topic o't conversation here for days t' come." She laughed in a gravelly voice.

"Let's get on with it," Selena said with an uneasy smile. "Alex, would you serve the cake?"

"With pleasure." He was actually relieved to be out from under the scrutiny of Matka's eyes. He felt the old woman could see more than what met her eye.

He cut generous slices of cake and handed them to the guests, asking each one their name and where they were from. He found to his delight these people were not senile or demented or even very infirm. They were just old. Which gave them a lot of stories to tell, which they did freely over the next two hours.

At last the party ended, as one or two of the guests dozed off and Matka admitted that her arthritis was hurting. Margaret started to maneuver her wheelchair, but Alex interrupted. "May I?"

Selena looked up at him in surprise. Matka nodded, and Margaret said, "Be my guest."

Matka motioned Selena to her side. "Thank y', daughter, for my birthday party. I was much surprised." She glanced up at Alex. "In many ways. I like your young man. And I have a favor t' ask."

"Sure, Gran."

"Let him take me back t' my room. Alone." She winked. "'Tis been many a year since I was tak'n t' bed by such a handsome man." This last she said loud enough for everyone in the room to hear, and there was a roar of laughter.

Selena looked at Alex, her cheeks scarlet. She shrugged and grinned apologetically for the old woman's ribald behavior, but Alex laughed, appreciating the witty old woman's joke.

"It's not often I get such an invitation," he replied, with a meaningful glance in Selena's direction. "Wait here. I'll be back in a little while."

He turned the wheelchair toward the door before Selena could change her mind or insist on going along. Alex guessed the old woman wanted him alone to interrogate him about his intentions toward her granddaughter.

It didn't take her long. They were barely out of the Community Room when she asked, "Wher'd y' meet my granddaughter?"

"Actually, I saw her artwork before I met her."

Matka snorted. "Her artwork, eh? What's it like? She never brings any o't for me t' see."

Alex was surprised. "She doesn't? Why not?"

"Ask her. Wher'd y' see her work?"

"In London, first. Then I came across another piece in Haworth."

"Haworth? What're y' doin' in Haworth?"

"I'm there . . . on business."

Matka considered that a moment, then nodded. "So how'd you come t'meetin' Selena, then?"

"I went to her studio. You see, something about her paintings intrigued me, and I wanted to find out more about them. As part of the business I'm in, you understand."

They reached Matka's room, which Alex found surprisingly homelike. The bed was a regular hospital bed, but the rest of the room was furnished with personal items: an armchair, a bureau, pictures on the wall, an old-fashioned mirror.

Matka pointed to the chair. "Sit. We must talk more."

It wouldn't have occurred to Alex to argue. He sat down in the armchair as instructed.

"Tell me more," Matka insisted. "Wha' 'tis 't about Selena tha' y'be int'rested in? Her work? Or herself?"

"At first I was interested only in her work," he began, hoping to avoid any mention of his nonexistent client. "It's quite remarkable."

"How so?"

Alex was sorry he had to describe her granddaughter's paintings to Matka secondhand, and wondered why Selena, who seemed to care so deeply for this woman, hadn't shared her work with her. "They're a series," he began. "Each one is different, but similar, too. They are surrealistic in style. Are you familiar with that?"

Matka frowned. "No. But I c'n guess't means they're not realistic. Is she paintin' those awful abstract things?"

"No, they're not exactly abstracts. The figures and images are definitely identifiable. There is a lot of imagery I think she got from you, actually."

The old woman raised her eyebrows. "From me?"

"Selena has told me a little about you, about your days as a Gypsy. . . ."

"I still am a Gypsy, young man, 'n proud o't."

"I didn't mean . . . well, your days when you traveled in your caravan."

"She's usin' Gypsy images in her paintin's?" Matka was clearly surprised. "Why, she don't want naught t'do with bein' Gypsy."

From Selena's earlier reactions about the subject, Alex wasn't surprised at Matka's comment. "Well, there are black stallions and campfires and organ grinders and monkeys and red roses . . ." His voice trailed off as he saw the wistful look on the old woman's face. ". . . and a piece of a letter in each painting," he finished.

At that, Matka looked up at him sharply. "A piece o' the letter? What d'y'mean?"

"It's what attracted my attention in the first place." Alex leaned forward, eager to hear the old woman's comment on the letter. "In each of her paintings, there is a small piece of paper with writing on it. I asked her about it, and she said it was just something she made up."

Alex's pulse beat a little harder when he saw Matka's reaction to what he was telling her. She was shaking her head side to side, slowly at first and then more adamantly. He was about to ask her if she knew something more about the letter when the door opened and Selena came in.

"Are you two about finished with your romantic interlude?" she asked. "It's getting late, and we need to be on our way."

Matka didn't look at Selena. Her gaze was somewhere far away. Her head was still moving slightly from side to side, and Alex was afraid he might have caused her to have some kind of seizure.

"We were just finishing our conversation," he said

hesitantly, chagrined that Matka hadn't been able to comment on the letter fragments, for he knew she had something more to say. Alex stood up, leaned over to the old woman and took her hand.

"We'll come back soon," he said, and his voice seemed to bring her back to the present.

She reached a twisted hand to his jacket and pulled his ear close to her lips.

"Y' must come back. But come alone. There's more tha' y'must know."

June 10, 1846
My heart is torn between the joy I feel over Mikel's return and the torment I experience each day over Branwell. We learned recently of the death of his former employer, Mr. Robinson, not something anyone should rejoice over, but it fired hope anew within Branwell's breast that he could be reunited with the one he loves. Knowing that joy myself, I could only wish it were true for Branii. It is not to be, however. He has received word from Lydia Robinson that her husband added a codicil to his will stating that if she had any further communication with Branwell, she would forfeit any claim to his fortune. Seeing no hope of support from Branwell, the woman has no choice but to forbid him to court her again. He is mad from this turn of events, even more so than before, if that is possible. I don't know how long I will have the courage to endure as his sole friend in this household. His demands are many and sometimes he becomes too deranged to be left alone. I have my own needs now, too, and although I would never begrudge him my love, I am beginning to do so of my time.

June 24, 1846
We have all three finished our novels, and Charlotte has bundled them off to whatever fate awaits them. As I reread

my own work, now that my "Heathcliff" has returned, I worry that I have created in him such a dark character. Mikel deserves better. But it is too late, for the work is done, for better or for worse.

I have just returned from the moors, and although it is late, the sun is still high. In spite of Branwell's fits and Papa's increasing blindness, my days are happy, for my heart is full knowing that Mikel is nearby. I have learned not to fear him, nor myself, for he has made no improper overtures, and I, for the most part, have learned to control my own desires. As much as I find happiness in the company of my new friend, I must always remember the pain of last winter. I must never leave myself open to such pain again. Control of the will allows me to spend parts of my days with him without fear I will lose my senses, and our enterprise together is safe and sufficient for two friends. He is an eager and intelligent student, and although I have always loathed the role of teacher, he is a special and beloved pupil. He has already mastered the alphabet and has rudimentary skills with words. His handwriting is childlike, but that is to be expected. My own is little better.

We spend some time in this endeavor, and then we walk on the moors and he tells me about places strange and foreign. I am learning gipsie folk tales he says they tell by firelight or beneath the light of the moon. What a carefree life it must be to live as a gipsie, and yet I would not trade places with him. My home is here, in the Parsonage, and although I have often pined for more freedom in the outside world, if it were offered, I would likely not accept. It would be too frightening, and the idea of such enormous freedom serves to keep my thoughts straight as concern Mikel. We come from separate worlds. There is no hope for a future life together, and so I must not indulge in those fantasies I once held. I must maintain control, and distance. I must let him be my friend, and nothing more.

July 18, 1846

    I sometimes feel as if I am in a maelstrom of terrible things going on around me, and yet I remain sublime. My sisters wonder at my calm demeanor, whilst Branwell rages and threatens murder and suicide and Papa is so blind we must be his eyes these days. I have much to be thankful for, however, for my life suddenly has more meaning than ever before. Our poems have been praised by the Critic *and* Athenaeum, *and although I still retain little hope of their providing any financial solvency for our efforts, they may perhaps lay a solid foundation should our novels be well-received. It is not the poems that give me such peace of mind, however. It is my student on the moors. He has progressed quickly, and we have invented a game, since he must come and go at odd hours as the chase of the ponies leads him. We have a special place, the message rock, we call it, where we leave written correspondence to one another. His notes, of course, I do not save, lest they be discovered by prying eyes, and he promises he burns mine in the campfire when he returns. Part of the magic of our world together is that it is a secret between us. I am reminded of when I was a young girl and Charlotte and I created our secret bed plays. This is very different, of course, and far more delicious!*

August 18, 1846

    Tomorrow Charlotte travels with Papa to Manchester to see if the cataracts which are causing his blindness are sufficiently ripe for surgery. I pray they be so, for I need his eyesight restored, for other than myself, Papa is the only one who seems to be able to cope with Branwell, and I am growing weary of carrying the burden alone.

    Tonight I said farewell as well to Mikel, who leaves on the morrow for his winter in Wales. He has collected many handsome ponies this season. I have seen them myself. I am happy for him, but knowing I will not see him again until next year grieves my already heavy heart. I longed for him to kiss me again, as he did last summer, but he has honored my wish, my insistence, that our encounters be within the realm of friendship, nothing more. But my hand trembles, I must admit it, recalling how he held it tonight, as if he never would let it go. He looked into my eyes as the firelight burned into the encroaching darkness, and his eyes said what his lips would not. I am in love with this man, I know it, but it is impossible for our love to exist in this world. Perhaps like Heathcliff and Cathy, we will be re-united in that greater world beyond, but until then, I can only hope and pray for his return again in the springtime.

✎ *Chapter 16* ✎

Alex and Selena said good-bye to Matka and made their way down the polished hallways to the exit. He opened the heavy glass door for Selena, placing his hand in the small of her back as he did so. But unlike her reaction when Tom Perkins had made the same gesture, Selena found it protective rather than controlling, and she made no move to escape his touch.

She knew the next time she talked to Gran in private, she would get an earful about the marriage thing again, but somehow it didn't matter. She wasn't interested in marrying Alex Hightower, but his attendance at the party today was the best present she could have given her grandmother.

Outside, the afternoon had shed its clouds and turned brilliant and warm. Selena shook her head, letting her hair blow freely in the warm breeze. Then she turned to Alex with a sunny smile.

"Thank you for doing this."

"What's there to thank me for? I would have missed a great event if I hadn't come along. Want to put the top down for the ride home?"

"Sure. Might as well get some sun while we can."

Alex dropped the convertible top and fastened it securely, then opened the car door for Selena. She watched him in the rearview mirror as he walked behind the car, taking off his lightweight blazer and exposing the substantial breadth of his shoulders beneath the pale yellow fabric of his shirt. He dropped the jacket on the backseat and got in beside her, and she caught the pleasant fragrance of aftershave mingled with his own masculine scent. Her heart picked up a beat in spite of her determination to keep a level head when she was around Alexander Hightower.

She waited until he'd settled his tall frame behind the steering wheel, then said tentatively, "You know Matka will have all kinds of designs on you."

He started the engine and grinned boyishly at her. "What kinds of designs? She's not into voodoo or anything, is she?"

"Gypsies don't do voodoo, Alex," she said coldly.

"Sorry. That was meant as a joke." Neither spoke as he backed the car out of the space and maneuvered it into the heavy traffic. "You want to stop for lunch, or are you anxious to get back?" he asked.

"I'm not really hungry right now. I snitched a piece of cake when you took Matka to her room. Why don't we get back to Keighley or Stanbury and stop for tea? My treat."

Alex glanced at his watch. "By then, it might be time for something more substantial than tea. How about dinner? My treat."

"We'll argue about it when we get there."

Selena was anxious that her grandmother had not led Alex to any false expectations. "I hope Matka didn't jump to the wrong conclusions," she said cautiously.

"What conclusions would be the wrong ones?"

"Well, it's just that she's always trying to convince me that I ought to find a man, settle down, you know what I mean. . . ."

"And you're not interested, I take it."

Selena didn't answer for a long moment. "No. I'm not interested."

"Why not, if you don't mind my asking?"

Selena thought only an American would come up with such a reply. Whether she minded or not, he had asked. She shifted uncomfortably in her seat and began to twist a lock of hair.

"I've never had a very high opinion of the state of marriage," she said at last. "I guess it's because my parents were so miserable in their own relationship."

"That doesn't mean you would automatically be miserable in one of your own."

Selena thought instantly of the curse. She had told herself for as long as she could remember that she didn't believe in it. But it was always there, just under the surface, whenever she thought of getting involved in a relationship that might lead to marriage.

"No, I suppose not," she answered carefully, not liking the direction this was leading. "But my . . . my whole family, for generations, has . . . well, as Matka would put it, has been, quote, unlucky in love." How ridiculous that sounded in her ears, but she heard herself reveal her own beliefs in her next statement. "I guess I've just never wanted to run the risk."

"Unlucky in love? What does that mean?"

Selena attempted to hide her bitterness behind levity. "It's the Gypsy way of saying that I come from a long line of dysfunctional human beings."

She saw Alex shoot her a quick glance, but he didn't reply. He only took her hand in his, and they drove on in silence. Selena was grateful that he'd finally stopped asking questions, and she liked the feel of his large, strong hands around hers. She recalled her wish the night of the party at Harrington House to meet a man who wasn't like all the rest.

Was that man sitting next to her right now?

She knew so little about him. She had been unable to answer Tom Perkins's questions about him when she'd spoken to him by phone, and Tom had intimated that the American might be after more than just her artwork. Considering Tom's own lechery, she had only laughed.

But today she wasn't laughing.

After this afternoon, Selena believed Alexander Hightower's interest in her extended beyond her artwork. The question was, how far? And how far did she want it to go?

Selena felt the wind rushing through her hair and saw the brilliant sunshine reflecting on the lush summer leaves as they sped through the tranquil countryside. For a brief electric moment she let herself conceive the inconceivable. What if she allowed herself to fall in love with Alex?

The terror inherent in such an idea brought her back to her senses. She didn't love him, because she wouldn't allow herself to. Perhaps that was the curse in action after all, but it was her best defense against ending up miserable and destructive like her parents. Something dark and terrible crawled across her memory and then was gone before she could grasp it, like a fleeting dream. But suddenly she was filled with feelings of shame and dread.

She eased her hand from Alex's grasp. She should break this off now, before it went any further. She shouldn't give Alex any sign of encouragement if his interest did extend beyond a business relationship.

But perversely, she found she wanted just the opposite. There was something about him that had captured her imagination, if not her heart, and suddenly she felt an overwhelming urge to learn all about this man who threatened everything she had so carefully laid out in her life.

"What about your family?" she asked abruptly, surprising herself by the intensity in her voice. "It seems the questions have been pretty one-sided today."

They were at a busy intersection, and Alex didn't answer right away. Surely he'd heard her question. Selena thought she caught a glimpse of distress on his handsome features, and she wondered why he seemed so reticent to talk about himself. Was he hiding something? She pressed on. "Well, turnabout's fair play, isn't it?"

Alex maneuvered the sports car skillfully around a traffic circle, then gave her one of those sexy smiles that sent her heart into overdrive. For the first time she noted golden flecks in his deep gray eyes. "Yes. I suppose it is," he said. "What would you like to know?"

Selena decided it was best not to get too personal. "Tell me what it's like in America. Is it so much different from here?"

He laughed and ran his hands through his thick, dark hair. "No, it's not that much different. We drive on the other side of the road. Use different money. But I'm afraid that our world has become pretty homogenized, for better or worse."

"How so?"

"Well, for instance, the last night I was staying at the Black Bull, the young couple who manage the place wanted a pizza after they closed the doors. Who did they call? Pizza Hut, for God's sake. It seems almost sacrilegious that in Emily's very backyard, an American franchise is delivering pizzas."

"Emily? Who's Emily?"

Alex swerved into the right-hand lane, almost colliding with an oncoming car. Swearing under his breath, he regained control. "Sorry," he said after a moment. "Like I said, we Americans are used to driving on different sides of the roadway." She saw him focusing on the highway, trying to steady himself, but she guessed what he was hiding.

There was another woman in Alex Hightower's life.

That cold, dreadful feeling returned, and Selena regretted having entertained any thoughts about entering into a relationship with him. And she was deeply embarrassed that she had so easily fallen into his arms on the terrace at Harrington House. Why had it never occurred to her to ask the same question of him he had of her? Was he married? She'd never even considered it.

But it hadn't mattered to her.

Until today.

And then his next words were so surprising, they threw her completely off balance.

"Emily is Emily Brontë," he said casually. "The writer. You grew up around here. You must know a lot about the Brontës."

Selena blinked at his most unexpected reply. Here she was tiptoeing terrified into his personal life, and he wanted to talk about Emily Brontë? She found herself inexplicably irritated. Still, it kept them on neutral ground, so she answered evenly, "Not really. I know the Parsonage is up in Haworth, and as a schoolgirl I went there on field trips. But I never really paid much attention. They've always been sort of like, well, neighbors who live nearby but you never visit." She looked at him. "Why? Does your work have something to do with Emily Brontë?"

She saw him open his mouth to speak, then close it again. He thought for a few moments, then said, "Henry Bonnell donated a lot of priceless Brontë works to the Parsonage Museum in Haworth. I've been working there for the past several weeks, and I guess Emily and her sisters and brother have become sort of like, well, like family to me."

Selena wanted to ask about Bonnell's interest in her

work, but she'd headed her line of questioning down another track, and she was determined to follow it through.

"Are you married, Alex?"

She saw a deep furrow form between his heavy brows, and his expression grew dark. "No. I'm not married," he replied, then, with an obvious effort, he expanded. "I used to be. My wife divorced me almost three years ago."

"I'm sorry," Selena said, ready to drop the subject. It obviously wasn't something he wanted to talk about. But surprisingly, he continued.

"I was sorry too, for a long time." He paused and studied the traffic, seeking, Selena thought, detachment. Then he added, "I guess I still am. The fact of the matter is that I was a lousy husband."

Selena was afraid she'd opened Pandora's box. She didn't really want to know what had gone wrong between Alex and his ex-wife.

She didn't, and she did.

In a curious way, it made her feel like less of an oddity for avoiding relationships. She didn't speak, and in a moment Alex went on. It was as if he wanted to let her know what a bad guy he was, like he was putting up a warning sign for her.

"I'm a dedicated workaholic. I put my career ahead of everything. My wife didn't find much satisfaction in our marriage, and looking back, I can't say as I blame her. I didn't give her the attention she needed. Deserved. And she . . . found someone else who would."

In spite of his attempt at remaining unemotional, Selena could tell he was still fighting deep pain. She withdrew her foray into his personal life. She'd learned what she needed to know. She wished there was something she could say or do to ease his pain, but nothing she thought of seemed appropriate, so she didn't try, and they drove in silence the remaining few miles to the lower end of the village of Haworth.

Alex stopped for a red light and looked across at her, and when he spoke, there was no hint of his earlier distress. "Want to stop for a bite now?"

Selena glanced at her watch. Five-fifteen. The late June sun was still high above the moors. She thought of her recent trip to the market and the unusual stock of supplies she had purchased in her moment of madness. Like red wine. Paté de fois gras. Three of her favorite cheeses. Some pears and apples.

Then she thought of the options for dining out locally, and all of them seemed to include smoky pubs and heavy, rich food. She ran her hands through her hair, pulling it away from her neck and then letting it fall again, daring herself and then quickly taking her own challenge before she could change her mind.

"I'm hungry," she began, her heart pounding, "but I have an idea. I really detest pub food. I . . . bought a few things recently that would . . . make a wonderful picnic. It's such a lovely afternoon. Would you like to stop by my place, pack a hamper, and climb to the top of the moor?"

There! She'd done it. Her pulse drummed in her ears. Never had she so boldly approached a man before. What would he think? What would he say? Apprehension turned her mouth to cotton, and suddenly she wished she could take her words back. He probably had other things to do this evening. After all, she'd already consumed most of his day with her grandmother's party. Maybe he hated picnics. Or had another date. She was certain he'd say no. She hoped he'd say no. Maybe he'd save her from her own insanity.

But when she turned her face to him, she saw that grin that turned her insides to butter.

"Sure. Why not?" he said. And then he shifted into gear and turned the car toward Bridgeton Lane.

September 14, 1846

> *Why ask to know the date—the clime?*
> *More than mere words they cannot be:*
> *Men knelt to God and worshipped crime,*
> *And crushed the helpless even as we.*
>
> *But, they had learnt, from length of strife*
> *Of civil war and anarchy,*
> *To laugh at death and look on life*
> *With somewhat lighter sympathy.*
> >   —Emily Brontë

September 20, 1846
Charlotte and Papa remain in Manchester, where he is recovering from cataract surgery which Dr. Wilson assures us was successful. It will be a happy miracle indeed if his eyesight is restored. My sister writes that she has begun another novel as she sits in Papa's darkened room next to his bed. "Jane Eyre" she calls it. Like Anne's Agnes Grey, Jane is a governess. It is an ordinary idea, but the only calling Charlotte finds realistic for an impoverished young woman, and a fate we ourselves narrowly escaped.

I seldom walk these days upon the moors, for the memories of the golden summer hours I spent there with Mikel haunt me and I return melancholy and filled with that unnamed desire. The dreams have returned as well, and there is a fire in my soul stronger than that of last winter, since now I believe that Mikel is my own true friend. Will I see him again? I do not know, for he is of gipsie ways and promised me nothing but his earnest attempt to return next summer.

October 8, 1846

Papa and Charlotte have returned and the miracle has happened. Papa can see to read and get about on his own once again. It is at once a blessing and a curse, for now he can also see the pitiful creature Branwell has become. We came near to disaster only yesterday on Branii's account. Anne thought she smelled smoke and ran into his room to find him unconscious on the bed with the bedclothes aflame. She screamed and I followed up the stairs. I am larger and stronger than Anne, who was rendered quite witless by it all. I dragged Branii off the bed and dumped his drunken carcass in a corner, then managed to put out the fire. Then I put Branwell, still unconscious, into my own bed, and I slept on the sofa in the dining room. Papa has such a terror of fire, I pleaded with Anne and Charlotte not to let him know what had happened, but the odor of burned bedclothes told him for us. He has now proclaimed that Branwell must sleep in his room, and I fear for both their lives. Branwell is insane, quite mad, and makes dire threats against us all. Oh what, what will come of this? Perhaps he shall murder us all in our sleep, and I will not have to wonder whether I will see Mikel again.

Eleanor Bates was taking tea in front of her favorite daytime television program when the phone rang.

"Drat," she said, punching the mute button on the remote control. She picked up the portable phone, wondering who would be calling her at this time. She'd educated most of her friends that she didn't want to be disturbed during this particular time every day.

"Yes? Eleanor Bates here."

"Good afternoon, Mrs. Bates. My name is Tom Perkins. Perkins Galleries, London. In case you don't remember me, I was a guest at your daughter's recent *soiree.* The one who misplaced his date for the evening, if you will recall."

Of course she recalled. She also recalled that Tom Perkins's date was the lovely young woman Dr. Alex Hightower seemed so taken with. "Yes, yes, certainly," she said, keeping her tone neutral, although an inner sentinel sent up a warning flag. "What can I do for you, Mr. Perkins?"

"First, let me thank you for your assistance that evening. I'm afraid I overreacted terribly when I couldn't find Selena. She's . . . well, she can be rather absentminded, if you know what I mean. Artists often are, and I was concerned that she might have forgotten her obligation, uh, I mean, that she had a group waiting to discuss her work with her."

Intuitively, Eleanor hadn't liked the man the first time she'd met him, and his gratingly patronizing tone on the phone only reinforced her first impression. "She seemed to be in good hands when we met up with her," Eleanor said pointedly.

Tom Perkins cleared his throat. "Actually, that is the reason for my call. I understand from your daughter that Alexander Hightower is a friend of yours."

So that's what he's up to, Eleanor sniffed. Wants to check out his competition. Well, she would help him as little as she could. "I would call Dr. Hightower more of an acquaintance than friend. We have only recently met. Why?"

"Apparently Selena, my, uh, client, is under the impression that Dr. Hightower is a personal representative of an American collector who is interested in her work. Let me see, I wrote the name here somewhere . . . yes, a Mr. Henry H. Bonnell. I would very much like to get in touch with Mr. Bonnell, as Selena's agent. Her work is becoming quite in demand, and I wouldn't want Mr. Bonnell to miss an opportunity to invest in a most promising young artist."

Stunned, Eleanor sank into a damask wing chair that

was fortunately close by. Bonnell! She was speechless. On the terrace at Harrington House she'd taken Selena's introduction of Alex as someone's personal representative as a joke, one that Alex himself had brushed aside lightly. But now it would seem as if Selena's agent was taking it very seriously. But how could that be? Obviously, the man had no idea who Henry H. Bonnell was.

Her intuition warned her not to tip him off, at least not at the moment. Not until she had a chance to get to the bottom of this. "I wouldn't know anything about all that, I'm afraid. You'll have to take it up with Dr. Hightower."

There was a protracted silence, then Tom Perkins replied, "I would, but I have no idea how to get in touch with him. Selena says he is staying in Haworth. Would you, uh, happen to have his address or phone number?"

"I see Dr. Hightower from time to time," Eleanor replied noncommittally, still reeling from the bombshell dropped apparently unwittingly by this noxious little man. "I could tell him you are looking for him."

"I see."

Eleanor detected disappointment in his tone. "I'm afraid I cannot be of more assistance to you, Mr. Perkins, and I am rather tied up at the moment."

"Before we ring off, Mrs. Bates, would you be so kind as to take my number? In case you see Hightower, perhaps you could pass it along?"

"Certainly." Eleanor wrote down the number.

"Thank you for your help, Mrs. Bates."

"I can't have been of much help. And by the way, it's Ms. Bates. With an M-S." She heard the twit at the other end of the line making apologetic noises, which she ignored as if she was hard of hearing. "Good day, sir," she said, and hung up in his ear.

Eleanor Bates would do nothing to harm Alexander Hightower, because she'd taken a liking to him. Perhaps in her own elderly way she'd even fallen a little in love with him. He was so handsome, after all, and charming. And so dedicated to the Brontës.

Or so it seemed.

But this phone call ignited serious concerns about the man's integrity. What was he up to, parading as an art agent? And claiming to represent Henry Bonnell, for God's sake. It was preposterous.

Picking up the remote, she switched the TV on again, noting with irritation the program was almost over. She couldn't concentrate on it anyway, agitated as she was over Tom Perkins's phone call, so she turned it off for good and sat staring out of her window into the sunny rose garden below.

What's your game, Alexander Hightower?

Eleanor decided to find out. Bonnell was an important, almost sainted figure to the Brontë Society. And Hightower was recognized as a renegade, academically speaking. No matter how much she liked him personally, she couldn't stand by like a witless teenager and let anything destroy the credibility of either the Society or the Bonnell Collection.

She picked up the phone and called the Parsonage Library and shortly had Alex's phone number in hand. Alex deserved the opportunity to explain his curious use of the Bonnell name and to know that Tom Perkins, at least, didn't realize it was a joke.

Eleanor was certain Dr. Hightower would set things straight.

The phone rang four times, then was picked up by an answering machine. As loath as Eleanor Bates was to leave a message on one of the damnable contraptions, she concluded that the reason was important enough to overcome her personal dislike of the technology.

"Dr. Hightower, this is Eleanor Bates. I must talk to you at your earliest possible convenience. It concerns the art collection of Henry H. Bonnell. . . ."

❧ *Chapter 17* ❧

January 2, 1847
   This is the coldest winter I can remember. I cannot seem to get warm, even in the kitchen where I find every excuse to spend my hours. Outside, the darkness never seems to end, and within my own world, I suffer from a dark foreboding that I will never again see my beloved. Oh, it hurts to think of him now, camped in some wild place, freezing in the snow. How do the gipsies stay warm? It is visions such as these that remove the sting from my lack of freedom. I envy Mikel in some ways, and yet I do not wish at the moment to exchange places. . . .

March 5, 1847
   The earth is showing early signs of spring, although it will be some while before the weather is warm enough to walk on the moors. I am weary of winter, and I long to stretch my housebound spirit with a good run with Keeper up the hills and down. Even though I know Mikel could not possibly arrive before summer is fully upon us, I doubt not that my footsteps, when finally I break loose of this infernal prison, will lead directly to the beck at the back ravine. Until then, I pass these dreary hours in a new writing endeavor. I have begun another novel, although our efforts of last winter

have yet to see the light of day. This work springs from a far different source than did "Wuthering Heights." I do not feel the same energy for it, perhaps because this time I have no demons to drive away.

May 13, 1847

The world is shed of winter at last, and my spirit soars once again with the winds of spring. I have only the rudiments of my novel on paper, and I find surprisingly that I simply do not care. There is no evidence that "Wuthering Heights" or "The Professor" or "Agnes Grey" have made any friends on their rounds of London's publishers. Our poems have been published almost one year, and we have sold but two copies. How easy it would be to become discouraged, but my days are now preoccupied with other thoughts. When will he arrive?

June 15, 1847

I expected Mikel before now, and as each day passes, I fret for his return. He made no promises when he said farewell, only that if he did come near this area, he would leave a message under the rock. Charlotte has invited Ellen to visit in July, now that Branwell has tamed his temper somewhat. I hesitate to think what our dear Ellen will think when she sees his much diminished appearance, but she has been duly warned. Ellen is no fool, and I fear that I might give myself away should Mikel be within my sphere, so perhaps it is as well that he not come during her visit.

July 8, 1847

I have done the outrageous, and yet I am pleased to have done so. Ellen insisted that we go to Bradford to do some shopping, and although it is not my normal pastime, I decided to go along. We each selected cloth for new dresses. Charlotte and Anne chose dark-colored silks, while I, in a fit of delirium, have brought home a white fabric with pur-

ple lightning and thunder imprinted upon it. I will sew it into a dress that I hope Mikel will like. Ellen looked at me oddly, as if she was desirous of questioning my new taste in clothing, but she said nothing. We also played at hairdressing late yesterday, and I pulled my dark locks up and fastened them haphazardly with a Spanish comb. Ellen said I looked like a gipsie! If only she knew . . .

July 18, 1847

The unimaginable has happened. Both "Wuthering Heights" and "Agnes Grey" have found a publisher. But not poor Charlotte's "Professor." It will continue on to the next publisher on her list, whilst Anne's work and mine will soon be published by T. C. Newby. We must pay him for the honor, not exactly the way I had envisioned earning a living as a writer, but after 250 copies are sold, he will refund our fifty pounds. My heart goes out to Charlotte, for it was her idea to sell the novels, and hers was not accepted. Perhaps she will have better luck in the future. It is difficult to keep our secret, that we are novelists, with Ellen in the house. I fear she has suspicions, for she was in the dining room yesterday when the postman rang the bell with this news, and the three of us could scarcely contain our excitement.

July 21, 1847

Ellen knows of our careers, I am certain of it. Today upon the moors, we witnessed a strange and haunting sight. Three suns shone down upon us in rainbow-hued light. I was standing apart from the others, awed by the parhelion, when Ellen suddenly commented that we were the three suns—Charlotte, Anne, and I—and that our suns were on the rise. Charlotte only scoffed and denied Ellen's statement as nonsense, but I have a strange notion that she may be right. Perhaps I want it so because I have begun to lose hope of seeing Mikel again. As each day passes, the chances diminish that I will look into those flashing dark eyes or feel

*the pleasure rush through me when he rewards me with a
rare but winsome smile. Each night as I lay upon my cot, I
pray for his return, but if he comes not this year, I will take
heart knowing that our time together on the moors last
summer meant much to him, as my friend. The dreams,
however, continue to haunt me. They frighten me, for they
leave me wanting more than friendship from this wild creature I know and love.*

Alex turned into Bridgeton Lane, parked the Jaguar in
the driveway and decided to put the top up once again,
even though the weather appeared as if it would hold for
a while. It had been a splendid day, in more ways than
one. But his sense of elation at the prospect of Selena's
picnic was tempered by the nagging trepidation that she
might throw him out on his ass when he came clean
about his little prevarication concerning Bonnell. It was
what he deserved. But not what he wanted. Well, the die
is cast, Alex thought, following Selena and a yapping,
tail-wagging Domino up the steps and into the kitchen of
the old house. Whatever the outcome, at least he'd have
to suffer no more of Emily's "anticipation."

Inside, his concerns vanished as he surveyed his surroundings. Ancient board flooring creaked beneath his
feet, and the faint musty smell of decay met his nostrils.
Cracks clawed their way across the panes in the two large
windows of the room that faced the front of the house,
and faded wallpaper hung in peeling scales from ceiling
to floor. A bare lightbulb at the end of a long black cord
strung through a hole in the ceiling swung slightly in the
draft that seeped through the cracked windows.

He had seen squalor in the poorer sections of New
Orleans when as a boy he'd gone with his mother, a
home health nurse, to care for an indigent person. This
place was only one notch up on the scale. His face must

have reflected his dismay, because he heard an apology in Selena's voice, if not her words.

"This is going to be a great place one day," she said with forced brightness. "I plan to gut it and renovate the entire thing. I might turn the downstairs into a gallery." She shrugged and pulled a large picnic hamper from a shelf above a squatting, half-sized refrigerator. "All it takes is money."

"How long have you lived here?" Alex wondered how she could stand to inhabit such a place.

"Are you joking? I don't. I just keep my food in the fridge and my clothes in the armoire in the bedroom." She turned and looked at him, her face a mixture of humor and practicality. "There's not even any hot water down here."

He watched as she busied herself loading the basket, observing unabashedly the inviting curve of her hips beneath the soft skirt.

She continued her explanation, talking more rapidly than usual, he thought. "I bought this place for almost nothing, which, if it's true you get what you pay for, should be self-evident," she said with a nervous laugh. "That was almost three years ago, and I had planned by now to have it completely restored. But like I said, it takes money, and although I haven't exactly starved yet, my career, shall we say, has been a little slower taking off than I'd hoped. So I did what I could. The studio was my priority, and since that's all I have been able to afford so far, that's where I live as well as work."

Alex recalled the barn's new roof and windows, the small kitchenette, the modern free-standing fireplace. "You did all that yourself?"

Selena wiped her hands on a small towel and leaned back against the kitchen sink, her breasts pressing against the fabric of the white knit pullover. "With a loan from a local bank and the work of a carpenter in town."

Alex tried to ignore the distinct outline of her nipples and kept his gaze on her slightly flushed face. Her dark hair curled in shiny tendrils across her cheeks and fell in ribbons of ebony silk on her shoulders. The deep pools of her eyes held his gaze for a long moment, and he felt himself drowning in them. He groped for words to save him.

None came.

He stepped closer to her and brushed a curl away from her face. "You're an extraordinary woman, Selena," he said at last, his voice husky. It was an inane thing to say, he knew, and it wasn't what he wanted to tell her. But it was all he could come up with at the moment to put a safe distance between him and the libidinous thoughts that were flooding him with desire.

Her head was raised to his, and although she didn't move away at his touch, Alex could see she was trembling. "Not so terribly extraordinary," she replied, her own voice strained. She raised the picnic basket between them, handing it to Alex. "For the same money," she said, clearing her throat and nodding toward the door, "I could be living in a one-bedroom flat above the butcher shop with no room to paint in. I guess it's worth putting up with this for a bit. Come on, let's go before we miss any more of this fabulous sunshine."

Domino romped ahead of them out of the door and stood guard against Alex while Selena took a moment to dash upstairs and check on her cats. Alex felt the hard discomfort of his body's unquenched need, but knew he must exercise restraint with Selena. He wanted her too much.

They walked briskly up the steep lane, which ended just past a large gate that prevented sheep from wandering too low on the moors. Alex carried the basket in one hand and slipped the other around Selena's and gave it a squeeze, noting her fingers were like ice. She looked up

at him, and he saw an uncertain smile striving for her
lips.

"Beautiful day, isn't it?" she said. "We don't get many
like this."

Alex's hungry gaze devoured the sight of the dark-
haired lady at his side, striding with vigor up the hill, her
long cotton skirt swishing against her legs, her hair drift-
ing in midnight waves in the wind. Danger here, a warning whispered in his mind.

The late sunshine spilled down the hillsides, tinging
with gold the heavy heads of the long amber grass. A
different variety of much greener grass apparently ap-
pealed more to the sheep, for it was cropped short, revealing the sandy soil beneath. On the next rise, a utility
vehicle was parked near a crumbling drystone wall, and a
man in a yellow cap waved from the distance.

"That's Andy Mahoney," Selena said, returning the
greeting. "He used to be a schoolteacher around here,
but he found he could make more money putting these
stone walls back together again." She explained the joint
venture between the government and private property
owners to restore the hundreds of miles of drystone walls
that were the historical signature of Yorkshire. "The
original farmers in this area stacked the stones as they
removed them from their fields, building these walls
which have stood for centuries."

Alex paused and looked across the vast expanse of
verdant hillsides that spread in every direction. The walls
crisscrossed them in a haphazard pattern, dividing the
land into odd geometric shapes. "Did the walls separate
property or something?"

"Nope," she answered with a laugh. "The farmers just
had to put the stones somewhere. The walls do provide a
windbreak and shelter for the sheep, though."

They continued their journey upward until they
reached a rise high above the farmhouse.

"This is the place I had in mind," Selena said, indicating a shallow dip in the terrain. "I come here often. The grass is soft, and the sky seems so close you can reach out and touch it." She looked up and added, "Do you suppose the yellow balloon that broke loose this morning is responsible for this sunshine?"

Alex looked up, too, feeling the sun's warmth on his face and having the distinct impression that it was spreading downward into other regions of his body. "Perhaps it is." He didn't care what had brought the welcome change in the weather, nor whether he could touch the sky.

He wanted to touch Selena.

They spread the coverlet she'd brought over the thick grass, creating a soft pallet beneath an azure sky. A few clouds had begun to gather at the crest of the hill behind them, but their misty gray offered no threat at the moment.

"I must have subconsciously wanted to have a picnic," she said, bringing the paté and cheeses out of the basket and placing them on the wooden cutting board. "I never buy this kind of thing at the market."

Alex found himself at a loss for words. On one hand, he was immensely glad her subconscious had been so astute, but on the other, he suspected that by coming to this idyllic spot with Selena he'd irrevocably violated his own hard and fast rule against becoming emotionally involved with a woman. He must be very, very careful.

He helped himself to a slice of cheese and tried to think of something safe to talk about. "I used to go on picnics when I was young, but I haven't done this in a long time."

She handed him the bottle of wine and the corkscrew. "Where did you go to picnic then?"

He eased the cork from the bottle and poured them each a goblet full of the robust red liquid, noticing how the sunlight played on Selena's hair. "My favorite place was a park, down along a bayou near where we lived. There were picnic tables, and people brought charcoal to cook out. Sometimes somebody caught a fish and cooked it over an open fire."

Alex raised his glass to hers. "To your future as a rich and famous artist," he said, and they drank deeply of the wine.

With her tongue, Selena retrieved a drop of wine from her full lips and laughed. "I'll take the rich part. Then I can afford to fix up the house so I can properly entertain my guests from afar." She paused a moment, then asked, "What's a bayou, and where was this picnic place?"

Alex hadn't missed the way her tongue licked away the wine, nor the way his body reacted to it. Slow down! he demanded of his thudding heart. He spread some of the rich paté onto a slice of crusty French bread and handed it to Selena. Then he refilled the wineglasses and took another deep swallow before answering. "A bayou is a slow-moving river or stream that comes out of a swamp, and the place was south Louisiana. That's where I was born and raised."

"But you live now in New York?"

Another large sip of wine. It was a natural supposition that he lived in New York. After all, didn't most important art deals happen in New York? He lowered the glass and looked at her, knowing the moment was at hand. "Virginia," he replied, expecting further questions that would allow his confession about Henry H. Bonnell to unfold in a natural and hopefully not too condemning manner.

But surprisingly, she did not pursue it. She raised her glass to her lips and sipped the wine, her eyes holding his in a steady gaze. "Do you like the wine?"

Alex refilled their glasses, noting the bottle was already over two-thirds empty. "It's wonderful. Italian?"

Selena nodded. "So is this Gorgonzola. Try it."

She stuffed a small slice of the Italian blue cheese between his lips, letting her fingers linger long enough for him to lick the crumbs from her fingertips.

The touch of his tongue against her skin was his undoing.

The desire he'd been struggling to control the entire day unleashed itself, leaving him helpless in its wake. Alex took her fingers in his and kissed them lightly. His eyes searched hers for permission to continue, and his heart raced when he saw it in their midnight depths.

Alex lowered his lips to hers, savoring their wine-sweetened tenderness. Their fingers entwined, and he drew her hands against his chest, letting his kiss speak to her of his desire while their bodies were yet apart. Her lips opened to his gentle searching, setting Alex on fire with the realization that she wanted him as much as he did her.

Restraint vanished, and the walls of his resistance crumbled.

Alex shoved the cheese board aside and nestled their wineglasses carefully in the tall grass. Selena lay back against the side of the hill, and Alex leaned over her, gazing steadily into her eyes, dropping his head slowly, slowly, until their lips met.

"Selena," he breathed, and her name was a prayer on the wind. He grazed the flawless olive skin on her face with the back of his fingers, tracing them lightly down her throat and over the crest of her breasts to the nipples that rose to greet his touch.

She was everywhere in his senses. He knew he should stop, but the scent of her perfume, encouraged by the quantity of wine he'd consumed so quickly, inebriated his will. He felt the gentle pressure of her hands against his back, almost as if she were pulling him against her. He tasted her kiss, sweet and demure at first, and felt it intensify as her lips parted to receive him. A loose strand of her hair struck his cheek. lashing him toward the edge of uncontrolled passion.

A nameless emotion suddenly tightened his throat, and he pulled away from her. "My God," he whispered, holding her face in his hands, kissing her lips, cheeks, the tip of her nose, her forehead. What was he thinking? He felt her trembling in his hands. Or was he the one who trembled? Alex sat up, trying to catch his breath, which was coming in ragged gasps. He had to regain control.

Selena looked up at him, her eyes questioning, asking without words why he had pulled away from her.

The nameless emotion took on a name, and Alex knew the answer to her question.

Fear.

It was fear that clawed its way upward from his belly and wrapped icy fingers around his heart. It had been forever, it seemed, since he'd felt this way toward anyone. Maybe he never had. Not exactly like this. Emotions seemed to spiral from deep within, swirling from a dark vortex and surrounding him with a power so strong it threatened to overwhelm him. He couldn't do this. He had to stop. Get away. Now!

A cold drop of water dashed across his cheek, as if a giant tear fell from the sky.

They looked up in unison. The misty cloud that earlier had nestled peacefully at the top of the moor must have been but a scout for the warrior storm that had invaded the heavens from behind the crest of the hill. The wind picked up, sending more cold raindrops earthward.

"Grab the wine!" Selena cried, twisting from Alex's arms. She whistled for Domino and began to toss the picnic fare into a plastic container. "Looks like we're going to get wet after all."

He hoisted the hamper and took her hand, and together they hurried back down the hillside. The sudden downpour served as a much-needed cold shower for Alex, restoring his senses. When Selena was safely back in her house or studio or wherever the hell it was she lived, he would, he swore, get in the Jag and make a permanent exit from her life.

❧ *Chapter 18* ❧

As the afternoon turned into evening, Eleanor Bates grew restless, anxious to hear from Dr. Hightower. But her phone remained silent. The longer the time stretched out, the more questions built up in her mind. I wonder what Brian Wescott knows about this man? she thought. A longtime friend and fellow Society member, Wescott was in charge of organizing the debate between Maggie Flynn and Alexander Hightower. Had Brian checked out Hightower's background carefully enough? They all knew his reputation was that of a renegade scholar. But being an unconventional thinker was one thing.

Being a liar was another.

And it was obvious that Alexander Hightower had lied to the artist and, she supposed, to her agent as well.

Ordinarily, Eleanor Bates was not one to police the actions of others. But in this case, she felt compelled to investigate Alex's veracity completely, because the lie he'd told had outrageously involved the Society's most important benefactor. Questions shouted through her mind and kept echoing there until she could no longer ignore them.

Was this man a fraud, and if so, should there even be a debate?

At last she could stand it no longer. She picked up the telephone and dialed Brian Wescott.

"Brian, my dear fellow," she said, "Eleanor Bates here. How have you been? And do tell me things are going well for the debate. Will we have a good crowd?"

"El! What a delightful surprise." Brian Wescott spoke in the thick accent of his native Yorkshire. "Yes. Yes, I do believe so. We have already started receiving reservations."

"Splendid! However, I was thinking perhaps I could help out. You know, make some personal phone calls, that kind of thing. I feel this will be an extraordinary event."

"No doubt. I understand Dr. Hightower is already in Haworth. What do you suppose he's up to?"

I wish I knew, Eleanor thought silently, but replied, "It's probably a last minute effort to support his theory, which I believe will be quite difficult to do. Actually, he was the reason for this call. I know when I call my friends to talk up this debate to them, they will want to know all about Dr. Hightower and Dr. Flynn, and I was wondering if you could provide me with a vita on them both?"

"Certainly. I'll drop them to you by post tomorrow morning. Don't you think it's interesting that they used to work together?"

Caught by surprise, Eleanor didn't reply right away. "Well, actually, I wasn't aware of that. Where was this?"

"Flynn was a visiting scholar at Strathmore for a year." The man hesitated a moment, then continued with a hint of humor in his voice. "There's talk, you know, that they . . . know each other quite well, if you get my meaning."

Eleanor Bates didn't miss much, but this news quite astounded her. "You don't say? When was this?"

"Oh, a year or so ago, I believe. It's just gossip, of course. But still, it should make things very interesting, don't you agree?"

Nonplussed by this news, Eleanor answered somewhat absently, thanked her friend for his help and rang off. Her mind was chewing on a lot of things, including her own misguided efforts to make a match between the two scholars. She'd been too late, she thought, amused in spite of herself. Maggie and Alex had already played that game.

And lost, it would appear.

Or at least one of them had.

She recalled Maggie's eager willingness to invite Alex to her daughter's affair at Harrington, and Alex's distress when he'd discovered Maggie was in attendance. Had Alex rejected the beautiful Maggie Flynn? It was hard to fathom.

Although with the newly planted seeds of doubt concerning Alex's personal integrity, Eleanor thought that maybe Maggie was better off in the long run.

What was between them now? she wondered. Was it only professional disagreement that fueled the debate, or was there more going on than met the eye? Intrigued by this latest news, Eleanor placed a third call. Who would know more about Alexander Hightower than his former lover?

"Dr. Flynn? Eleanor Bates here. I hope all is going along well with you?"

"Yes. Things are fine, Ms. Bates." She sounded distracted, perhaps in a hurry. Or uncomfortable with the call.

"I won't keep you long, dear. I'm calling to ask a favor."

"I'll be happy to help if I can."

"I've volunteered to do some personal promotion to increase the attendance at the debate, and I was wondering if you could give me some insight as to how this whole thing developed in the first place?"

"Well, I guess it was because I called Alex's hand on

his ridiculous suicide theory," she said, and Eleanor didn't miss the scorn in her voice. "You see, I spent a year at Strathmore, and we . . . came to know each other quite well. At first I thought he was, uh, interesting. Creative. You know. The rogue scholar. But then I realized that he really didn't have anything solid to base this thing on, and frankly, I got tired of hearing him espousing something he could not substantiate."

Eleanor got her answer as to Maggie Flynn's motives for the debate loud and clear.

Professional jealousy.

A painful emotional involvement with her opponent.

Perhaps even revenge.

"Yes, I do understand Dr. Hightower is something of a renegade, but without new thoughts and theories, don't you think we could get stuck in a rut, academically speaking of course?"

"I think you would be the first to agree, Ms. Bates, that when it comes to the Brontës, we do not need any more wild, unsubstantiated rumors. Our work is too full of that kind of nonsense already."

"Perhaps you are right, my dear." Eleanor then carefully worded her specific inquiry so as not to make it seem too important. No matter what she found out, she still owed Alex a chance to speak in his own defense. "Still, Dr. Hightower does seem to be an interesting man. So involved academically, and an art connoisseur as well."

It was Eleanor's turn to hear a long silence on the line. Then Maggie laughed, loudly and harshly.

"Art connoisseur? Wherever did you get that idea?"

"I've heard he's in the market for some rather expensive art he's come across in the area."

"Surely you're kidding? I've been in Alex's . . . Dr. Hightower's home many times, and I can assure you the only art on those walls came already framed from the discount store."

"Well, perhaps I'm mistaken. Unfortunately, it happens when you get to be my age. Thank you so much, Dr. Flynn, for your input. It will help as I prepare my pitch for your debate."

"Feel free to call if I can help you further," Maggie said, then added with open malice, "As far as I'm concerned, Dr. Hightower is a dilettante and a boor, and the more witnesses to his downfall, the better."

Eleanor raised her eyebrows and rang off quickly, settling the phone back into its cradle as if it were red-hot. A dilettante and a boor? Alexander Hightower had seemed neither to Eleanor.

But then, he also had not seemed like a liar.

August 10, 1847
Charlotte's "Professor" has once again been rejected, but this time with encouragement from the publisher who wishes to see her next novel, which is almost complete. I continue to scratch away at my work, but nothing pleases me about it. I have created a gipsie hero, but I know nothing of gipsies except what Mikel has told me, and this story does not ring authentic to my own ears. Perhaps I should tear it up and start over.

August 25, 1847
"Jane Eyre" is off to Smith Elder in yesterday's post. I pray that it is accepted, for Charlotte is having increasing difficulty in holding up under continued rejection, especially since Anne and I are receiving the first proof sheets on our novels. It would be sad irony if Charlotte's was to go without a publisher, as she is the most adamant that we can earn our living as novelists. To this end I should be concentrating on my writing, but as I sit by the fire at night with my sisters, my mind wanders not into my story, which lies fal-

*low on my lap desk, but into the arms of a gipsie named
Mikel, whom I may never see again.*

September 1, 1847

*Good tidings arrived today from George Smith of Smith
Elder. He has accepted Charlotte's manuscript in less than
one week since she submitted it to him! She is a changed
person since receiving the news. Papa has remarked about
it, so we must be cautious, for he does not know that all
three of his daughters are soon-to-be-published novelists.*

October 19, 1847

*We have received by post copies of some London news-
papers which are carrying rave reviews of* Jane Eyre. *Charlotte is stunned that it is apparently such an overnight
success, but Mr. Smith writes that many bookshops have
already sold out. We are all three ecstatic at this turn of
events, but I am not so surprised, for* Jane Eyre *is an
excellent piece penned by that talented writer Currer Bell.
"He" has told a masterful tale!*

Even though Wuthering Heights *and* Agnes Grey *have
been with our publisher far longer than* Jane Eyre *has been
with Smith Elder, Newby has yet to give us a publishing
date. Perhaps "Currer's" popularity will spur him to bring
forth our books as well.*

December 13, 1847

*I question my ability to make sound decisions, at least in
the case of Mr. T.C. Newby. So eager was I to have my
novel published that I fear I have signed up with a charla-
tan. Now that Currer's* Jane Eyre *is all the rage in London,
Newby has seen fit to publish the efforts of Ellis and Acton,
but he is busy confusing the work of the three Bell brothers
and intimating that Currer is the author of all three. He has
done a frightful job of getting the books out as well. They
abound with errors, and it appears as if Mr. Newby did not*

bother with our corrected proofs. Wuthering Heights *has, however, finally reached the light of day. Will my dear Mikel ever read it? It is unlikely, and I am as glad so, for I should wish him never to know he was the model for the dark personage of Heathcliff.*

Man, woman, and dog were soaked to the skin by the time they made their way up the stairway and into the studio. The storm was increasing in violence, with wind wailing down the moors and lightning streaking across the skies. Peaches and Hizzonor jumped down from the sofa and rubbed against Selena's legs as if relieved that their human had returned safely to protect them from the gale.

"How'd that happen so fast?" Alex said, catching his breath and pulling at his wet clothing.

"It's like that all the time," Selena replied, breathless. "One minute it's beautiful, the next it's a mess." She headed for the small linen cupboard in the cubicle she called a bathroom, trying not to think about what had happened on the moors between her and Alexander Hightower. Her hands shook as she pulled two clean towels from the shelf. "Here," she said, tossing one to Alex from across the room, as if she were afraid to get too close to him again.

She was having difficulty reconciling the fact that her normally well-disciplined emotions had not only wavered beneath his touch, they had exploded into shards of intense desire.

She didn't blame him for what had happened. She knew she'd invited the kiss. She'd wanted to feel the light touch of his tongue against her fingertips. She'd wanted to press her breasts against his solid chest and feel the strength of his arms around her.

She had wanted, still wanted, him.

And as she stared at him from across the room, she

read the sexual hunger in his eyes as well. A hunger that was at once both frightening and intoxicating. A hunger that matched her own. Her belly contracted and she was aware that it was more than the cold that caused her nipples to stand erect beneath her clammy, drenched shirt. She reached for the woolen shawl that hung over the back of the couch and pulled it around her shoulders protectively.

She had to ask him to leave.

Soon.

But she couldn't throw him out soaking wet. Like her own clothing, his was sodden and mud-splattered, and she saw a shiver crawl down his spine. "Let's warm this place up," she said, finding her voice at last. Quickly, she went to the stack of neatly piled firewood in the corner and laid several sticks in the large round firebox. With shaking hands, she crumpled some old newspaper for kindling and lit the fire with a match. Soon a flicker of warmth began to dispel the chill. Domino was especially appreciative, and stretched out nearby on his blanket, keeping one eye cocked on Alex.

Alex threw the towel around his shoulder and went to the window, where raindrops struck thick and fast from the outside and firelight reflected from within. "Guess I should make a run for it," he said, shivering again. "My jacket's in the car. Glad I put the top up."

Selena stood with the sofa between them, her heart pounding. "That's for sure!" Go ahead, she ordered herself silently. Send him on his way! But instead she said, "I have hot water up here. And some brandy. Why don't you warm up in the shower, and we'll finish our picnic, at least. The storm will likely subside before long."

She imagined she saw his back straighten slightly, but he didn't turn to face her, and a small ache nestled around her heart. So he didn't want to stay . . . But he rubbed his hair with the towel, then turned and looked at her with an unreadable expression in his eyes.

"Yeah," he said after a long moment, surprising her again. "Yeah. I guess we ought to do that."

A knot of apprehension suddenly tied itself in the pit of her stomach. Where was this leading?

"You go first," she said, indicating the shower stall. "I have a clean smock you can wear till your clothes dry." She gave him a small grin and went into the back room of the studio. She returned and held up a paint-stained garment that loosely resembled a muslin choir robe. "Not exactly haute couture, but I think it'll fit. At any rate, it'll be warmer than what you're wearing now."

He came across the room and took the smock with a doubtful smile. Holding it out in front of him, the smile turned into a laugh. It was obvious to both of them that if it fit at all, the effect would be hilarious. "I don't know, Selena. Maybe I'd better just bite the bullet and go on home."

"Your choice." His laughter caught up with her, and she felt the tension that had steadily been mounting between them ease somewhat. "Brandy and brie by the fireplace, or a cold, wet ride home with your dignity intact."

He hesitated, dropping his head to one side and contemplating her from smoldering gray eyes. "When you put it that way . . ."

Selena waited until he'd shut the door behind him and she heard the water running before considering the ramifications of the offer she'd made him. She poured herself the rest of the red wine that remained from their aborted picnic and drained the glass swiftly. She knew better than to drink so much, but she was counting on the wine to steady her nerves now that Alex had taken her up on the invitation to stay.

What was the harm in it? She'd meant it only as a

hospitable gesture, nothing more. She threw another log on the fire and busied herself unloading the picnic basket. Relax, she told herself, her heart pounding, trying not to think of the sexy man taking a shower only inches away from where she stood at the sink. She laid out the remains of their picnic on the table in front of the fireplace and went to the cabinet beneath the sink to retrieve the brandy she'd promised Alex. She'd give him a drink and send him on his way when the storm subsided. After all, she hadn't asked him to spend the night.

Or had she?

Selena blinked, considering the possibilities.

Behind the brandy bottle she spotted another bottle of red wine. She hesitated. Then she heard her guest turn off the water in the shower. With a deep breath, she brought out the wine, located the corkscrew, and uncorked the bottle.

One more glass of wine wouldn't hurt.

One more glass.

✒ *Chapter 19* ✒

Warmed from the hot shower and dried with the towel, Alex peered into the steam-shrouded mirror, trying to evaluate the absurdity of his attire. He wiped the glass with the towel and grimaced at what was reflected there. He looked, he thought, like a fallen angel at best, or perhaps a misplaced Roman in a paint-speckled toga. But he was covered, sort of, and he was dry.

The yoke of Selena's painting smock didn't pretend to make it all the way across his wide shoulders, forcing the armhole seams to strain upward toward his neck. What should have been long, loose sleeves tightly covered his well-developed biceps and ended just at his elbow. He would have to call on the aid of his own belt to achieve decency where the smock gaped open in front. The hem fell not quite to his knees, and his muscular, hairy legs looked ludicrous in the skirt.

"Jesus," he muttered. Then he considered his options. His trousers, shirt, socks, and undershorts lay in a puddle on the floor.

Dirty.

Cold.

Wet.

Annoyed, Alex scooped up the clothing and fastened

the belt around his waist, pulling the soft muslin fabric together in front as securely as possible. He cracked the door and peered out. He could see Selena's silhouette in the firelight where she sat, her back to him, brushing her wet hair.

"Are you sure you're ready for this?" he growled, asking himself the same question.

She turned, and when she saw him emerge, her eyes danced in merriment. "You look . . . great!" Then she covered her mouth with her hands to capture the howl that escaped only seconds later.

"Maybe I should have left with my dignity intact after all," he uttered, but when he saw that Selena had changed into a similar frock, he changed his mind. Whereas he looked ridiculous, she was spectacularly beautiful in the garment. Her hair fell soft and black against the white smock, which clung to her as if custom fit by a master tailor. It was open at the throat, and coming toward her, Alex could see her breasts were bare beneath it. His breath caught for a moment, then raggedly escaped.

"I've poured you a brandy," she said shakily, averting her eyes from the front of his makeshift robe, where the belt was all that kept the fabric from revealing his naked self. "Why don't you sit here and warm up while I jump in the shower?"

Warm up? he thought, suddenly perspiring. If I got any hotter, I'd explode. He waited until Selena made her way around the opposite end of the sofa and into the bathroom before he turned fully to the firelight. He didn't want her to see the force of his desire, which stood erect beneath the thin material. Hastily, he drew a chair as close as he dared to the fireplace and hung his clothing on the back of it to dry. Perhaps in a short while they would be fit to put on again and he'd be on his way.

Alex picked up the snifter of brandy she'd set out for

him and downed a large swallow, noticing her nearly empty wineglass on the table. He laughed to himself, guessing she was as nervous as he. He tossed back another large swig of brandy and felt its fingers of fire scratch down his throat. She didn't have anything to be nervous about, he thought, but he knew he was lying to himself. Trying to quit thinking about the possibilities the evening held in store, he settled into one end of the sofa, and only then did his eyes fall on the paintings.

They hung, as they had the day he'd photographed them, along three walls of this room of the studio, giving it, in the flickering firelight, the look of a macabre gallery from an alien world. A streak of lightning lit up the room, washing the mauves and grays with an electric white. Thunder followed a split second later, and suddenly the lights went out.

"Oh, damn it all," he heard Selena's voice from the bathroom. She shut off the shower abruptly. "Alex, be a love and find the candles so we can see what we're doing. They're in the cabinet over the sink. The matches are on the table."

Alex hitched his smock together and picked up the matches. Another flash streaked from the heavens nearby, this one even closer, for it simultaneously cracked the nighttime sky with ear-splitting thunder. He fumbled in the semidarkness and found the candles. He lit one and melted some wax onto a china saucer that waited unwashed in the sink. Firmly, he anchored the candle in the wax, then repeated the process with another.

He carried the two lights toward the bathroom. "You'll have to open the door. My hands are full."

She did, and emerged fully clothed again in the smock. The olive skin of her face glowed soft and healthy in the candlelight. "Some storm," she said, her voice throaty.

Which one? Alex wondered. The one outside, or the

one that was raging fiercely inside his own breast? "Yeah. That last bolt of lightning must've hit pretty close around here."

They made their way to the fireplace, set the candles on the low table, and sat down awkwardly at opposite ends. "It's like that often out here," Selena said, picking up her wineglass and refilling it. "Lightning crashing, thunder booming."

"Don't you get scared?"

"What's there to be scared of? The only one it seems to bother is my brave and fearless Domino." She laughed and looked at the poor creature huddled miserably in his bed. Then she turned back to Alex. "Well," she said, "after all that, I really am starved. Shall we?"

The earlier picnic was spread in a smorgasbord on the table in front of the fireplace, just out of reach from where they sat. Cautiously, Alex leaned forward, moving a scant two or three inches closer to Selena.

Selena did the same. Still, neither could comfortably reach to take the first bite.

Alex grinned over at Selena. "Want to try that again? Maybe after two or three more scoots we can reach dinner."

Laughing, they moved closer and reached for the cheeses, fruits, paté, and French bread, which unfortunately by now had gone a little soggy. His appetite sated, Alex downed the remainder of the golden brandy in the snifter. He leaned forward, his hands on his knees, and stared at the fire. "Will the lights come on soon?" he asked, stifling a yawn. Selena's prescription of a hot shower, food, and a snifter of brandy was working its magic, but unfortunately, it was also making him damnably sleepy. He should leave soon, but he didn't want to leave her alone in the dark.

She stretched like a sleek satisfied cat and said with a

not so stifled yawn, "Who knows? The local power company isn't the greatest at restoring electricity quickly."

Thunder continued to rumble overhead, but it was more distant now. The rain pattered rather than beat against the windowpane. The wind sighed, and Alex did, too. He leaned back against the worn sofa, braced from the stiff drink and as ready as he'd ever be to explain about the Henry Bonnell thing. It wasn't a big deal, but seeing the paintings had reminded him he needed to get past that little hiccup.

"Selena." He touched her shoulder, and she jumped. "Come here," Alex said with a low laugh. "I won't bite."

He held out his arm and she moved into its shelter, snuggling up next to him, her feet behind her and her body leaning against his. He ran his hand down her back, noting the disconcerting absence of either a bra or a panty line. He felt her shawl on the back of the sofa, and he pulled it over them, protecting them from the darkness of the room behind them.

They sat in silence for a long while, adjusting to the unfamiliar warmth of intimate closeness. Alex rested his cheek against Selena's damp hair, inhaling the perfume of her freshly shampooed locks. He wanted more than anything to raise her lips to his and bury himself in her kisses, but he knew if he did, for him there would be no going back. He felt her body relax into his, the curve of her breast pressing softly against him. He glanced down to make sure his gown still covered the lower portion of his body.

At last Alex spoke, brushing a soft kiss into her hair. "Listen, there is something I need to, er, straighten out with you," he said, feeling her even breathing as her breasts rose and fell against his ribs. "That day when I first came here, I . . ." His hand had traveled down her back again and across the rounded flesh of her bottom. He paused, realizing she had made no move to stop him.

His interest in telling her about his little mendacity turned into a desire to explore other possibilities further, even though the rational, sane side of him knew better than to tempt fate. But that rational, sane side was slightly inebriated. Lightly, he traced small circles across the surface beneath his hand, allowing his fingers to graze ever so lightly the cloth-covered crevice they crossed along the way.

Incredibly, she still didn't move. If anything, her body felt even more solid against his. Alex continued his finger dance along her back with one hand, while employing the other in similar strokes alongside her cheek and down the inside of her arm, coming to rest at last at the roundness of her breast. He held his breath, feeling need surging painfully in his groin.

Knowing he had to stop this.

Now.

Her breathing was light and even. Her head rested against his shoulder. The nipple that had stood erect so invitingly earlier beneath the wet sweater was now soft beneath his inquiring touch. It was as if she felt none of his ministrations.

Which she didn't, he realized with dismay.

Selena, innocent as a schoolgirl in the white muslin smock, was sound asleep.

January 21, 1848

Today Charlotte has told Papa about our books. We decided it must be done, for last week Charlotte saw an old clergyman she knows reading Jane Eyre, *and in it he recognized Cowan Bridge School and that infamous Mr. Brocklehurst. It would have been only a matter of time until Papa heard about the books, we supposed, and we decided it would be better for us to tell him than for him to find out we had been hiding our endeavors from him. At any rate, he seems pleased. Branwell remains uninformed about our work, and it is our desire for it to continue as such.*

February 18, 1848

I have written Mr. Newby about this new novel which I am struggling with. He seems eager to see it and has written that he would indeed be interested in publishing it. Charlotte upbraids me for my loyalty to the man, for he has not done for Anne's and my books what Smith Elder has for Charlotte's. What she doesn't understand is that at times I find her domineering attitude overbearing, and I would rather remain with my own publisher, independent from her, for then she is less likely to attempt to impose her will upon me.

The sun edged steadily up over the distant moors, streaming golden morning light through the windows of the loft studio and directly into the eyes of the man asleep on the sofa. Alex awoke, dazed and disoriented. The fire had died and the room was chilly. He was dressed in a ridiculous sort of nightshirt. On the table nearby stood an empty brandy snifter, a half-empty wineglass, and the remains of last night's supper. Two cats napped on the windowsill. The dog was nowhere in sight.

And neither was Selena.

It all came back to Alex in a hangover-filtered haze. He groaned and rubbed his eyes and made his way into the bathroom. A splash of cold water on his face only slightly diluted the fuzziness of his consciousness. He wished he had a toothbrush.

He found his clothes still draped on the back of the chair where he'd hung them to dry. They were a little stiff and less than clean, but he was happy to put them on again, and he dressed quickly. Where was Selena? he wondered, running her brush through his own thick dark hair. He felt suddenly as if he were an intruder.

Alex went to the window and looked out onto the drive
below. There was no hint of last night's tempest other
than beaded drops on the two automobiles parked there.
He couldn't see into the house, but he surmised Selena
had gone to dress.

Selena. He felt the stirrings of arousal just thinking
about the night before, how Selena's feminine form had
felt beneath his caress. Thank God she'd fallen asleep, he
thought. He was certain he would have done a really
stupid thing if she hadn't. Hightower, he admonished
himself, for a smart guy, you sure are making some asi-
nine moves.

With a sigh, he turned and tried to decide what to do
next. Collecting his socks from the back of the chair, he
was in the middle of donning one of them when he
looked up at the wall of paintings. It was full daylight
now, and the room was the brightest he'd ever seen it
illuminated. Each scrap of the painted note seemed to
flutter at him in invitation from the canvases.

Hastily, he finished putting on his socks and shoes and
went over to where the earliest painting hung. He read
the clearly printed lettering on the canvas, and his heart
started to beat a little faster. He glanced over his shoulder, as if what he was doing was somehow clandestine.
He remembered how Selena had suddenly clammed up
when he'd asked her about the source of these images,
and he guessed she'd not welcome his snooping this
morning. But the tiny words called to him anyway. He
read the second and third notes, and hastily moved on to
read the others while he had the chance. Suddenly, one
of the messages claimed his total concentration, and he
stopped in his tracks, adrenaline screaming through his
body.

One word jumped out at him and chased his imagination like the large yellow wolf dog that had pursued him
in a dream he only vaguely remembered.

Keeper!

Keeper was the name of Emily's faithful dog, which, according to Brontë legend, had howled for weeks after she died. A large yellow mastiff.

Keeper.

Capitalized.

Of course, it could be the beginning of a sentence, but what kind of sentence would start with Keeper? Keeper of the keys? Keeper of the kingdom? Or was it Keeper, a dog, in mid-sentence? Alex stared at the handwriting, knowing at gut level he had stumbled onto something far more important than a word game. That was Emily's handwriting. Keeper was Emily's dog. This was Emily's territory.

And something that Selena kept painting over and over had to do with Emily Jane Brontë.

Alex looked around, desperate for something to write on and with. He found a ballpoint pen and a small note-pad on the counter in the kitchenette. He raced back to the painting and copied what he saw, exactly as the words fell together:

Keeper
Time. I kn
opening
gazing
for tha
bor
De

His ears were ringing with the aftereffects of the brandy, and his pulse pounded in acknowledgment that he shouldn't be doing this without Selena's permission. Why didn't he just wait until she returned? he asked himself from the small corner of his mind that seemed to still retain reason.

Because, the much larger, madder mind replied, what if she denied him access to the message? This was no ordinary missive. He was certain of it. And she had clearly been hesitant to talk about it before. He felt compelled to snatch as much as he could at the moment and explain later.

He went back to the first painting and scribbled its contents hastily onto the notepad:

> *and*
> *s o'er, I weary*
> *ere we were*
> *all meet our*
> *ffering*
> *to*

"Sounds like part of a poem," he'd remarked to Selena when he'd first seen it. A part of one of Emily's poems? Without remorse, he moved on to the next painting and captured the contents of the letter fragment painted there:

> *fully, sh*
> *wish only*
> *put an end*
> *brought upon*
> *use pay for*
> *y foolish and*
> *ear not death*
> *in death I shal*

put an end. His mind began playing a theme it already knew well.

ear not death. Fear not death? Alex was certain Emily had no fear of death.

in death I shal. Shall what? What!? Alex's breath came

in short, harsh gasps. He felt as if electricity coursed through his veins.

Where in hell did Selena come up with these images?

Torn between continuing his theft of the words on her canvases and calling to her and demanding to know what this was all about, Alex turned around to find himself facing the image of fury itself.

Selena stood in the doorway, a cup of steaming coffee in each hand. Her face was white with rage, and he knew she'd seen him scribbling her words as fast and furiously as possible. "What are you doing?" she demanded.

Alex stared at her, hardly seeing the woman for the potential literary discovery she stood for. "What are these . . . these messages?" He spoke in a low voice, straining to control his excitement, his frustration.

"Get away from my paintings. Nobody gave you permission to trespass there."

"Trespass! I could have sworn I was an invited guest here last night."

Selena stormed into the room, fully clothed now in jeans and a long-sleeved T-shirt. She banged the cups down on the counter, slopping coffee onto the laminated plastic. "My mistake, I can assure you, if this is the way you show your gratitude."

Alex stared at her, not believing her vitriolic response. Where was the softly welcoming woman of the night before?

"What is it that's eating you about these paintings?" he demanded. "These messages? Every time I ask you about them, you go ballistic."

"What I paint is none of your business," she hissed, glaring at him, then added, "unless you've come up with a buyer for them."

Alex grimaced and replied in a low but steady voice, "No, I haven't come up with a buyer, but—"

"Then it's time for you to go." Her voice was sharp and cold and brooked no argument. Alex clenched his fists, crumpling the note paper. Yeah, he agreed silently. It's time to go.

❧ *Chapter 20* ❧

Selena watched from the high north windows as the handsome, dark-haired man in rather rumpled clothing climbed into the antique Jaguar and slammed the door behind him. Her entire body quaked, but she wasn't sure whether it was from anger, fear, or something even darker, something that lay buried at the depths of her soul. She picked up Peaches and went to the couch, hurting clear down to her fingertips.

She was angry with herself, and mortified at what apparently had happened the night before. She'd awakened sometime around five o'clock, just as the first faint rays of dawn began to prove to the world that the storm had subsided. Her head was splitting, and she was lying half naked next to Alex, her smock barely covering the essentials. His arm was thrown protectively over her, but the shawl that had served as a coverlet earlier in the night had crawled down their entwined legs, leaving them both exposed.

She had remained still for a moment, suppressing her first inclination, which was to jump up and run. Slowly, she'd regained her composure, and with extreme care not to awaken him, she'd disengaged herself from his unconscious embrace and moved a cautious few feet toward the door. The room was cold, and since she hadn't had the good sense to dry her own clothes by the fire, she'd decided to make a dash for the house. Domino was at her side, awiggle to escape to the out-of-doors, and she'd petted him, praying he would remain silent. Turning to make sure Alex was asleep, her mouth had fallen open.

He lay on one side, fully stretched out, and the open-fronted smock was gaping in a rather major strategic area, leaving nothing concerning his masculinity to her imagination.

Selena had turned and, with Domino ahead of her, fled down the stairs. What had she done last night? What had they done? Surely she hadn't had that much to drink. Surely she would have known if he'd tried anything with her body. She'd run into the house and slammed the door behind her, dropping the bolt into place. Leaning against the door, she'd fought to catch her breath.

And her wits.

Hugging herself in the chill morning air, Selena had dropped her head to her chest and closed her eyes. Nothing she could remember indicated that Alex had violated her trust in any way. They had been sitting together, he wanting to talk about something. And then the full day and the fresh air and sunshine and the run home in the rain, and the red wine . . . especially the wine, had taken their toll on her energy.

The last she could remember, she was leaning against his side, relishing his warmth and the strength of his arm around her.

That was all. That had to be all that had happened.

On weak knees, Selena had gone into the kitchen and swallowed two aspirin. In the bedroom, she found her long flannel nightgown on a hook inside the armoire. She'd pulled it on over the smock and dug for socks in a drawer. Thus fortified against her headache and the cool morning, she had pulled back the covers on the bed and climbed between the icy sheets, huddling knees to chest for warmth.

The last thought she'd had before falling asleep again was of the long, mostly naked masculine body whose warmth had sheltered her for most of the night.

Now, Selena stroked the cat and gazed absently into the ashes of the long-dead fire. Behind her, thrown casually over the back of the sofa, was the smock that Alex had worn so good-naturedly. Selena reached for it and brought it to her face, inhaling the scent of the man she had spent the night with. The man who had come to her rescue for Matka's party. The man she had just railed at like a madwoman.

Why?

Holding the smock in a bundle next to her heart, Selena stood up again and went to where he had been studying her paintings. He'd seen something in them he hadn't seen before, something that put a hard gleam in his eye. It was the letter, she was certain of it. He'd asked her point-blank about the messages, as he called them. "What are these messages?"

Selena stared at one of the painted fragments. What were they, indeed? Parts of an ancient letter. Remnants of a curse. Obviously, something Alex wanted badly enough to attempt to copy them behind her back. Selena shivered. Was that his only interest in her? Was he just using her to get access to the letter?

It didn't make sense, but the thought sent a searing pain through her heart.

The alien sound of a telephone ringing jangled Selena out of her dark thoughts. She jumped, unaccustomed to the instrument's intrusion. It rang again, but she did not hurry to answer. Only one person knew her number, and she was in no mood at the moment to speak to Tom

Perkins. He was insistent, however, and on the eighth ring she finally picked it up.

"Hello?"

"A phone won't do you any good unless you use it, you know." Tom's voice grated in her ear.

"What do you want, Tom?" Selena hoped she didn't sound rude, but since the debacle at the inn the night of the Harrington gala, she found it increasingly difficult to be civil to him.

"I've been doing some checking on that Hightower fellow. The client he claims to represent is not anyone known to my contacts in the States."

Selena frowned. "So?"

"So nothing. It may just be some obscure collector out in the boondocks. You never know about the Yanks. I wouldn't hold out much hope that anything will develop on that front, but in case it does, you know to—"

"Yes, Tom," Selena said, disgusted at his greedy possessiveness. "I know to call you right away. Don't worry, I won't go behind your back. You'll get your commission," she added dryly.

"Now, Selena, don't get upset with me. It's just that you . . . all artists, rather, can be rather naive when it comes to sales and promoting your work. That's why I am so insistent that you work only through me. It is in your best interest."

My best interest? Selena doubted her agent gave a damn about her interests. He was a user, and she the usee.

Unfortunately, he was right about one thing. She was naive. And she knew she needed him. At least for a while longer.

"Thanks for the call, Tom. I have to go now."

"Wait, wait before you ring off, love, and do tell me how those commissions are coming along?"

"They're coming, Tom. They're coming. I'll let you

know when I'm finished." Selena hung up on Tom unceremoniously before he could inquire further. She didn't want to give him any hint that she hadn't been able to finish even one of the four.

Leaning back against the sofa, Selena felt her thoughts spiraling downward. She didn't like Tom, and she liked even less what he'd just told her, perhaps because his insinuations only amplified the doubts that were beginning to throw shadows across her mind. Going to the table in front of the fireplace, she picked up the dishes and glasses that loitered there from the indoor picnic of the night before.

A night that seemed almost as if it never happened. Should never have happened.

She carried the dishes to the sink and washed them absently, her thoughts on the well-built American with the hint of a grin ever-present in his deep gray eyes. Who was he and what was he up to? And why in God's name had she let him get so dangerously close?

She stuffed the cork back into the second bottle of wine, distressed to note that it was more than half empty. But on second thought, Selena decided that maybe it had been for the best that she'd had too much to drink and dozed off. Her face grew warm as she recalled the intimacy of their bodies when she'd disentangled herself in the cold, predawn hours. What would have happened last night, she wondered, if she hadn't nodded off?

She swallowed hard. She would have made the Major Mistake. Her skin tingled at the thought, and Selena knew she could no longer trust herself when she was with Alexander Hightower.

And after his strange behavior this morning, she felt she couldn't trust him, either. With any luck, she thought with a deep sigh, her tirade had sent him off for good, and she wouldn't have to worry about Alex Hightower again. Why, she questioned herself over and over again, had she so overreacted when she saw what he was doing? Was it because he seemed so "caught in the act"? What act? Writing down the words from her paintings wasn't exactly grand theft. And why did she give a flip if he wanted those words? Was it because she feared that somehow he would learn about the curse? That it would affect him? Them?

Damn it all, Selena thought, throwing the smock onto the sofa. For once, she wished she had a best friend, someone she could call and talk to about all of this. Someone with whom she could share her concerns about Alexander Hightower. Her concerns, and her dangerous attraction.

But she had no one she could confide in, except her grandmother, and she wasn't sure she could tell Matka about her mixed feelings for Alex. Even though Gran loved her and would understand, still, she was . . . Gran.

And besides, the old woman always related matters of the heart to the curse, and Selena simply didn't want to hear it.

Didn't want to hear it.

She thought about that for a moment, and then realized that despite her efforts and intentions not to allow the Gypsy legend to influence her life and affairs, it was doing so anyway. Hadn't it already infiltrated her work? And now, when she'd finally taken a chance and let a man even tangentially into her life, was the curse, that cursed letter, going to destroy any possibilities she might have had for developing a deeper relationship with Alex?

Selena felt as if she wanted to cry from anger and frustration, and from the strange sense of loss she felt that Alex might indeed be gone for good. Was he?

She didn't want to hear about the curse, but suddenly it was a matter of great urgency that she understand it

better so that she could confront her own irrational
thoughts and fears. She had to talk to Matka.

Today.

And then she remembered her disabled vehicle. Well,
maybe Matka would have to wait until tomorrow.

With a heavy heart Selena thumbed through the directory that came with her telephone and rang the number
of a nearby garage.

Maggie Flynn opened the refrigerator door in the ul-
tramodern, ultrasterile kitchen that had cost her half a
year's salary when she'd remodeled the town house upon
her return from the States. She retrieved a carton of juice
and slammed the door behind her. It had been daylight
since just past five A.M., and she'd had to fight to remain
asleep for the next hour and a half, her mind echoing and
re-echoing the odd phone call from Eleanor Bates the
night before. She knew Eleanor was keen on the debate,
but after the rather strange twist in their conversation,
Maggie knew the shrewd old woman was up to more than
publicity.

Maggie had been too tired to think when Eleanor's call
had come in. She had barely arrived home, even though
it was after seven o'clock. She'd had time only to kick off
her shoes, pour a glass of wine, and shuffle through the
mail. The meeting she'd attended had been aggravating
—a panel of fools, in her estimation, wanting to institute
even more bureaucracy into an already cumbersome re-
porting system for professors. Maggie did not gracefully
abide fools, and had managed to make herself unpopu-
lar, not so much for her opposition to the plan, but rather
for the outspoken, brash manner in which she did it.

Speaking of fools . . . She sipped her juice and gazed
out into her small garden, refocusing her thoughts on the
unexpected phone call from Eleanor Bates. What was
that idiot Alex doing investing in art? He knew nothing

about art and had never shown any interest in it. In fact, she literally had to drag him to that show in London.

That show in London.

The artist named Selena.

Maggie frowned, recalling vaguely the dark-haired woman who had entered the Perkins Galleries that afternoon. Recalling the hungry look on Alex Hightower's face as his eyes followed her from the front of the shop to the back. The look Maggie had craved but never elicited from him during the short months of their relationship.

Her mind crawled back over the past couple of weeks to that dreadful encounter at Harrington House, picking up the pieces of an unwanted memory. A memory that not only included the ugly scene that had taken place between them, but also encompassed the image of Alex on the dance floor with a dark-haired woman Maggie hadn't recognized . . . until this moment.

They were one and the same. The artist. The dance partner.

Selena.

And then all the pieces fell together.

It wasn't art that Alex was after. It was the artist.

Maggie's cheeks burned, and she slung the remainder of the juice into the sink, splashing the immaculate countertop with sticky nectar. She strode into the bathroom and turned the tap on full force, wondering why she gave a damn about Alex's taste in art. Or women. He'd made it clear their affair was over.

If you could call it an affair, she thought bitterly, removing her robe and examining her lithe body in the mirror while the tub filled. From the beginning, she admitted, it had been relatively one-sided. She picked up a brush and ran it vigorously through her hair. She had wanted him far more than he'd seemed to want her, at least at first. They'd shared some good times, but whenever she got too close, he seemed to retreat behind an emotional wall she didn't understand and he chose not to explain.

Maggie Flynn did not regret her fling with Alexander Hightower. In fact, if she were honest with herself, she still wanted him. Desperately. For in spite of his initial reluctance to extend their relationship beyond the boundaries of friendship, once she'd successfully eased him across that barrier, in bed he was the best she'd ever sampled. His body was hard, his lovemaking fierce, the way she liked it.

After she'd taken him to her bed, his earlier reluctance seemed to disappear. In fact, his passion had seemed insatiable. Whatever emotions had held him back before appeared no longer in the way. His need was very great, and she had been there for him, believing that somehow she was helping to heal the old wounds he never spoke about.

But she'd been wrong.

Something had happened. Abruptly and with little explanation, he'd become like a different person. Quite literally overnight. Although she remembered the pain in his eyes and the apology in his voice, she'd never believed it was because it was too soon after his divorce, as he'd told her.

She didn't think it had been because of another woman. And she was positive it wasn't because of anything she had done. The whole thing continued to confound her.

But Maggie detested the fact that she hadn't had the class to walk away and not look back. Instead she'd engaged in schoolgirl tactics to rekindle his affection. She'd written notes. Left small gifts on his doorstep. Even after she returned to England, she'd indulged in her fantasy that one day he would want her back.

But he didn't want her back and never would.

And now it looked as if there *might* be another woman.

Maggie stepped into the bath, which was heaped high with bubbles. What are you up to, Alexander Hightower? she asked silently, massaging the soft foam into the sensitive areas of her body he had once found so enticing.

Later that morning, after her classes were over, Dr. Maggie Flynn shut the door to her office and picked up the large telephone directory for the London metro area. Without hesitation she quickly located the number she sought. She knew intellectually that Alex's newfound interest in art was none of her business.

But her interest at the moment had nothing to do with intellect.

Two rings. She tapped her nails nervously on the hardwood desk in her office.

"Perkins Galleries. How may I help you?"

"I wish to speak with the owner," Maggie said, improvising her inquiry.

"That would be me. Tom Perkins."

"Very well, Mr. Perkins. My name is Maggie Flynn. Dr. Maggie Flynn. I am calling to inquire about the work of an artist I believe you represent, the one who goes by the name of Selena?"

"I do indeed represent her. A marvelous young talent. Have you seen her work?"

"I was able to make it the last day of her exhibit at the end of May. Quite remarkable work. Where is she in residence?"

Tom Perkins paused. "I . . . uh, she's asked me not to give out that information specifically, although I can tell you she's from Yorkshire. You can see the influence of the mists on the moors in her paintings, don't you think?"

"Oh, yes. Certainly."

Yorkshire.

Well, that answered one question. It was geographically possible that Alex could have run across her somewhere near Haworth. Her curiosity was not yet sated, however.

"When I visited your gallery, I was there with a friend whom I understand is very interested in purchasing one of Selena's paintings, and I . . . I was wondering if you could tell me from your records if he has done so? I was considering giving him one as a gift, but I wouldn't want to duplicate—"

"I will be happy to check for you. What is the gentleman's name?"

"Hightower. Dr. Alexander Hightower."

"You know Alexander Hightower?" The man's voice almost squeaked with excitement, and Maggie wondered how Alex had become so notorious in the few short weeks he'd been in England.

"Yes. Yes, I do. Do you?"

"I met him only briefly. But I have been trying to get in touch with him." The gallery owner's voice became more guarded. "In answer to your question, no, he hasn't purchased a painting yet, at least not that I know of. But he has told my client he represents an American collector who is interested."

Alex's antics got curiouser and curiouser.

"An American art collector? Who?"

"Henry H. Bonnell."

"Bonnell!" Maggie almost choked. "Let me get this straight. He claims to represent an art collector named Henry H. Bonnell?"

"That's what he's told Selena. But quite frankly, I haven't been able to locate any known collector in the States by that name. Perhaps you know of him?"

Maggie sank into the large chair behind her desk, not knowing whether to laugh or cry. "Yes," she replied at last. "I know of an American collector named Bonnell. But I didn't know he collected contemporary art."

"Perhaps you could be so kind as to put me in touch

with him. I am afraid your friend is moving very slowly, and if Mr. Bonnell is interested in Selena's letter series, he will have to move quickly. She is almost sold out, and she doesn't plan to paint more in this style once this is complete."

"I doubt if time matters much to Mr. Bonnell, or Selena's paintings. You see, Mr. Perkins, Henry H. Bonnell has been dead for over sixty years."

The fury and accusation Alex had seen in Selena's face had joined forces with his own guilt over copying the messages without her permission and sent him out of her door without an argument. His emotions were in chaos. He wanted fiercely to turn the car around and go back to the studio and find out once and for all what her problem was with those images. If she'd let him in. At the same time, the word fragments he'd copied kept racing through his mind. Keeper. The poetic style. The handwriting.

He accelerated the Jag as fast as he dared over the narrow winding road leading toward the photo lab at Keighley. He was determined to try to make some sense of it all. Alex was mystified by the vehemence of Selena's reaction. Not that he didn't deserve her wrath, but the look on her face had included not only anger toward him for trespassing, as she put it, but also what could best be described as fear. The paintings, he surmised, were more to her than a source of income.

Significantly more.

Painfully more.

But what was it about those images that sent her into such a rage?

His thoughts shifted to the other mystery he'd just uncovered. It was inconceivable that those words Selena had painted in bits and pieces on her canvases could somehow be connected to Emily Brontë, but there was no denying the resemblance of the handwriting. And the words . . . "Keeper," and the poetic nature of the composition . . . He pressed the accelerator still closer to the floorboard.

Alex didn't bother to open the envelope he picked up a few moments later at the photo lab. Either the enlargements were readable or not. If not, there was nothing further they could do to enhance the images, the technician had told him. Alex felt adrenaline shoot through his veins as he made his way as rapidly as possible up the steep incline toward his flat.

Racing up the stairs, he pulled the crumpled sheets of the notepad containing the fragments he'd copied earlier out of his pocket and laid them carefully on the small table next to the packet of photos. He could hear his heart pounding in his chest, feel the nerve endings tingling at his fingertips.

As anxious as he was to see what he could piece together from his clandestine collection of Selena's artwork, he wanted to savor the expectation as well. He gulped two Tylenol for his hangover, took a quick shower, donned fresh clothing, and made coffee, trying to still his mind, get his feelings under control.

But when he finally approached the chore at hand, he found no peace. The image of Selena's accusing face continued to loom in his thoughts, in spite of his efforts to justify his actions. He should have asked her permission. But what if this was the evidence he'd been seeking, something that had never before surfaced concerning Emily's life, and what if Selena had said no?

Hogwash, he replied equally as vociferously. You're only trying to justify your deception.

And yet . . .

Alex brought over a small lamp from the end table and turned it on. He retrieved his strongest magnifying glass, ambivalently hesitant to undertake what he was dying to pursue. His hands shook as he opened the envelope and removed the grainy prints inside.

He worked slowly, painstakingly, as he'd been taught as a scholar, searching each blurry image for the secret it might hold. Most of the prints were totally unreadable, and one of the few readable messages was the same as one he had copied. In all, when he raised his head thirty minutes later, he had three usable images from the photos. These, plus the three he had pirated at Selena's and the one he'd copied from the gallery in Haworth, would have to suffice.

He wiped his brow and leaned back in the rickety chair. Would they be enough to reveal anything that made sense? He wished now he'd copied the one he'd seen at the Perkins Galleries his first day in England.

Alex stood and went to the kitchen to pour another cup of coffee, debating on the next step to take in piecing the puzzle together, when a tiny red light flickered at the edge of his vision. Someone had actually left a message on his answering machine. He stared at it a moment almost in disbelief. He'd purchased the machine on a whim a couple of days after he'd given Selena his phone number, not wanting to take a chance on missing her call.

Which of course never came.

He pressed the Retrieve Messages button, hoping that by some miracle Selena had calmed down, decided to forgive him, and called while he was on his way home.

But the voice on the phone was old, not young, and its message, though short, left no doubt he still had some explaining to do about Henry H. Bonnell.

❧ *Chapter 21* ❧

May 24, 1848

It is that time of year again when all my thoughts turn to a certain gipsie I once met upon the moors. Two winters have passed since I last looked upon his face, and yet it is as clear in my mind as if he sat across this room from me. So much has happened since I talked with him, and I long to tell him the news as concerns Wuthering Heights, Jane Eyre, *and* Agnes Grey. *I wonder what I would do if he were to return, for my longings are desperate and dangerous. If he were to make camp once again in the back ravine, I fear I would become depraved, my unquenched desire is so strong within me. How can I feel this way, when I know the world within is always there for me, and I do not need to know the pleasures of the flesh in reality. I have my imagination, and it has sufficed for nigh unto thirty years. Still, I wonder as I see the full moon creep across the spire of the steeple yonder what it would be like to know love in the arms of this man.*

June 10, 1848

He has returned! My joyous heart is filled to overflowing. My deepest desire has been realized. I have not seen him yet, and I only know of his presence in the area from the mes-

sage he left beneath our rock at the back ravine, which I found yesterday on my rambles with Keeper. He wrote only "emily, i am come back. i miss you." My heart is wild with anticipation and fear.

June 12, 1848

There is much reason for me to fear, I find, now that I have met him once again in person. He stood against the rock outcropping, his long locks whipped by the brisk evening wind. I could scarcely hold myself together as I approached, for the sight of him filled me with such delight. I held my skirts high and ran toward him, and he broke into a radiant smile and ran to me as well. I was in his arms before I realized what happened, and his lips were upon mine with hungry passion. It was as if we were Cathy and Heathcliff, reunited for all time. I should feel shame for what I have done, and yet nothing seems more natural. Is this not the way it should be between men and women? This feeling of utter oneness when we are together? I allowed him to hold me in his embrace for a long while, and I felt comforted and complete for the first time perhaps in my entire life. How can this be wrong?

Attempting to ignore the implications of Eleanor Bates's laconic message, Alex returned to the table where the pieces of the mysterious letter were laid out in an odd assortment of media. He ran his hands through his hair and down the back of his neck. He stared at the words that he seemed driven to connect, regardless of the cost.

The price was becoming steep. First, Selena. Now, his credibility with Eleanor Bates and the Brontë Society.

It had better be worth it, he reflected, picking up a pen and yellow legal pad. Carefully, he copied the words from each specimen onto the paper, making sure they were exactly in the same form as they appeared in the photos. When he had all seven pieces reproduced in a uniform style, he took a pair of scissors and cut them apart again, creating his own jigsaw puzzle.

The morning sun stretched toward noon. Traffic rambled noisily in the street below. A faucet dripped in the bathroom sink. But Alex was oblivious to all but the fascinating narrative taking form in front of him. He had been able to connect all but one piece in some relation to each other, creating a still incomplete picture, but one that was tantalizing in its contents:

> *my days*
> *is failin*
> *fail fast*
> *which I*
> *the pri*
> *with you*
> *behavio*
> *welcom*
> *In death my sh*
> *never to hurt*
> *forgiveness*
> *is of you a*
> *retributio*
> *no hell he*
> *the hell he*
> *I will miss you and the mo*
> *Keeper and the rest, but o*
> *Time. I know there is a bl*
> *opening its ports for me a*
> *gazing Time's wide waters o're, I weary*
> *for that land divi   ere we were*
> *born, where you a   all meet our*
> *Dearest when we di   ffering*
> *   to*

Stunned, Alex went into the bedroom and picked up his well-used paperback copy of Emily's poems. His hands trembled as he opened the book and fumbled through the pages for the familiar lines he sought:

> *But, I'll not fear—I will not weep*
> *For those whose bodies lie asleep:*
> *I know there is a blessed shore,*
> *Opening its ports for me, and mine;*
> *And, gazing Time's wide waters o'er,*
> *I weary for that land divine,*
>
> *Where we were born—where you and I*
> *Shall meet our dearest, when we die;*
> *From suffering and corruption free,*
> *Restored into the Deity.*
>   —Emily Brontë

Alex sat very still for a very long time. His face was burning and his heartbeat was fast and irregular. There was no doubt the words on Selena's canvases, or at least some of them, had been penned by Emily Brontë.

The evidence was in front of him in black and white.

The question that remained was more difficult: Was this message something Emily had written, or had Selena or whoever penned the letter only used a fragment of Emily's poem to illustrate a point?

Either way, Alex had to know what the rest of the message conveyed. And who wrote it.

That it was despondent was clear. That it spoke of death and hell and retribution could also mean it spoke of . . . suicide.

Emily's suicide?

Good God.

Alex paced to the window and back to the table. He glanced at the telephone. He rubbed the back of his neck again. He thought of Selena. He thought of Eleanor Bates. He thought of a lonely, depressed young woman taking her own life a hundred fifty years ago in the old stone Parsonage less than a block from where he stood.

He thought of the cryptic message that lay in pieces in front of him.

And then he thought of an old woman named Matka.

An old woman who had invited, no, insisted that he come back to see her.

Alone.

In reference to the letter her granddaughter painted in all of her work.

Alex looked at his watch. It was not yet one o'clock. It took an hour to drive to Leeds. He had plenty of time. Carefully, he taped the pieces of the message together and slipped it into the envelope from the photo lab. Then without another moment's hesitation, he snagged his umbrella from its hook and hurried out the back door.

"She should just be getting up from her nap." The volunteer led Alex down the shining corridor toward Matka's room. "Was she expecting you?"

"Sometime, but probably not today."

The woman turned and smiled at Alex, glancing appreciatively at the bouquet of flowers he carried. "Maybe you'd better give me a minute alone with her. A lady likes to look presentable when a gentleman comes to call, you know."

Alex leaned against the wall in the hallway outside the door, nervous energy screaming through his body. This was crazy. The whole idea of Selena's painted message having something to do with Emily Brontë seemed so far out it was ludicrous. And yet, there was no doubt whoever wrote that letter had used in it a portion of Emily's poem known as *"Faith and Despondency."* And whoever wrote it did so in a handwriting that distinctly resembled Emily's.

The coincidences were too incredible to ignore.

He wished he was standing in Selena's studio instead of outside her grandmother's room at the nursing home. He'd rather get his answers from her, but from her violent reaction to his snooping and his questions earlier in the day, he surmised it would be a futile effort.

And he knew something about the letter caused her deep and personal pain. As badly as he wanted to know about the painted fragments, he wouldn't, couldn't, cause Selena pain.

And so here he was, standing like a suitor outside a sweetheart's door.

Only it wasn't the sweetheart he was courting. It was her grandmother.

Crazy.

The volunteer came out of Matka's room and held the door open for him, jarring him back into the moment. "She's waiting for you."

Alex returned the volunteer's smile and went into Matka's small room. The old woman was seated in the armchair with her feet propped on an ottoman. Shafts of afternoon sunlight streamed through the window behind her, brushed across her shoulders and fell into her lap where her hands lay, deformed and virtually useless. Next to her, in the corner, a tall round table held a number of small curios, a lamp, and an arrangement of dried flowers and herbs, all organized on top of a large lace doily, yellowed with age.

She looked up at him with unreadable eyes, scrutinizing him slowly, purposefully.

"Sit down," she said at last, indicating a chair on the other side of the table.

Instead, Alex handed her the flowers. "I brought these for you."

"Why?" Her voice was gruff, and her deep-set eyes harbored other, unspoken questions.

Alex donned his famous grin. "Because I always bring flowers to the ladies."

She looked at him noncommittally. "Why don't y' put 'em in tha' pitcher there by the sink? I can't do nothin' wi' these hands anymore."

He arranged the blossoms and placed the stainless steel pitcher on her bureau, hoping he hadn't made a mistake in coming here. "How's this?"

Matka slowly moved her head up and down, never taking her eyes off him. "Y'be here about the letter?"

Alex took the seat she had indicated before, leaning forward and resting his forearms on the denim of his jeans. He was on fire to know the message contained in the letter, and who wrote it, but even more so to understand the impact of those words on Selena. With any luck, this old woman would shed some light on both. He massaged his temples and looked up at Selena's grandmother with tired eyes.

"Yes. The letter, and more."

Again she seemed to size him up with her gaze. "What more?"

"About Selena. I must know—"

"About Selena y' must ask Selena. I canna help y' there. T'would be an intrusion int' her life, would t'not?"

"What if she won't talk to me?"

Matka's head jerked up. "Won't talk to y'? Why'nt she not?"

"I'm not sure. But I think it has something to do with the letter."

Matka looked at him, a knowing, mysterious smile spreading slowly across her face. "Perhaps I can help you after all. Here. Hand me that," she said, indicating a large, clear, crystal globe that rested on the arched backs of three miniature bronze dragons who nested amidst the antique lace on the table.

Alex reached for the object, which seemed to emit a soft golden glow where it was touched by the sunlight. It was cool and round and heavy in his hand. He placed it in her lap, wondering if she could clutch it. The ball balanced precariously in the palms of the twisted hands, but Matka didn't seem concerned.

She stared into the globe. "'Tis been a while since I give a look in here," she said in a low voice. "Might take me some time."

Alex suddenly realized with dismay the old Gypsy was gazing into the crystal ball to tell his fortune. He groaned silently and remembered Selena's warning that Matka might surprise him with her Gypsy mumbo-jumbo. Still, he didn't dare interrupt her. Maybe if he humored her, she would eventually get around to telling him what he wanted to know.

"I see many things about your life," Matka croaked. "You've been unlucky in love yourself, haven't you?"

Alex blinked. "Uh, well, yes, I suppose you could say that."

"Twice."

Alex hesitated. "Yes. Twice," he admitted at last, wondering how she knew that. He remained silent, allowing her to continue the hunt for his story. It was her way, he decided, of checking out his background.

"I see y' surrounded by books and papers. Do y' be a writer?"

"Teacher."

"More than a teacher. I see y' be searchin' for somethin'."

Alex leaned forward. The old woman was remarkable. "Yes, actually, I am." He watched the crone bend even closer to the ball, then slowly raise her head, her dark gaze boring into him.

"Selena's got what y' want."

In more ways than you know, Grandmother, Alex thought.

She returned her attention to the ball, concentrating so long he thought for a moment she'd forgotten what she was doing. "Yes, Selena's got somethin' y' want. But it isn't the letter."

Startled, Alex frowned. "I don't know what you mean."

The old woman's face crinkled into a smile. "Y've fallen in love with her, ha'nt y'?"

Alex didn't answer, but he felt his face grow crimson, and Matka nodded with satisfaction. "Well, let's see what comes up about tha'." She resumed her contemplation of the crystal ball. "I see . . . possibilities for you with Selena. Hope. But there's much work t' be done."

Alex stared at the old woman, astounded. She had seen the other things about him clearly enough. Had she seen a truth that even he didn't know? Had he fallen in love with Selena? "What kind of work?" he asked, alarmed.

Matka raised her head. "Y' must know about the letter and the curse," she said matter-of-factly. "And then y' must do somethin' about 'em. Here . . ." She attempted to raise the ball toward him. "Take this and put it back on the table."

He did as she asked as if in a daze, his blood pounding in his ears.

"Now," Matka said, smoothing her skirts as best she could with her crippled hands, "I'll tell y' a tale, and listen well, for in't y' might find all that y' seek." She leaned back in the chair, her eyes seeing something far away and long ago.

"There once was a Gypsy king who lived in the land of Wales. Abram Wd be his name. His wife was the famous Black Ellen. Together with their sons and daughters and grandsons and granddaughters and great-grandsons and great-granddaughters, they moved about the country-side, campin' on the banks of Tal-y-llyn lake or the river Alwen.

"Rich he was, Abram Wd, rich in those things tha' count. He had not so much money, but always sufficient, as the land provided for his every need. No, this Abram Wd was rich in family. He and Black Ellen had many, many children, who also had many, many children. Rich they all were, too, in the Romany tradition. Tied together by the unwritten laws tha' all held sacred.

"Now, all was well with the descendants of old Abram and Black Ellen, until one day the eldest son of the eldest son, harkin' down the line directly from the first king o' the Gypsies, broke with the sacred law. Lo! His name was Mikel, and he was a trader of horses. He rode the countryside, capturin' the wild ponies and tamin' them before takin' them to market.

"Now Mikel goes into a faraway land, as the horses are more plentiful there. He stays away longer than he ever has before, and his old father falls ill. So they send his brothers far and wide to find him, and when he is brought home, he is half lame from a fall from his horse. 'Father,' he says, 'My life was saved by a miracle.'

" 'What miracle?' says his father. 'A *Gorgio* woman healed me, Father.' " Now, the Rom be wantin' no more t' do with *Gorgio* than *Gorgio* with Rom, and women, too, have been thought impure by some Romany traditions. So Mikel's father was stern with his son. 'Y' must forget it,' he commanded. 'Y' must go into tha' country no more. Trouble will only follow. And now as I lay dyin', I must be comforted to know my eldest son is here to become the new king.' "

Matka paused and cleared her throat. "Can y' bring me a glass of water, son?"

Anxious for her to go on, Alex hurriedly poured some

water into a glass and waited for what seemed like forever for the old woman to raise the glass to her lips,
drink, and return it to him. At last she continued.

"So the old king dies, and Mikel is named new King o'
the Gypsies. Winter passes, and spring, and Mikel grows
restless to ride again for the wild ponies. His lameness is
gone now, and he is in full health and strength. He rides
away, and again he is gone for many weeks. 'Don't worry
tha' I am gone so long this time,' he tells his family. 'I
ride far and wide, for I must collect enough horses to
count at market.'

"Now, when the heather bloomed purple upon the
high moors, Mikel returned home. He brought many
horses, and sold them for a pretty price. There was much
gladness and rejoicin'. But his family sees he is changed.
He knows new words. He can even read an' write, something few Gypsies had ever learned until then. 'Where
did you learn these things?' his brothers ask him around
the campfire. 'They were given me by a spirit on the
moors,' he replies, laughing. 'Ask me no more, for I will
tell y' nothing further.'

"The next year, he does not go to the moors on the far
side of the mountains, for there is strife and disputes
among the men. Mikel stays with the caravan, but he is
cross and easily vexed. But come the following summer,
he returns again to the far country, and again his family
enjoys good fortune from his ponies. When he returns,
however, he seems strangely changed, and his brothers
fear he is enchanted, or his mind is weak. Now, Mikel
does a strange thing. It is the end o' summer, and the
ponies have all been sold. It is the time to make preparations for the winter ahead. But, no, Mikel does not do
this. 'Do my part extra,' he tells his brothers, 'and I will
pay you well.' And he leaves even as the snow begins to
fall.

"The family waited and waited for Mikel's return, until

his brothers could bear it no more. 'I will ride to find him,' said the one who had found him before. And so off he rode, and he went straightaway to the same high moor, and there was Mikel, hovered shiverin' by a camp-fire. His heart was heavy and his mind was numb. He spoke little, but offered no fight when his brother urged him to return home.

"There he remained for the rest of his life. Never again did he ride away for the ponies. He spent much time alone in the woods, and became ill-tempered when approached at the wrong time. At last, he seemed some-what better, and he married a beautiful woman of the tribe. She bore one child, a son, but after that, Mikel could stand no more to look upon her or his son. Many believed he had gone mad, and indeed, it so seemed, until one day he brings his wife and son into his wagon.

" 'I have wronged you both greatly,' he says, and he is in despair. 'I have deceived you even as I tried to deceive myself tha' I am still of the Rom. But I have not felt of the Rom for many years, since the days I traveled to catch the wild ponies beyond the mountains. I met there a *Gorgio* woman who healed me and taught me many things. I loved her and became one with her. I begged her to marry me, vowing I would forsake my Gypsy blood, but she sent me away. From that moment, I no longer wanted to be of the Rom, nor was I in my heart. I did not know the sorrow my actions would bring, but soon a curse befell me, a curse so strong it killed the one I loved.' "

Matka wheezed, and Alex handed her the water glass again, her last words still echoing in his ears:

. . . *a curse so strong it killed the one I loved.*

The old Gypsy resumed her tale. "Mikel shows his woman a letter, but she cannot read, and so he tells her what is in it. 'She was with child . . . my child, when she fell ill. This message she left for me beneath the rock, and this grief and burden I have carried in my heart for many years. I returned and in time tried again to become of the Rom, but I cannot. I have betrayed our law, and I have brought a curse upon my house. I have not made you happy, wife, nor have I been a good father. I fear tha' forever our line is fated to be unlucky in love.'

"So he stated, and so it has been. He died shortly thereafter, and the letter and its curse were passed on to his son. It is tradition, and a reminder to the Rom to respect and keep sacred our heritage. There has been no escaping the curse. In each generation since, there have been many tragic losses the likes of which had never visited the family Wd before Mikel's trespass against the ways of the Rom.

"In my own time it was not me, but my brother, who was cursed with a loveless life. Selena's father and mother as well suffered until death.

"And now," Matka concluded with a heavy sigh, "it is Selena's turn."

❧ *Chapter 22* ❧

A lex stared at the old woman in disbelief. "You can't be serious," he said at last, his mind reeling. "I mean, this is the twentieth century."

Matka looked up at him sharply. "Don't underestimate the power of this curse," she snapped. "'Tis likely t' affect your life as well, if you love Selena, that is."

Alex doubted that any such curse had power over him, and he didn't want to think about whether or not he loved Selena. So he turned his thoughts in another direction. "This ancestor, Mikel, where did he live? How long ago did this all happen?"

"He lived about a hundred and fifty years ago, according t' the tales tha' were handed down t' me. He was a Welsh Gypsy, and he lived wherever the Gypsies camped in the forests and fields."

"And he traveled afar to capture the wild ponies," Alex said, thinking out loud. "Do you suppose he might have traveled as far as Yorkshire?"

Matka's eyes narrowed. "I suppose it'd be possible. What's on your mind?"

"You saw there in your crystal ball that I am a teacher, and that Selena has something I want. Well, you are right on both counts. But in addition to being a teacher, I am also a student of history. I have been studying the life of a woman who lived in Haworth about a hundred fifty years ago and wrote many poems and a novel."

"One o' them Brontës?"

"Emily Brontë."

"What does tha' have to do with the curse?"

"Maybe nothing. But I have reason to believe that Selena has copied part of one of Emily's poems into the letter fragments she puts in every painting. But I haven't been able to get her to talk to me rationally about her work. Every time I ask questions about the contents of the letter fragments, she gets . . . very upset."

Alex reached for the envelope he'd laid on the bed. "This morning I was in her studio, and I was able to copy a few of the fragments, although when she saw what I was doing, she got furious and threw me out." Taking care not to loosen the tape holding the message together, he slipped it out of the envelope and placed it on Matka's lap. "I have managed to piece together this much," he said, then added carefully, "What I want from Selena is the rest of the message. I want to know where it came from, and who wrote it. I'm curious why she painted it into her work, and why," he added, "she won't talk to me about it."

"Hand me those glasses," Matka said, "and help me put 'em on my nose." She stared at the words for a long while, saying nothing. Then she looked up at Alex. "These words are the same as in the letter tha' carries the curse."

"Does Selena have the letter?"

Matka shook her head. "I gave her a copy of it once, but I thought she'd thrown it away. Because she so strongly denied her belief in the curse, I never trusted tha' she would not break Romany law by destroying the letter. I could not take tha' chance, for she doesn't understand the fate tha' would befall her for doing so."

"What fate?"

The expression on the old woman's face grew dark. "Oh, a terrible fate. The curse must be lifted before the letter can be destroyed."

Matka's fatalism troubled Alex more than he wanted to admit. "But surely the curse can be lifted?"

"Mikel brought down a curse upon his family because in his heart he left the Rom. He left the Rom because he wanted to marry a *Gorgio* woman. 'Twas the curse tha' killed the *Gorgio* woman. Just before he died, Mikel told his wife tha' the only way for the curse t' be lifted was for the *Gorgio* family to grant forgiveness for his reckless actions," she said. "But tha' has been impossible, since no one knew who the *Gorgio* woman was." Matka's eyes pierced his own. "Until now."

Neither spoke for a long moment, then Matka added, "Y' know her, don't y'?"

Alex leaned back with an audible sigh, overwhelmed by the possibilities. "I don't know anything for certain. I have suspicions, but until I can see the entire letter, have the paper and ink analyzed, and the handwriting, it would be impossible for me to prove what we both suspect."

The old woman stared at him, as if contemplating a decision. "In the crystal ball, I saw something else," she said at last. "I saw hope tha' the curse might be lifted. Perhaps y' be tha' hope." She reached for the small drawer under the lace covering on the table, but her fingers were unable to grasp the metal pull. "Help me wi' this, will y'?"

Alex opened the drawer and watched with growing excitement as she painstakingly retrieved a yellowed piece of paper that was the sole content of the drawer. Her hands quivered as she unfolded it slowly, slowly. Alex yearned to reach out and accomplish the task for her, his mind screaming to know if this was the evidence he had been searching for that would prove that Emily did indeed take her own life. But he held his eagerness in check, waiting respectfully for Matka to make her move.

"If I entrust y' with this letter, will y' be able t' prove who wrote it?" she said at last, looking up from the paper with brooding eyes.

Blood sang in Alex's ears. He was in agony to examine what Matka held in her hand. He could see from where he sat across from her that the handwriting on the paper was tiny and cramped. Familiar. Brontë.

But he couldn't promise what she was asking him to deliver.

"I can only try," he said at last. "I don't know for sure. . . ."

She held it out to him. "'Tis our only hope. And take care tha' nothin' happens to it. If it be destroyed before the curse is removed, someone will die a terrible death."

Alex stared at her, thinking of the responsibility she was placing in his hands. Even if he didn't believe in the power of a curse, she did. And if something happened by accident to destroy that letter, Alex was afraid the old woman would somehow fulfill its fatal legend.

He also needed to explain to her that even if the letter proved to have been written by Emily Brontë, there would be no way to petition forgiveness of her descendants, for there were none, but before Alex could say a word, the door flew open and Selena raged into the room.

"What the hell are you doing here?" she demanded, her face flushed and eyes wide with anger.

Alex jumped out of his chair. How did she know he was here? He groped for words, something that would secure his innocence of wrongdoing in her eyes. "I came to get some answers that you wouldn't give me, Selena." Truth was easier than fiction, he found, even though he risked making her even angrier. If that was possible.

"Answers? Or nonsense? I don't know what you're up to, Alex, but you have no business invading my privacy, or my grandmother's. So just get out."

"I was invited here," he pointed out, unable to rise to an argument with her. Matka's story had explained many things to him, and though he was no psychologist, he understood, even if Selena didn't, that the so-called curse might have more influence over her life than she would ever admit.

Selena looked from Alex to her grandmother, who sat watching them serenely, a small smile playing on her lips. Alex saw Selena clench her fists tightly in frustration. Then she turned on him again.

"Get out," she hissed. "Just get out!"

Alex picked up the envelope and slid his homemade jigsaw puzzle back inside, but made no move to take the letter from where it lay in Matka's lap. He turned to the old woman.

"It's been a delightful visit," he said, bending to kiss her cheek. "But I think it's time for me to go now. I will help in any way I can," he added, looking into her clouded eyes, "but I can do nothing without . . . uh, certain tools."

Matka only nodded but made no move to give him the letter. "Perhaps in time," she said.

July 7, 1848

I have attempted to tame my passion, but I fear that door has been opened and the beast unleashed. There may be no turning back, nor am I certain that I wish it to be so. I must only be very careful not to reveal my secret. I have spent my lifetime protecting my privacy, and there is reason to believe I can continue this practice, a most necessary endeavor where Mikel is concerned.

Charlotte and Anne have impulsively left for London, where they intend to reveal their feminine identities to

*George and William Smith. There is much confusion, cre-
ated by Newby, that Currer Bell is the only novelist, publishing under three names, and Charlotte is in a furor to clear
the situation. I have forbidden either to mention my name
or that I am a woman. I want no part of their notoriety. I
know not where I wish my future to lie at the moment. Anne
has already published her second novel,* The Tenant of
Wildfell Hall, *and Charlotte is finishing up a work she calls
"Shirley," while I continue to battle my way through a work
I no longer have an interest in.*

*My interest is in discovering the outside world, with Mi-
kel's tutelage. Once I showed him how to read and write;
now he is showing me things secret and forbidden. I have at
last kissed a man, a true and vigorous kiss, and in so doing
have changed my life forever. I have no illusions that there
is any future for me with this gipsie, but I have no intentions
of having a future with any other man, either. This is an
interlude at best. Perhaps I am sinful, but because I believe
not in sin, how can that be? I am hurting no one, and I am
learning at last what it is to be a woman.*

July 30, 1848

*It is my birthday, and Mikel has made me a special
present of polished rocks tied in a kerchief. I hold them in
my hand as I write this, their presence cool and comforting
in his absence. I shall sleep with them beneath my pillow.
He fried up a fat rabbit, which we shared by the campfire.
(Keeper is as in love with my gipsie friend as I, especially
when Mikel throws the scraps his way.) We lay upon his
cloak on the hillside beneath the stars tonight, giving them
fantastical names such as my brother and sisters and I used
to do in Angria and Gondal. I began to tell him Gondal
stories, for I was afraid if I did not keep talking, I would
succumb to the desire that flamed through me as I lay next
to him. He leaned on one elbow, and with his free hand
touched me, here, and I could no longer speak. He leaned*

*into me and kissed me, parting my lips with his, letting his
hand roam across my body as he roams the wild moors on
his pony. I must write this, although I live in terror that it
will be discovered. I must write it, just as I had to write
W.H., for in the writing I gain some semblance of control
over feelings I do not understand. I had no wish to cease the
madness that had overtaken us, even though I am terrified
of that passion he stirs within me. Tonight we did cease, but
I know that if we are together in such a manner again, there
may be no such escape.*

August 21, 1848
*It has happened. My most terrible fear and my most
rapturous desire. I know now the secrets of love, for right or
wrong. Oh, such fools we are to think we can control the
urge of nature, for that rashness to which I have succumbed
is nothing more than the force of nature moving upon itself.
I can hardly write of what I have done, for there are no
words to describe the quenching of that secret fire which has
burned so long in my dreams. I have experienced true freedom today, in a bed of soft grass upon the moor, beneath a
sky so blue the forget-me-not would pale against it. It is a
freedom unlike any I have dreamt of, a freedom that released my spirit to join its counterpart in the Invisible. But
to experience such limitlessness, I had to relinquish the control I have always held so dear. It was not such a high price
after all, at least in that temporary moment, for the passion
of two souls unleashed together cannot be controlled. Mikel
speaks of love, and I myself have discovered another aspect
of the love I have held for him since the days I nursed his
injuries by the beck. There is no hope for any tomorrow
between us, and I expect none but the memory we will be
able to share when he is once again called back to his
people in Wales and I return to my own dear family who
know nothing of this secret.*

September 1, 1848

Mikel has astounded me by declaring he wishes us to wed! Never did I encourage such a thought, for it is impossible. He is a gipsie, born to wander and to live a life of such freedom that it would frighten even me. I am content to find my freedom within, while he is destined to be free in the outside world. He claims he no longer feels part of his tribe, or of his culture, so changed is he by our love. I am saddened at his words, for I never meant this to happen. I love Mikel, but I am content with what we have had and I want no more. I cannot marry this man. My own family would desert me, and that is a price I am not willing to pay, even if he is. I wish he had not urged this upon me. It is not my wish to wed, Mikel nor any other man. I must make my feelings clear when we meet tonight. He must return to his people in Wales. He must! And perhaps he must never come back to me.

September 15, 1848

The air grows chill even as the purple heather nods and dances upon the moors, and today my heart grows chill as well, for I bade farewell to my own true love. Oh, how can I bear this anguish? It would seem the freedom I found in his love has now bound me to the most tormenting agony. No torture I could have dreamt of in the dungeons of Gondal can compare to the misery of seeing my beloved ride away to the west, stopping before he disappeared over the erest of the moors to wave one last salute my way. But it is as it should be, although we are both in torment. He pressed me until the end to marry him, saying we could run away, move to America, not knowing how ill I fare whenever I leave Haworth. I am a prisoner here, and he is my freedom. To send him away was the most difficult decision I have been called upon to make in this lifetime. I sent away my freedom, my love, my life, but in so doing, I regained my world within once more. Will he return to the moors when spring-

*time makes the world alive again? I do not know, nor do I
know if I wish it so. The world within is safer, less compli-
cated.*

"Be careful of that man, Gran," Selena warned, hoist-
ing herself up onto the tall hospital bed, glad now that
the mechanic had been able to repair the Land Rover in
such a short time. If she hadn't walked in on Alex and
Matka, there was no telling what he would have cajoled
out of her trusting grandmother.

Since talking to Tom earlier in the day, Selena had let
her anger build up a healthy head of steam. Where once
she'd thought Alex might have been using a pretended
interest in her work to get to her sexually, now she wasn't
sure it wasn't the other way around. She didn't understand Alex's strange behavior in sneaking the copies of
her word pictures, but his guilty exit from her studio had
generated all kinds of questions. Maybe he was some
kind of crook, although Selena was mystified as to what
he was after. Whatever it was, seeing the vintage Jaguar
in the nursing home parking lot had been the last straw.
Now he was conniving to get whatever it was he wanted
from her grandmother. Maybe he was selling something.
She'd heard of people preying on innocent elderly people.

Then Matka spoke, her voice barely above a whisper.
"He lóves y'."

Selena, startled out of her suspicious accusations, was
sure she hadn't heard correctly. "What?"

Her grandmother raised her head, a satisfied smile on
her lips. "He loves y', daughter. I saw't in the ball, and in
his face as well."

Selena scowled. "He's just using you, Gran. He knows
what you want to hear. Did he try to sell you something?"

Matka let out a low "harrumph," her version of a

laugh. "No. He's not selling anythin'." Then she trained her clouded gaze upon her granddaughter and said, "You're not angry at him, y' know. Y'be angry at yourself."

"What are you talking about? Have you lost your mind?"

Matka snorted. "No. In fact, I think I be seein' things quite clearly today."

Selena stared at her grandmother, knowing that Matka's words, as usual, cut to the heart of the matter. It was true. She wasn't angry with Alex. She was angry with herself that she wasn't able to get past her own irrational fears and for once act like a normal human being. Her anger at his snooping was just an excuse to send him away.

Safely away.

She was unable to contain the tears that suddenly sprang to her eyes and spilled down her cheeks. Never had she been this frustrated or miserable. And never had she wanted a man like this, nor been so afraid of the consequences.

"Oh, Gran, I don't know what's the matter with me. I'm so . . . so confused. I want to believe what you're telling me, but if that's how he feels, why hasn't he said it to me?"

"I suspect he may not know it yet himself," she answered with a shrewd smile.

"He frightens me, Gran."

"Do y' love him?"

Selena turned her head to see a golden halo of sunshine surrounding her grandmother's silhouette against the window. Matka, her guardian angel. Selena was once again a little girl, running to the safety and shelter of this wise woman. "I don't know what being in love means," she said with a sob that ended in a hiccup. "You know how I have always said I would never fall in love."

"There comes a time, Selena, when y' have t' outgrow the hurts of your childhood. What happened t' y' then, and whatever went wrong between your mother and father, y' must learn t' let them go so y' can get on about your life."

Selena sat up again. "How can you say that when you have spent your life believing in a stupid curse that's been handed down for generations? Shouldn't you learn to let that go, too?"

Matka looked at her thoughtfully. "So tis the curse what y' be afraid of?"

"No," Selena retorted quickly. "I don't believe in the curse, you know that."

"But y' be afraid of somethin'?"

Selena hesitated, then retorted, "Yes, damn it, I am afraid. But not of the curse. I'm . . . I'm afraid of losing all that I have worked for. Afraid of giving up my independence. Afraid that all men might be . . . might be . . . like my father." She broke down again and cried like a lost child.

"I can't get up n' come t' y', daughter," Matka said. "But my lap be here for your head, if y've come t' me for comfort."

And like a child, Selena slid off the bed and crumpled into a heap at Matka's feet. She rested her head in the old woman's lap and let the tears fall.

"What makes y' think this one be like your father?" Matka asked at last, stroking Selena's dark hair with her gnarled fingers. "Has he shown y' any sign o' violence?"

Selena shook her head.

"Has he ta'en too much t' drink?"

Again Selena shook her head, knowing it was she, not Alex, who had tried to drown her fears the night before in a wine bottle.

"Do y' want t' love him?"

Selena thought about that for a long moment, then

raised a tearstained face to her grandmother. "I . . . I don't know. I think so."

Matka wiped Selena's face with a soft handkerchief from the table. "Sometimes, daughter, we can't always know tha' what we be doin' is right. We have t' take a chance. The best we can do is listen t' what be deep inside. Y' be afraid t' let yourself fall in love? What if fallin' in love be the best thing for y'? Would y' not be makin' a mistake not t' listen t' your heart?"

Selena had never been very good at overcoming Matka's sensible arguments. And her grandmother's words released her from the terrible weight of doubt and fear she'd been carrying since kissing Alex the night of the party.

"What should I do, Gran?"

"Trust yourself. Go to him, if you think he is the man for you."

"I've acted like such a fool," Selena said, half to herself. "What if he doesn't want me anymore?"

"Do y' really believe that?"

Selena gave Matka a small smile. "No."

"There is somethin' y' must do, however, if y' want t' take every precaution t' protect yourself from the curse."

"Gran! I keep telling you, I don't believe in the curse."

"Y' don't. And y' do. Do I not be right?"

Selena looked away from her grandmother, into the shadowy corners of her own mind. Yes, she admitted finally, she feared the curse. It was that fear that plagued her every working hour and had caused her so much agony in her painting. And, she supposed, it was a sub-conscious fear of the curse that was nagging at her now. Taunting her. Convincing her not to get involved with Alexander Hightower, no matter what she felt for him.

"Okay," she said, turning to look at Matka again. "You win. Yes, I'm . . . I'm uneasy because of all the horror stories you've told me about the curse. But I truly think it's only a legend. How can such a thing hold power over people's lives?"

"Who knows how the spirits work? But I think I have found a way t' break the spell, once and for all."

Selena's heart skipped a beat. Never had she heard such an idea out of Matka's usually pragmatic but pessimistic mouth. "How?"

Matka pulled the worn and tattered piece of paper from beneath the one hand that never moved from her lap anymore. The hand that had cradled Selena's head while the other stroked it. "The time has come for me t' give this t' y'. In so doin', I be honorin' Romany law, and as much as it hurts me t' do it, I also be passin' along t' y' the curse of the line of Mikel Wd. But daughter, there is more," she said in reaction to Selena's shaking head. "I also give y' a way for t' break the curse."

"You've always told me there was no way out," Selena reminded her grandmother, curious at the old woman's change of mind.

"Your young man, the one y' love, holds the key. Here. Take this. Give it t' him. He can free y' and all your children and grandchildren t' come."

Selena decided that Matka had truly taken leave of her senses. "What does Alex know about breaking curses?" Her eyes narrowed. "And what does Alex know about this curse, Gran? What have you told him?"

"I have told him all. And I be tellin' y' now, if y' love him, give him the letter. He knows what he must do."

Matka motioned to the crystal ball on the table. "Take that, too, daughter. Y'll know when to use it. And now, I'm getting hungry. Will y' wheel me t' tea on your way out?"

ꕥ *Chapter 23* ꕥ

Alex sat behind the wheel of the Jaguar in the parking lot of the nursing home, his heart slamming against his rib cage. He drummed his fingers on the dash, trying to slow his thoughts enough to make some sense of everything that had happened in the last two hours.

Matka's tale intrigued him, and his mind reeled when he considered the implications of both the story and the letter he'd caught only a tantalizing glimpse of. If the woman involved was who he suspected it to be, it would be one of the most important literary discoveries of the century.

He'd been agonizingly disappointed at having to leave that letter behind in Matka's lap, but that did not hurt nearly as much as being vigorously shown the door twice in one day by Selena. Could he do nothing right?

"Damn it!" he swore, and struck the steering wheel with the palm of his hand. Sweat trickled down Alex's back in the warm afternoon as he reviewed his options for the future. As far as Selena was concerned, he doubted he had any. And as for the letter, unless Selena talked her grandmother out of giving it to him, Alex was uncertain what to do with it once he had possession of it. The only thing he was sure of was that if the letter's

existence became known, a flock of literary and merce-
nary vultures would descend upon it at once.

That Emily Brontë might have had a lover, or at least a
boyfriend, was a continuing topic of speculation among
Brontë scholars, especially in connection with the issue
of the unexplainable passion in *Wuthering Heights.* But to
date, no one had been able to produce a single shred of
evidence to substantiate the notion.

And now this.

That not only did Emily have a lover, but that she also
became pregnant by him! It was unthinkable. Inconceivable.

Sacrilegious almost.

But it was the strongest motive Alex could think of for
her to have taken her own life.

Emily would not have considered suicide immoral, for
spiritually she believed that everything was Eternal, and
death was simply a doorway back into the One. It would
have been, Alex believed, far preferable to her than the
alternative—the terrible shame that public knowledge of
her predicament would have brought to the family she
loved so much.

And her choice of weapons, willful self-neglect, would
have created no suspicion from her sisters. Emily had
often used personal deprivation as a means of getting her
way. Self-imposed fasting had brought her home from
more than one hated boarding school. And it was how
she had eased Heathcliff into the hereafter to be reunited with his beloved Catherine.

Although the thought of Emily taking a Gypsy as a
lover sounded at first like an improbably romantic notion, the more he considered it, the more feasible it
seemed. Emily, who frequently sought freedom on the
moors, could have encountered a roving horse trader.
Alex recalled the story of her finding a wounded hawk
and nursing it back to health.

What if she'd found a wounded man?

She would probably have called a doctor. But there was no record anywhere of such an incident, or at least none that had been found. Perhaps he should have been going through old medical records in Haworth instead of Brontëana.

However, in Matka's tale the Gypsy told his father he had been healed by a *"Gorgio* woman," not a doctor. Would Emily have had the skill? Alex knew little of Emily's medical abilities, but he did know that she and her sisters often accompanied Patrick Brontë and most likely the village doctor when they visited the sick.

Alex ran his hands through his hair, trying to decide what to do next. He desperately needed someone to talk to about all this, to advise him on proper procedures. But who? He wasn't about to let it out, even among Brontë scholars, that such a document had been unearthed until he could substantiate its authenticity. If he made premature claims only to have it later proven to be a fake or written by someone other than Emily, he could kiss his credibility, and his career, good-bye.

Not only that, but if it was the real item, it would be worth a bloody fortune. Security became a sudden and real concern. He thought of the wilted, fragile paper lying crumpled beneath Matka's twisted hands. It was as safe there as anywhere, he supposed, as long as no one knew it existed.

But if he was lucky enough to convince Matka and Selena to release it, when it came to light he must make certain that it remained in the stewardship of legitimate and reputable trustees who would oversee the stringent forensic and academic analysis it would have to undergo to be proven authentic.

He knew the academic world only too well. If word of the letter's existence leaked out, professional jealousy would pit scholar against scholar, school against school,

museum against museum, for the privilege of conserving
the artifact. Ownership would come into question, although undoubtedly it belonged to Matka at the moment.

Would she see its historic and literary significance and
trust him with it, or would she fall prey to the offers she
would invariably receive from representatives of private
collectors? If it fell into the hands of the private sector,
Alex thought with dismay, it could be lost again to a
wealthy collector, who, unlike Henry Bonnell, would
likely see no reason to share it with the rest of the world.

Alex felt almost sick to his stomach at the thought. He
must know someone he could trust, someone who, out of
respect for the Brontës, would keep Emily's letter a secret until it was proven to be an artifact.

If indeed it was Emily's letter.

Only one name came to mind.

He placed a quick phone call, and thirty minutes later
Alex rang the doorbell of a stately stone mansion in a
prestigious neighborhood in Leeds. A uniformed woman
opened the door and ushered him in with a quiet smile.

"Follow me." She led him down a wide, mahogany-
paneled, portrait-encrusted hallway and indicated for
him to enter the parlor. "Ms. Bates is waiting for you."

Eleanor Bates stood to greet him. "Come in, Alex. I
was glad to receive your phone call."

Alex stepped into the intimate, richly appointed room.
Oriental carpets adorned polished wood floors. A graceful Chippendale sofa and two side chairs surrounded the
marble fireplace, and a tall, ornately carved clock ticked
solemnly in one corner. Eleanor was, as always, immaculately groomed, today handsomely dressed in a suit of
black and white houndstooth check.

He shook her hand. "Thanks for seeing me on such
short notice," he said, feeling his earlier panic subside

somewhat. "I have a lot of things . . . we need to talk about."

"Starting with the art collection of one Henry Houston Bonnell?" she replied sardonically.

Alex looked directly into her magnified blue eyes. "Yes. That, and a whole lot more."

"Sit," she commanded, but her tone had softened. "Would you care for tea? Or perhaps something stronger. I'm having a gin myself."

"Gin. Yes, gin, thank you."

Eleanor rang a small bell, and the woman who had answered the door stepped into the room. "Two gins, please, Anna. Mine with tonic." She looked at Alex. "Do you like tonic, or would you prefer it neat?"

Two neat, Alex wanted to say, but he knew he had to stay in control of his already frazzled wits. "Tonic would be fine."

Their drinks served, the door closed behind them, Alex decided to get straight to the point. "About Bonnell's art collection," he said, unable to cover a small, self-deprecating grin. "I do owe you an explanation. But I don't recall giving his name the night I was introduced as, er, someone's personal representative there at Harrington. How did you know about that?"

"I had a call from Tom Perkins, the art dealer who represents Selena." Eleanor sat stiffly in the armchair. Her voice was candid, bordering on impatient, and Alex knew she did not take his misrepresentation as a joke. "He was trying to locate you, or your 'client,' Bonnell."

"I see. It doesn't surprise me, although I think Perkins is more interested in the artist than her work." He laughed bitterly. "I'm sure he has the same designs as I have on Selena. And I'm afraid I may have unwittingly given him the means to discredit me in her eyes." Alex sipped the gin and leaned forward in the chair. "I did a really stupid thing, although at the time it seemed harmless enough."

Then he described his visit to the Perkins Galleries and his first impression that the words in Selena's paintings resembled the handwriting of Emily Brontë. He told her about the second painting in Haworth, and how he'd ended up at Selena's studio door in the pouring rain.

"I never meant to mislead her, but I couldn't think of any reason she would let me in unless she thought I might be a buyer."

"So you told her you were an art agent?"

"I implied as much, and it was going to stop there, but then she asked me who I represented. I'd just spent days working with the Bonnell Collection, and his name just sort of . . . popped out."

Alex saw Eleanor's expression thaw, and a smile crept into her eyes. "You didn't know then that you were going to fall in love with her, or that your little fib would come back to haunt you?" she finished the story for him.

Embarrassed, he shook his head. Why did everyone keep insisting that he was in love with Selena? But he didn't bother to deny it to Eleanor.

"Does she know the truth now?" Eleanor asked.

"I've tried to tell her several times, but either it doesn't seem like the right moment or something has interrupted us."

"So you drove all the way to Leeds to tell me this?"

"Actually, no. I was here visiting Selena's grandmother."

"Her grandmother? Why would you be visiting her grandmother?" Eleanor was clearly surprised.

"Well, that's another long story and the real reason I came to see you." He looked up at her with a steady gaze. "Ms. Bates . . . Eleanor, I'm sorry about that foolishness with Bonnell. I don't know if the end justifies the means, but because of that foolishness, I think I may have come across a significant discovery, possibly the most important Brontë artifact uncovered in our time."

He paused, noting the gleam of intrigue he saw in her faded blue eyes. "It is something so incredible it will set the literary world on its ear, or else it is nothing."

"My God, dear boy, do go on. What is it you've found?"

Alex leaned back and crossed one leg on top of his knee. He hoped he wasn't making a mistake in trusting Eleanor Bates.

"I think I may have come across . . . Emily's suicide note."

Eleanor rang the bell again. "Another gin please, Anna." She looked into the open face of the young man who sat in front of her, astounded at what he'd just told her. Not the part where he'd used Bonnell's name to gain entrance to the artist's studio. That was relatively understandable.

And forgivable.

But the rest. Was he deluded? Reaching so hard for evidence to use against Maggie Flynn in the debate that he was willing to fabricate an even larger lie?

Or was he telling the truth?

"What brought you to such a conclusion, Dr. Hightower?" she said, trying to contain her growing excitement. She listened carefully as he expanded on the details and his own interpretation of the possibilities. The more he talked, the more she believed. Then he reached inside the envelope he'd brought along and withdrew what appeared to be several little bits of paper taped together.

"This is what I was able to piece together on my own from the photographs I took and what I was able to copy from four of her paintings," he explained, holding the paper to her view. "What caught my attention first was this, the word 'Keeper.' Then when I put this together, I recognized the words down there toward the bottom."

He laid the piece on the table between them and pointed to the lines. "They are clearly from Emily's poem *'Faith and Despondency.'* Either she wrote that letter, or someone whose handwriting seriously imitates hers used those lines to make their own point."

Eleanor frowned. "Have you actually seen the letter? What does it say?"

Alex nodded. "I saw the letter. I know it exists. But I only got a quick glance at it. But I could tell, Eleanor, I could see that the handwriting was so . . . tiny and cramped. It looked just like . . . hers."

"Where is the letter now?"

"The old woman was just about to give it to me when Selena came in and all hell broke loose." He sighed. "I suppose right now it's back in a drawer in Matka's room at the Sunnyside Nursing Home."

"Can you get it?"

"I can try. But if I do, I need your help in protecting it. No one must know it exists until we can examine it and take appropriate steps to prove its authenticity."

Eleanor nodded, then saw a frown crease his brow.

"You already know," he continued, "that my reputation as a scholar is, shall we say, nontraditional. I can't afford to have this come to light only to be proven a fake. I'd rather have it turn out to be something totally insignificant, written in the twentieth century maybe by some crazy Gypsy, than to have my peers think that I would stoop to fabricating something just to prove my point in the debate."

He paused and looked at her meaningfully. "Maggie would suspect that of me, I'm afraid."

Eleanor was nursing her gin as he talked, and at his last words, the glass tilted away from her mouth, spilling several drops of the clear liquid onto the lapel of her suit. Calmly, she brushed them away and looked at Alex.

"I have a confession to make to you as well before we go on. After I heard about your use of the Bonnell name, I became so perturbed that I called around to check on you. I . . . I couldn't imagine a scholar of integrity doing such a thing, you see. Still don't exactly. At any rate, I learned that you and Dr. Flynn had . . . known each other before."

"We had a brief affair last year when she was in Virginia," he said, holding her gaze steadily.

"Yes, so I understand. When I didn't get a call back from you, I called her. Now, I didn't tell her exactly what you had done, but I did mention I'd found out you were an art connoisseur, just to see if she would validate that much of the story."

She heard him groan and saw him lean back and rub his eyes. She regretted her hasty action now, but there was nothing to be done about it. "I guess we have both told our little white lies lately. Will you forgive me mine?"

He raised his head and gave her a slow smile, that sexy grin that seemed to be his trademark. "Then we're even?"

Eleanor nodded. "For now. But we must decide what to do next."

"Maggie mustn't know about this, not yet," Alex warned. "She is a top scholar, to be sure, but . . ."

"I understand. If this proves out, your theory is set in concrete. There will be no need for the debate."

"And if it doesn't, I don't want to load any more ammunition as to my lack of credibility into her cannon."

Eleanor wasn't sure why she was so willing to believe Dr. Alexander Hightower, but his story seemed straight. And it would be ever so much to the Society's benefit if she could steer that letter into its hands rather than let such a treasure wind up, like so many others, in the British Museum.

"I'll make a few discreet calls to locate reputable forensic experts," she said. "But you . . . it's up to you to get your hands on that letter."

September 15, 1848

I sent away my love, and since that day, my heart has been as lead. At times I feel physically ill, especially in the early hours of the morning. I find many days I can scarcely face the gruel I must cook for the rest, and this morning I was wretchedly ill in the privy. I must work to overcome this weakness of spirit or I shall lose my vitality altogether. I am coming to understand even more of love. It is the most powerful force in the universe! It removes mortal control, defies convention, and changes destinies. I pray now that Mikel will return next summer, and perhaps if he still wishes to wed, I will consider it. Thoughts of our reunion must sustain me through the lonely days and nights that stretch endlessly in front of me.

September 25, 1848

Would that Mikel's arms could enfold me now and comfort me in the grief that enshrouds me instead. Branwell has died, and I have scarce been able to make it through the past two days. Despite his degradations of the past years, he was our beloved brother, and we are all in a sorry state. The house is as still as the stone floor of St. Michael's where we shall bury him on Thursday. No more shall we hear his ravings, as vile and repulsive as they were, and yet perversely we shall miss them, for they were his life, and now that life is no more.

I take solace from knowing he is free at last from his torment, and I am thankful for the peace that seemed to come over him in his last hours. After years of near insanity, Branii seemed suddenly to come to his senses yesterday, only a few hours before his death. He spoke as the person he once was, clear-headed, affectionate, our brother. We were recalled from Sunday services by John Brown, who had come to sit with him for that brief hour, for Branwell knew that he was dying. Papa held him in his arms and prayed aloud while Anne, Charlotte, and I looked on. I have never witnessed death firsthand, although it has touched my life often enough. Before he took his final breath, he asked forgiveness for his mortal sins and for the duress he had inflicted upon us. Oddly, he did not mention Lydia Robinson, but wanted only to make amends with his family. And then he suffered his final convulsion . . . it is hard to bear the memory. I shall miss him maybe more than the others, although Papa is inconsolable at losing his only son. I am continually awed at what love can forgive.

September 30, 1848

Two days ago we laid Branwell's body to rest, and grief has us all in its tight clutches. Papa is morose and stays in his room. Charlotte feels ill and won't eat, and in addition to the malady of the stomach which has visited me in recent weeks, I suffer from a cough which came on the afternoon of the funeral. I was chilled already from inside and out, and I stepped into a marshy puddle, wetting my feet thoroughly. I should have watched my step more carefully, but my thoughts were with my brother, not myself. I am paying for that carelessness now.

Chapter 24

Something about her conversation with Tom Perkins
had bothered Dr. Maggie Flynn all day. The fact that
Alex had claimed to represent the interests of an art
collector named Henry Bonnell was ludicrous, but Maggie knew Alex possibly better than any human on earth.
He wouldn't have done something like that unless . . .

Unless what?

That was what bothered Maggie.

What was Alex up to? Was it just some kind of absurd
ruse to play up to that artist? She didn't think so. In their
year together in academe, he'd never given her reason to
believe he was less than honest. A renegade in his thinking, to be sure. But not a liar.

And yet, he'd obviously lied to this woman, misrepre-
senting himself blatantly, and foolishly, for if anyone with
any knowledge of the Brontës heard about it, they would
know the name Bonnell.

So what was his game?

Maggie tapped the end of her pencil on the ancient
hardwood desk in her office. Maybe Alex had actually
found something to support his ridiculous contention
that Emily Brontë committed suicide. . . .

Her razor-sharp mind went back to the afternoon

they'd spent together in London, to their visit to the gallery, and it honed in on a comment she recalled:

"Looks like Emily's writing . . ."

Hastily, she picked up the phone and dialed the Perkins Galleries in London.

"Mr. Perkins? Dr. Maggie Flynn here. Do you have a minute?"

"I will make time. Have you come up with any ideas as to why your friend Dr. Hightower would pose as an agent for a dead man?"

Maggie cleared her throat. "Dr. Hightower is not exactly my friend. I'm afraid I misled you just a bit in our last conversation. But I've been thinking. What do you know about those paintings your client creates?"

"Nothing other than they seem to sell well. Why?"

"Dr. Hightower seemed strangely taken with the tidbits of writing she has in all of her pictures. Do they mean anything?"

There was a long pause on the line. "Now that you mention it, Selena told me that those images were a message that made sense if pieced together."

Maggie smiled. "Did she say what that message was?"

"Something about a lover's farewell note or some such gibberish. What are you getting at, Dr. Flynn? I'm a busy man. Too busy for word games."

"Too busy to investigate the possible existence of an extremely valuable literary artifact?"

A long silence. "I don't deal in artifacts, Dr. Flynn. I deal in art."

"Then would you consider allowing me to examine the paintings? Perhaps I could discern if those scraps of painted words mean anything of importance."

"At the moment, I have none of Selena's paintings in the gallery. She took them all back to her studio. The pieces of the note she used in the paintings are there as well." He hesitated. "I take it from your earlier comment you are no longer interested in one of those hangings for Dr. Hightower?"

Maggie smiled coldly. "I'm interested in *hanging* Dr. Hightower, not a hanging *for* him."

"Perhaps, then, we have something in common, Dr. Flynn."

A brisk but warm wind blew Selena's hair as she drove home from Matka's in the recently repaired Land Rover, her mind and her heart at war with one another. Intellectually, she could accept Matka's argument that it was time to get over old hurts and fears and take a chance on love, but on another level, she didn't know if she could do that. There was more to it than just an irrational fear of the curse, but she didn't know what exactly was continuing to emotionally paralyze her.

She turned into Bridgeton Lane and in a few moments into her own driveway, where Domino gave her his usual frenetic greeting.

Normal.

Familiar.

Home.

But somehow things seemed different, as if the world had shifted. The horizon seemed wider, the sky more expansive. There seemed to be more . . . possibilities.

"Come on up, boy," she called to the dog.

Inside the studio, things were just as she left them, and yet, it was as if she were looking at them through different eyes. A paint-spattered smock hung over the back of the sofa, alongside her woolen shawl. A half-empty bottle of wine and a well-sampled bottle of brandy stood on the counter. Paintings in haunting shades of mauve and gray hung from floor to ceiling. Ashes lay in the fireplace in silent testimony to last night's intimate encounter.

Intimacy.

For the first time in her life, Selena had experienced

intimacy, and the memory of the time spent in Alex's arms warmed her as she stood alone in the empty studio. She liked the feel of his arms around her, the strength of his body next to hers, the feeling of being protected, sheltered in his embrace. For the first time in her life, she'd felt safe, secure, and loved. Yes, Gran, she thought, I want to love Alex. If I only knew how.

And if only I knew it was me he wanted as well. His furtive behavior in copying the words from her paintings and his secret visit to her grandmother had raised Selena's suspicions that Alex might be more interested in the letter than in her, and that he was just using her to get his hands on that letter. But why? What interest could he possibly have in that cursed piece of writing?

More than any other time in her life, Selena needed answers.

Going to where the paintings hung like opaque windows on the walls, depicting a strange and alien world, she stared at the silent riders and the monkeys and the organ grinders, and especially the torn scraps carrying their jigsaw message. "Is it you the man wants?" she whispered. "Or is it me?"

She surveyed her work in much the same way she had the day she'd tried to chant the images out of her life, and strangely, they seemed far less threatening than before. She saw anger in the paintings, and fear. Perhaps even hatred. But somehow these emotions no longer had a stranglehold on her. They belonged to the images now.

And suddenly, with great relief, Selena realized it was unlikely she would ever finish the commissions, no matter how much she needed the money. Painting the rest of the letter was no longer necessary. In fact, it might be impossible.

The demons were departing.

All that remained was a need to sort through the residue of a lifetime of fear of intimate relationships to find the key that would unlock new hope, new possibilities. A key that would allow her to trust, to open herself and take a chance on love.

The one you love holds the key. Give him the letter . . ."

Selena slid her handbag from her shoulder and dug through it until she found the letter. She went to the window and squinted, reading the tragic message in its entirety.

What was it about this message that Alex wanted so badly? And what made Matka believe Alex would be able to dispel the curse?

Selena remembered the other gift Matka had pressed upon her. It, too, was nestled in the depths of the large bag. She felt for its cool, hard roundness and brought the crystal ball into the light.

Holding it up to the window, she wondered if Matka really could see things in its depths. Selena saw nothing there except the swirling clouds and shadows and angles formed by nature when the quartz had crystallized untold ages ago. She had often witnessed her grandmother reading the ball for others, but she had never really believed in scrying. At the moment, however, she wished she did. Perhaps the ball would give her answers to the questions she harbored in the deepest, darkest corners of her heart.

Selena turned the ball over in her hands. Actually, when she thought of it, Matka had given accurate guidance to many people using this cool object. But how did it work?

The shrill ring of the telephone shattered her thoughts. "Hello?" she finally responded after the fourth ring.

"Selena. It's Tom. How are you getting along?"

"Only so-so," she responded truthfully. "I'm afraid I'm a little . . . stuck on those commissions."

"Oh, dear." His voice reflected serious concern that

she wouldn't fill his coffers as quickly as he'd intended. "Well, I am certain that whatever block you're experiencing, it will pass. Listen, love, I have a favor to ask."

Selena was in no mood to grant Tom Perkins any favors, and so she didn't reply. She listened, however, in growing aggravation as he continued.

"As you know, I have been trying to trace down that American collector Bonnell, and I'm afraid I'm having no luck. Have you spoken with Hightower lately?"

"Not about Bonnell. Why?"

"I'd . . . like to get together with him, you and I. Maybe between us we could stir up some action there, you know?"

"I'm sure when Alex has some news about Bonnell, he'll give you a call, Tom."

There was a long pause on the wire. Then Tom said pointedly, "Don't you think it's time we worked together to move some of your paintings, Selena? It's difficult to sell your work when I have none to show in the gallery. We had some success from the exhibit and those two social affairs, but sales are lagging. I'm only doing my job in trying to pursue all possible avenues."

Selena let out an audible sigh. She supposed he was right. "What favor?"

"I'd like to drive up there tomorrow. Perhaps we could take Hightower to dinner. Get to know him, talk up your work, you know the kind of thing I mean. Would you be able to set it up?"

The last two times Selena had seen Alexander Hightower, she'd been in a fit of rage. Her interest in him now had nothing to do with his role as the representative of the American collector. And her emotions concerning him were so confused at the moment, she didn't want to encounter him right away, much less set up a meeting with Tom Perkins involved.

"I don't think so, Tom. I . . . I haven't been feeling well lately."

"Perhaps you could give me his number, then?" Tom's tone of voice revealed his irritation. "I'll try to set it up myself."

"I . . . I don't think I have it," she lied, strangely wanting to protect Alex from Tom's avaricious invasion.

"I can get it from the telephone company, then, I suppose. But I am going to set it up. For tomorrow. And Selena," he added, a hint of menace in his words, "I expect you to be there."

Alex left Eleanor's house with a much lighter heart than when he'd arrived. At least now, he believed, he had an ally and a trustworthy confidante as he moved forward in his inquiry into the authenticity of Matka's letter.

If he could lay his hands on it.

He stopped back by the nursing home, but it was after nine o'clock, and the nurse at the desk informed him that the old woman had gone to bed. His own fatigue began to creep up on him, and he drove with extra caution as he made his way up and down the narrow roadway leading back to Haworth.

At the edge of Stanbury he was tempted to turn into Bridgeton Lane, but thought better of it. He needed to regroup his energy, clear his thinking, before confronting Selena again.

If she would give him the time of day.

When he finally opened the door to his tiny flat, Alex wanted nothing more than a hot shower and a good night's sleep. Eleanor had insisted he stay for the evening meal, and the two had talked eagerly about the letter, Gypsies, and the possibility that Emily might have encountered Selena's great-great-something ancestor. In addition to finding appropriate resources for the forensic study of the artifact, Eleanor had also promised to look into the history of the Welsh Gypsies and their possible forays into Yorkshire in the mid-1800s.

Alex walked past the table and into the postage-stamp-sized kitchen and saw that the red light was blinking on his answering machine. His heart skipped a beat. Selena?

But when he heard the message, he scowled.

"Dr. Hightower, Tom Perkins here. Perkins Galleries. I will be in Stanbury tomorrow to visit with Selena about a commission she is working on, and I would like to invite you to be my guest for dinner. Perhaps I could be of assistance to you in placing one or more of her paintings in the collection of your American friend. I'll be leaving the gallery shortly, and will be out for the evening, so there is no need to return this call. Dinner say sixish at the Lion and the Bull in Keighley?"

When pigs fly, Alex thought. He'd planned to see Selena tomorrow himself, to clear the air about the Bonnell thing and see if he could get her to talk rationally about the images in her paintings. He wanted to explain why he'd gone to visit Matka and about his suspicions as to who the author of the letter might be. He wondered what time Perkins would arrive from London. It was two and a half hours by train, perhaps as much as four by car. Alex figured he had until noon.

Depressed by the prospects of the following day, he showered quickly and climbed into bed, where he spent the night in a fitful sleep. The sun was already above the rooftops the next morning when he was awakened by the telephone. At first he was tempted to let the machine pick up the message, but if it was Selena, he didn't want to take the chance on missing her.

"Hello?" he answered, his voice still sleepily sluggish.

"Hightower? Tom Perkins. Did you get my message?"

"Uh, yes, but you see, I will be unable—"

"Before you beg off, let me share one fascinating discovery I have made recently about Selena's surrealistic series. She has never told me much about their origin, and so I had never considered that the little fragment of a letter she paints into each one had any meaning. . . ."

Tom Perkins now had Alex's full attention. "What do you mean?"

"One of my, uh, colleagues has pointed out to me that the messages might have some meaning if they were put altogether. Selena has verified this and told me she plans to paint only as many paintings as it takes to complete the message. Don't you see, this will make this series a very special collection. One I'm sure your client wouldn't want to miss out on."

"Did Selena tell you what the message said?"

"Something about a farewell note from a lover. I admit I was not paying much attention at the time. She took all her work back to Stanbury with her after the exhibit, so I haven't been able to work out the puzzle myself, but I plan to copy the messages while I'm there today. Which reminds me, I'd better be off. It is a long drive. So we're on for tonight, then?"

Alex wanted to hang up on the disgusting little man, but he couldn't. And he knew he had no choice but to meet him for dinner and try to dissuade him from pursuing his investigation further.

"I'll meet you at the Lion and the Bull at six," he replied unenthusiastically.

He settled the receiver heavily in its cradle, wishing he had Selena's number. He dialed for information, but the number was unlisted. So he made coffee and dressed quickly, more anxious than ever to talk to Selena before Tom showed up.

But three-quarters of an hour later, when he arrived at the old farmhouse, the Land Rover was not in the driveway. Discouraged, Alex returned through the streets of Stanbury, driving slowly and keeping an eye out for her vehicle.

No luck.

He drove into nearby Keighley, thinking perhaps she'd gone to market there, but again there was no sign of the old car.

Discouragement turned to alarm.

Perhaps, he thought, trying to reassure himself that she was all right, she stayed over with her grandmother. Alex returned to his flat and placed a call to the Sunnyside Nursing Home. The volunteer who answered the phone happened to be Margaret, who remembered him from the birthday party.

"No, Selena didn't stay in the guest quarters, and so far she hasn't been in today," she replied to his anxious inquiry.

"Please, if she shows up, give her this number," he said, and added, "Tell her it's urgent."

Morning moved toward noon. Two trips back to Bridgeton Lane produced no Selena. And there was no blinking message light to greet him when he returned from both excursions. By one o'clock Alex became seriously concerned, but he decided not to risk an encounter at the studio with Tom Perkins, who possibly had made it to Stanbury by this time.

So Perkins would have the pleasure of discrediting him after all, Alex thought, as he was certain to do, by introducing Selena to the facts about Henry Bonnell. That didn't matter to him nearly as much, however, as Selena's innocently giving the toad the chance to discover what Alex believed to be the truth about the letter. If Tom Perkins had so much as an inkling that Emily's letter existed, he would latch onto it like the greedy bastard he was, and Alex feared it would disappear into the hands of the highest bidder.

❧ *Chapter 25* ❧

*O*ctober 15, 1848

My illness worsens even as the cold descends upon us once again. Today dark clouds spilled heavy snow into the garden and churchyard, and I cannot seem to get warm. I will write here briefly, then attempt to bake the bread. Perhaps the warmth of the oven will take this chill from my bones. I cough incessantly, and the sickness in my stomach seems as if it will never end. My monthly flow has not come since Branwell's death, although I expect it any day. Once that has passed, perhaps my health will return.

October 21, 1848

In the kitchen last night, I listened to Tabby's gossip, and the turn of her conversation has struck terror in my heart. There is a village girl, she related, who indulged in an indiscretion, as she called it, with the son of a wealthy farmer nearby. She is with child, and the shame of it has caused her family much grief. The boy's family refuses to acknowledge his responsibility, and her own family has sent her away, abandoning her to a fate of poverty and disgrace, as if she were not of their own flesh and blood. "Where is their compassion?" I cried, unable to believe such callousness.

*"We all forgave Branwell." Tabby looked at me as if I had
lost my head. "It is not the same, Emily. You know that."*

*I know so little of troubles such as these, but I fear I, too,
may have fallen victim to my indiscretion with Mikel. It has
been two months now since our time together, and since
that time, I have not been visited with my monthly flow. If it
doesn't come by next week, the most unthinkable fate may
be mine.*

November 3, 1848

*I am convinced of my predicament, after making careful
inquiry into certain symptoms which I have suffered since
the summer. My clothing is loose, so no one has yet suspected, but my melancholy continues to cause both Charlotte and Anne great concern. How would they feel if they
learned the truth? Would I, like the village girl, be turned out
by my family? If my plan works, it will not be so, for I will
turn myself out, into that Invisible world where I will be with
Branwell once again, and there will be no pain and suffering, no shame for my beloved father and sisters.*

*But until I succeed, there is pain like I have never borne
before, an inner sorrow that the little happiness I knew with
Mikel could turn to this. Oh why did it have to end this
way? Was I never to know happiness on this earth? I know I
will never see him again, but it is the price I must pay for
losing control. I have written to him, and yesterday when
Charlotte and Anne went with Papa to tend the sick in the
village, I crept out of the back door and made my way to the
back ravine. It was a terrible journey, as the wind was bleak
and I could not catch my breath. But I had to let him know.
I left a brief message beneath the rock. Perhaps if the winter
does not destroy it, he will learn my fate when he returns in
the summer, and know of my deep love for him. I am worse
for the effort, but it is my wish now only to get it over with. I
will see no doctor, take no nourishment, until nature col-*

lects my withered body and turns this wasted lifetime into sand.

I think of the lines I once wrote, and I laugh at my false courage. No coward soul indeed. I fear not death, but I tremble before the dying. How could I have so severely misplaced my control?

I will write no more. It is finished, and now it, and I, must be destroyed.

Domino jounced happily in the seat beside Selena, his nose out the window, hungrily capturing the wild smell of the moors as they drove higher and higher into the desolate countryside. Selena did not know exactly where she was headed, nor why she felt compelled to make this early morning journey. It was as if some unseen hand was guiding her, and she could only hope that it would point out what to do next.

Cresting a hill, she spotted a wide place in the road, the first she'd come across. Instinctively, she pulled over and turned off the engine, and the world grew suddenly quiet. The air was breezy, with thin clouds brushing a soft mist over the swaying grasses. The cry of a meadowlark in the distance was the only sound that pierced the silence.

"Well, let's see what happens next," she said resolutely to the dog, who was doing a turnabout in the seat, anxious to spring free into the moors. Selena had never allowed herself to think about inner guidance before, although her grandmother had often talked about listening for directions from some invisible source. Selena had considered it all just old-fashioned Gypsy stuff, but this morning she had awakened with an inexplicable urge to go deep into the moors to sort out her confusion. Not that she hadn't often sought tranquility in the peaceful countryside, but this morning was different.

It wasn't tranquility she sought, but rather direction.

Guidance.

All night she had tossed restlessly on her bed while her fears and her desires battled each other for supremacy. By first light neither had won and she was exhausted. At last she'd drifted off into a heavy, dream-filled slumber, and when she awoke, she knew in some deep part of her that an answer was at hand. She had only to seek it, and the place to do so was here, high on the moors, at the juncture of earth and sky.

She opened the door and barely made it out ahead of the exuberant dog, who bounded away through the grass. Selena reached for the bag she'd brought along, then turned to survey the landscape. Far below she could see the haze of civilization hovering in the air over the valley. Behind her was a ravine with a large outcropping of rock. She could hear the sound of water trickling over stones, and she soon discovered a small beck flowing in the crack of the hillside.

This was the place.

She settled on a large flat stone and leaned back against a rock that stood perpendicular to it, her face to the sun. A sense of peace surrounded her, and she breathed deeply. Only then did she allow the troubling thoughts to take center stage once more.

Alexander Hightower played the lead. Why was she so afraid to let herself love him? It was the crux of the matter, and she knew that until she came up with an answer to this one question, there could be no future with him.

Fear.

Selena recognized she had lived with fear for a very long time. Not an overt, identifiable fear, but one buried deeply within her soul.

But what was she afraid of? She knew now with certainty it wasn't the curse. No, there was something else . . .

Selena reached into the bag and found the crystal globe. It was irrational, she knew, to believe she would find any answers within its glistening depths. But perhaps it would give her something to focus on until her subconscious let loose the dragons she suspected lurked in the midnight caverns of her soul. Dragons she must now bring to the surface and face in the light of day.

Selena stared into the glass for endless moments, watching the sunlight play among the formations that swirled inside the globe. She was reminded of swirling water, swirling skirts, music that awakened her with its loud blast from the next room. She saw herself as a little girl, maybe three or four years old. The room she was in was cold and dark, and voices came from the next room.

She heard her mother's voice, taunting her father, scolding him like a shrew, demanding things he could not deliver.

Her father's voice replied in angry, insulting threats.

Selena saw tiny fingers widening the crack in the door that allowed light into the darkened room. She saw shadows in silhouette against the low lamplight and heard her mother's drunken, derisive laughter as she swirled her skirts high on her legs, teasing, tempting her father. Then she screamed in hateful rejection, repulsing her father's advances.

In the crystal depths, Selena recognized the angry man who was forcing her mother beneath him, shredding her clothing and twisting her slender arms, pinning her beneath his weight. She heard a scream, and it sounded like her own voice, only younger. She saw the child dart forth from the room, running to protect her mother. The child beat its small fists with all its might against her father's back.

The images took on a deeper aspect, as if she were not only seeing and hearing them, but could feel them as well. Her father was like an angry animal, turning blindly and striking out with the force of thunder.

Red hot pain shot through her body, pain that filled her until she knew nothing else. She felt herself stumbling, falling terrified into midnight darkness.

A hoarse cry escaped Selena's throat, and the horrible images faded abruptly, but suddenly she remembered it all—that terrible night when her father had beaten her so badly he'd broken her arm. His deep grief when he sobered up and realized what he'd done. Her mother's rage against him, and her fear.

And then the tears came. Selena sat hunched over the globe of crystal and let herself cry from the most inner depths of her soul. She cried in anguish for that small girl. She cried in despair for her mother and her father. She cried for all the dark nights she'd huddled in her bed, fearing, not understanding, trying to forget what had happened so she could get up in the morning and somehow manage to still love her parents. She cried in relief, at last understanding.

The dragons had surfaced at last. Now it was up to her to conquer them.

Selena sat beneath the brilliant morning sun trying to regain control, dazed by the intensity of the memories that flooded through her now. Memories of this incident, and others, that she'd buried deeply and thoroughly throughout a childhood of violence.

Denying.

Denying.

Invisible memories that had frozen her emotions even as Matka had spun her tales of the curse, laying the blame for her parents' cruelty and self-indulgence at the doorstep of some long-dead ancestor.

Selena sobbed. The curse. A convenient excuse for inexcusable behavior. But was that how a curse worked? Had her parents, believing they were cursed to be "unlucky in love," fulfilled its prophecy with their own reckless behavior?

Likely.

She considered the idea of a curse and where such a thing originates. What kind of father would bring down such a damnation on his family? A tormented, guilt-ridden father, or one like her own, willful and self-absorbed?

Suddenly, Selena wanted to know what kind of man was Mikel Wd, King of the Gypsies.

Staring again into the crystal, Selena let her focus go soft once again, let her mind wander freely back into a greater Mind that might encompass all time. She heard water running over rocks, and she knew it was the beck nearby, but she was hearing it from a great distance of time. Her skin grew cold and she shivered in the wind, which seemed suddenly icy.

She saw a man standing on the flat rock where she now sat, his eyes searching for something, then catching the flicker of white against the dark shadow of a moss-stained stone. Leaping across the snow-clogged beck to where the tiny flag of paper flapped in the wind, he stooped to retrieve it, almost losing it in the winter blast.

Frowning, he strained to read the tiny words printed on the crumpled paper. The color drained from his face, and Selena felt his anguish and disbelief. Surely he had not read correctly! She watched as he read the paper again, then fell to his knees in the snow.

"No!" A cry was torn from his mouth and carried away by the wind. "No!" he cried again, and then, "Emilie . . ." And then his voice was drowned in bitter tears.

Selena heard a horse whinny. The sky grew dark and the snow fell in thick flakes, whitening his long, dark hair and dusting the shoulders of his rough hide jacket.

Silence.

Darkness.

The image blurred before Selena's eyes, then formed again. The man stood beside his horse at the top of a hill, gazing down at a village below, where gray stone houses huddled beneath snow-covered roofs. Vague lights shone from small windows, the only sign of life in the winter darkness. One house stood alone at the edge of the moor, isolated from the rest by a vast churchyard with snow-covered tombstones shining ghostly in the cloud-veiled moonlight. It was a house he had seen many times before, Selena sensed, although the dwellers within were unaware of his observation. It was the house of the *Gorgio* woman. Does she still live there? Selena felt the man ask himself.

Does she still live . . . ?

As she watched, Selena had the strange sensation that she actually became the man. He tethered the horse to a gnarled, ice-clad tree, and a clump of frozen heather caught his eye. He stooped and snapped off a brittle stem. It had been a symbol between them. He will place it on her doorstep. Perhaps she will know and will somehow come to him.

If . . .

He couldn't bear the terrible thought that death might have already taken her from him. With a leaden heart, he strode through the drifts toward the village, but he did not knock on the door of her house. He would not be welcome there in any case.

Clinging to the shadows of the night, not knowing for sure where he was going, the man knew only that he was being led toward an answer he did not wish to learn. His footsteps came to a halt at the doorway of the old church, only a few yards from the darkened house. Her house. Does she sleep in that house, he wondered, or here beneath one of the grim, snow-draped headstones?

He tried the door of the church, not expecting it to open, but it gave beneath his firm insistence, and he stepped inside. The wind howled to be let in, but he closed the door against its shriek and took refuge in the silent darkness. On stealthy feet he made his way to the front of the small sanctuary, but barely halfway there, he stumbled on a large stone in the floor which had been dislodged.

Recently dislodged.

Kneeling, he ran his hand over the outline of the stone, his eyes searching through the thick darkness. She was here. He knew it. He could feel her presence. "Emilie," he whispered, and the word ached as it struggled over his unshed tears.

The only reply was silence.

Deathly silence.

And a knowing.

The man placed the stem of thawing heather reverently on the stone that sealed her tomb, its purple bloom now black as death. And as silently as he entered, he returned into the night.

Selena's fingers were cold as ice as she forced herself to reclaim her consciousness and return into the present. She replaced the crystal ball in the bag, her mind numb. She managed to stand up and, on unsteady legs, made her way back to the Land Rover.

Who was that man? What had she just experienced? A dream? An hallucination?

Uncertain of the state of her sanity at the moment, she felt exhausted and emotionally drained. She whistled loudly for Domino, and the sight of his black and white form wriggling toward her through the tall grass gave her a welcome dose of reality.

"C'mon, boy," she called, not caring that the dog silted the car seat with sand as he leaped into the vehicle. She sat behind the wheel for a long while, breathing deeply, an intense sadness enveloping her. It was as if the emotions of the man kneeling in the church's darkness had left their residue in her heart, and Selena allowed a tear to slip down her cheek in his behalf.

Who was Em-ilie? she wondered as she switched on the ignition. Whoever she was, Selena knew that it was Em-ilie who had written the letter she now carried in her own purse. She turned the vehicle around and headed back toward the village of Haworth. Intuitively, just outside of town, she felt compelled to pull over once again. Parking the car in the shade of a stunted tree, she rolled down the windows. "Stay," she commanded Domino. "I won't be long."

She went to stand at the crest of the hill. Below her, the scene was strangely familiar. A building nestled at the edge of the moors, a two-storied house, with an addition that hadn't been there that dark, snowy night. But it was the same place, Selena knew, as she had just seen in the crystal ball. In front of it spread a grimly overpopulated cemetery, on the other side of which stood a church.

Selena remembered visiting this place as a schoolgirl on special outings. It was the Brontë Parsonage Museum. She began walking toward the structure, as she had seen the man do. She paused at the gate to the museum, then moved on down the cobblestones to the church. Looking up, she saw a blue and gold clock face, newly painted. Two o'clock.

She went into the church.

It, too, was the same as she had just envisioned, and yet not. Or perhaps her vision had not been accurate. She walked to the far aisle and went halfway to the front of the church, then stopped, feeling the hair rise on her arms. Looking down, she saw she was standing on a large, flat stone. Selena stepped off the stone, then with the toe of her shoe tapped the slab.

It moved. Ever so slightly, it rocked against its neighbors, and she knew the place was the same.

At the front of the church a bronze plaque was set into the floor, a memorial to the writers Charlotte and Emily Brontë, whose graves were sealed beneath a nearby pillar. And on the plaque, someone had placed a sprig of heather in a small vase.

Emily.

Em-ilie?

Haunted, Selena left the church and went directly to the Parsonage. Had this been the home of the *Gorgio* woman her ancestor had loved? Or was her imagination wildly out of control? She paid the entrance fee and stepped inside. It seemed strange that this had actually once been someone's house, for it felt undoubtedly like a museum now. Rooms were cordoned off with gold braid roping. Items were displayed behind glass.

It wasn't large, and it took only a short while for Selena to make the tourist's rounds. She had grown up in the area and of course knew of the Brontës, but she hadn't paid much attention to her famous neighbors. Now, her eyes scanned each room hungrily, searching for something, she knew not what, the reason she'd been drawn to this place on this hot summer afternoon.

She found it almost immediately upon passing into the display area on the second floor in the new wing.

There, safely ensconced behind glass, were what appeared to be miniature books, written in a hand that Selena recognized instantly.

"My God," she whispered, staring. And then the pieces of the puzzle of the curse began to fall into place. The *Gorgio* woman. The writing in the letter. Her vision on the moors. This house. Em-ilie. Could it have been? Could that *Gorgio* woman have been Emily Brontë?

It seemed preposterous. Who would ever dare claim such a thing? Then Selena's pulse quickened. Alex had told her he was working in the museum. Doing what? No wonder he'd been curious about the letter. The handwrit-

ing was virtually identical to that in the miniature books
in front of her. Did he suspect that the letter Matka had
so innocently revealed to him was written by Emily
Brontë? Selena had a sudden sickening feeling that he
did. And that he wanted that letter. And that he was
willing to seduce her to get it.

And the part of her that wanted to fall in love with him
wept in bitter acknowledgment of the truth.

Tearing her gaze away from the little books and the
handwriting that had given her the ugly answer to her
questions about Alex, Selena looked for the exit. She
hurried down the back stairway and was almost out the
door when a name jumped out at her from one of the
historical exhibits.

Bonnell.

Henry H. Bonnell.

Her eyes widened as she read the history of the collection of manuscripts, letters, drawings, samplers, and
other items of Brontëana donated by the philanthropist.
"After Bonnell's death in 1926, his widow oversaw ar-
rangements for the shipping of the collection from
America to Haworth . . ."

Selena stared, even more stunned than she had been
when looking at the handwriting upstairs. Was there no
end to this man's audacity! She didn't know whether to
laugh or cry. Henry Bonnell was no art collector. He was
a dead man! Alex must want that letter badly, she
thought, furious, to make up such a stupid story.

Yes, he wanted the letter.

And Matka had almost given it to him!

The one you love holds the key. Give him the letter . . .

Not on your life, Gran.

Hot tears filled her eyes, blinding her. She never saw
the man coming up the steps toward her until she ran
squarely into his rock-solid body.

❧ *Chapter 26* ❧

Alex had searched all day for Selena, never thinking to look in his own backyard. What was she doing here at the museum? And why was she crying? He held her, steadying her, then felt her stiffen when she recognized him.

She pulled away from him. "Sold any paintings to Bonnell lately, Alex?" she snapped, wiping away her tears. "Where does he hang them, in his crypt?" Then, with a sardonic glare, she pushed past him and stormed up the path away from the Parsonage.

Oh, shit, he thought, and started after her. "Selena, wait, I can explain."

"Leave me alone, Alex. I don't know who you are or what you want from me, but whatever it is, you can't have it."

He rolled his eyes heavenward. "Will you calm down and let me explain?"

"No!"

"Look, I'm sorry about that little story. I should have set it straight before now, but—"

Selena wheeled around to face him, her cheeks burning bright pink. "You know, you have a lot of nerve, parading around pretending to be somebody you're not, invading my privacy, harassing my grandmother. I've a good mind to call the authorities. It's the letter you're after, isn't it? Who the hell are you, anyway?"

The afternoon sun bore down on them as they stood in the sandy lane, but he was oblivious to all but the shining black eyes boring into him, demanding answers. Anger poured from her in torrents, and he withstood the blast, knowing he deserved every bit of it.

"I am who I said I was, Alexander Hightower," he began, trying to sound calm in the face of disaster. Why couldn't he seem to hold to his determination not to get emotionally involved with women like Selena? He always seemed to find a way to screw it up. And he could see that history was about to repeat itself. "I'm an historian," he continued, "like I told you. And yes," he said after a short pause, "I think the letter your grandmother showed me might have incredible historical significance."

"That's all you've wanted all along," she charged reproachfully, her eyes flashing. "That's what it was all about, wasn't it . . . the made-up story about Bonnell, you bringing flowers to Gran. The . . . the night in the rainstorm—" At that she broke off, and he saw the tears glistening in her eyes once again.

"You're wrong, Selena," he said, groping for some way to make her understand. He touched her shoulder, but she jerked away.

"Am I? Then why the stupid masquerade?" Her voice was high-pitched, almost hysterical.

Alex felt his temper rise. "Well, damn it, I'm trying to tell you. Why don't you shut up and listen?"

She looked as startled as if he'd slapped her. He'd been rude, but at least he finally had her attention. Alex ran his hand through his hair, wondering how this had gotten so blown out of proportion. "I didn't mean to lie," he said simply, "and I'm sorry. And no," he added, taking a chance, "the letter isn't what it was all about."

She sniffed and gulped down a sob. "Do you care to expand on that?"

"Do you care to listen?"

She shrugged and nodded.

Alex took her hand, encouraged. "Like I said, I'm an historian," he began again. "My field of specialization is Victorian English literature, especially the work of the Brontës." He described how he'd noticed the similarity between the handwriting in her paintings and that of Emily Brontë. "At first, it was just something that struck my fancy," he told her, "but when I was able to get a closer look at the message on the painting here in Haworth, something clicked, and I couldn't get it out of my mind. When I found out your studio was nearby, I knew I had to try to get a look at the rest of the paintings."

"But why the charade? What was the point?"

He slowed to a halt and put one hand on her shoulder. With the other, he tipped her chin up. "Tell me the truth," he said. "Would you have let me in if I'd walked up to your place in the rain that day and said, 'Hey, you don't know me, but I need to take a look at your paintings because I think the handwriting looks like Emily Brontë's?' "

She hesitated. "No, I guess not."

"I didn't think so either."

"You could have written me, explaining what you wanted."

"Would you have answered?"

Slowly, she shook her head, again acknowledging he was right. "Normally, I don't let anybody into my studio. That's why I work through Tom. I . . . I'm used to being alone."

I'd like to change that, lady, Alex thought, but doubted if he could do much about it at this point. Better just to get the truth out, and with luck, find out about the damned letter. After that . . . well . . .

Selena looked up at him, and he saw that she was still deeply troubled. Why was she making such a big deal out of this?

"What are you working on at the museum?" she asked.

Alex was surprised by her change in direction. "I'm here for the summer researching the possibility that one of · the Brontë sisters might have committed suicide. . . ." He saw her eyes widen.

"Suicide?" Selena rubbed her arms as if she were cold.

"Yes," he replied, watching her closely. "You see, I think it's entirely possible that Emily Brontë took her own life."

Selena frowned. "Don't the history books tell you how she died?"

"They tell how she died, but I think they stop short of revealing the full story." Alex explained the circumstances surrounding the author's death, and his own theory that she took her life through willful neglect. "I didn't think too much about the words in your paintings other than I found a fascinating similarity in the handwriting," he continued, "until yesterday morning after the storm. I should have waited and asked your permission to study them, but you weren't there when I saw something in one of the paintings that set my imagination on fire. It was the word 'Keeper.' "

"Keeper?"

"Keeper was the name of Emily Brontë's dog. I saw 'Keeper' in the painting, along with some other familiar-sounding words, and I began to wonder if maybe your letter might convey a message relating to the Brontës."

"Why didn't you just ask me about it?"

He hesitated. "If you'll recall, I did," he replied slowly, "and you sort of, well, lost it. Like you didn't want to talk about those images."

Selena looked up at him, and her expression told him

she remembered that he *had* asked her, and she'd told him to get the hell out. "You're right. I wouldn't have answered you anyway." Her voice was soft, and he felt pain behind her words. He continued as they began to walk down the path.

"After I left your place, I went to the photo lab where I'd had those pictures enlarged, and between the few that were readable, the words I copied at your place, and those I got from the painting in Haworth, I pieced together a message that . . . that contained a line from one of Emily's poems.

"I wanted to come to you with what I'd found," he went on, "but you'd made it clear that I was persona non grata around you. Then I remembered that your grandmother had asked me to come back to see her. She said she wanted to tell me about the letter, and she asked me to come alone." He paused. "And so I did."

He could tell that rather than easing the tension between them, his words were somehow causing Selena even more distress.

"Do you think Emily Brontë wrote that letter?" she asked.

"Unless you wrote it, or know who did, I think there's a good chance it could have been Emily. It would have to be examined by experts, of course, but I am myself something of an expert, and I'd be willing to put money down to prove its authenticity." His gaze penetrated the depths of her eyes. "I have a feeling that your grandmother's letter may have been the last thing Emily Brontë ever wrote," he said, probing for her response, hoping she'd tell him what was in the letter. "Maybe even something of a suicide note."

Selena glanced at him but offered nothing. They had almost reached the Land Rover, which hunkered beneath an isolated tree. Suddenly, Selena started to run toward the car. "Domino! Oh, damn! I forgot!"

But Domino was nowhere in sight.

"He must have jumped out," Selena agonized. In tomboy manner, she placed two fingers between her teeth and produced a shrill whistle. "That'll bring him running."

But Domino must have had other things on his mind. She whistled and called again while Alex walked on up the lane alone, his eyes searching the sea of waving grass for some sign of the black and white dog. As he called out to the dog, he considered his conversation with Selena. He knew she thought that all he was interested in was the letter, and he hadn't taken the opportunity to tell her any different, even though it was clear to him by this time that he'd lost his heart to her. Now that she had calmed down, and her anger seemed to have abated, he could risk telling her how he felt about her, but he doubted if she wanted to hear it. Their future together, he surmised, would be limited to any contact they might have in the search for the truth about Emily Brontë's death. Just as well, he tried to convince himself, but a too-familiar ache settled around his heart.

Half an hour passed, and Alex could see Selena visibly sinking into despair. "Maybe he's found his way back to your place," he suggested, hoping to ease the forlorn look from her face.

Selena turned to him and smiled wanly. "Perhaps you're right. He's obviously nowhere around here." She looked at her watch. "I need to get back anyway. I'm supposed to have dinner with my agent this evening."

Alex scowled. "Yeah. I guess you know he's cornered me into that meeting, too. I think Mr. Perkins has some suspicions about the content of the letter. He said he wanted to tell me about that aspect of the paintings, to pique the interest of my, uh, erstwhile client Bonnell." He shot her a self-deprecating grin and was relieved when she smiled back.

"Guess you'll have to come clean," she said, and her tone indicated that she might enjoy watching his discomfort when he did so.

Alex shrugged. "Paybacks are a bitch."

They stood close to one another beside the car. Selena's dark hair was tossed by the warm wind, and her face was smudged, but Alex had never seen her look more beautiful. The defenses that were supposed to protect him from intimate involvement continued to fail him.

He lowered his head and kissed her lips gently. "Let me know if you find Domino," he said. "See you at dinner tonight."

Selena could no longer restrain the tears that had threatened to spill over as she and Alex had searched for her dog. Large teardrops fell across her cheeks and blurred her vision, forcing her to drive slowly. She wiped them with the back of her hand and sniffed. Damn it, Domino, she cursed silently, hoping that her pet would be waiting for her at their doorstep.

But it wasn't the dog that brought the tears to the surface. It was the man. Alexander Hightower. The man —and the frustration and confusion he seemed to engender in her. Why couldn't she seem to think clearly about him?

Gran had said he loved her, but he'd never mentioned any such thing, even though the times she'd allowed herself to get close to him, he'd acted tender and protective. Or was that just another ruse to get at the letter?

She herself had admitted that she wanted to love Alex, and a very large part of her knew that maybe she already did. But how could she love someone she wasn't sure she could trust? It wasn't that ridiculous story he'd made up about Bonnell that gave rise to her misgivings about the handsome American. It was his motive behind it.

His explanations had been plausible enough, and Selena knew he was right in surmising that she would not have let him in had he been straight with her. She should not have let him in regardless. Why did she?

She thought about his claim that the letter might have been Emily Brontë's suicide note. After what she'd envisioned in the crystal ball and seen at the museum, she knew intuitively he was right. If it could be proven that the letter had actually been written by the famous author, it would be priceless.

And that's what Alex was after, Selena decided with a heavy heart.

A priceless relic. Nothing more.

She turned into Bridgeton Lane, thinking of the letter she now carried in her handbag. The letter had held a cruel curse over her family for generations. Was her heart to be its next victim?

The one you love holds the key. Give him the letter . . .

Matka's words echoed once again in her mind. Under other circumstances, she would have gladly turned it over to him, or anyone else who could help her rid the family of its hateful presence. But she doubted sincerely that Alex could break the spell of the curse, and she'd be damned if she'd just give it to him like some lovesick schoolgirl, especially after the rather underhanded way he'd gone about trying to obtain it. No. If it was as valuable as she now suspected it to be, she would consider all the options before making up her mind what to do.

Her thoughts shifted to the upcoming dinner party, which she now faced with dread. She wondered what Tom's real motive was for making the long drive from London.

"Guess I'm about to find out," she said out loud, frowning at the sight of two cars parked in her driveway.

No Domino romped to greet her, but Selena scarcely

noticed. "Who's here?" she called out, alarmed at this curious intrusion.

Tom Perkins stuck his head out of the upstairs window. "Up here, love. Thanks for leaving the place open. It's bloody hot this afternoon."

Selena stared at him with unmasked hostility, but Tom seemed oblivious to her anger. "Come up. We've just discovered the most remarkable thing. Perhaps you can explain it."

We?

Selena didn't recall leaving her studio unlocked, but she supposed it was possible. With a sigh and a quick glance up the hillside in case Domino was lingering on his Lassie-come-home journey, she went inside. She was hot, tired, emotionally spent, and had just lost her dog. She was in no mood to confront Tom Perkins or any of his cronies he'd dragged along.

The crony sat next to Tom on her sofa and didn't stand to greet her. The woman's red hair fell to her padded shoulders, a gleaming helmet. Selena had seen those coldly intelligent green eyes before, that milky white skin. Her memory rewound until she could play back the recollection, and she discovered Alex Hightower was also in the movie.

"What are you doing here?" Selena raged at Tom. "Nobody gave you permission to come into my studio." Her face was blazing, and it wasn't from the sun's heat.

Tom stood and held out his hands toward her. "Now, now, calm down, Selena. We didn't mean to intrude. Like I said, the door was open. I thought you might have had to run an errand and left it open for me. You *were* expecting me, after all."

Selena glanced at the woman, who seemed to be enjoying the scene from an icy distance. "Who is she? You know I don't let strangers in here."

Tom turned to Maggie, who at last condescended to rise for her introduction.

"This is Dr. Maggie Flynn," Tom said, a note of inexplicable triumph in his voice.

Neither woman extended a hand to the other.

Selena stared, trying to recall what Alex had said about this woman. A colleague, he'd called her. Was she, too, a scholar? A Brontë scholar? She hadn't believed him then, but now that she knew who might have written the letter, she thought it entirely possible.

"Dr. Flynn. What brings you to Stanbury?" she finally managed.

Maggie forced a smile. "Your work, my dear." Her tone was disdainful, patronizing. "I find it quite . . . fascinating."

Selena looked at Tom, then her gaze fell to the table-top in front of the couch. To her horror, she saw the tiny pieces of the photocopied letter scattered about.

"What in bloody hell do you think you're doing?" Selena shrieked, swooping to scoop the fragments into her hands. "Where did you get these?"

Tom surveyed her mildly, as if measuring the importance of her reaction to his invasion. "They were in the next room. We found them to be . . . a pastime . . . while we waited for you."

Red-hair spoke again. "Where did you get this?" It was a demand, as if Selena had stolen something from her, not the other way around.

"You are trespassing, Dr. Flynn," Selena said, ice in her voice. "And you as well, Tom. I did not invite you here, nor did I leave the door open for you. Please leave, or I'll call the police."

Tom came toward her and attempted to put his arm around her. "Now, Selena, aren't you overreacting? We meant no harm. It was an honest assumption that you wanted us to wait up here rather than in our hot cars."

Selena pulled away from him in disgust. "And you assumed it would be all right with me for you to rummage about my studio as well?"

"I *am* your agent," Tom said sharply. "Part of the reason I came here was to see what's holding you up on those commissions. I do assume it would be natural for me to take a look at your work."

Selena wadded the bits of paper between her sweaty palms. "And what is your interest in coming here, Dr. Flynn?"

Maggie Flynn attempted another smile, but it, too, never reached her eyes. "Let's get to the point, Tom," she said, avoiding making a direct statement to Selena.

Selena looked at Tom, demanding an answer. She could see beads of perspiration encircling his fat forehead. He glanced at what she held in her hand.

"Dr. Flynn has discovered something about your paintings that I'm afraid has eluded me all along," he said at last. "She is a professor. At Oxford."

Selena waited, her nerves taut, for him to continue, but she already knew what he was going to say.

"She saw your work in London, and she noted the written images in the paintings. She approached me with the idea that perhaps those messages meant something, if they were pieced together." His eyes narrowed. "You had told me they did, and I knew I would be meeting with you this afternoon, so I invited her to drive up and join us. I thought . . . perhaps you could shed some light on the subject. It could give us," here he cleared his throat, "another sales angle."

"Is Dr. Flynn interested in purchasing my work?" Selena asked Tom, ignoring the other woman in kind.

"Let's cut through this, Tom," Dr. Flynn said, annoyed. She turned and spoke to Selena. "Unlike other . . . colleagues of mine, I have no penchant for lying. I am interested only in the message which you have been

painting. I am a scholar of English literature, and I have
reason to believe that either you have read the poems of
Emily Brontë and have used some of her work here in
your paintings, or," she paused, "this letter you are painting was written by Brontë herself. Tell me, which is it?"

"It is none of your business, Dr. Flynn, how I arrived at
the images in my work. And you are not free to examine
my paintings further, unless you wish to buy the entire
series."

"Perhaps I will, if that's what it takes. But I must advise you, Miss . . . uh, Selena, that if you are indeed in
possession of an original document penned by one of the
Brontë sisters, its value will far outweigh anything you
will ever receive for your art. I came along with Tom
today to see if I could validate my conjecture that the
message is Brontë-related, which it clearly is." She attempted to add warmth to her smile.

"Now I hope to be able to convince you that if this
document exists as an original and is not a photocopy of
a forgery," she nodded toward Selena's clutched fists, "it
would be in your best interest, as well as in the interest of
history, to turn it over to the safekeeping of my university, where we can examine it for its authenticity. We
would, of course," she said this to Tom, "be willing to pay
handsomely for such a prize, once it was proven to be a
Brontë artifact."

She turned back to Selena, who stood stunned at the
woman's temerity. "It is of utmost importance that it not
fall into the wrong hands. I understand you have been
approached by Dr. Alexander Hightower, who claims to
be the representative of an American art collector?" Her
inflection indicated she expected an answer, but when
Selena remained silent, she continued.

"I must warn you that Dr. Hightower would stoop to
anything to obtain this letter. His . . . scruples, shall we

say, are questionable. It has come to my attention that he is using the name Bonnell in his deception."

Selena straightened and inhaled deeply. It was difficult to remain calm when she wanted to fling this odious woman out the door. Instead she smiled as sweetly as she could force herself to do.

"Dr. Hightower and I share a little joke concerning Henry H. Bonnell. An innocent little joke." Selena's eyes penetrated Maggie's gaze of ice, daring her to push the issue further. "Bonnell wouldn't be interested in my art or anyone else's, now would he? It would be difficult, don't you agree Dr. Flynn, for a man who has been dead for almost seventy years to be interested in much of anything?"

❧ *Chapter 27* ❧

"**H**ere, boy," Alex called to the bedraggled dog, snapping his fingers and pointing to the front seat of Eleanor's Jaguar. He'd tried to protect the red leather by covering it with his bedspread, but the dog's enthusiasm over having been rescued from the animal shelter quickly turned the spread into a tumbled mess. At least, Alex hoped as he climbed in beside the animal, the fabric might have wiped off some of the grime.

"Settle down," he said, patting the frightened dog's head. "That'll teach you to run off." Alex slipped the car into gear and headed toward Bridgeton Lane, pleased that he would see a smile back on Selena's face, if not for him, at least for the return of her lost pet. She had looked so distraught when they parted, he could barely stand it, so when he returned to his flat, he rang the RSPCA kennels just in case the dog had been found, and there was a dog matching Domino's description.

He wasted no time in getting to the facility, where he was greeted by a confused and frightened Domino. Alex was not sure the animal would come to him, but he'd paid the fine anyway and suffered through the stern admonitions of the keeper against letting dogs roam free. Domino apparently preferred human company to caged canines, however, and came at a run when Alex called him.

Alex was looking forward to this visit to Selena's, thinking that by bringing her dog home, he would make a giant stride in restoring her confidence in him. But he frowned as he drove up to the old farmhouse. It looked like a car lot. The Land Rover was there, along with a small white Honda and a red BMW.

Perplexed, he parked the Jag behind Selena's car and got out, motioning for the dog to follow. It had been only a little over an hour since he'd kissed Selena, and she hadn't mentioned that she was having a party. She'd said she had to get ready to meet Perkins for dinner.

Perkins.

His would be the red car.

But who did the other one belong to?

Alex decided he might as well have his standoff with Perkins here. It would save the aggravation of forcing politeness over dinner. He knocked at the studio door, then opened it and let the dog scoot past him, fur flying up the stairs.

"Selena!" Alex called. He heard a squeal of delight as the dog rushed into the studio, then Selena appeared at the top of the stairs.

"Alex!" she cried, dashing down and into his arms. "Where did you find him?"

"He was at the wrong place at the wrong time this afternoon, and the animal control people picked him up." His words were casual, and then he realized her whole body was quaking. "Selena. What's the matter?"

She released her viselike hold on him and looked up the stairs just as Tom Perkins stepped onto the landing. "Well, well, look what the dog dragged in," Tom scoffed.

Alex glanced at Selena, who said, "I have unexpected visitors, Alex. They were just leaving."

But Perkins only laughed. "Not now. Things are beginning to get interesting."

Alex squeezed Selena's hand. "It's all right," he said in a low voice.

"No, it isn't—" she started to reply, but he had already started up the stairs.

He was face-to-face with Maggie Flynn before he realized what Selena had been trying to tell him.

He read smug amusement in Maggie's green eyes and sheer enjoyment that she had obviously shocked him with her unexpected presence.

"Dr. Hightower," she said in a voice of silken steel. "How nice to see you. However, I was looking forward to surprising you this evening. Tom had graciously invited me to join you for dinner."

Alex glared at her. "At least I'll be spared that case of indigestion," he growled, then looked at Tom. "You're just full of surprises, Perkins. What's this all about?"

"Perhaps you could tell us that, Dr. Hightower. By the way, have you spoken to Henry Bonnell lately?"

Before Alex could reply, Selena came to his side. "They know about the letter, Alex. Your . . . colleague, Dr. Flynn, has graciously offered to keep it safe from predators like you." Alex felt her slim hand slip into the crook of his arm. "Of course, she doesn't know if such a document really exists. She can only surmise from the torn pieces of the photocopy she and Mr. Perkins helped themselves to before I returned home."

Alex heard a strength in Selena's voice that hadn't been there before, and he felt her unspoken support in the touch of her hand.

Maggie groaned impatiently. "Quit playing games. Alex, what in bloody hell possessed you to pretend to be an art agent on behalf of Henry Bonnell, for God's sake?"

Alex felt a slight squeeze on his arm, and he glanced

down at Selena. Her reassuring smile told him all he needed to know.

"It's none of your business, Dr. Flynn," Alex said, returning his attention to the redhead, whose face seemed to be even more pale than usual.

"It becomes my business when you manipulate Brontë history for your own advancement."

Alex stared at her. "I don't get your drift."

"If you think you can resurrect Henry Bonnell, Alexander, you might also create phony evidence to prove your point in the debate. Evidence such as a letter, forged in Emily's handwriting, copied in pieces on your lover's canvases, and later 'revealed' as proof that Emily killed herself."

The room echoed the silence that followed her tirade.

"You're insane, Maggie," Alex said at last, shocked at her accusation.

"Am I? Then prove me wrong. So far I don't know that any such letter exists. All I have seen is a crumpled and torn photocopy of what might or might not be such an artifact."

"I don't have to prove anything to you," Alex snarled. "You're way out of line."

"Perhaps Dr. Flynn's imagination has run away with her a bit," Tom Perkins interjected, himself visibly shaken by Maggie's vehemence. "I can understand if you have run across such a valuable artifact, you would indeed want to hold onto it until the right buyer—"

"Wait a minute. Wait a minute." Alex held up his hands. "Let me make one thing perfectly clear. I don't have any such artifact. I suspect that it exists, and I would give my arm to know what it says and if it might possibly be authentic. But I have nothing more to go on at the moment than you, Dr. Flynn." Then he added dryly, "Perhaps even less, since I have not had access to the photocopied pieces you mentioned."

Selena spoke up, her voice quiet against the shrill accusations the others were slinging at one another. "There was a time, not long ago, when I wanted nothing more than for the images in my paintings to release me from their spell. I couldn't seem to paint anything else. You called it a series, Tom. I call it an obsession. The only image that has any basis in fact is the letter, those pieces you were putting together when I came in."

She looked at Maggie. "The letter does exist, Dr. Flynn. It is an ancient letter, written to one of my ancestors. It is a terrible letter, and its words have cursed my family for generations."

Then she turned to Alex. "My grandmother seems to think you hold the key to breaking the curse. Perhaps the time has come to trust in her Gypsy nonsense."

With that, Selena went to her purse, which she'd tossed in the corner, and brought out a slightly bent envelope and handed it to Alex.

His eyes widened, knowing the treasure she was entrusting to his care. "Are you sure . . . ?"

Selena nodded. "Maybe you should read it aloud. Tom and Dr. Flynn seem to have gone to a great deal of effort to learn of its existence. They deserve to know what it contains."

With his heart beating heavily in his chest, Alex took the fragile paper out of the envelope and unfolded it. He read:

"November 2, 1848
To my dear love:
I write this to leave under the message rock,
to bid you farewell for the last time. I will
never see you again on this earth, for
my days are thankfully short. My health
is failing, and I wish only that it would
fail faster, to put an end to the misery

which I have brought upon myself. It is
the price I must pay for my indiscretion
with you, for my foolish and uncontrolled
behavior. I fear not death, in fact I
welcome it, for in death I shall at last be free.
In death my shame will go undiscovered,
never to hurt my beloved family. I beg
forgiveness only from you, for this child
is of you as well, but I fear not
retribution for what I do. There is
no hell hereafter to torment me as
the hell here on earth does today.
I will miss you and the moors and
Keeper and the rest, but only for a
time. I know there is a blessed shore
opening its ports for me and mine, and
gazing Time's wide waters o'er, I weary
for that land divine. Where we were
born, where you and I shall meet our
Dearest when we die; from suffering
and corruption free, restored unto
the Deity. So do not mourn, my
only love, just remember me when
the moon rises above the moors and
the wind blows the heather in the
sunshine, for my spirit will be there."

They stood in stunned silence, and finally Maggie collapsed into the sofa cushions.

"Could it be?" she whispered, and Alex looked up in time to see her brush an uncharacteristic tear from a mascara-encrusted eye.

Tom peered over his shoulder, looking at the piece with covetous eyes. "Do you suppose it's authentic?" he said with unveiled awe.

"I suppose it could be," Alex replied. "We have a lot of

work to do in order to prove it, though. Eleanor Bates has already contacted the top forensic experts we'll need. . . ."

Maggie looked up at him sharply. "Eleanor Bates? Don't you think the authorities at Oxford would be more appropriate?"

Alex studied her. "You'd like that, wouldn't you?"

"You're damned right I'd like that. I'd like to see this thing handled for once in a professional manner."

"What makes you think Eleanor isn't a professional? You told me yourself what high esteem you had for her."

"I didn't mean it that way. Of course, I hold her in high esteem. But she's not . . ."

"An academic? You're right about that. And as far as I'm concerned, so much the better. Perhaps the Brontë Society is a better home for that artifact than anyone's university."

"I can't believe that is coming from you, of all people. Unless . . ."

"Unless what?"

Abruptly, Maggie Flynn stood and picked up the large leather purse she always carried. "Unless, Dr. Hightower, you still have something to hide." She made her way to the door, then turned. "Tom, please forgive me, but I think I just remembered an urgent appointment back at Oxford. I won't be able to join you for dinner." She glanced once at the letter, which lay exposed to the world on the table, then marched out of the room.

"I think the reservations have just been canceled anyway," Tom said gloomily, following her out. "Selena, when you get past all this nonsense, give me a call."

Selena and Alex held their breaths until the outer door slammed. Then Selena ran into his arms.

"Who is that awful woman?" she whispered, as if Maggie might overhear.

Alex held her close, his heart hammering, scarcely daring to believe what he'd just read, or that Selena had trusted him enough to give the letter to him. Even more, not believing that she was here now, in his arms. He wished she hadn't asked about Maggie, but he had no choice, nor desire, to hide anything from her ever again. "I won't lie to you, Selena. She and I once—"

"I don't want to hear it." Selena suddenly pulled away with an uncertain laugh. "Just tell me that whatever was between you is over."

Alex kissed her nose. "Long, long over. If it ever was." He kissed her cheeks. "But what's not over, I hope, is what's between us."

Lowering his arms, he let her slip from his embrace. He walked to where the letter lay like a ragged tissue on the tabletop. This bit of paper and ink could make his career, if it was authentic. But it was time for history to stop repeating itself.

He reached for the paper, not looking at it. His eyes held Selena's. He folded the letter as he walked back to where she stood in silence. He took her hand and held it palm up.

"There was a time in my life when I would damn near have killed to lay my hands on something like this," he said, curling her fingers around it. "But I've found something far more important, Selena, and I don't want to lose it. I don't want to lose you. I love you."

His eyes searched hers and saw the earlier doubt begin to dissolve. She put her arms around him and laid her head against his chest.

"I . . . I want that more than anything, Alex," she murmured. "I've never felt like this toward anyone before." Her breathing was ragged as she talked. "And I know I can trust you. It's just that it's all so strange. The way you came here. The paintings. The letter. What happened today on the moors. I haven't told you the half of it."

She looked up at him with troubled eyes. "I'm afraid, Alex," she admitted at last. "I love you. I know it from the bottom of my heart. But I'm afraid the curse will . . . destroy us as it did my mother and father." She attempted a small laugh, but it only emphasized her deep distress. "I know that sounds stupid, but—"

Alex drew her close to him once again. "Don't be afraid, Selena. The curse is nothing unless you believe in it."

"That's what I thought, too, until . . . I couldn't stop painting those images."

"Maybe your subconscious was trying to tell you to deal with this once and for all. You know intellectually the curse doesn't need to have power over you or anyone else. And yet, deep down, you still believe in it. Maybe your paintings were your way of dredging up the fears and bringing them to the light of day." Alex had often used poetry the same way, long ago when his own dark doubts threatened to overpower his sanity.

Selena didn't reply right away, and Alex knew she was considering what he'd said. He expected her to agree, but when she answered, he knew his psychological explanation had lost out to Gypsy tradition.

"Matka thinks you're the one who can break the curse." She looked up at him. "Can you?"

Alex led her to the sofa and drew her into his lap. He brushed the dark hair away from the delicate face, loving her beyond all being. How he wanted to take away the demons that haunted her! If only he knew how. He thought back to his visit with Matka.

"Your grandmother told me the only way the curse could be lifted was if the family Wd attained forgiveness from the family of the *Gorgio* woman who died."

"And you think that woman was Emily Brontë?"

"Yes."

He saw hope in her suddenly eager expression. A hope he had to dash with his next words. "But Emily died unmarried, as did her brother and sister, Branwell and Anne. Charlotte married and conceived a child, but died before it was born. Old Patrick Brontë outlived all of his children, and when he died, it was the end of their line." He brushed her cheek with his fingers. "There is no family to grant forgiveness, Selena."

"Oh, dear," she said quietly, and Alex saw the dark impact of these words in her destitute expression. "Then there is no way for the curse to die. Unless I die, and there are no more descendants of the family Wd as well."

Alex felt his heart break, and he bled for her pain. He had to clear his throat to speak. "I guess that's one way to look at it," he said, his voice husky. "Another way is to believe the curse died with the end of the Brontë family."

"But what about my ancestors? My great-uncle? My . . . my own parents?"

"Do you really believe they were cursed, or could their problems be explained differently? Isn't it possible they would have had the same troubles had they never known the curse existed?"

Selena frowned. "I've always believed that my mother and father suffered from alcoholism and hopelessness, and I've tried to deny the curse all of my life. But when those paintings started to control me, I had to pay attention, Alex. I had to! Even if my family's problems could be explained away by psychology or something, I still believe the curse influenced their lives."

"Then you do believe . . ."

Selena nodded ever so slightly. "I suppose I do."

Alex swallowed. "Then I guess you have a choice."

"What choice?"

"You can continue to believe in the curse, or you can believe in us."

"It's not that simple, Alex. You just don't understand."

Alex understood only that he wanted this woman and that he was not going to allow any curse, real or imagined, to stand in his way. He wasn't sure how, but he would find a way to either break the spell, or convince Selena it didn't exist.

At the moment, he would do his best to persuade her that he was a better bet.

Unable to control his desire for her any longer, he framed her face with his hand, raising it slightly. He saw no resistance in her eyes, only an igniting passion that fueled his own. He dropped his lips to hers, and he felt her body melt against him. Her lips parted to receive him, and hunger for her welled within his soul. A wild, dangerous, animal hunger. He teetered on the edge of control.

Forcing himself to slow down, he said in a low voice, uttered between short breaths, "I understand . . . what is important, Selena. . . . I love you, with all my heart. Curse or not, I want you to be mine for all eternity. I'm willing to take that chance if you are."

He saw her eyes were misty with tears. "My own *Gorgio* love," she murmured before she returned his kiss with a fire that said what his heart wanted to hear.

Selena closed her eyes to the mauves and grays and wild Gypsy riders that hung on walls only a few feet away. She nestled in the strong arms that held her, protected her. Safe. With Alex, she felt safe. He would not hurt her. He would not leave her. There was no curse.

At least not for him.

And for her?

Take a chance. Take a chance.

His words echoed through her mind and reached deep into her heart. She wanted to take a chance. She felt Alex trace the back of his fingers along her jaw and down her neck. She wanted this man. His finger edged free the top button of her blouse.

She wanted . . .

Her tongue searched for a deeper taste of him, and she heard him groan and move beneath her.

He wanted . . .

Selena splayed her hand across his chest, then moved it down and away, giving him room.

Take a chance.

Alex released another button, and then another, and she made no move to stop him. Her heart pounded as she felt the intoxicating rush of passion filling her soul. His kisses were desperate and hungry, and she returned them with a fever she hadn't known possible.

Take a chance.

He laid bare her soft breasts, revealing their tender beauty in the late golden sunshine. Her nipples, dark and erect, invited his fingertips to graze and his lips to explore, and she quivered beneath his touch. Arching her back, she felt fire in her belly when his hand moved downward, seeking the silken inner curve of her slender thigh, shedding the soft cotton skirt that once hid it from view. She lay naked before his eyes, which ravished her body even as his hands, large and strong, stroked every inch of her skin with abandonment.

Seeking, finding, private hidden places.

Lighting even greater fires, until she wanted to cry out in her delicious agony.

She didn't know how it could be, but her desire for him seemed more than physical. It was a raw, demanding need that ripped through the source of her very being. She felt as if she must melt into him and become him. Desperately, she freed him from the loose shirt that remained between them and raked her fingers through the wiry wisps of dark hair that covered the taut, hard planes of muscle on his chest.

Selena felt him move beneath her to remove the last barrier to their intimacy, and with a boldness born of long-controlled passion at last unleashed, she placed her hand on him, exploring his masculine hardness beneath her feminine fingers. She heard him emit a low groan and felt his arms tighten around her, his kiss deepen as he moved against her.

Any lingering doubts Selena might have held dissolved as her love for Alex commanded expression. She lay back against the old sofa and closed her eyes, her heart pounding wildly as she awaited her lover. She could feel the heat from his body, the scratchy texture of his chest hair against her breasts. Her breath mingled with his for an instant and then seemed to cease altogether as they became one. Daylight was plunged into darkness, and she felt the sexual energy, ancient and sacred, the very force of life itself, rising within her with each movement, each surge into oneness. She knew the dance. It was as old as time: A man, strong in his nakedness, enfolding woman, woman enveloping man, until at last, with a silent primal scream, all consciousness exploded into a thousand infinite stars.

Chapter 28

"**S** top here," Eleanor Bates directed her driver. "I'll walk the rest of the way. You can wait for me in the pub on the corner."

The well-dressed elderly woman waited for the man to open the door for her, then nodded, straightened her back, and walked off in the direction of the Sunnyside Nursing Home at the far end of the block.

Eleanor hated going into a nursing home. It reminded her of her own mortality, she supposed, and as the years passed, the age of the residents seemed to more closely equal her own. But today her visit was unavoidable, even though she did not know the woman she'd come to see.

"Matka Wood," she said to the volunteer at the reception desk. "Could you please direct me to her room?"

"It's 115-B, down the hall there and to your left at the drinking fountain. But I believe," she looked at her watch, "that you'll more likely find her by the fireplace in the Community Room, in there." She pointed to a set of double doors, and Eleanor nodded.

"Thank you, my dear." She looked down the hall toward Matka's room, wishing she could accomplish her mission in privacy. Well, she thought, taking a deep breath and trying to ignore the semihospital smell of the place, might as well get it over with. Alex might be furious with her for interfering in his love life once again, but Eleanor thought that perhaps she could rectify her earlier error in attempting to set him up with Maggie Flynn.

Going through the heavy doors, Eleanor saw that the room was occupied by only two people. An old man sat on the window seat, looking out upon the gray morning. An old woman in a wheelchair read a newspaper by the fireplace, which glowed with a low flame. Even though it was August, the day was wet and cool, and Eleanor welcomed the warmth of the hearth.

"Mrs. Wood?" she queried, approaching the woman.

An ancient face appeared from behind the paper and peered up at Eleanor, who suddenly felt immensely younger. "Who be askin'?"

Eleanor smiled, recognizing mettle when she saw it. "My name is Bates. Eleanor Bates. I have recently become acquainted with your lovely granddaughter, Selena, through a mutual friend, Dr. Alexander Hightower."

The old woman frowned, as if sorting through her memories until she came upon the right names. "Hightower." Then the frown turned into a smile that reversed the direction of the myriad wrinkles in her face. "That nice young man." She leaned forward and added conspiratorially, "I hope the girl has the good sense t' keep holt o' him. He's a looker, in't he?"

Eleanor pulled up a chair, liking the crone better every minute. "Yes, Dr. Hightower . . . Alex is quite handsome," she agreed. "And Selena is in love with him, you know."

"Ah, I thought maybe, but I didn't know f'r sure. She can be stubborn, that'n."

Eleanor cleared her throat. "Well, that's what I have come to see you about," she said, hoping for Alex's sake Selena's grandmother would accept what she had come to offer. "Alex has told me about the . . . curse, Mrs. Wood."

"Matka. Nobody calls me Mrs. Wood. I wouldn't know t' answer."

"Matka, then. He says Selena is still not sure she will say yes to his marriage proposal, because she feels this ancient curse might . . . well, as he put it, make her 'unlucky in love.' "

The words sounded almost ludicrous as they rolled off Eleanor's tongue, but she was never one to laugh at another's idiom.

Matka shook her head slowly from side to side. "I'twas as I feared," she murmured. "She told me tha' Alex had proven who wrote the letter, but tha' there be no family left t' grant forgiveness."

"Technically, that is true, Matka. But I have come as something of a proxy, because I believe the Brontës have quite a large family, of which I am a member."

Matka's head jerked up. "What y' be sayin'?"

"I am saying that there is a large group of us who feel a kinship with the Brontë family. We call ourselves the Brontë Society, and for over one hundred years we have worked to protect and preserve the Brontë name and heritage. Many of us, like myself, feel as if there might be a little Brontë blood flowing in our veins, although I am sure that is just wishful thinking."

The older woman's eyes searched Eleanor's face. "Go on."

Eleanor reached into her purse and drew out the letter. "Alex gave me this into safekeeping until the debate, day after tomorrow. We have worked closely together to examine it, and from the chemical makeup of the paper and ink, we're certain it was written around the time Emily Brontë wrote *Wuthering Heights*. Alex is an expert on Emily Brontë's penmanship, and with the consensus of other experts in the field, he firmly believes it was she who wrote it." She opened the letter and gazed once again at the almost unbelievable message it revealed.

"If it is forgiveness you believe will end the curse," Eleanor said, looking up into Matka's eyes, "I am here on behalf of the Brontë Society to offer it, although I know that Emily Brontë would never have wished such a thing onto anyone."

Matka's eyes grew moist. "'Twasn't the girl who brought on the curse," she said. "I'twas Mikel himself, and believin' he was responsible for the girl's death, Mikel named forgiveness by her family as the only possible release from the curse." She stared into the fire for a long time, a distant look in her eyes.

"Yes. I think i'twill work," she said at last, bringing her gaze back to Eleanor. "Let me see the letter again."

Reluctantly, Eleanor gave the letter back to its rightful owner, who clutched it between gnarled fingers. She closed her eyes, as if listening to a voice Eleanor could not hear. When she opened them again, there was a look of deep peace and gratitude on her face.

"It is done."

The auditorium was filled to overflowing, and latecomers had to stand in the rear of the university's small theater. Word had leaked out over the past few weeks, largely with Eleanor Bates's help, that some sensational new material concerning Emily Brontë was going to be revealed at tonight's debate, and there were more than twice the number of people than had originally been expected.

Alex and Maggie were seated at opposite sides of the stage with a podium between them.

A podium, and palpable tension.

Alex ran his hand through his thick, dark hair. It was warm in the room, and the starched shirt and navy blazer he wore with a tie threatened to suffocate him. Sweat beaded on his forehead and trickled down his back. Outside, the sky had turned an ominous color, and the warm summer day threatened to end in a nasty storm.

Sort of like my career, Alex thought grimly, doubting seriously that he would now be appointed to the vacant Chair in English Literature at Leeds University he'd applied for, even with the clout of Eleanor Bates behind him.

Eleanor Bates and about a dozen other members of the Brontë Society had arrived early and were sitting in the front row, looking at him expectantly. Alex knew that Eleanor had delighted in tantalizing her friends with the "secret" she'd been in on, letting them know something big was about to be revealed without telling them what.

She'd been a good friend and a trustworthy colleague. He'd even accepted her generous offer to stay in her home after the debate for a "celebration" toast without a long drive back to Haworth after.

He hated that he would be unable to deliver the victory she expected.

He should have told her before tonight what had happened, but he himself was still in a state of shock. In fact, he could hardly think. Everything was out the window. He should have called the debate off instead of trying to wing it. Nobody, with perhaps the exception of Maggie Flynn, was going to be happy with his performance tonight.

Outside, heavy thunder rumbled.

Glancing over the heads of the audience, Alex saw Selena enter the auditorium pushing her grandmother's wheelchair, and his heart lurched. She was sensational in the red dress she'd picked out especially for the occasion. At least there would be someone in his court tonight, and no matter what else happened, Alex thought with a melancholy smile, he had come out the winner with the dark-eyed beauty. He'd find something to do, anything, to remain here with her in the moorland country they both loved so well.

Selena's grandmother, dressed in black and wearing a large strand of pearls, would never know how appropriate her funereal attire was. Matka gave him a broad, semitoothless smile, and he found it hard to be angry with her.

What was done was done.

The moderator began the proceedings, introducing each debater in formal, eloquent style. Alex, as the affirmative side, spoke first.

"Resolved, that Emily Jane Brontë, author of *Wuthering Heights* and numerous poems, committed suicide through willful neglect."

Alex looked out across the sea of faces in the audience, wishing he was anywhere else but behind the podium at the moment.

"I am convinced of the truth of this statement based upon extensive studies of the work of this Victorian writer," he said unenthusiastically. He knew it was the truth, but that truth would now have to be anchored only by old arguments.

Which he made, point by point, quote by quote, carefully reasoning each through to a logical conclusion. At the end of his ten minute presentation, the audience was visibly restless, wondering when the big news was going to be forthcoming.

Maggie, statuesque in an immaculately tailored cream-colored suit with black trim, approached the podium. Before beginning her own arguments, she shot Alex a "what the hell is going on here" look.

Alex looked away. Although Maggie remained diametrically opposed to him on the issue, he knew she could not overlook the impact of the letter, and he figured she'd planned her counterproposal accordingly.

But he hadn't introduced the letter.

So what was she going to do? he wondered. He was not sorry she was going to find the debate as difficult as he. In fact, he found it amusing that she would be floundering as badly as he in this first segment.

"Resolved, that Emily Jane Brontë died of natural causes following a serious illness." Her voice was crisp and British.

Like Alex, Maggie was forced to take the fall-back position she would have used had she not known about the letter. Her argument was predicated not upon Emily's work, but rather on biographical accounts that were old news to those in the audience.

The audience stirred, whispering among themselves, their restlessness and growing disappointment punctuated ever more frequently by the rattle of thunder overhead.

The first segment completed, the moderator approached Maggie and Alex, a perplexed expression on his face.

"Is there something wrong?" he asked. "I mean, we all expected—"

"There damn sure is something wrong," Maggie hissed at Alex. "What the hell do you think you are doing? When are you going to get to the point?"

"I have already."

She stared at him. "The letter, Alex. What about the letter?"

"I'm not going to use the letter," he stated flatly, and it was worth all his own disappointment to see the shock in her eyes.

"Not use it! Why? I don't understand."

"I can't use it, Maggie, because I don't have it."

Her face turned to ash. "Someone's stolen it."

"Not exactly."

"Surely you have copies?"

"I'm not about to introduce a photocopy without the

real thing to back it up," Alex replied with a sardonic smile. "That would set you up real nicely, wouldn't it? No forensics. No authenticity. Only a document that you would eagerly try to prove that I forged."

Alex could see by the rising color in Maggie's face that he had accurately surmised her strategy.

"Where is the damned letter, Alex?" she demanded in a guttural voice.

He looked at her evenly. "Let's just get this over with as fast as possible." Turning to the bewildered moderator, he added, "I'm ready for my second presentation, if I may."

Alex, having prepared for months against Maggie's predictable biographical arguments, laid out his theory again, using other biographical material to support his case.

There was only a smattering of polite applause when he was seated.

Maggie fared little better, and in fact made several errors. Alex knew she was beside herself with fury, and he found it ironically funny that she should be the one to be thrown off by the unexpected turn of events the evening before. He wondered what she would do for a rebuttal, as he surmised that she had planned a scathing denouncement of the authenticity of the letter.

She had been furious to learn she would not be on the research team, which was comprised of scientists, scholars, and selected representatives of the Brontë Society. Alex, being the trustee of the letter on Selena's behalf, had helped to select the committee, but he had not recommended Maggie, believing that her intense emotional negativity toward him might create unnecessary delays.

When Maggie finished, the moderator took the podium and called for a five minute recess. Alex, who sat leaning forward on his arms, looked up into the faded blue eyes of Eleanor Bates, eyes that silently but

staunchly demanded an explanation for this sorry debacle. He nodded and scribbled a message on his notepad.
Eleanor came to the edge of the stage and said nothing
as he handed her the paper.

The program resumed under the noisy drumming of a
downpour on the roof. It was Maggie's turn to go first,
and she took the podium loaded with all the resentment,
anger, and hostility she had stored up against Alex in the
past year.

"Tonight, Dr. Alexander Hightower has proven himself to be the dilettante I have long suspected him to be,"
she began. "He has provided no new evidence for his
foolish and unworthy claim. I believe more than one of
us here tonight expected something rather more dra-
matic than what he has presented, and I for one feel
deceived and misled."

Alex heard a rustle of agreement in the audience, and
he didn't blame them. He had not deceived nor misled
anyone, but neither could he produce what he'd hoped
would prove once and for all that scholars should never
rest as long as there is a shred of doubt surrounding an
issue.

He watched his former lover—how could he have let
that happen?—sink from academic counterpoint into a
diatribe that turned clearly into a personal vendetta
against him. Her words were harsh, emotional, and un-
professional, and he found himself feeling perversely
sorry for her. The audience, as unhappy as they were
with him at the moment, appeared uncomfortable and
embarrassed as she took her seat.

Alex looked out at Eleanor Bates, whose demanding
eyes had lost some of their wrath after reading his note,
although they remained inquisitive. He saw Selena and
her grandmother at the end of the aisle, and suddenly
Eleanor Bates, Maggie Flynn, even the letter no longer

mattered. Things had worked out as they should. He could see that now.

He had but one thing left to do.

Dr. Alexander Hightower stood to his full six feet and went to the podium. He carried no notes, for he needed none for what he had to say.

"Ladies and gentlemen, I regret that tonight's event did not meet up to your expectations. Some rather . . . er, unusual circumstances precluded my presentation from being all that I expected as well. Life is like that sometimes. It takes a turn around a corner we least expect, and it is how we cope with that turn that forges our future.

"I submit that Emily Brontë met with just such an unexpected event, and that she coped with it in the only way she knew how. I cannot in this assembled group provide proof of what that event might have been, and so I must ask you to imagine, if you will, what sort of unexpected tribulation could have befallen this young woman that would have caused her to take her own life.

"We are all devoted to the Brontë sisters, and I have a special place in my heart for Emily Brontë, for I believe she is the least understood. We scholars tend to raise her to the level of a saint, this supposedly celibate preacher's daughter, and we forget how young she was, how lonely at times, how vulnerable she might have been. She was a woman just entering her prime. She had feelings. She laughed and she cried. She hurt, just like we all do, when things go wrong.

"Because she was so fiercely private, we call her rude and unbending. Because so little of her work is available to us, we judge her by what we see and do not consider that there may have been much that would cast an entirely different slant upon this talented creature.

"It is my contention, ladies and gentlemen, that it is our job as scholars not to close our minds and dig our heels into the sand when it comes to a theory such as my own, but rather to explore it fully, with an open mind. We must never rest as long as there is doubt in a single mind that Emily's death might have been self-induced. Because if it were, ladies and gentlemen, if she did make a conscious choice to die, and execute that choice with her will of iron, as I firmly believe she did, then history as we know it is not only incomplete, it is incorrect.

"Why am I compelled to force this issue into discussion and examination by my reluctant colleagues, such as Dr. Flynn, whose rigid views leave no room for the 'what if'? Why do I not just leave the poor woman alone? I am compelled, ladies and gentlemen, by the desire to know the truth about an inexplicable life and an equally unexplainable death.

"Perhaps in time you will learn the contents of the document I had hoped to produce here tonight. But since I cannot bring it forth and prove its authenticity, I will not challenge your integrity by asking you to accept something that lacks tangible viability. Rather, I ask only that each and every one of you rethink your image of Emily Jane Brontë. Allow her to be human, for God's sake. Set aside for just a moment the outworn images of Emily the old stoic, and think of her as the wild, free creature of the moors that she was. Allow the possibility that there was more to her life than housework and writing and Branwell's insane ravings.

"Allow the possibility that she knew love. That she loved and was loved in return. Grant her the humanity to make mistakes, and pity her in her sorrows.

"Emily Brontë was a remarkable woman, in every respect. Her strong will, her devotion to family, her belief in the eternality of all things would have supported a decision to allow herself to die in dignity rather than live with whatever troubles beset her in those closing months of her life. I ask you to open yourselves to the possibility that there might have been a different, more human side of Emily than we have known before. That there remain many unanswered questions which demand our examination. Do not close your eyes, nor your ears, nor your minds. We as scholars simply cannot afford such complacent ignorance. Thank you."

Alex returned to his chair, agonizingly conscious of the fact that there was no sound, even politely, of applause. The darkened room was hushed, and a hundred faces stared at him. A hundred faces who would call him a fool and denounce him in tomorrow's press.

And then Eleanor Bates stood up and began to applaud. Her friends on the front row did likewise, and in a brief instant the entire audience was on its feet. The sound of their acclaim grew louder and louder, and it remained unabated for several minutes. Out of the corner of his eye, Alex saw Maggie stand up, and he guessed she assumed they were clapping for her, which they may well have been. But she left the stage abruptly, and the moderator seized the moment to restore order.

"Thank you, Dr. Hightower. And thank you for coming this evening, ladies and gentlemen. I believe we all have new food for thought, and speaking of food, refreshments are now being served in the lobby," he said. "You are welcome to stay and share your own views on this matter directly with Dr. Hightower and Dr. . . ." He looked over his shoulder at Maggie's empty seat. ". . . Flynn."

The gin burned all the way down, and Alex thought a martini had never tasted so good. A fire crackled in the marble hearth, and Selena sat next to him on the brocade sofa in Eleanor Bates's elegant parlor. Their hostess had excused herself momentarily to see that their rooms were readied to her satisfaction. Outside, the storm had turned into a much needed steady rain, cooling and cleansing a summer-dried land.

Alex reached his arm across the back of the sofa and drew Selena close to him. "Is your grandmother exhausted from her big night out?" he asked, kissing her lightly on the forehead.

"She had a great time. It was thoughtful of you to suggest she come, but after last night, I wasn't sure it was a good idea."

"She did what she had to do."

Selena raised her lips to his cheeks. "I love you, Dr. Alex Hightower. I know how much Matka's mistake cost you, and yet you seem to be taking it . . . better than I would have."

"Maybe it was the right thing to happen after all," Alex murmured, dropping his head and tasting her lips for the first time that evening. If that's what it took to convince this sexy Gypsy lady she was safe in marrying him, so be it, he thought.

Their kiss was interrupted by the sound of the parlor door opening behind them. Eleanor cleared her throat noisily before entering.

"It appears that things are in order upstairs. Now where's my drink?" She bustled into the room dressed in a floor-length satin robe and slippers. "Do forgive me, dears, but as soon as I get to hear about Emily's retribution, I'm headed for bed. But not without my nightcap," she added, going to the sideboard and pouring herself a brandy.

She returned and took a seat next to the fireplace. "Now, Alex, will you please tell this befuddled old woman just exactly what is going on? Where is that blasted letter anyway?"

"Matka burned it."

Eleanor's eyes widened. "Burned it? Oh, my God. But I thought you said it would be safe with her."

"When you called to tell me Matka had kept the letter after your . . . visit . . . on behalf of the Brontë Society to convince her the curse could be broken, I had no idea she would do something like this."

"How . . . when . . . ?" It was the first time Alex had seen Eleanor Bates rendered speechless.

"Last night. Selena and I went to tell her that we had decided to be married, regardless of any so-called curse. She told us we didn't have to worry about the curse anymore because you had called on her and brought the gift of forgiveness needed for the family Wood to be released from it." He hesitated and smiled, remembering. "If you could have seen the look on her face, Eleanor, what happened next wouldn't seem so terrible."

"What happened next?"

Alex glanced down at Selena and then looked back at Eleanor. "We don't know how she did it so quickly," he began. "She was sitting in her usual spot by the fireplace when we got there. I didn't even know she had the letter with her. We chatted for a while, then told her what we had come there for, that we wanted to be married. She got this strange look on her face, and then she just sort of leaned over with her hand out. I thought something was wrong with her, that she was having a reaction to our news. Then she opened her fingers and dropped something squarely onto the fire. It was the letter. It was gone before we realized what it was."

He cleared his throat and continued. "Then she looked up at us, and she was crying. She said, 'There 'tis, my dears. There be an end t' the curse. Y' be safe now t' wed.' "

Selena wiped a tear from her cheek. "She thought she was doing us a favor by burning the letter. She said that with your forgiveness, the letter could be safely destroyed, and should be, to completely rid the family Wd of the curse."

Eleanor stared into the fire that burned quietly in her own grate. "That's what you meant in your note, then, that Emily seems to have reached out from beyond the grave to protect her secret. . . ."

Alex only nodded. They sat in silence for a long while, listening to the rain dripping from the eaves. At last Eleanor stood up. "Your room is at the top of the stairs, on the left," she said. She kissed Selena on the cheek, then looked slyly at Alex. "I figured I didn't need to prepare two rooms." She made her way to the door, then turned and smiled wearily at them.

"By the way," she said, "my rose garden would be a lovely place for a September wedding reception."

I was going to the Grange one evening—a dark evening threatening thunder—and, just at the turn of the Heights, I encountered a little boy with a sheep and two lambs before him; he was crying terribly, and I supposed the lambs were skittish and would not be guided.

"What is the matter, my little man?" I asked.

"They's Heathcliff, and a woman, yonder, under t'Nab," he blubbered, "un' Aw darnut pass 'em."

I saw nothing; but neither the sheep nor he would go on; so I bid him take the road lower down. He probably raised the phantoms from thinking, as he traversed the moors alone, on the nonsense he had heard his parents and companions repeat—yet still, I don't like being out in the dark, now; and I don't like being left by myself in this grim house—I cannot help it; I shall be glad when they leave it, and shift to the Grange!

"They are going to the Grange then?" I said.

"Yes," answered Mrs. Dean, "as soon as they are married; and that will be on New Year's day."

"And who will live here then?"

"Why, Joseph will take care of the house, and, perhaps, a lad to keep him company. They will live in the kitchen, and the rest will be shut up."

"For the use of such ghosts as choose to inhabit it," I observed.

"No, Mr. Lockwood," said Nelly, shaking her head. "I believe the dead are at peace, but it is not right to speak of them with levity." At that moment the garden gate swung to; the ramblers were returning.

"They are afraid of nothing," I grumbled, watching their approach through the window. "Together, they would brave satan and all his legions."

As they stepped onto the door-stones, and halted to take a last look at the moon—or, more correctly, at each other, by her light—I felt irresistibly impelled to escape them again; and, pressing a remembrance into the hand of Mrs. Dean, and disregarding her expostulations at my rudeness, I vanished through the kitchen as they opened the house-door: and so should have confirmed Joseph in his opinion of his fellow-servant's gay indiscretions, had he not fortunately recognized me for a respectable character by the sweet ring of a sovereign at his feet.

My walk home was lengthened by a diversion in the direction of the kirk. When beneath its walls, I perceived decay had made progress, even in seven months; many a window showed black gaps deprived of glass, and slates jutted off, here and there, beyond the right line of the roof, to be gradually worked off in coming autumn storms.

I sought, and soon discovered, the three headstones on the slope next the moor—the middle one grey, and half buried in the heath; Edgar Linton's only harmonized by the turf, and moss creeping up its foot; Heathcliff's still bare.

I lingered around them, under that benign sky;

*watched the moths fluttering among the heath and
hare-bells; listened to the soft wind breathing through
the grass; and wondered how anyone could ever
imagine unquiet slumbers for the sleepers in that quiet
earth.*

"He played a cruel and cunning game with me. What I took for love, to him was only a conquest."
— *The ghost of Lady Caroline Lamb*

Her parents' tragic death has led Boston heiress Alison Cunningham to seek them out at a seance. Instead, she encounters the troubled spirit of Lady Caroline Lamb, whose scandalous 1812 liaison with the charming, erotic Lord Byron ended in bitter betrayal and vengeful madness. Soon Alison finds herself buying Dewhurst Manor, near London, where the winsome apparition begs her to search for Byron's secret memoirs.

Also looking for the memoirs is sexy, arrogant Jeremy Ryder. Together, Alison and Jeremy must reckon with that beautiful capricious phantom, and find out what happened nearly two centuries ago. But will their obsession bind them together or drive them apart?

My Lady Caroline

Jill Jones

"A terrific tale...Jill Jones is one of the top new writing talents of the day."
—*Affaire de Coeur*

No one believes in ghosts anymore, not even in Salem, Massachusetts. And especially not sensible Helen Evett, a widow who lives for her two teenaged kids and who runs the best preschool in town. But when little Katie Byrne enters her school, strange things begin to happen. Katie's widowed father, Nat, begins to awaken feelings in Helen that she had counted as dead. But why does Helen get the feeling that Linda, Katie's mother, is reaching beyond the grave to tell her something?

As Helen and Nat each explore the pain of their losses and the joy of their newfound love, Linda Byrne's ghost plays a bold hand, beseeching Helen to uncover the mystery of her death. But what Helen finds could make her the target of a jealous killer and a modern Salem witch-hunt that threatens her, her family...and the magical second-time-around love that's taking her and Nat by storm.

BESTSELLING, AWARD-WINNING AUTHOR

ANTOINETTE STOCKENBERG

Beyond Midnight

BEYOND MIDNIGHT
Antoinette Stockenberg
_____ 95976-1 $5.99 U.S./$6.99 CAN.

Against the backdrop of an elegant Cornwall mansion before World War II and a vast continent-spanning canvas during the turbulent war years, Rosamunde Pilcher's most eagerly-awaited novel is the story of an extraordinary young woman's coming of age, coming to grips with love and sadness, and in every sense of the term, coming home...

Rosamunde Pilcher

The #1 *New York Times* Bestselling Author of *The Shell Seekers* and *September*

COMING HOME

"Rosamunde Pilcher's most satisfying story since *The Shell Seekers*."

—*Chicago Tribune*

"Captivating...The best sort of book to come home to...Readers will undoubtedly hope Pilcher comes home to the typewriter again soon."

—*New York Daily News*